JUL · 2017
CH

BY TERRY BROOKS

SHANNARA

SHANNARA

First King of Shannara
The Sword of Shannara
The Elfstones of Shannara
The Wishsong of Shannara

THE HERITAGE OF SHANNARA

The Scions of Shannara
The Druid of Shannara
The Elf Queen of Shannara
The Talismans of Shannara

THE VOYAGE OF THE *JERLE SHANNARA*

Ilse Witch
Antrax
Morgawr

HIGH DRUID OF SHANNARA

Jarka Ruus
Tanequil
Straken

THE DARK LEGACY OF SHANNARA

Wards of Faerie
Bloodfire Quest
Witch Wraith

THE DEFENDERS OF SHANNARA

The High Druid's Blade
The Darkling Child
The Sorcerer's Daughter

THE FALL OF SHANNARA

The Black Elfstone

PRE-SHANNARA

GENESIS OF SHANNARA

Armageddon's Children
The Elves of Cintra
The Gypsy Morph

LEGENDS OF SHANNARA

Bearers of the Black Staff
The Measure of the Magic

The World of Shannara

THE MAGIC KINGDOM OF LANDOVER

Magic Kingdom for Sale—Sold!
The Black Unicorn
Wizard at Large
The Tangle Box
Witches' Brew
A Princess of Landover

THE WORD AND THE VOID

Running with the Demon
A Knight of the Word
Angel Fire East

Sometimes the Magic Works:
Lessons from a Writing Life

THE BLACK ELFSTONE

THE **FALL** OF
SHANNARA

◆

THE BLACK ELFSTONE

TERRY BROOKS

DEL REY
NEW YORK

Copyright © 2017 by Terry Brooks
Map copyright © 2012 by Russ Charpentier

All rights reserved.

Published in the United States by Del Rey, an imprint of Random House, a division of Penguin Random House LLC, New York.

DEL REY and the HOUSE colophon are registered trademarks of Penguin Random House LLC.

The map by Russ Charpentier was originally published in *Wards of Faerie* by Terry Brooks, published in the United States by Del Rey, an imprint of Random House, a division of Penguin Random House LLC, in 2012.

Hardback ISBN 978-0-553-39148-0
Ebook ISBN 978-0-553-39149-7

Printed in the United States of America on acid-free paper

randomhousebooks.com

2 4 6 8 9 7 5 3 1

First Edition

FOR JUDINE
AT THE BEGINNING AND END OF
EVERYTHING THAT MATTERS

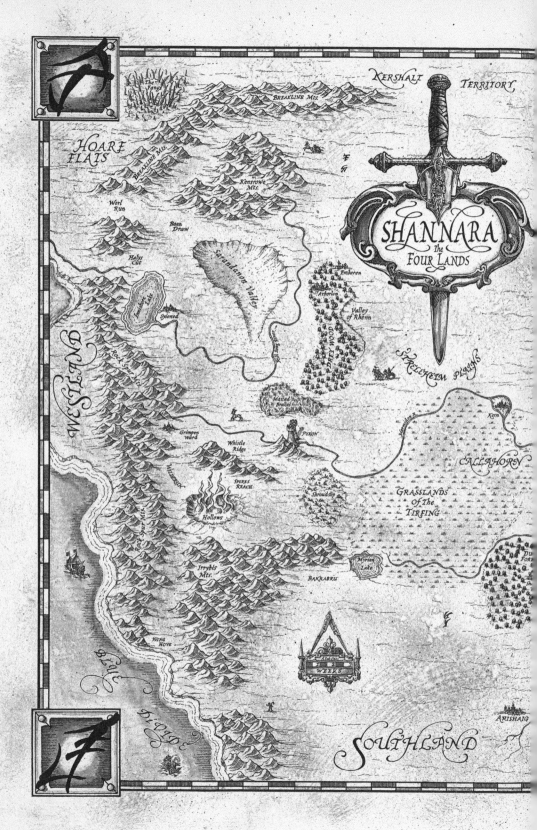

THE BLACK ELFSTONE

ONE

———————————◆———————————

TIGUERON, THE LEADER OF Orsis Guild and one of the most feared assassins in all Varfleet, sat alone at a table in the back of the Bullfinch tavern, waiting. Smoke from pipes clamped between teeth and oil lamps set upon tables clouded the air with a pungent haze, wafting to the rafters and along the walls. Smokeless lamps were discouraged in places like this where so many of the customers preferred anonymity. It was crowded enough that such anonymity would have been impossible otherwise, and Tigueron did not necessarily disagree with the reasoning of his fellow patrons. The noise was ferocious—shouts and laughter and conversations fighting to reach the ears of those seated just across the table from each other. Pitchers filled glasses, which rose to meet eager mouths, which gulped and swallowed until the ale was gone and the glasses refilled to begin the process anew. Much of the amber liquid was spilled on the wooden boards of the worn tavern floor, and more than a little stained the clothes of the customers. Manners were not anywhere near as popular as raucous behavior.

Tigueron hunched over his glass, watching everything around him without seeming to do so. Watching, but mostly waiting.

He was a big man, burly and muscular, his head heavy on his shoulders, his face rough-featured and scarred, his hair cut short and close to his scalp, his broken nose prominent, and his eyes hard and empty. He wore a heavy cloak with the hood pulled back and the drawstrings unfastened. It was warm in the cavernous drinking room, but he ignored it. The cloak served a more useful purpose than providing warmth. Beneath it were seven blades, all hidden in various sheaths within his clothing, all readily within reach—any one of them so sharp it could cut through bone. He never went anywhere without them.

His eyes shifted to the tavern's front doors. A client was coming but had not yet arrived. It was unusual for Tigueron to meet with a client under such circumstances. Normally, such meetings took place in the cellars of his fortress lair, Revelations, where he was surrounded by protections and protectors and in complete control of any situation. But this client had been insistent. The meeting was to take place in a public house—a demand Tigueron would have ordinarily dismissed out of hand. But a rather large number of credits placed in the hands of those who vetted such requests—some of which were passed on to him—persuaded him of the other's seriousness and proved an inducement too persuasive to ignore. No advantage to either party, the client had insisted. No danger that one or the other might act inappropriately.

Which clearly meant Tigueron, since the client would have had no advantage at all available in Revelations.

Yet the promise of further credits in such large amounts was intriguing. What harm could it do to hear the client out? His enemies would never invite Tigueron to a tavern to do him in. They would be subtler in their efforts. Besides, he was too cautious not to guard against such attempts. After all, he was in the business of bringing harm to others rather than to himself.

He glanced over to the men sitting at a table nearby. Three hardened, experienced killers who worked for him and would come to his aid in an instant if he was threatened. Not to mention that he was his own best weapon. Others had tried to kill him in the past. He had buried them all.

Outside, the wind was howling. The shutters, closed and latched, rattled against their casings with its force. Tigueron had seen the storm approaching on his way to this meeting, huge black clouds rolling in from the west filled with lightning and thunder, a dark promise of the deluge yet to come. But he made no move to leave, even though the client was late. He simply waited. He was good at waiting. It was very much a requirement of his work. Still, he could see that his associates were growing restless, their bodies shifting in their chairs, their gazes turned away from one another, their conversation exhausted.

It was not his problem. They would wait as they had been instructed to wait.

A black-cloaked figure appeared through the doors, pausing at the entrance and looking around the room. Droplets of rain dotted his cloak, and his head and face were hidden in the deep shadows of a hood. This had to be the client. Tigueron stood to signal and waited as the stranger crossed to his table.

"Tigueron?" the stranger asked.

A man, from his voice and now his face, as well, his features coming into the light as the gleam of the oil lamp burning on the table etched them out of the hood's blackness. He was smooth-faced, with a serene look on his countenance. His skin was unusually pale, and his hair quite blond. His features were calm and expressionless, as if carved from stone.

Tigueron nodded and gestured to the seat across from him, then sat himself. The stranger slid into place smoothly and silently, his eyes on Tigueron all the while. "Nasty weather coming," he said, his voice soft.

Tigueron nodded again. "What services do you require of Orsis?" he growled, eager to get down to business.

"You perform assassinations, do you not?"

Tigueron leaned forward. "Keep your voice down. The walls have ears in places like this." He leaned back again. In point of fact, the din of the tavern room was sufficient concealment, but he wanted to intimidate this confident stranger just a bit. "Do you wish to purchase my services?"

"What are the terms?"

"Depending on whom you wish killed, we set a price. The harder the job, the higher the price. I will require the name and payment in full. If we succeed on our first try, fine. If we do not, we will continue until we succeed. You are guaranteed to receive what you pay for. That is our pledge when you enter into the agreement."

"This one may be more difficult than others."

Tigueron shrugged. "Nothing is impossible."

He signaled the serving girl who had been attending to him since his arrival and placed an order for two tankards of ale. The girl nodded and left at once to fetch the ale. He took note of the fear in her eyes. She knew who he was, but he was paying her well for good service. Credits always trumped fear.

The stranger seemed not to notice any of it. He sat back, glancing toward the rattling windows, hearing a fresh change in the wind. A new sound reached their ears. Rain was falling heavily. The storm had arrived. The last of the mooring lines for the airships docked on the quay would have been lashed in place. The light sheaths would have been brought down and gathered in and the radian draws pulled in close. Windows and doors of homes and businesses would have been secured. The storm was expected to continue through the night. Rain would be heavy, and there would be some flooding.

A few of the tavern patrons had risen and were heading for the doors, wrapped in their cloaks and hooded against the downpour. But most stayed put. The storm was an excuse for adding a little more enjoyment to the evening—another tankard or two, another hour or so. Voices shouted and laughed and chased back the sounds of the storm, brave and alive with confidence.

"The man you are looking for should be in a village called Emberen," the stranger said. "He was at Paranor before, but he has been gone for a while. In any case, I don't want you to act against him right away. Not until after a date I will set before I leave. Can you wait?"

"As long as you like. But why wait?" *Paranor?* Tigueron was suddenly wary. There were only Druids at Paranor.

"That would be my business." A pause to be sure the point was made. "So, then, how quickly can we bring the matter to a close?"

Tigueron leaned forward. "I don't know. It would depend on the client and circumstances. You mentioned Paranor. If he is there, it would be much more difficult. Elsewhere, not so much. Usually, we settle matters in no more than one day."

"You can do it so quickly?"

"Orsis Guild is unique. We have special skills. Special tools to call upon."

A pause. "Do you have the use of magic?"

"Magic?" Tigueron gave him a look bordering on disgust. "Magic is for weaklings and charlatans. Besides, it is outlawed in the territories of the Federation. It is outlawed virtually everywhere but in Elven country and one or two other enclaves still wedded to its uses."

"Just because it is outlawed doesn't mean it isn't employed. The Druids use it as they see fit. And who is going to stop them? Even the Federation seeks to avoid that sort of confrontation. It would take a bold effort indeed to challenge those who inhabit Paranor. You let some sleeping dogs lie."

The stranger paused. "Besides, aren't assassinations outlawed, as well? And are they not employed on a regular basis, too?"

The tankards of ale arrived, and the serving girl carefully placed one before each man, accepting the coin the stranger offered as payment before departing. The stranger picked up his drink and took a long pull, swallowing with relish.

"Wonderful," he pronounced. "A fine batch they brew here. Now, I want this done at month's end and not before."

"As you wish." Tigueron was growing irritated with this whole business. Irritated, as well, with this unflappable stranger he now regretted agreeing to meet. "Tell me, who is it we are to remove from your life?"

"Not yet. I want to hear the price first. Let me say that you will know the victim, and he will not be easily killed. In fact, it will be hard even to get close enough to carry out my wishes. He is trained to protect himself against men like you and yours."

"I will have the name before you have the price," Tigueron replied, his face dark. "Do you take me for a fool?"

"You should know he has magic at his disposal."

Tigueron nodded slowly. "That means a higher price, then. Such men can prove troublesome."

"Cost does not matter. Only success. Once you take this job, you must complete it. You cannot change your mind later."

Tigueron stared at him. This client was being inordinately demanding. Most men who wanted another killed didn't spend time worrying about what it might take to accomplish the job. They only cared about the cost. This stranger had the exact opposite concerns. And Tigueron was suddenly troubled in a way that he had not been earlier.

"What are you not telling me?" he asked pointedly, glancing at the men sitting at the other table.

"Do not even think about calling those men to your defense, Tigueron. You would be dead before they got out of their seats if I wished it. Let us try to stay on point. I desire your services and nothing more. You do not get to ask my name or the details of why I am doing this. You either accept the job or you don't. The choice is yours."

Tigueron glowered at him. "The name, first."

Being stubborn, digging in. If word got around that he was letting his clients dictate the terms, he would be out of business in a flash. He held the stranger's gaze, unmovable.

The stranger nodded. "Very well. His name is Drisker Arc."

Now Tigueron understood the other's concern. A Druid of Drisker Arc's skill and reputation would not be easily dispatched. But the amount of money he could demand for such an endeavor would be enormous.

He named a ridiculously high figure—so high that, if he were the client, he would have walked away.

But the stranger just nodded his agreement with a shrug. "Done."

Tigueron was suddenly unsettled. He felt oddly trapped, as if the bargain were a snare into which he had stepped. But he was not afraid of risk, so he nodded in turn. "You must pay me now."

The stranger passed a slip of paper across the table. "Take it to any Bluestone Credit Agency outlet in Varfleet by tomorrow morning and it will be honored. The credits will be waiting."

Tigueron read the amount written on the paper greedily. "If the agency fails to honor it," the stranger continued in his soft, calm voice, "you have no obligation to me and you may keep what I have already given you to meet with me tonight. But the credits will be there."

Tigueron sneered. "They had better be."

The stranger's face showed nothing. "Send word to Paranor when the matter is concluded. I will be there. Make sure your message reveals nothing about yourself. Make it a general announcement intended for all."

He rose from the table, tightened his cloak about his shoulders, and pulled its hood forward over his head so his face was hidden once more.

"Do not fail me," he whispered.

Then he walked to the doors of the tavern and went out into the stormy night.

TWO

---◆---

Tavo Kaynin remembered enough of his early boyhood to know that he hadn't always been like he was now.

When he was very little, the magic wasn't yet a part of his life. He was a normal boy in most ways; he fit in with his family and he loved them. His sister was his closest friend, and they played together every day. She was younger by five years, and although now and then she told him there were things about him she didn't understand, he never had reason to think much about it.

Still, he would catch her looking at him strangely sometimes. She would study him, as if trying to see something that was hidden. He would ask her what she was doing, and she would always say the same thing: Nothing. Even though he was the older sibling and he could intimidate her easily enough, he always let the matter drop.

After all, she was his little sister and he loved her.

But then, once she turned ten, she started to go off by herself, telling him he could not go with her, saying she wanted to go alone. Even though he did as she asked, he was hurt and angered by her secretiveness, and he told her so. But even knowing this, she refused to confide in him.

At first, he asked his mother.

"Oh, that's just Tarsha," his mother told him. "Girls are like that sometimes. Just give her some space. It won't last."

He had no idea what she was talking about, so he let the matter drop.

But soon, some of those secrets began to reveal themselves. He had just turned fifteen and was already beginning to test the boundaries of his parents' control. He was beginning to disobey directives—sometimes because he felt it was necessary and other times because he simply felt like it. Disobedience was a part of growing up, although he didn't understand this at the time. But he was noticing something else troubling about himself, too. His temper was getting the best of him with increasing frequency. Sudden rages, quick bursts of anger, and feelings of hostility toward almost everyone, including his sister and his parents, were becoming the norm. Most of the time there wasn't even a reason for it.

His parents and his sister all commented on it, asking him to hold his temper, to think before he acted. But he found that hard to do, particularly when the release of his anger seemed to calm him—or even provide him with a strange sense of satisfaction.

Then one day he followed his sister when she went on one of her mysterious outings, in spite of his promise not to do so, and discovered what she was trying to hide. Concealed within a stand of trees, he watched her kneel in a clearing and begin to sing words he could not make out and motion with her hands in ways he did not recognize. At first, he thought she was performing a ritual of some kind, perhaps a giving of thanks to Mother Earth. But then she shifted just enough that he could see the results of what she had been doing. From the soil in front of her, a slender green stalk emerged like a snake, twisting and reaching for the light, maturing much more swiftly than a normal growing cycle would require. The stalk budded with leaves that within seconds were fully formed, and then with scarlet flowers that blossomed like starbursts.

Unable to help himself, he burst out of the trees and rushed over to her. "How did you do that?"

She looked up, not as surprised as he would have expected. "You followed me, didn't you? Even though I told you not to."

He made a dismissive gesture. "I wanted to see what you were doing."

"It's my business." She frowned. "You shouldn't have come."

He felt a surge of anger at her presumption. "But I did, so tell me." He pointed at the tiny plant. "How come you can do that, and I can't? You have to teach me!"

"I can't. You don't have the gift."

"What gift? What are you talking about?"

"Magic."

"You can do magic? Then you can teach me. If you can't teach me the trick with the plant, then teach me something else."

The frown deepened. "I can't. That's all I know how to do!"

Abruptly, he grabbed her by the shoulders and shook her. "You teach me, Tarsha, or I'll tell Mama about this!"

Tarsha paled. He had guessed right. Their mother didn't know. "If I show you how I do it, you must promise not to tell her. Will you?"

"I don't tell her lots of things."

"All right. Sit down."

He sat, legs crossed in front of him, leaning forward eagerly. She was only ten years old, but smart for her age. Teaching him would not be difficult.

"You have to sort of sing to it," she said, pointing to the plant. "You think about what you want it to do when it is a seed, and you sing to it to make it obey. I only found out a few months ago that I could do it. That's why I have been going off by myself—to discover what else I can do. There's more, I think, but so far that's all I've learned."

"But you can teach me that much?"

"Not if you can't do the singing right. It's a sort of humming, a kind of . . . I don't know. A kind of reaching-out. I can't explain it."

"But you have it and I don't!" he complained.

She shushed him. "Not yet, maybe. But you are my brother. You might find out it's hiding inside you. Do you want me to help you find out?"

He nodded eagerly. "Let's try!"

They did so for almost an hour, but Tavo could not make anything happen. Eventually, he grew frustrated. She recognized the signs of his growing rage and hastened to calm him.

"Maybe it will just take a little longer for you to find it. I didn't know I had it until it just happened one day. Maybe that's what will happen to you. I can keep working with you, but you have to keep your promise. You have to keep this secret from Mama and Papa. You can't tell them. At least until you find out you can do it, too."

He had accepted her explanation and asked only that he be allowed to go with her while she practiced using the magic so he could practice with her. That way, he could better understand what it was like and how it might feel when he discovered it, too. They were still close then, still very private in their sibling relationship—less a part of the larger community and more a community of two. Tavo loved his sister enough that he understood the nature of his responsibility for her. He was protective of her in the way a brother often is of a younger sister. He adored her. And even when he was angriest, he knew he would never hurt her.

Because in those days, he had no doubt that she would always be there for him, and they would always be close.

But even with her efforts to help him, even with all her coaching and support, he was almost seventeen before the magic revealed itself. It happened all at once—unexpectedly, shockingly, just as Tarsha had told him it might. He was off by himself, not far from his house, playing inside a fort he had constructed of old tree branches, deadwood, and heavy stones, pretending at heroic conquests and daring deeds, his thoughts so far from the magic it would have been difficult to measure the distance. His sister was elsewhere, gone off to the village with her mother to shop. Two years had passed since Tarsha had told him for the first time about the magic, seemingly a lifetime ago. In all that time, no sign of the magic had appeared in him. Her own use had grown considerably, allowing her to change things of all sorts and even sometimes to make herself disappear into her surroundings. Her skills were raw and unschooled, and often she failed to make the magic obey her. But at least she had some use of it. He had none—and he was beginning to believe he never would.

Inside the fort, peering out at the forest and the animals and birds, he was practicing being a hunter, spying on game, choosing his target. He had a slingshot with him, his favorite weapon, and he was usually quite accurate with it. Sometimes it bothered him when he killed small creatures, but mostly he considered it necessary so that they would not overrun the forest. Where he had come up with the possibility of this happening he had no idea, but he was having many strange thoughts lately—increasingly dark and unpleasant, but at the same time rather intriguing.

Upon spying a squirrel not too many yards from where he lay concealed, he shifted his position within the fort so that he was aligned with his target while staying hidden, sighted through the Y of his sling, and released a smooth, round stone.

And missed.

The squirrel shot away and was gone.

He tried again a few minutes later with a bird. Same result. He began to grow angry with his inability to do something he had done so often before—and without any problem. He got to his knees, settled himself in place, and waited. The minutes slipped away and he grew impatient as well as angry.

Then a raven landed close by, and he knew he had his target marked and readied himself. This time he would not miss. Deep breath, steady hands, and release!

The stone caromed off a patch of bare earth a good two feet from where the raven strutted.

Another miss.

He lost all control of himself, leaping to his feet within his enclosure, screaming and howling, stamping his feet and swinging his arms like windmills, so furious he was shaking with rage. He wanted to destroy something. He wanted to destroy everything!

And all at once everything seemed to explode from inside him. He felt it rise into his throat and exit through his open mouth like a giant wind. The fort he had built flew apart, pieces of it spinning off in all directions. It shocked him so greatly that he went silent and motionless. The fort was leveled, and he was left standing amid the wreckage, staring into the trees beyond—now emptied of animals and birds alike.

But immediately, he knew. He felt a mix of satisfaction and fear, because he now wasn't quite sure what to do with this thing he had wanted so much. How could he manage something that could be triggered so spontaneously? How could he find a way to make it do what he wanted?

He spent the remainder of that day trying to find out but was mostly unsuccessful. Either the magic refused to respond or it refused to do what he asked of it. By sunset he was so frustrated he was using what power he could manage simply to destroy things—trees and shrubs, small animals that wandered into view, birds that foolishly tried to fly overhead. He went home dismayed and disgruntled, but eager to tell Tarsha.

It should have gotten easier after that. Tarsha should have been able to teach him how to control the magic, how to make it do what he wanted. But for some reason, she couldn't seem to find a way to explain it so that he could understand. She told him what to do, how to do it, what it would feel like, and how to keep the magic from breaking free. She had him practice using his powers over and over again, out in the forest, away from everyone. But he struggled with everything he tried, the magic elusive and stubborn, his efforts repeatedly falling short. He worked so hard, but nothing helped.

In the end, she told him it would take time for the magic to settle within him. His gift was incredibly powerful, and he was still very new to it. In time, he would learn to command it better. He would just have to wait.

But Tavo Kaynin was not patient and never would be. He was reckless and wild and infuriated by his failures. He never quit trying to do as Tarsha told him, and after a time he gained a measure of control—but never like the control Tarsha had mastered, and never to a point where he could feel comfortable with using it. It was odd, but the only times he felt comfortable were when the magic broke free of its own accord, spiraling out of him like fire fed with accelerant, hot and raw. The destruction was terrible, but it eased his pain and sense of failure.

After a time—months after his discovery of the magic within him and while he was still struggling to come to terms with it—he began to actively court these spontaneous releases, encouraging them with his wild, irrational behavior. Tarsha warned him against doing this, but what did she know of his suffering? She meant well, but no one could understand what it was like to try to fight back against the dominating influence of such power. There was no escaping what it did to him when he repressed it, how it diminished his sense of self, how it scrambled his thoughts and preyed on his mind.

Eventually, his parents discovered the presence of the magic within their children and tried to stop them from using it, but they were woefully inadequate to the task—at least where Tavo was concerned. Tarsha pretty much did as they asked and used the magic only sparingly. But Tavo was less controlled, more susceptible to his anger. His use of the magic became wilder and more destructive. Property damage became rampant in the village of Backing Fell. Other children who taunted him into fits of rage found themselves mysteriously cast away by sudden winds. One of those children—a boy who bullied Tavo relentlessly—mysteriously went missing and was never found again.

Tarsha Kaynin could remember the exact day when they took her brother away. It was two days after her thirteenth birthday, one her brother had helped her celebrate in the family home with their parents. Tavo was being punished at the time, but Tarsha made her parents promise they would release him from his room where he was serving out a five-day disciplinary sentence for killing a neighbor's cow.

Even with all the guidance and encouragement she had given him, even though he knew what would happen if things went wrong, events like this continued to occur. It was as if he couldn't help himself.

"Listen, Tarsha," he'd told her. "These are things I have to do, even if they go wrong. I need to find out what is happening to me. Why can't I control this like you do? It's so easy for you, but for me it is like pulling out my fingernails. I'll try my best; you know I will."

He always tried his best—or so he claimed. It was just that his best was never enough.

So he had used his gift—yet again, in spite of her repeated warnings—and the effort had failed and the cow had died. It was just a cow, he had argued as his parents locked him in his room and left him there. What difference did it make? No one cared about a cow.

But Tarsha did. She loved saggy-bellied old Bella with her whiskered face and her big dark eyes, and she cried when she was gone. She loved the way Bella had followed her around the field like a puppy when she went to help care for the old cow's new calves. She loved how Bella nuzzled her with her soft nose. She was sorry for her brother, but he should have known better. He shouldn't be so stubborn. Her parents, however, had gone way beyond the limits of their patience. For them, it was the last straw. They had put up with their son for as long as they could. The neighbors hated him. The people of Backing Fell hated him. If he'd had any friends, they would have hated him, too. He didn't know how to win people over, to make them like him, even a little. No small part of this was his fault. But he would blame others, of course, as he always did, saying they picked on him, made fun of him, played nasty tricks on him, and sometimes hurt him, so that was why he hurt them back.

But she knew better. He did it because he wanted to see if he could. Just as he did with Bella.

So, two days after her birthday, her parents made the decision to send him to his uncle—his father's brother—who lived ten miles south on a small farm. There he was to remain until he had outgrown his dark proclivities and learned to manage both his temper and his gift. His uncle would let them know when he was beginning to come around and become the young man he was supposed to be. His uncle would tell them when he had ceased to misbehave.

In the meantime, he would not be allowed to use his gift for any reason. He would remain on his uncle's farm and do the work he was given. He would see them now and again, but he was not to come home on his own.

Tarsha was still young then and not fully aware of all that had happened because of Tavo's foolish acts. She knew of some of what he had done, but some her parents had kept hidden from her. She knew enough, however, to understand that everyone was afraid of Tavo—

especially her parents—and letting him continue to live with them in the family home was no longer an option.

Nevertheless, she begged them not to send him away. She cried and wailed and pleaded and demanded, but nothing would change their minds.

Later that same night, Tavo came into her bedroom and sat at her bedside and told her not to worry. Sending him away was not going to mean they would never see each other again. It did not mean they wouldn't continue to be each other's best friend. He would serve out his time on the farm and come home again. He would show them that it didn't matter what they did to him; he could endure any punishment and still be strong. He wouldn't stop using his gift, either. He would not let his uncle know, but he would keep using it. And he would be careful, just as she had told him.

"No, Tavo, no," she had pleaded. "Don't do it. Don't take the risk. Please don't use the magic without me there to help you!"

But he talked right over her, repeating himself. He kept saying the same thing, over and over.

He would show them. He would show them.

When he left, she was afraid she would never see him again, that he would never return to her. And eventually, she decided to do something about it.

THREE

◆

TARSHA WAITED TWO WHOLE years before taking action. She had asked her parents repeatedly when Tavo was coming home, ever since the day he had been taken away to live with his uncle, but their responses were always the same.

"It's too early for a visit, Tarsha."

"He needs time to adjust to his new life."

"We don't want to interrupt his rehabilitation."

"We have to be patient."

By the time she was fifteen, she was done with being patient. Only seeing her brother again could reassure her that he was all right. There had been no communication between them, even though she had written him notes, which her father had promised he would deliver. But Tavo had never replied.

So now she would go see him on her own. She had no other choice.

It was a big undertaking for a fifteen-year-old girl. But her entire life had been a big undertaking, right from her birth, when she had emerged almost two months early from her mother's womb weighing a little more than three pounds. She should have died. That's what everyone told her later. She shouldn't have survived such an early birth in such a small body. But it was clear from the first that she was no ordinary child. She was tough and resilient, and she gained weight as she grew and fought off childhood illnesses and even recovered from the bite of a neighbor's dog that tore a chunk from her leg. She worked hard from an early age because she had to; her parents were poor and struggling with her brother. She endured beatings and advances from older boys and a few girls; she taught herself to read and write when no one else had the time; she learned to ride horses and plow fields and harvest crops; and she tended to both parents on numerous occasions when they became too sick to tend to themselves.

Her looks were striking, and not in the usual ways. She was pretty enough but not especially so. She was more exotic than beautiful, with a complexion pale as fresh cream and hair so blond it was almost white. Her eyes were a strange lavender color. She was narrow-featured, with prominent cheekbones and a spray of freckles across her nose and cheeks. When she laughed, the sound was bold and lusty and seemed as if it should belong to an older person.

At fifteen, she knew little of the larger world, but she was capable enough, in her judgment, to make the daylong journey to her uncle's farm. She would have to walk it because she had no other means of transportation. She would have to make up a story, too—one to explain where she was going without being entirely honest about it. To her friend Albaleen's home in the nearby village of Quenn Ridge, perhaps. She would have to cover her tracks and make certain she was back by the following day. Eventually, her parents would find out what she had done, but she hoped they would understand her reasons and not punish her for her deception.

But if punish her they did, she would accept it and not feel regret for doing something she felt so strongly about. She was not the kind to back away from a challenge.

However, her plans went wrong almost from the start. When she told her parents she was going to spend the night with Albaleen, her father insisted on driving her there in the cart. At fifteen, he said, she was too young to be out on the road alone. Young girls at that age were far too vulnerable to men whose moral principles had been abandoned long ago. She wasn't sure she understood exactly, but she got the gist of it. So she chose to reveal the real reason for her journey, trusting that her father would understand and help her. She was mistaken. He told her flatly she would not be going—not then, and not until Tavo was better. And nothing she said after did anything to change his mind.

"You are a young girl with no real understanding of the problems of the world, let alone your brother's," her father said.

"Papa, I am almost grown! I have the use of magic. It can protect me against anything I might encounter. It is important that I see Tavo!"

But her father shook his head. "You must accept my decision and abide by my rules so long as you live under this roof."

"That is so unfair!" she had snapped back in fury.

"You are entitled to your opinion. But the decision is mine and it is final."

"Fine! Mama might see things differently. I'll go to her!"

But arguing the matter with her mother was futile. She deferred to her husband and said Tarsha must do the same. So after several days of brooding, Tarsha decided simply to slip away without their knowledge and make the journey anyway.

That effort failed as well. She got as far as the end of the lane leading away from the house when her father appeared in the doorway to call her back. Desperate to go anyway, she tried to convince him once more of her need to see her brother, but nothing would sway him. And when she tried to run, he caught up to her and dragged her back into the house and locked her away for two days.

"I hate you!" she screamed through the door, sobbing. But he made no response.

In the end, the best she could manage was to extract a promise that sometime soon he would take her to see Tavo himself.

But that "sometime" never came. Almost two more years passed with no visit to or word from her brother. Life distracted her, as life tends to do, and before she knew it she was nearing her seventeenth birthday, and the absence of her brother was becoming comfortable in a way she increasingly found disturbing. Soon, she feared, she would forget him entirely, content to consign him to the past and leave him there—and she could not bear the thought of that happening.

So she decided to try again.

Only this time, she was older and better prepared. The confidence she had lacked at fifteen had blossomed. She was bigger and more capable by now; she was tough and ready. She had learned from old Stoll down in Backing Fell how better to protect herself, the hunter giving her lessons in self-defense in exchange for repairing and painting his cottage porch railings and the fence surrounding his yard. More important, she was continuing to develop her use of magic. She still didn't know its origins, but her ability to create images and to virtually disappear into her surroundings was vastly improved.

So she made up her mind. She would go to Tavo. And this time, she vowed, her father would not stop her.

She left early one morning, slipping silently from the house before sunrise and setting out along the road to her uncle's farm, leaving a note saying she would be back in a day. She crossed open fields and passed through forests, cutting cross-country to save time and to avoid the pursuit that would come once her father discovered what she had done. But by the time she arrived at her destination, she had not seen him even once during her journey and did not find him waiting for her.

Still, it was not the end of her troubles.

Her uncle was a stranger to her. She had seen him no more than a handful of times when she was younger, and not at all since Tavo had gone to live with him. He was a large, shaggy-haired man with a gruff voice and a dark look, his big hands always flexing at his sides, his words slow and rough-edged. He was restless and short of patience, and he made it clear how he felt about her arrival immediately.

"You turn around and go on home, girl," he told her.

He did not say this in a way that suggested there was any choice in the matter, but Tarsha stood her ground. "I want to see my brother."

Her uncle worked his jaws as if chewing on something. "Can't allow it. He's in the punishment shed. He's to stay there until he learns his lesson. He's not to see anyone until then."

"What's the punishment shed? What's he in there for?"

"Disobedience. He's bad clear through." He pointed to a weathered shed standing off to one side of the barn, close to where the animal pens were situated. "That's where he spends most of his time these days. His choice, for not doing what he's supposed to. He won't change."

Tarsha hesitated. "I want to see him anyway."

Her uncle shook his shaggy head, his face stern and set. "He ain't what you remember. He ain't been since he came here. He was trouble from the moment he arrived, and not much has changed. I keep him because my brother wants it, but I don't much like it. He's a millstone around my neck, and if it wasn't for your parents' insisting . . ."

"Then let me take him home," she interrupted. "I can manage him."

Another shake of the head. "Tried to send him home already. Your parents wouldn't take him back. Said he had to stay here until he changed. They won't let you bring him back neither, I expect."

She stared at him in shock. Mama and Papa wouldn't let Tavo come home? They were forcing him to stay here with her uncle? Locked in a shed like an animal? He had to be lying! "They wouldn't agree to that!" she snapped. "They probably don't even know about it!"

"Well, they do know, so change your thinking." He paused. "Do you know what he was like when he first got here?"

She shook her head. She didn't know anything. "He didn't write me. Mama and Papa wouldn't let me come visit."

"No, I don't guess they would." He looked over to the punishment shed as if considering it. "First week he was here, he was so angry he wouldn't speak a word. Second week, he started killing things. Small animals, at first. Wild or tame, didn't matter. Then he killed my dog. Did it for no reason I could understand. I loved that old dog. He was my best friend after Mayerling died and I chose not to wed again. Boy crossed a line on that one, and I had to teach him a lesson. I put him in the punishment shed for the first time. But it wasn't the last."

"This has been going on for four years?" Tarsha was practically shouting at him. "You've been locking him up for four years?"

"Had to. He just got worse and worse. Started coming after me.

Once he got hold of a knife and tried to use it on me. And it's getting worse. He's bigger now, stronger. I can't take chances with him. But my brother pays me to keep him, so I do. His wife, your mama, begs me, too. She's terrified of him. They came once, early on. Couple of months into his stay. Did they tell you that?"

They hadn't. They'd told her nothing of a visit.

"That was when they said I had to keep him. He was too dangerous to go home, too wild and unpredictable. Doesn't think right. Doesn't know what he's doing. I agreed. Thought I could reach him in time. Thought I could teach him to work the land, learn something useful. I tried to teach him. I tried to show him how to have fun."

He paused, looking off into the distance as if remembering, a disturbing smile creeping over his worn face. "We had a few good times, him and me. We had some fun times. He learned to play some games. I taught him how. He liked them well enough. He was happy to play them. We was close for a bit, him and me." His gaze shifted back to her, his face suddenly hard again. "But that's all ended. Can't be doing anything like that anymore. Can't risk it. Can't trust him not to hurt me. I got to watch him close. He's smart, but he's crazy, too. He gets out of control too easy. He thinks I'm doing stuff to him I'm not."

"What do my parents think about what you're doing?" she asked him, wondering suddenly what he was talking about. The dismay in her voice was unmistakable. "Don't they worry about him?"

"They don't ask, I don't tell. They mostly worry for themselves. You don't know, girl. He's like a wild animal. They just want him out of their hair. They didn't tell you that?"

They hadn't, of course. They hadn't told her anything of what was happening here. But it was clear now that they didn't want Tavo back. That he wasn't their son anymore.

And they had known better than to tell any of this to Tarsha.

"I need to see him," she said finally, her voice softened. "Please."

He started to object and stopped. Studied her a long minute and then sighed. "All right, then. But only for a few moments. And you got to do what I tell you, do what I say. First off, stand right in the doorway once it's open. Don't take another step. Don't let him get near you. He's dangerous, girl. You might not want to believe it, but he is. He might not even know who you are, and he can hurt you. So you stand with me and you don't move. You just talk to him. If you can get him to talk."

She nodded at once. If this was the best she could do, it would have to be enough. But if there was more to be had, more to be gained, she would press him again after she had seen how Tavo was. She had taken too long already to come here. She was not going to leave without having achieved something.

He hesitated a moment longer—perhaps thinking, wrongly, that she might change her mind. When she just stood there staring at him, he turned and started for the shed, Tarsha at his heels. The path was well worn, suggesting her uncle had come and gone to the shed often. A larger, wider track, more a road than a path, followed in parallel fashion to the barn. Tarsha was aware of her uncle's bulk as he lumbered along the smaller path, and she wondered momentarily if she might be in danger, but she dismissed that as foolishness. He had no reason to want to harm her.

At the door to the shed, he stopped and turned back to her.

"Remember what I told you. Stand beside me and do not attempt to enter on your own. Stay in the doorway and keep clear of his reach. Sometimes he don't even know who I am. Might be so with you. You just speak to him and see if he responds. Understood?"

She gave him a brief nod, worried now about how she would find Tavo. She felt her heart racing as he used a key to release the huge padlock that held the door secure. She listened to its loud snick, watched her uncle slip it free. The door swung open, and she peered into the gloom.

At first, she couldn't see anything. The shed was clapboard-built with gaps in the walls between slats where the light shone through. There were no windows. There was a floor of hay and a stall; some empty hooks fastened to the walls here and there. The smell was rank and pungent, and she wrinkled her nose.

Then she saw Tavo, huddled at the back wall. At least, she assumed it was her brother. He was curled into a ball with his face turned away and his arms about his head. She caught a glimpse of the iron clamp locked onto his ankle and the heavy chain leading away to a ring set into a massive stone block.

Her uncle nudged her, nodding toward the creature lying on the floor. Tavo. Her brother. She was so shocked and appalled that for a moment she couldn't speak. How had this happened? How could her parents have allowed it?

"Tavo?" she called softly to him. "It's Tarsha."

He did not respond.

"Tavo, please talk to me."

He lifted his head to look at her. Mumbled something, and then lowered his head again.

"Tavo, I need you to talk to me. I miss you so much."

"You don't miss me!" The words came out a low, harsh growl filled with anger and frustration. "You've never missed me. You abandoned me!"

She cringed at the rebuke, fighting not to cry.

"I was trying to help you. I was trying to find—"

"*Liar!* You shut your filthy lying mouth! I know what you did! *I don't want you here!*"

He sprang to his feet, his face twisting into something horrible and demonic, his scream primal. Then he lunged at her and would have had her if the chain hadn't brought him up short and yanked him backward. He collapsed in a heap then, hunched over and beaten. But his eyes were still fixed on her, their glare as hard as stone.

His voice changed to a soft, cajoling purr. "I like it here. I love Uncle. Uncle is good to me. Uncle treats me well. When I am bad, he punishes me, but it's for my own good. But when I am good, he lets me play those games with him, the ones he says are good for me. Uncle loves me. He does things for me that feel good and pleasant. Uncle . . ."

He trailed off, going silent once more. Tarsha started forward at once, but her uncle grabbed her and dragged her from the shed, slamming the door behind him and locking it.

"You listen to me, girl. He isn't who he was. He isn't a boy anymore. He's a man, and he must learn to act like a man. He is finding this out. I am trying to teach him. You are nothing but a disruption, a distraction! Go home and you tell your parents whatever you choose about Tavo. See what they say. See if I'm not right. Now get out of here!"

He practically threw her down the pathway. She caught herself just in time to keep from falling and stumbled away in shock. Some part of her knew that what her uncle was saying was the truth. Tavo wasn't the boy who had left her four years earlier. He wasn't a boy at all. But he wasn't a full-grown man, either, and he wasn't right in his mind. Something was seriously wrong with him, and she knew that, whatever else had helped bring it about, it was the magic at fault, too. And his inability to control it.

But her uncle? Loathsome, terrible, vile! She hated him and she feared him at the same time. She should have used her magic against him. She berated herself for not doing so.

She continued down the path, thinking about what she could do to help her brother, and decided she must first talk to her parents and describe what she had seen. She must find out if they had indeed given up on Tavo, if they had abandoned him for good. She must know that first.

Then she would decide what else needed to be done.

So she returned to Backing Fell. And before her parents could get a word out to question where she had been and what she had been doing, she exploded.

"Do you have any idea what's happening to Tavo? He's locked in a shed and chained to a wall! Uncle said you knew of this. He said you didn't want Tavo back. He practically threw me off his farm! What's wrong with you?"

"Sit down!" her father roared back at her. "And don't say another word!"

Scowling, but hesitant to say more, Tarsha did as she was told.

"Now you listen to me," her father said, his voice gone soft again, low but still dangerous.

Her mother was standing at his shoulder. Tarsha could tell they had been expecting this. They knew where she had been, what she had discovered, and what she would say when she arrived home. She also knew, with a sinking feeling in the pit of her stomach, that everything her uncle had told her about her parents and Tavo was true.

"When we took your brother to live with your uncle, we did so knowing he might not come back to us. By then he was dangerous, Tarsha. He had threatened your mother several times and struck her, as well. He had attacked me. He had hurt some of the children he played with. He had killed animals for no good reason." He paused and took a deep breath. "There were rumors he even killed that boy who had been teasing him. I never believed those rumors, but they kept resurfacing. They never found that boy's body. I didn't like to believe my son was a killer, but Tavo told us once that he was glad the boy wouldn't ever tease him again, and I was never entirely sure."

Her father took a chair across from her. Her mother remained standing. She was crying, her head bowed, the tears running down her face.

"Your brother is a danger to everyone," her father continued, still speaking softly, still with an edge to his voice. "Your mother is terrified of him. The village is frightened, as well. We don't know what's wrong with him or what to do about it. Maybe it's the magic and maybe it's just his nature, but he's better off where he is. Jorris agreed to try to help him recover. He feels your brother needs discipline and structure, even sometimes punishment. He says Tavo has started to grow comfortable with the routine of his life and familiarity of his surroundings, so I'm leaving him there for now."

"But it's been nearly four years!"

"And it might be more than that, Tarsha. You cannot put a time limit on these things. We have to lead our lives, too, your mother and I. We have a right to our peace and quiet. We have a right to feel safe. With Tavo here, all that would be gone. Now, I don't want to talk about it again. I won't punish you for going to see him, but I don't want you doing it again. Just let things be. Let Jorris do what he needs to do to help the boy."

Tarsha was not convinced. She rose, went outside, and walked through the woods, thinking. Tavo's professions of happiness with his life and love for his uncle did not feel real. His condition did not seem to have improved. If anything, it had deteriorated. But she understood that, even if she wanted to help him, her options were limited. Going back now would only get her in worse trouble, and she wouldn't be able to achieve anything. She had the use of her magic, but it wasn't much compared with her uncle's size and brute strength. Even if she freed Tavo from the shed or from his shackles and took him away, where would they go?

She was halfway through her wandering when she made her decision. What she needed was to find another way to help Tavo. His problems were largely the result of his inability to control the magic that he, like she, had been born with. But she was limited herself. While able to control the magic, she was largely ignorant about how to use it. What she needed to do was to find someone who could teach her to be more skilled.

Right away, she thought of the Druids at Paranor. Teaching the uses of magic to students was a large part of their mission. If anyone could help her, they could. She would have to make the journey to Paranor and speak with them. She would ask for their help and convince them to take her on as a student.

Then she could return to Backing Fell and help Tavo.

Keeping her plans to herself, she began a concerted effort to find out more about the Druids and how they chose their students. She knew from listening to stories passed around by other children that only those who possessed magic were admitted into Paranor. As the weeks passed, she gleaned more snippets of knowledge about the Druid order and its workings. Some of it was useless. Some of it seemed mostly to be gossip and rumor with little or no supporting evidence. Much of it was the speculation that goes hand in hand with a group as mysterious and secretive as this one.

But one shared point of agreement concerned Drisker Arc, the High Druid of the order and one of the most respected and skilled Druids ever to bear that title.

The more Tarsha heard about this man, the more she became in-fatuated with the idea of having him be her teacher. She had no idea how she would go about this. She did not know him personally; nor did anyone else in her village. She had no reason to think he would give her the time of day, let alone commit to teaching her.

Unless, she thought, he found her worthy.

As her seventeenth birthday approached, her parents asked her what she would like for a present. What she wanted was clear to her, but it was not something they could give her. Still, it was something she might be able to give herself.

She celebrated her birthday with her parents, all the while know-ing what she was going to do. What she *had* to do.

And on the morning following, without telling them anything or even leaving them a note, she set out on foot for Paranor.

FOUR

———————————◆———————————

PARFEND, MATUREN OF THE Corrax Trolls, stood with his army atop a rise facing northeast to where the waters of the Tiderace were visible in vague choppy heads of foam through layers of shifting mist. The army stood readied perhaps five miles back from the shoreline, but from the high ground they could look down on their enemies as they marched in loose formation to a second rise, somewhat below them and several hundred yards away.

The Corrax were a fearsome sight. Their faces were painted with terrifying images of blood and bones, and they were stripped naked to their waists to emphasize the huge muscles of their arms, shoulders, and torsos. They carried massive battle-axes and broadswords, their blades sharpened and gleaming even in the faint light of dawn. Were an adversary to be struck by any of these—even if it were only a glancing blow—death was almost certain. The Corrax fed on the fear of those they fought, and fear was unavoidable against creatures and weapons as large as these.

Parfend did not know who these enemies were, but they had invaded Corrax territory and were exhibiting a clear hostile intent to remain. Where they had come from remained a mystery. Efforts to speak with them had failed. Any chance at a reasonable resolution had evaporated when the heads of their envoys had been returned in a cart. The Corrax were warriors, fighters for as far back as anyone could remember. Nomads as well, which made their claim to the land on which they stood somewhat suspect.

But for the Corrax, wherever they were was territory that belonged to them until they decided to move on. They themselves were invaders with a long and bloody history of warring with the other Troll tribes. They had engaged most of them in battle at one time or another and, for the most part, triumphed. So they were not worried about this latest batch of fools.

The Corrax attack relied on brute force and a reckless disregard for personal safety to overwhelm and crush their opponents. It had always worked before. Strike hard. Give no ground. Show no mercy. It should have worked here. The Corrax should have been able to hammer their way through the invaders' lines with all the fury and bloodlust that had destroyed so many other armies.

Parfend took a moment to watch these latest enemies draw up in an uneven line on the lower ridge. They were lightly armored, tall, and fair-haired. With the ocean brume shifting and swirling, it was hard to tell much about them besides that. There did not appear to be as many of them as there were Corrax, which suggested they did not understand the nature of the enemy they faced. Anyone who knew anything of the Corrax people knew they were ferocious, relentless, and implacable. Once they engaged, they fought to the death. Once they attacked, they did not retreat.

But this enemy did not seem concerned. It simply waited for them to come, standing perfectly still in precise but loosely formed ranks, showing rather large gaps between individual soldiers. They stood with their long scarlet robes tightly drawn and their pale-tan boots set. Those in the front two ranks carried spears—eight-foot poles with hafts of pale ash, smooth, iron-tipped points affixed to one end, handgrips carved into the wood at the other. Those in the rear ranks bore short swords—held loosely at their sides, balanced and easily maneuverable in combat.

Parfend waited to see what they would do, but it soon became apparent they intended to do nothing. If the Corrax wanted a battle, they would have to do the attacking. This was fine with Parfend. The Corrax were used to attacking, to seizing the advantage, to striking swiftly and surely and making a quick end to any conflict. So it did not trouble him that they would have to do so here.

Nevertheless, he held his ground longer than usual. There was something odd about these men lined up across from them. There was an ethereal quality to them, a sense of ghostliness. The wind off the Tiderace whistled and the mists swept all around the invaders, and at times they seemed to fade and then reappear. Everything about them—even their weapons—seemed curiously insubstantial. They were creatures made not of flesh and blood but of smoke and mirrors. They were there, clearly revealed in their paleness, and yet they were not.

It was unsettling, but the Corrax were not accustomed to being troubled by things they couldn't explain. That was the nature of the world and those that inhabited it.

A moment longer, and Parfend gave the signal to attack, his sword arm raised high as he roared the Corrax battle cry. His warriors took it up. When his arm fell, the army rushed forward, screaming like madmen. They tore down the slope toward the waiting enemy, brandishing weapons while keeping their lines intact, one on point and two to form the body of the charge. Their cries shredded the sounds of the ocean and the wind, and the pounding of their feet on hardpan and rock sent up a fearful roar.

But the enemy did not stir. It continued to wait.

They will break, Parfend thought. *They will break and run.*

But they did not. They held their line, the butts of their spears firmly planted on the ground, their swords still sheathed. They remained so still they seemed to be statues rather than men. Not even a shifting of feet was visible. Not even the faintest whisper of voices could be heard.

The Corrax reached the valley between the two ridges and continued on. They slowed slightly with the incline, but their war cries remained undiminished. Even the bravest and most resolute of adversaries had always fled from them in the end.

The Corrax were within fifteen feet when the invaders shifted slightly, the entire line taking on a curious shimmer all along their ranks as they did so. While nothing seemed to change, there was an odd sense that something *had* happened. Then those in front lowered their spears and a bristling forest of long, steel-tipped shafts faced the Corrax. And all of a sudden it was unclear where any of them were. In another instant, they were not there at all. They had simply vanished.

The Corrax were caught completely by surprise and had no chance to adjust. By then, they were on top of the enemy, weapons slashing and stabbing, finding only empty air as the enemy ranks dissolved before them. They experienced a few quick moments of confusion and then sword blades and spear points were skewering and slashing the Corrax from places where no one seemed to be. The Corrax fought back in a frenzy, still screaming their battle cries as they died, but there was nothing they could do to protect themselves. They couldn't see their attackers. All they could see were empty images, insubstantial and no more solid than air.

Their enemies had become ghosts.

The Corrax fought on anyway, because that was all they knew to do, struggling as they did so to understand what was happening, to restore things to the way they should have been. But it was hopeless. Blood flew everywhere, painting the ground and the faces and torsos of the living. The Corrax swung wildly at nothing, trying to find their adversaries and failing. And still they were cut down.

They died still wondering what had killed them, still blind to what had happened.

At the center of the line, where the fighting was fiercest, Parfend tried to rally his warriors. He called them to him, had them form a solid line of defense, their weapons pointed out, their bark-skinned mass surging forward toward the enemy. Or to where they believed the enemy to be. But by now, the enemy was no longer where they had been. By now, the enemy was behind them, attacking their rear, felling the unsuspecting Trolls before they could defend themselves. All around the Corrax Maturen his friends and family died. All around him, his warriors perished. It was a slaughter, and there was nothing Parfend could do to stop it.

The battleground had become a charnel house, and the dead were piling up all around him. The Corrax were down to less than a hundred men, and those who remained alive were reduced to fighting for their lives individually or in small groups. A few even fell to their knees in abject surrender, begging. They were not spared. The wounded cried out for mercy. They were ignored.

One by one, they fell—the entirety of the Corrax attack force, all five hundred. Parfend battled on because he knew no other way, watching in dismay and fury as his warriors succumbed. All of his efforts at saving them, at rallying them, at turning the tide, failed. They were battling ghosts. They were fighting spirits of the air.

Parfend watched it all until one of those horrific eight-foot spears was driven through his body, and the strength went out of him. He fell to his knees, his great ax falling from his fingers, his arms limp at his sides. He looked up in time to see a vision approaching—a slender, cloaked form all in white, a broadsword gripped in two gloved hands. In a dream, he watched the sword lift and fall in a mighty swing.

Then his head fell from his shoulders.

FIVE

◆

NORTH OF ARBORLON AT the borders of the Elven nation, a new day had begun in the village of Emberen. In skies somewhat grayer and less friendly than those of the previous night, clouds massed on the western horizon, suggesting the approach of another storm. There was a metallic taste to the air and a smell of dampness that warned of what was coming. Winds had begun to gust, and the leaves of trees surrounding the village had begun to shiver with expectation.

Drisker Arc paid no attention to any of it. Instead, he continued to read his book, sitting on the porch of his cottage, absorbed in a study of shape-shifting. He had been up since dawn, an early riser, his breakfast consumed and his ablutions completed hours ago. His was a mostly solitary life, a life of study, contemplation, and practice with magic. Sometimes more experimentation than practice, but both always led to the same thing—an acquired or improved skill. His cottage was a mile removed from Emberen proper and surrounded by heavy forest, which allowed him to carry out his work undisturbed. His nearest neighbor was far enough away that even shouting was unlikely to attract any attention. Drisker preferred it this way. He valued his privacy more than the company of others. He always had— and now more than ever, since he had almost nothing else. He lived alone. No one came to visit. No one came to seek his advice. Traders and vendors passed him by. The past was past, and that was the way he liked it.

Although on mornings such as this one, he wished that, for a single day, he could go back in time and gain temporary access to Paranor and the Druids. There was trouble afoot, and it was the kind of trouble that the Druids should know about and investigate. Probably, at some point, they would. Some, at least, would think it worth doing. Some would manage to put aside their petty squabbles and constant bickering and look to the north. Some would find a way to ignore the politics and game playing that the others engaged in on a daily basis and realize that more important things were at stake than gaining a momentary advantage over their fellows by raising their status in the Druid pecking order.

Maybe. But maybe not. Maybe no one would do anything. He hadn't been able to change this attitude when he was there.

And he had been the order's High Druid.

He sighed, put aside his book, and stared off into the trees. It was hard even to think about it now. So much infighting. So many attempts by members of the order to advance their own causes. So little tolerance for the opinions of others. So little willingness to engage in reasonable discussion and compromise. How had it gotten so bad? Even now, looking back on it, remembering all the little details that had brought it about, he wasn't sure. It had happened slowly, if inexorably. Perhaps choices of who to admit as Druids in training had hastened the degeneration of the order's smooth operation. Perhaps the increase in size had weakened the earlier stability that he and a handful of others had enjoyed and been better able to control. There had always been periods of turmoil over the years, deaths and departures, changes in the structure of the order, periodic attacks from within and without. But the Druids had survived the worst of it, emerging stronger each time, ready to continue their work. They had put the past behind them and continued to seek out foreign magic, collecting or neutralizing the more dangerous forms, determining the sources of power that showed on the scrye waters, and housing those artifacts that needed watching over so that they could not be misused.

A struggle, to be sure. A work in progress that had no discernible end and might never be finished. In the world of the Four Lands, magic was everywhere and much of it was unstable. Science had failed in the Old World and been abandoned. Magic had filled the void, and for many years now had been the dominant power in the reborn world of the Races. But always there had been the threat that magic, like science, might be misused, might be left untended, might break free on its own, or might give birth to new ills and sicknesses that would match those that marked the time of science. That had happened, sometimes with devastating consequences. But each time the magic had been brought under control and turned back before growing too dark to contain.

It was always the Druids who made this possible. It was the Druids who shepherded and bound close wild magic, standing against the worst of it and mastering the best.

Now the world was changing once more, and the Druids were changing with it. Wasn't that why he was here instead of at Paranor? New science was emerging, mostly from the Federation, forms unknown in the Old World that had come alive in the new. Forms that relied to a substantial extent on diapson crystals and the power that could be unleashed through skilled faceting and a harnessing of sunlight. There were airships and ground vehicles that utilized both. There were flash rips and thunderbolts, railguns and shredder slings all capable of releasing power that could shred and destroy enemies and their weapons. There were new communications devices that allowed conversations and visuals between people who were hundreds of miles away from each other. There were machines that could affect the weather, machines that could generate storms to provide rain for farmland. There were transports of such size they could carry entire armies. So much changing, but the Druids weren't changing with it.

The magic was all they needed, they kept saying.

The magic was the only power that mattered.

It wasn't necessary to employ these new sciences. They didn't need to embrace a future others claimed to own.

They held the balance of power among the nations, and they would continue to do so forever.

Drisker Arc pursed his lips. *Not if you tear yourselves and your order to pieces from within first.*

He rose and stretched. He was a big man—enormously strong, broad-shouldered, and muscular. Of all the Druids since the time of Allanon, he was physically the most impressive. At almost seven feet, he wore his hair long and braided. He was not a young man, his dark skin lined by weather and the demands of magic's use, but neither was he old. He had not slept the Druid Sleep while High Druid, so his aging was a natural process. His eyes were bright and alert and a curious pale blue that suggested an unexpected gentleness. His smile was warm when offered, but his gaze was piercing enough that most would look away rather than meet it.

He was a mass of contradictions.

He adhered to order and ethic, as did few others, yet he was forgiving of those who could not match his discipline. Magic and its uses were his life's passion but he understood those who did not share his feelings or even thought them foolish and dangerous. He was famously mercurial, his temperament going from calm and steady to borderline out-of-control—in spite of the warmth reflected in his eyes. He sounded the same when he was patient and when he was not; his moods were often hard to determine.

He was unreadable. Inscrutable. No one could ever be quite certain what he was thinking before he revealed himself.

He lowered his arms out of his stretch and sat down again. He knew all these things about himself. Others had witnessed it often enough that he would have had to be obtuse not to notice their reactions. He accepted what was true about himself but did not much admire any part of it save his compulsion for studying and mastering magic. That meant something. That had value.

Although no longer, perhaps. No longer, when this latest Druid order threatened to throw away all that had been accomplished. Not when the Four Lands were in danger and there might be no one who would come to the rescue.

He shook his head, bitterness flooding through him.

Word of terrible violence had come down out of the Northland, bits and pieces of rumor that filtered through vast distances. The rumors were neither clear nor reliable, because they were carried to him by strange visions sent in dreams and the shrieks of birds and the whispers of winds rustling in the forest. But he was a magic wielder, and he knew better than to discount such signs. His eyes in that part of the world would send word at some point if it were true, a confirmation of the magic's vestigial warnings. Still, he sensed even now that it was. And his instincts seldom betrayed him in these matters.

The Druids should be wondering the same thing. Especially if the scrye waters indicated magic had been used. The scrye responded to all magical disturbances in the Four Lands, and one of this size could hardly have been missed. Surely, the waters of the reading bowl had recorded it, and someone would be sent to investigate.

He would have gone to Paranor to inquire if he had thought for one minute anyone would admit him. Or even listen to him. Just to hear what they had to say about it and what they intended to do would ease his concerns. Doing nothing ate at him, yet what choice did he have? He was no longer one of them. He was no longer welcome at Paranor. Balronen had made sure of that when he assumed the position of High Druid. Never one to leave anything to chance, he had banned Drisker from the Keep on the spot, proclaiming him a Druid no longer but an outcast. He was making sure that Drisker could not change his mind at some point and choose to return.

In truth, Ober Balronen was afraid of him—and not without good reason. Drisker had always found Balronen to be little more than a political animal with ambitions that far exceeded his abilities. When he had come to Paranor to ask for admittance to the order, Drisker had voted against it. But enough others were persuaded to embrace it that his veto was overridden. Years later, when Drisker decided to step down as High Druid and depart Paranor for a new life, Balronen had been quick to seize the opportunity to claim his position and find a way to persuade the majority of Druids that he was the right choice for the job. Drisker had never imagined Balronen would have been accepted as High Druid or even have the audacity to lay claim to it. If he had known, he would have thought twice about giving him the opportunity. He would have held on to his office.

But he knew that wasn't the truth. He would have left anyway, so maybe Balronen's ascendency was inevitable in any event. Balronen was the epitome of what was wrong at Paranor. Wasn't he representative of the many reasons Drisker had chosen to leave in the first place? Wasn't he just another of those men and women mired in self-indulgence and inattentive to the needs of others who had soured him on the Druid order? Wasn't he another example of the recent failure of Druids to adhere to a commitment to finding and protecting magic for the betterment of the Four Lands rather than as a way of gaining personal power?

All true, but the extent to which Balronen and his kind had abandoned this professed cause was stunning. It troubled him to think he had left things in such disarray. It haunted him even as he tried to tell himself it didn't matter anymore.

A slight movement in the trees to his right caught his eye. Pretending not to notice, he picked up his book and began to read again.

Someone was out there.

He waited patiently. He felt the other's presence, sensed rather than saw or heard the movements. Someone. But who, exactly? Who would come sneaking around like this? The movement continued, a sort of shifting from one place to another, almost taunting him with tiny reveals between long gaps marked only by stealth and swiftness as one position gave way to another. Whoever was responsible was extraordinarily skilled.

It occurred to him that maybe this was one of his enemies come to bring him down, but he abandoned the idea almost as fast as it surfaced. That was ridiculous. What would be the point of the small reveals? If his enemies wanted to harm him, why would they hesitate like this? Besides, he didn't sense any ill will in what was happening, and he could almost always tell.

Still, better to make sure before he took anything for granted.

He put down his book once more and looked directly to where he had last sensed his uninvited guest. "I know you're there."

"I wanted you to know," a voice answered coming from a different place entirely. "I need your help."

A girl, her voice still young enough to make her recognizable as such.

"Well, now that we both know you're here, why don't you come out of hiding so we can say hello face-to-face?"

"No. I have to prove myself. Do you think you can find me?"

He hesitated. What was this about? "Why would I bother?"

"To prove you can."

He stood up, looked over at the woods, and shrugged. "Seems like I ought to be the one testing you, not the other way around."

"You are testing me," the voice replied, now coming from another new place. "This is how I can prove to you I would be a good student."

"I don't want a student."

"But I need you to teach me. Why don't you see if I'm worth it? Test me."

"You won't like how this turns out."

"Maybe not. Let's make a bargain. If I can sneak up on you, you agree to teach me how to better use my magic. I do have magic, in case you were wondering. But if you get the better of me, I'll walk away."

"You sound very confident of yourself."

"I'm not confident at all. I'm desperate. Will you test me?"

"You'll be walking away however this goes. I don't teach anyone these days. I am retired. Do you know who I am? I guess you must."

"I know all about you. I knew of you before I came to find you. People were more than willing to tell me where you were once I reached Elven country. It's not a big secret. Come on. Test me to see if I am worth teaching. You are famous for your magic skills. Try to find me."

She was somewhere else by then. He smiled to himself. He admired her audacity. She was good at shifting her position without showing any movement when she did so. He hated to admit it, but he rather enjoyed the idea of a fresh challenge. It had been awhile since he had faced one.

"All right," he said. "How do we play this game?"

"You see me and call me out before I can get close enough to tap you on the shoulder."

"And are there rules?"

Her laughter was muted. "What do you think?"

Drisker Arc smiled in spite of himself.

SIX

◆

FROM HER HIDING PLACE, Tarsha Kaynin saw him smile and smiled back. It was a shared moment she would treasure always, no matter how this turned out. She had come a long way to find him, escaping one set of hardships at home only to encounter more on the road. But she was a determined sort and so certain of herself that she had not considered the possibility she would fail. Find Drisker Arc. Demonstrate her magic in a way that would impress him. Convince him to help her improve on and master her skills. Help her save her brother before it was too late.

She waited on him, thinking he would act quickly to find her. She was humming softly to herself, the sound no more than a whisper of breezes passing through the limbs of the trees surrounding her. It hid her from anyone seeking her out so completely that for all intents and purposes she was rendered invisible. It was her strongest magical skill—a skill she had mastered early on. She had never been a fighter, never big or strong enough to be physically capable of standing up for herself. But use of the magic let her escape the worst of what others would do to her as a result of being Tavo's sister, and she had decided this was how she could best impress Drisker Arc and persuade him she was worth teaching.

Thus, this game. Thus, everything that would follow.

She remained where she was a moment longer before moving on. She was wearing loose-fitting forest clothing, fabrics colored in mottled greens and browns, material that made no sound and reflected no light. Her boots were soft leather, cut ankle length. She carried no weapons or jewelry—nothing that would clink or flash and give her away. Her white-blond hair was wrapped in a headscarf, tied up and tucked away. Her freckled features were blackened to hide her pale skin. She wore gloves. She had thought this through carefully. This was a game she needed to win.

The Druid was looking around now but only casually and not with any evident intentions in mind. She began moving left, hiding her movements and sounds, screening herself as she slipped among the black trunks of the old growth that warded the Druid's small cottage. He did not turn with her, did not look her way. He took a step right and turned from her momentarily but nothing more.

She would say nothing more, she decided. She would cease taunting him. It was only important now that she be able to convince him of her promise. Anything else was a distraction.

Wind whistled hard through the upper branches of the trees, and she glanced skyward momentarily. Leaves shivered in a soft rustling, and limbs swayed. The sky overhead was a brilliant blue.

When she looked back, he was gone.

For a moment, she couldn't believe it. Then she realized he was doing the same thing to her that she was doing to him. He, too, had the ability to fade.

She shifted to another place, moving more cautiously now, searching for him through the trees. Once, she thought she caught sight of him, a momentary glimpse of his dark-robed form. But then he was gone again, smoke in sunlight. She must trick him, then. She must force him to reveal himself so that she could win the game. Swiftly. The longer it went on, the more likely she was to make a mistake. With this man, as storied as his skills with magic were, she knew it would take only one wrong move for her to give herself away.

Then she saw him. He was standing at the edge of the clearing, just back in the trees, seemingly no more than another dark trunk at first glance. A closer look told her otherwise. He had positioned himself carefully so that he blended into the forest. He was unmoving, waiting on her. He would stay there until she gave herself away and then call her out. It was a clever ruse. He had waited for her to look away just for a moment—perhaps even caused her to look away—before shifting out of her sight lines and fading into the trees. It was what she would have done, had their positions been reversed.

But she had him now.

Tarsha forced herself to remain calm, to move so she was coming at him from behind. She waited for him to turn her way, but he did not. She continued to advance, taking her time, but moving steadily closer. She thought about causing a distraction that would keep him looking away, but then decided it was too risky and could easily have the opposite effect and bring him around to face her.

Slowly, she told herself. *Slowly.*

Time ground to a crawl. Wind rippled the Druid's dark cloak, but still he did not turn. She was almost on top of him now, no more than ten feet away. She hesitated, wondering suddenly if this wasn't too easy, if this might not be a trap to get her to reveal herself. But how could it be a trap? He was right there. All she needed to do was tap him on the shoulder and the game was over.

She moved up swiftly and reached out her hand.

But when she touched his shoulder, he wasn't there. It was only an image of him, and her hand passed right through it.

She gasped in spite of herself and then felt his hand on her shoulder, tapping softly. "You lose."

Disappointment and frustration flooded through her, but she turned to face him anyway, putting on a brave face. "That was very clever of you."

He nodded, smiled. "Years of experience that you don't have yet. How old are you?"

She thought about lying and decided against it. "Seventeen."

"So skilled at such a young age. I'm impressed. What is your name?"

"Tarsha Kaynin."

"Do you understand the nature of the magic you possess, Tarsha Kaynin? Do you know what it is called?"

"I don't know anything about it. Do you?"

"Your magic is called the wishsong. You can trace it directly back to a family called Ohmsford. It was within their bloodline, centuries ago, that it first found life. Its power lies in your voice, does it not?"

She nodded. "It's a sort of singing or humming. Sometimes just shouting or screaming is enough. As far as I know, I am the first in my family to possess the magic. Well, the second, actually. Tavo has it, too. He's my brother. But my parents don't and none of our family earlier did, either. Do you have the wishsong magic?"

He shook his head, a rueful expression on his face. "I wish I did. But it is magic passed on through genetics, and the Ohmsfords were not part of my lineage. No, my magic is of a different sort."

"It was good enough to beat me and win the game."

"It would have been embarrassing not to have beaten you. I am far more experienced than you, and much more skilled in magic's use. You, I am guessing, have been self-taught."

She nodded ruefully. "That's what brought me here. I want to get better at using it."

"So I gather." His smile returned, surprisingly warm. "Well, even if you've lost our little contest, it doesn't mean you have to leave right away. Would you like to come sit on my porch with me and share a cup of tea and some sweet cinnamon bread?"

She had not eaten in more than a day and been traveling for two weeks, so she was happy to agree. If he was still talking to her and not yet ready to dismiss her out of hand, perhaps there was still a chance. She had to hope so. Persuading him to teach her was all she had left. If he sent her away, there was nowhere else for her to go.

He took her into his cottage and directed her to a pump and basin so she could wash off her face and generally clean up a bit. As she worked on herself, he stood watching, speaking softly.

"You have considerable skill already," he told her. "Few others could have done what you just did. Had I been a little less practiced, you might have won our game. But you failed to take into account the fact that I might have the same skill as you and be better at it. My image was made of stronger stuff than you expected or you wouldn't have allowed yourself to be lured out of hiding. A good lesson there, Tarsha."

"I need such lessons," she said, looking up from the basin, water dripping off her face as the blacking washed away. "It's why I've come. Even knowing you would probably say no. My parents are farmers in the Westland village of Backing Fell. They have no money and know no one who uses magic. My brother can use it, too, like I said. But he's not good with it."

She trailed off, deciding she had already said enough. But the Druid was watching her closely.

"You came all the way from the deep end of the Westland to ask me to teach you?" Drisker shook his head. "Not very sensible of you. Why not go to the Elves in Arborlon?"

"I don't want Elves teaching me. I want you. You're the best magic user of all. Everyone says so. You're the most accomplished, the most talented, and the most experienced. I thought all I needed to do was persuade you."

"How did you even find me?"

She had finished washing off her face. He beckoned her to a seat at his kitchen table, where he had already set out the tea and bread. She began to eat without a word. After several bites, she looked up again. "As I said, it wasn't that hard. I just asked around. I thought you were in Paranor at first, but that turned out not to be the case."

"Someone told you I was here?"

"Not right off. At first, people ignored me. They told me to go away. But I don't give up easily. I kept asking. I finally found someone who was happy to tell me where you were."

"Who was that?"

"I have no idea. Whoever he was, he didn't seem to like you much. He said you were thrown out of Paranor and good riddance."

"So it appears Paranor is not the only place where I'm not so popular these days."

"Why were you thrown out?" she asked.

"I wasn't thrown out. I was exiled."

"So you left," she said, finishing her bread and licking her fingers. "Why did you do that? Why didn't you fight it? There must be more to the story."

"Do you think that's your business?"

She shrugged. "No. I'm just curious. Paranor was your home. You lived there for years. You were High Druid. You were respected. Why would you give all that up?"

He leaned back in his chair, giving her a look. "Some things aren't worth keeping. Sometimes, you have to let go. Sometimes, you have to follow your conscience and put aside your pride."

"You wanted a different life for yourself? Like me?"

"Maybe not like you, but yes, I wanted a different life. The Druid order isn't what it once was, and I couldn't seem to change the direction it was going or the mindsets of my fellows. I have a strong sense of purpose when it comes to being a Druid, but those around me didn't seem to share it. I tried to change their minds, but I failed. In the end, I decided I couldn't stay. So I left."

"What do you do now?"

"You are curious, aren't you? Some might call you nosy."

"Some might. Some have. I wasn't well liked in my village. People are afraid once they sense there's something different about you. I don't have any friends except for my brother, and he is only a sometimes-friend. Even my parents are a little afraid of me. And a whole lot afraid of him."

"You are right about having magic. It doesn't win you friends. It makes people fear you, but sometimes, if you are lucky, it makes them respect you, too. Another good lesson, Tarsha."

"That one I've already learned." She looked around at the cottage. "So what are you doing here?"

"Reading. Studying magic. Enjoying the peace and quiet of the forest."

"Sounds boring. Why don't you teach me, instead? At least, that would be interesting. I'm not afraid of hard work, and I could be good with magic if someone would show me how to use it properly. You could do that."

"I left teaching magic behind when I departed Paranor for Emberen." He poured them both another cup of tea, then shoved it all aside impulsively and brought out a pitcher of ale from cold storage and poured them each a glassful, instead. "Are you allowed to have this?"

Tarsha shrugged. "My mother probably wouldn't approve."

"From what I've seen of you so far, that doesn't bother you much. Does she approve of you coming here on your own?"

"She doesn't know. If she did, I wouldn't be here." She picked up the glass of ale and drained it. "Good. I've had better once or twice, but this is tasty. Did you make it?"

"I did. Now let's cut to the chase. Something about your explanation doesn't ring true. You spoke about your brother. It seems his need to learn to control the magic is much stronger than yours, yet you didn't bring him with you. Why is that?"

She held her glass out for more, trying to think what she should say. "I don't like talking about it," she said finally as he refilled her ale.

"Maybe not, but I think you have to. If he is the reason you are here, I have to know that. I have to know about him. You want me to be your teacher? Then you have to be willing to tell me all your secrets."

"You already said you wouldn't be my teacher."

Drisker Arc shrugged. "You decide."

She hesitated again, this time for longer. Then she sighed. "My brother is scary," she said.

"Too scary to bring with you, even given his condition?"

"Especially given his condition. It's gotten worse. He has little control over his temper and less over his magic. I tried to teach him what I could, but I must not have been a very good teacher. He just never understood. Much of the time, I was worried about what he might do to other children. I was afraid he might hurt them. When he grew angry, his temper was uncontrollable."

She paused, taking a fresh drink, lowering her eyes. "It was so bad having him at home that my parents moved him out four years ago. They sent him to live with my uncle on a farm in a nearby town. My uncle lives alone, no family. So now my brother works for him, laboring in the fields. He hates my uncle, but he has nowhere else to go."

"Sounds very unpleasant." Drisker eyed her the way he might a curious object. His brow furrowed. "Did you tell him you were leaving to come here?"

"No, I couldn't."

"Because he wouldn't have liked it?"

"Because neither my parents nor my uncle allow me to see him. But I am afraid for him. I did manage to see him once, and something was terribly wrong. My uncle spoke of games they played, and . . . It didn't sound right. I think he might be . . . doing something to Tavo. Something he shouldn't. I had to find some way to help him."

The Druid nodded slowly. "So you're here because of him, aren't you? If I help you, maybe you can help him."

Tarsha forced herself to meet his gaze. "Yes."

She was irritated that he had seen through her so easily. She had hoped to tell him in her own good time and on her own terms. She had hoped to keep this part of her life to herself. But he was too perceptive for that.

"You realize, of course, that teaching someone to use magic— especially magic as powerful as the wishsong—takes months, maybe years. By the time you learn enough to help him, everything might have changed in his life. Or yours. And there is nothing to say that anything you learn from me would even do what you want for your brother. His condition doesn't sound like something that can be mended quickly."

"I know that." She exhaled sharply and fought back the tears that threatened. "But I couldn't just sit back and hope things got better. I took a chance. He's my brother. Good or bad, sane or not, I love him."

"But that doesn't change the facts. Magic can't be mastered overnight. It can't be turned quickly to specific purposes. It has to be understood. You have to be inhabited by it. It has to be embraced by your heart, mind, and body."

"I know that, too. I know all that. But I have to get better at using it. I have to learn how to . . ."

She trailed off, suddenly engulfed in a feeling of hopelessness and futility. This wasn't working. She stood up abruptly. "Thanks for talking to me. And for the tea and bread and ale. I have to go."

Drisker shrugged. "I was hoping you would stay a little longer."

"I don't think I can."

"Giving up so easily?"

She wheeled on him. "Well, you made it pretty clear how you feel about helping me. You think I've gone about this the wrong way and don't deserve your help. You want me out of your hair. So I'm going."

She started for the door.

"Hold on!" he called out sharply. When she turned back, he said, "Maybe I'm rethinking my position."

"No, you're not. You're just saying that!" She was angry and petulant, and she heard it in her words. She blushed deeply and shook her head. "I didn't mean that. I'm just disappointed. I don't think that of you."

"Well, you won't find out if you leave, will you?"

She slowed at the door and turned. "If this is a game . . ."

His dark face was inquisitive and oddly encouraging. "You showed real courage and determination coming here. Not many could have done what you have. I think that's worth considering."

She hesitated and then came back to the table and sat. "So you might agree to teach me?"

"Don't you think you're worth it?"

She grinned. A little of the cockiness returned. "Of course."

"Then let's talk about it a little more. Let's see if maybe it might be possible." He paused. "You interest me, Tarsha Kaynin."

The discussion continued for a time, with Tarsha answering question after question about her magic and her ability to use it. The Druid seemed as interested in the extent of her understanding of how it worked and what it could do as he was in her personally. She let him take her wherever he wanted in this discussion, encouraged now that she could persuade him to take her on as his student. His words as she'd been about to leave convinced her she still stood a chance of winning him over, and she had no intention of letting that chance slip away.

"You realize you are committing yourself to a long period of serious study and practical experience, Tarsha," he said at one point.

"This isn't something you can undertake if you don't intend to stick with it. You have to be sure that no matter how difficult or unpleasant it becomes, you will not walk away."

"I made that decision before I came to find you," she assured him. "I've lived with the wishsong since I discovered it as a child. I didn't even know what it was back then. I didn't know what was happening to me. I don't think anything can be as frightening or confusing as that was. I have to master it if I'm to live with it."

"And help your brother?"

"I can't help him if I can't help myself."

"You aren't suffering from any of the same problems he is, are you?"

She hadn't thought about that. She hesitated. "If I was, you wouldn't teach me, would you?"

His smile was unexpectedly kind. "Just answer the question, please."

"I don't think I have his problems. I'm not like him. Even aside from his struggle with the magic, we have very different personalities. I think I'm stronger than he is."

He studied her a moment, as if judging the validity of what she had said. Or perhaps measuring her strengths as she had revealed them in this conversation. "I think you are probably right."

"Will you take me on?" she pressed, unable to stand it any longer. "I've done everything I can to persuade you. So will you?"

"Let's understand something," he said. "I am not a Druid. I am a once-Druid. So you will not be receiving instruction from the real article, only a semblance of one. I will be able to teach you magic, but I will not be able to make you a Druid."

"I care nothing for being a Druid."

"As well, if I agree to teach you, I will need something back in payment. Not credits but services. You must agree to stay with me for one year afterward, working as my assistant, using what I've taught you to help me out. Will you agree to do this?"

Tarsha hesitated. If she agreed, she would be away from her home and her brother for a year beyond the time it took her to complete her training. That seemed a very long time to let things go untended, given how she had left them. She had thought to go back sooner, to take what knowledge she had gained and use it to help him.

"I don't know," she said. "I don't think I can leave Tavo alone for that long."

"I understand," Drisker said quietly. "So I will make a bargain with you. Once I find you ready for it, I'll give you time to go home and do what you can. No more than two weeks, but at least enough time to find out what is needed. After that, you come back. If things are bad, we can talk about how it should be handled."

"You will listen to what I might think is necessary?"

"I will listen. And you, in turn, must listen to me."

Everything she could have hoped for was being offered her. Everything she had come to find, everything she had thought she had lost, was now gained back. The tears started again, and she took a moment to compose herself. It was a long moment.

When she was steady again, she looked up at him. "We have a bargain."

"Then let's begin, Tarsha Kaynin."

SEVEN

Two days later, within the walls of the Druid Keep at Paranor, High Druid Ober Balronen called his inner circle of advisers into a meeting, the subject of which he refused to reveal until all were assembled. It was typical of him to be coy about the purposes of these clandestine gatherings, which were routinely limited to a few trusted supporters. Darcon Leah stood against the wall behind the High Druid's chair and faced the seven gathered about the long table. It was a familiar cluster of faces, but that didn't mean he could afford to relax his vigilance. Though he doubted any would try to harm the High Druid, he was positioned so he could act instantly if one of them attempted to prove him wrong. It was his job, after all, as the High Druid's Blade, to do so.

And with men and women as fickle and mercurial as these, you never took anything for granted.

Balronen had not yet appeared, preferring as always to be the last to enter. He reveled in the authority he commanded, and never missed an opportunity to let others know it. He was more a schemer than he was a strong, inspirational leader. He led from behind, as those in the Druid Guard liked to joke among themselves—although they never did so in anything but the Troll language and never to Balronen's face. He was not well liked by the guard, who missed

Drisker Arc's relaxed, casual approach to command and detested Balronen's constant manipulations.

Dar didn't think much of the High Druid, either, but since he spent most of his waking hours either in his presence or doing his bidding, he did as much as he could not to think about it.

The men and women gathered at the table were a mixed bag. Selected for reasons known only to Balronen, they were not the sorts one might expect. A couple were nothing more than paper cutouts—men and women possessing few achievements or recognizable moral code, blackboards waiting for their leader to write upon. No original thought had passed any of their lips since Balronen had succeeded to the position of High Druid. Or at least, none they were sharing. What they were good at was squirming out of difficult situations and avoiding blame. If blame was to be found, it would not be attached to them.

That was half of them.

The other half, save one, were a little more problematic—smarter and more clever than their fellows, and not-so-secretly ambitious. They tried to hide it, but Dar saw through them easily enough and was certain Balronen did, too. But they had value because they enjoyed power bases of their own within the order. The High Druid would have known this, as well, and probably believed the old saying about keeping your friends close and your enemies closer. These members of his inner circle weren't enemies, but it was certain they harbored ambitions that could impact Balronen if carried out. So there was a constant tension among all of them that was difficult to mistake but hard to read.

Dar Leah didn't bother trying. These men and women repelled him—all save the one. He suspected it was precisely because they were antagonistic toward one another that Balronen found them useful. He was the sort of man who liked the idea of his followers rubbing up against one another and giving off sparks. He dismissed their plotting and manipulating because he was so much better at it than they were, content to let them wait for chances that would never come. But for Dar, as protector of the High Druid, they were an unpredictable annoyance with the potential for turning dangerous.

It all made him wish for earlier times, for the days when Drisker Arc was High Druid and things were less complicated. He liked Drisker and had even tried to persuade him not to leave after his decision had been announced. But the former High Druid was a tough-minded and stubborn man, and when things became bad enough that he could no longer stomach them, he didn't hesitate to remove himself from the situation. It wasn't necessarily the right thing to do in Dar's mind, but Drisker was his own man. Drisker had tried everything he could think of to change the order's direction, but the manipulations and scheming had eventually undone him.

Dar missed him and missed the atmosphere that had prevailed at Paranor during his tenure as High Druid. Now that he was gone, Dar found himself thinking about leaving, too.

There was a sudden stirring, a shifting of seats and bodies, and everyone turned as Ober Balronen entered the room to take his place at the head of the table. A tall, lean man with deceptively bland features and a stooped look, he seemed to be anything but what he was. As he passed Dar, he gave his Blade his customary nod. The nod was not intended as a friendly greeting but as an unnecessary reminder to stay alert. It was an example of the way Balronen liked to exercise his authority. As High Druid, he never hesitated to remind others of the power he wielded. Insecure and suspicious, he trusted Dar as much as he trusted anyone.

Which was to say, marginally.

"I've received a report of a massacre in the northern territories," he said. His sharp eyes shifted from face to face. "An entire Troll army, annihilated. Normally, this wouldn't be something we would even be talking about. The Trolls are warlike, and one batch is always killing off another."

There were a few knowing chuckles. A few less Trolls didn't really matter that much, after all. Dar kept his facial expression impassive.

"But in this case the scrye waters revealed the presence of an unknown magic. Substantial magic. Presumably wielded by whoever carried out the massacre. This happened three days ago. There have been no other reports. What should we do?"

As always, he was testing them, waiting to see who was sharp enough to offer the solution he had already determined on. As usual, Ruis Quince, his voice smooth and knowing, spoke first. "Who destroyed this Troll army? It wasn't another Troll army, I assume?"

Balronen nodded. "Exactly. It was someone else altogether. We don't know who."

"Well, we have to find out!" growled Prax Tolt. One of the leaders of the warrior Druids, he was aggressive and confrontational. He glared challengingly about the table. "How could something like this happen and we not know about it beforehand?"

"Are we expected to be prescient as well as magic-skilled?" Crace Adris was their historian, and a sharper mind did not exist in the ranks of the current Druid order. A small man with restless eyes and quick movements, he made a gesture to emphasize his point. "Seems you are expecting a lot from us, Prax."

"We should find out who they are and what they intend," Quince pursued, speaking directly to Balronen. "Confront them. Give them a taste of real magic. A kind of warning. Prax is trained as a warrior Druid; he should go. He could take a handful of the guard to back him up."

"And if they possess magic superior to our own, then what?" Balronen pressed.

There was a moment's silence. "I don't see why we bother with any of this just yet," said the Dwarf, Chu Frenk. "What does it matter if they destroy every Troll in the Northland? Until they demonstrate they are a real threat to us, we should let them be."

Frenk was one of the more sycophantic members of the inner circle. A corpulent and sour-tempered man who had little patience with or regard for anyone, he entertained himself by finding new ways to upset the others. Only Balronen mattered to him.

"You ignore my question!" the High Druid snapped, causing Frenk to flinch. "What if their magic is *superior* to ours? What if they intend to use it against us? What then, Chu? Do we wait until their blades are at our necks before we act?"

Frenk did a quick calculation and decided to backtrack. "I am not suggesting we do nothing. But it wouldn't hurt to wait a bit to make certain of their intentions. If we go looking for trouble, we are likely to find it."

"Why would you say that?" Tolt snapped. "This violent attack on a Troll tribe would suggest trouble is already on the way!"

"As usual, you and I disagree," Frenk replied dismissively. "If this army intends to attack Paranor, why alert us while still so far away? High Lord, I think only of what's best for you and for Paranor. Let's consider this a minute. What if this army intends harm not to us but to others? Maybe we can turn this to our advantage. Perhaps it can be made to serve our purposes. Perhaps we can find a way to use this army against those who already threaten us. There are more than a few of them, are there not? The Federation, for instance. Let's wait and find out what these invaders want, and then look at whether we can strike a bargain with them."

"Careful, Frenk," Crace Adris spat at him. "You seem to forget you are talking of my birthplace."

"An unfortunate burden you must bear as best you can," Frenk sympathized. "But this doesn't change that they would see us brought down. You haven't had a change of heart when it comes to your Druid oath, have you?"

Adris started to get to his feet, but Tolt pulled him back into his seat quickly. "You should show some manners now and then," he said to Frenk. He shifted his muscular bulk in an aggressive way. "It might help change our rather low opinion of you."

"I care nothing for your opinion. I care only for the High Druid's. Let's stay on point. What if I am right?"

Ober Balronen nodded as if in agreement. "All well and good. But what if you are wrong? What if this invasion force intends to come here next? Do we simply sit and wait?"

"We do as you wish, High Lord," Frenk answered and went silent.

"We should proceed cautiously," Quince added.

Clizia Porse spoke for the first time, leaning forward for emphasis. She was slender to the point of emaciation, tall and sharp-featured and of indeterminate age. Dar also thought her perhaps the most dangerous of the bunch. She had a reputation as a poisoner, and more than one of those foolish enough to cross her had died writhing in agony. No one had ever proved anything, of course, but suspicions were strong and conjectures endless.

"Ruis is right: This is a delicate situation." Her owlish eyes shifted from one face to the next, probing. "On the other hand, it must be dealt with. Sitting back and doing nothing is not a viable option."

"A delegation, then?" Crace Adris said, making it more a question rather than a suggestion. "Neither an attack nor a verbal warning but a simple meeting. A discussion. Approach them and ask their intentions. What can it hurt if we do that much? There is no threat in seeking common ground."

"He's right," Frenk agreed quickly. "And our very able and experienced Crace Adris is exactly the right man for the job. His obvious lack of warrior prowess will suggest no threat is posed to those he approaches and will allow him to assess the situation efficiently."

"Perhaps I disagree with you," Adris snapped.

"Perhaps that is irrelevant," Frenk replied.

"It is the High Druid's decision, not yours."

"Which might get you off the hook, might it not? Is that your wish?"

"*Enough.*" There was a deep impatience evident in Balronen's voice, and all fell silent. "Pescarin. Amarodian. What say you? Speak up."

"I defer to your decision, as always." Pescarin bowed slightly from his seat. "I am not a military-minded man."

"Just a simple-minded one," Tolt spit out. "The High Lord asks for your opinion. Give it."

Pescarin glanced over, his smooth face registering pity. "I do not answer to you, Tolt. Nor do I look to you for help with interpreting what the High Lord means when he addresses me. I can manage that for myself, I'm happy to say."

Balronen looked as if he would intervene and say something to both of them, and then apparently decided to give it up. "Zia. Let's have your opinion. No deferrals to me, please. Enough sidestepping."

Zia Amarodian was the only one of those gathered whom Dar liked, and the one who seemed most out of place with these backbiters and schemers. Her support of Balronen made no sense. He knew her well enough that he found her presence in the High Druid's inner circle odd. As far as Dar knew, she had never spent time with him before he was elevated to the position of High Druid. She was an Elf, though not in the mode of most other Elves. She was a Halfling, born to an Elf mother and a human father, but she looked entirely Elf on the surface. Her temperament, on the other hand, was all too human. She was quick to anger and slow to forgive. Frenk had gotten on her bad side over a year ago and remained there still. The two never spoke, even in meetings such as these.

Zia's reticence was famous. She seldom voiced her thoughts, and when she did she was succinct. Dar expected it would be the case here.

"I think we are wasting our time discussing this. If magic has registered in the scrye waters and a massacre is connected, we need to find out the reason. Waiting is a fool's game, and we are not fools. Crace Adris has voiced the proper solution to the problem. Let's do as he suggests. But let Ruis Quince be given leadership of the delegation. He is the more experienced negotiator and statesman. I will go with him. I'm curious to know what this incident means."

It was a bold declaration for someone who seldom bothered to make one. Moreover, it was a voicing of opinion that almost never happened. Zia must feel strongly about this business, Dar thought. Or at least more strongly than she had about much else in the time he'd known her.

But then he was prejudiced when it came to Zia. He glanced at her momentarily, unable to help himself. Theirs was a complicated relationship, and he had to take a step back before he attempted any objective analysis of her behavior.

Balronen seemed pleased. "This seems a reasonable course of action to me—although we mustn't act in haste. We should wait for further word on this army's movements. Then, if I deem it necessary to send a delegation, Ruis and Zia will go. Now let's move on. There are other matters that require our attention. Let's start with the Federation. What else do we have that needs to be dealt with concerning the machinations of our Southland friends?"

The conversation shifted to other, less interesting topics. The slaughter of the Corrax tribe should have had them all quaking in their Druid boots, yet none of them seemed overly bothered. Which was odd, because destroying an entire Troll army would suggest a rather powerful and dangerous enemy. Or perhaps the Elves were responsible. If there was magic involved, the Elves were the logical culprit. But it was unlikely the Elves would have attempted anything like this unless provoked, and the Druids would have heard about it in advance.

So it remained a possibility that this was an enemy they knew nothing about. If that wasn't cause for alarm, Dar didn't know what was. But the High Druid and the members of his inner circle were acting as if the matter was already resolved. It was one thing to consider sending Ruis Quince and Zia Amarodian on a mission to make contact. It was something else again to believe this response was sufficient without anything else being done.

The meeting dragged on with occasional bickering and flinging about of accusations and blame. It made Dar wonder how anything ever got done. He decided that it probably didn't, that whatever was currently accomplished within the Druid order happened without any help from the men and women in this room. He took a moment to stretch—irritated, bored, and fed up in general—and thought about walking out. But it was only a thought. He couldn't abandon his post, bored or not, without resigning his position, and he hadn't thought it through sufficiently yet to make the jump.

Instead, he shifted his attention to Zia, who was slouched back in her chair ignoring the tumult about her, looking as if she, too, wished she were somewhere else. She wasn't even bothering with making sure she was attracting Balronen's attention long enough to demonstrate her loyalty and give evidence of her importance as a member of his inner circle. If anything, she looked like she couldn't care less.

He caught her eye and nodded a silent greeting. She glared at him, as if her boredom was his fault, and he shrugged and looked away. She still hadn't forgiven him.

And there was much to forgive. He understood that now.

They had met in the second year of his service as Blade to Drisker Arc. At first their relationship was cordial but uncomplicated. She was a respected member of the Druid order and he was newly appointed as the High Druid's protector. A number of times, he had accompanied her on expeditions. On occasion, he walked with her in the woods, just the two of them, talking about the future of the order. Then his relationship with her slowly changed. He could feel it even as it was happening, a slow drifting toward something more personal, discovering an unexpected closeness that involved tender words and brief touching. He came to know her better and more fully, and she him. He welcomed this, because he found her to be interesting and compelling. Then he found her to be something more.

One night, woozy with sket and the warmth of the evening and a need that had grown undeniable, they crossed a line. The loving was sweet and urgent and intense. They found themselves in foreign territory and happy to be there. They were newly come to love and eager to know more of where it would take them. They were open about it because there was no reason not to be. He sensed they had started out on a journey from which there was no turning back, but he felt it was right to have done so. He did not fear the feelings she generated in him or the passion she aroused.

He should have.

At some point, shortly after Drisker had resigned his position and Balronen had become the new Ard Rhys, Dar was nearly killed while on a mission for the Druids into the deep Eastland. He survived, but it changed his thinking about Zia. Maybe trying to bind her to him was wrong. It wasn't that he didn't love her. He did. What was wrong was what he perceived for the first time to be a conflict between his position as Blade and her future as his life partner. Continuing the relationship would be a mistake. Everything he did put him in danger. Every time he set out on a fresh expedition for the Druids, he risked not coming back. His life hung by a thread when he came up against a dangerously wild or ill-used form of magic. There were too many ways he could be killed—and too many opportunities for it to happen. It was not fair to allow her to think they could have a life together. Not when that life was so tenuous. It was selfish and unreasonable. It was wrong of him to lead her on when he understood the realities of his work. He became convinced of it.

But he did not reveal any of this to her. He did not discuss it. He muddled through his regrets and doubts and uncertainties on his own, then decided it was best to put an end to things. He was thinking of her, and in a different way entirely not thinking of her at all. He believed he was protecting her while at the same time setting in place the foundation of an act that would damage her irreparably.

When he finally told her he was leaving, that while he loved her he did not want her to depend on someone who might be gone in the blink of an eye, she responded with shock, then tears, and then rage. She railed at him, called him a coward and a fool. She begged him to reconsider. She used arguments and threats. She tried physically to keep him from going.

But he ended it anyway. He was setting her free to have a life. At the time, that was what he believed he was doing. Eventually, he came to see he was doing something else entirely.

By then, it was too late.

So now here they were, former friends and lovers, sharing meetings as boring and unproductive as this one and not much more. Dissatisfied and unhappy. Drifting.

Zia was with Ruis Quince now, a condition Dar could barely manage to think about. Several months now, and it wasn't getting any easier for him to accept. He, on the other hand, was with no one, and not much interested in even bothering to look.

She looked back at him briefly, and he dropped his gaze. It was too hard for him to hold it. He could read too much of the past in her look.

He shifted his thoughts to the history of the Druids from Allanon to the present, retracing all they had accomplished, recounting to himself how many terrible threats they had helped overcome, how many wars and battles and individual struggles they had endured. The Four Lands had come a long way in three thousand years, and the Druids had been there every step of the way. They had helped make the transition from the devastation of the Old World to the hard-won but durable civilization of the present. Where once science had ruled and then failed, now magic held sway. The Druids had made this possible. They, more than anyone, including the Elves, had devoted themselves to gaining control of and managing artifacts and talismans and to finding ways to put a stop to the presence of rogue magic. They had dedicated their lives to being curators and protectors.

Except that now, all of a sudden, they weren't doing their job. Not since Drisker Arc had stepped down. Not since Ober Balronen had taken his place. Now, instead of aggressively pursuing an unknown magic employed by an unknown force, they were all but dismissing it, concerned only with how it could be turned to their political advantage. It was so wrong it screamed for a correction, yet there was no one other than Balronen with enough power to make that happen.

It gave him pause. It aroused anger and frustration. It caused him to take another long, hard look at what the future might hold. A single question kept coming back to him.

How long could this sort of casual disregard continue before the entire house of cards that was the Fourth Druid Order came tumbling down?

How long before something really bad happened?

EIGHT

◆

THE SLENDER BLACK-CLOAKED STRANGER appeared at the south gates of Paranor just after dawn, standing in place for a time and looking up at the walls of the Keep before calling to the sentries he knew would be watching to announce his presence. A side door opened, and two members of the Druid Guard appeared. Huge bark-skinned Trolls in heavy armor bearing halberds and short swords, they separated just outside the portal, one coming forward to meet with the stranger while the other stood just at the door, ready to seal it away again if the need arose.

The Troll who came out to greet the stranger studied him carefully. He was unusually fair-skinned when he pulled back the hood of his cloak to reveal his face. His appearance was pleasing, almost pretty, his skin smooth and unblemished, his build slender, and his expression placid. He was so nonthreatening that the Troll felt a disdain he could not tamp down. When the Troll asked him, in his Southland dialect, what he wished, the man replied in a soft, pleasant voice, using the same dialect, that he was there to be interviewed for a position in the Druid order and would like to speak to someone who could arrange for that. He said it as if it were the most natural thing in the world, but everyone in Paranor knew no one was given an interview save by invitation.

The Troll to whom he spoke stood looking at him for a long few moments, his features expressionless and unreadable.

"Wait here," he ordered finally, and together with his companion disappeared back inside the Keep. Once there, he went alone to the reception room to advise the Druid-in-Training on duty of the stranger's arrival.

Allis Errencarthyjorian, she of the unpronounceable last name, was one year into her training and shortly would be brought up for review to see if there was a possibility of further advancement in the order. As a result, she was deeply engaged in her studies, currently reading and rereading a book of spells and incantations that one of her teachers had advised she look into carefully before her examination by her Druid elders.

Allis was not naturally gifted in the way some other Druids-in-Training were, but she was a hard worker and a clever young woman. She had progressed measurably in the development of her skills since arriving at Paranor and passing her entrance exam into the order, despite the doubts she had harbored at the beginning of her chances for success, and by now she was determined to make her good fortune count for something.

Nevertheless, when Eskrit, the guard, brought her news of the black-cloaked stranger seeking entrance, she put aside her book and walked back to see what this was about. Admittedly, she was curious. Eskrit had conveyed a full description of the man, which included a mention of poise and confidence that she wanted to examine for herself. Perhaps he was one of the very few uninvited magic users that the Keep would want to admit. It would be remembered if she were the one to invite him in.

She walked through the service door and over to the stranger, who immediately executed a low bow. "My lady," he greeted her.

Allis was caught off guard. "You don't need to bow to me. I am no one special."

"It is my privilege to consider all women special," he said, perfectly straight-faced. "I do not make exceptions."

"Then, well met, sir," she responded, smiling. "Can you give me your name?"

"Kassen Drue," he said. "I am from Franschen Dell."

She had never heard of him or the place he was from. "You come from the deep Southland?"

"Deeper than most. On the edge of the Antra Sink, well below Arishaig and the larger cities."

So he was from somewhere in the regions of the lower ice seas. "And you seek entry into the order?"

"I seek a chance to prove I deserve admission. No favors, no gifts. I expect to be tested."

She liked his face. His was a fine-featured, open countenance that showed some weathering and much exposure to the outdoors. Yet it was kind, too. It showed him to have humor and a willingness to accept others.

"Do you have weapons on you?" she asked.

"I don't require weapons," he replied.

Coming from another man, such a claim might have raised a doubtful eyebrow. But with Kassen she found the claim believable, even though she couldn't have said exactly why. She folded her arms within her gray robes and gave him a studied look.

"I hope not, because I am required to have you searched. Eskrit?"

The huge Troll approached, and Kassen held out his arms from his body compliantly to allow the other to check him over from head to foot for any concealed sharp objects. Eskrit found nothing.

"Very good," said Allis. "Now, if you will come with me, I will show you to a reception room where you can wait while a panel of examiners is assembled."

Together, with Eskrit shadowing them, they went through the service door and into an antechamber, which contained a few weathered wooden benches and not much else.

She pointed to the benches. "Sit here, please. Eskrit will keep you company until I return. Do not go farther into the Keep until then."

She left him there and went to her mentor, the Druid Clizia Porse, who was the chief examiner on duty that day, to let her know that a stranger seeking admission as an initiate had appeared at the gates.

She did so with some trepidation, just as always—not only because Clizia was very old and very respected within the order, but also because the rumors about her history were dark and dangerous. Although Allis had never personally felt threatened in any way, it was hard to ignore stories about someone who was said to have used poisons to settle disputes and whose gift with magic was claimed to be nearly incomparable.

She found Clizia in her study, occupied much as Allis had been earlier: deeply engaged in reading a book of spells and incantations. The old woman looked up the moment she opened the door and in that initial moment her look was hard and threatening.

A second later it was gone. "Yes, Allis?"

"There is a stranger at the gates seeking admittance to the order. He bears no weapons; I judge him to be no threat."

She waited uncertainly for the response, but Clizia only nodded. "I will meet with him shortly. Take him to the examining room and stay with him until I arrive with the panel." She paused. "And Allis? Don't ever judge anyone to be no threat. Everyone is capable of being a threat, whether it appears so or not."

Allis went out again without waiting for more, happy to be able to retreat relatively unscathed. No matter how much time she spent with her mentor, it never got any easier for her to feel comfortable.

She found Kassen Drue waiting patiently on the wooden bench, hands folded in his lap, gaze fixed on the far wall. He rose as soon as she entered the antechamber. "Come with me," she told him.

She nodded to Eskrit, too, and the three of them left the antechamber and walked out into a courtyard and proceeded to the building where the examinations were conducted on the ground floor. The day was warm and pleasant, and Allis took a moment to enjoy the feel of the sunshine on her face before they entered the examination section of the building and went down the hallway until they were just outside the room Clizia had designated. They took seats on the benches they found waiting, but these were cushioned and the corridor was bright and open, windows letting in the light and the warmth of the day. Kassen sat where Allis indicated, and she took a seat next to him.

They were quiet for a few moments, neither speaking. Kassen was studying her openly, and she found herself looking back. There was something compelling about him, something beyond his physical attractiveness and poise that drew her to him. Eskrit stood to one side, looking out at the day beyond, at the courtyard and the outer walls of the Keep, a statue.

"Have you been a member of the order for long?" Kassen asked.

"I am not a member. I am a Druid-in-Training. I will be examined shortly to see if my studies have progressed far enough to warrant further consideration of my status."

"We would be classmates, would we not?" he asked. "If I were admitted as a student?"

"We would be."

"Then I will make it a point to ask you now if you would show me around a bit in these early days, so that I might have someone I know to school me on what's what."

No hesitation in asking, no suggestion that he might not be admitted. She found it presumptuous but not irrational. The way he spoke made it sound more inevitable than anything.

"You seem awfully confident."

"Do I? I suppose it's just how I look at challenges. Everything can be overcome if you try hard enough."

She nodded. "I agree with you. Well, if you are admitted I would be happy to act as your guide."

They went silent again after that and remained so for quite some time until finally Clizia Porse and two other Druids whose names Allis could not remember entered the room and took a seat behind a table at one end. Then in came Ober Balronen, with Dar Leah trailing behind him as usual, his black sword strapped across his back.

But she had no opportunity to learn anything more. Clizia caught her attention and made a dismissive motion. Allis rose and left the room feeling highly disappointed she had not been allowed to remain.

"Come forward," Clizia Porse said to the stranger

Dar Leah watched as the stranger rose to his feet in response and stood before the table, executing a bow in Clizia's direction. "Kassen, my lady. At your service."

The old lady seemed unimpressed. "Are you ready to begin with your examination, Kassen?"

"Ready, my lady."

The audience was intense and probing, question after question from the panel of four Druids in this small, secluded room. It was not exactly an interrogation, but it was close enough. Dar, positioning himself as always behind Balronen, found the process measured and thorough.

As the examination continued, Dar couldn't help but feel, after a time, it had gone on for too long. But, likely at Balronen's insistence, it was Clizia who was driving it—he did relish his little power games, and would have been attracted by the idea of being a silent observer manipulating events. The other two Druids were junior to Clizia in tenure and unlikely to interfere. Kassen seemed unfazed, answering everything fully, staying calm and patient and uncomplaining. He seemed entirely comfortable with the questions he was asked and provided the panel with what appeared to be sufficient information to satisfy their doubts.

Then, at last, Clizia asked him to provide a demonstration of his magic.

"A small example of what you think you can do," she suggested. "Let's have a look at your talent."

"I will do my best," Kassen answered with a friendly smile.

The Druids watched him closely, waiting for the promised demonstration, but Kassen just stood there. His interrogators grew restless and began glancing at one another. "Are you ready yet?" one of the others asked finally.

"Of course," he answered. "In fact, I'm finished."

There was a momentary silence. "But you haven't done anything," Balronen burst out.

Dar felt a twinge of doubt. The man *hadn't* done anything, in fact. Did he not have any use of magic after all?

"That's only how it seems," Kassen replied.

"You haven't moved a muscle," Clizia pointed out.

"Haven't I?" he said from behind them, even though he appeared to be right in front of them.

They whirled about in shock, finding that, without them seeing how he had managed it, he had moved from where he had been standing to the wall behind them. But a clear and indistinguishable image of him remained where he had been a moment earlier, and was just now fading.

The questions came quickly then, but Kassen deflected them and only asked if they believed him sufficiently talented that he might be worthy of admission into the Druid order for further training.

Dar knew the answer before the words were spoken. Kassen Drue would be admitted.

Allis found Kassen later that same day standing on the walls of the Keep, staring off into the forest beyond. He no longer wore the black robes with the cowl raised, as he had on his arrival, but was garbed in the gray robes of all Druids-in-Training with the cowl lowered and his face revealed. She approached him slowly, admiring his chiseled features, stayed from speaking to him by his contemplative look. It was as if he saw something in the trees that was hidden from her. As if his mind were somewhere else entirely.

"You seem deep in thought," she said finally, coming closer.

He turned at once to greet her. "Not so deep. Daydreams, mostly, Allis."

He remembered her name, which pleased her. She was not immune to flattery, even though friendships of this sort were discouraged. Druids-in-Training were supposed to be occupied with their studies, not with infatuations about one another. But she genuinely liked him and didn't mind letting it show. Although she had not asked for it, she had been delighted when Clizia had assigned her the task of showing him around the Keep and explaining how his studies would be conducted. After all, he was a stranger in a strange land, come from far away, and he would need friends to guide him in his new life.

Allis was more than willing to make herself available to help with that.

Engaged in her Druid studies for a year prior to his arrival, she'd had more than sufficient time to discover most of what there was to know about the intricacies of the Druid order and its functions. If Kassen had such a question, she could answer it.

"This seems such a large complex," he told her as she walked him to his living quarters. He had spoken barely a dozen words to her until then, content to let her offer what information she was willing to impart without pressure from him. "I'm afraid I will get lost if I don't have directions."

She looked at him. "How about a guided tour then?"

"From you? That would be very much appreciated."

It was better than she could have expected. She watched him unpack and deposit his few belongings and his spare student's robes, then she took him through Paranor's maze from one end to the other—anywhere and everywhere either of them was permitted to go. She explained what the rooms were used for and the reasons that certain places were off-limits. As she did so, he listened attentively and asked questions at almost every turn, seemingly determined to learn early on everything there was to know about Paranor. She answered willingly, pleased by the persistence of his curiosity and his obvious interest.

Afterward, they went to the dining hall to eat lunch together; there she introduced him to some of her fellow Druids-in-Training, and then the tour resumed. After two more hours, she had taken him everywhere and told him everything she could think of. She brought him back to the walls of the Keep where she had found him earlier.

Together, they leaned against the wall and looked off into the trees once more. "I feel better able to begin my studies now," he told her. "Thank you so much for helping me."

She smiled. "I am to help you in whatever way you require," she told him, and then realized belatedly how that sounded and blushed.

For long moments after that neither spoke, and she grew worried she had overstepped herself.

"Have you a need for company or shall I go?" she asked.

"Stay," he said at once. "Your company is welcome. You know that."

"I hoped for it, at least. I was afraid I was boring you."

His smile was warm and knowing. "I doubt you could ever bore me. Your knowledge of Paranor and its Druids is impressive."

She glanced over. "Adequate, at least. There are others here who know much more than I do." She paused. "Would you like to walk the walls?"

He hesitated. "You know where I would like to walk? On a beautiful day like this I would most like a walk in the woods. I miss the birdsong and the smell of wildflowers. Do you think we could go out together?"

She cocked an eyebrow. His blue eyes were bright and laughing as she pursed her lips. She found herself wanting to kiss him. She was wondering what it would feel like. "I have that privilege," she said, "since I am a senior student. I will share it with you. It would be my great pleasure."

Fifteen minutes later, they were walking through the gates and into the forest. He let her choose their path, his own sense of direction clearly limited by his unfamiliarity with his surroundings. As they walked, Allis remarked on the talent he had displayed in his examination. Few possessed such abilities when they'd first come to the Keep, and she believed he had a bright future within the order. She had overheard the examiners talking about it when they didn't realize she was listening. They admired him and approved of him, and she was eager for him to know how important that was. But it seemed to make him uncomfortable to listen to her go on like this, and he repeatedly reminded her of how far he still had to go. So eventually she quit talking about it, and the two simply walked in companionable silence.

When they finally returned to the Keep, he took her hand in his and bent to kiss it. "It has been a delightful first day for me," he told her. "Thanks to you."

They would spend many more days and much time together in the weeks ahead, but she would always remember how she felt at the end of that first day. How much she liked and admired Kassen. How excited she was for the future.

It seemed a good beginning.

NINE

$\blacklozenge$

ON THE SAME MORNING Kassen arrived at Paranor, Drisker Arc was sitting on his cottage porch, looking out at the surrounding trees very much the way he looked out at them almost every morning. He had brewed a pot of tea and was drinking a cup as he let the minutes pass and the sun crest the horizon. He had until midday, a sufficient amount of time to allow Tarsha to do what she wanted before he set out, and he felt no particular urge to rush things. As talented as she was, she still needed whatever edge he could give her to answer this latest challenge.

He repeated the words silently.

As talented as she is . . .

Who would have thought it? He had encountered some adept magic wielders in his time. A few he had believed might be his betters although it had turned out they were not. But Tarsha Kaynin was on another level entirely, so generously endowed with wishsong magic that he doubted any other member of the Ohmsford family—save perhaps the legendary High Druid Grianne, who eventually fell victim to her own magic—had been so naturally gifted. Tarsha was a prodigy, a girl who was already mature in most ways and whose lack of understanding and command of her magic was her sole weakness. Much of what she needed to know and what she needed to learn was still a mystery to her. That would have to change, but time and practice and study would accomplish that. What mattered was that her ability to intuit and grasp concepts was prodigious, and eventually she would come to understand everything he did.

He had wondered at first if she was up to the task he had set her. But her journey to find him had been long and difficult, and the fact that she had found him at all revealed much about her determination.

Once it had been settled that she would become his student and he her tutor, it only remained to set a rigorous course of study.

"How do you think she is doing out there?" he asked the air and what hid within it. He couldn't see hide nor hair of him at the moment, but most certainly he was there.

He sipped from his cup and leaned back in his rocker and breathed the forest air. Hard to match that woodsy smell, he thought. You could taste it like sweet spices. Best air in all the Four Lands and beyond. Clean and pure and so sharp it tickled the senses.

"She's doing well enough, I imagine," he answered his own question, resisting the urge to cast about. "Not much that girl can't do."

His method for teaching her was straightforward enough. Mostly, it began and ended with the two of them talking. He would explain the nature of an aspect of her magic, and she would question him. He would answer her questions, and she would ask a few more. She was quick enough to know what to ask, sharp enough to realize what she was missing. He would open the doors of knowledge a crack and wait for her to consider what was being revealed. She would see its hidden depths and want to know how far back they stretched.

In between all the talk, all the questions and answers, all the dialogue about metes and bounds, stresses and strains, and mostly limitations to be paid attention to, he would give her tasks to accomplish. No point in keeping a young girl chained to a desk with an old man who rattled on when what she really craved was experience. Or in her case, challenges. She was not one to hold back, content with what she already knew. She was always pressing, trying to figure out how far she could take things, how much of what she didn't know and hadn't tried she could master. He gave her enough rope to fail, pleased each time when she didn't, content to assure her it was only for the moment when she did.

"But oh, she does have talent!" he whispered, the sound of his words a hiss of approval.

"What are you muttering about, *chil'haen russ'hai*?" a voice asked sharply.

The speaker was only a few feet away, so close it was troubling to Drisker that he hadn't heard his approach. He had been so preoccupied with the girl and her magic that he had dropped his guard. Not a good thing when you were a discredited Druid.

"What does it matter?" Drisker asked, turning to meet the speaker's gaze.

The forest imp was rough-featured and sour-mouthed, and his face was crisscrossed by deeply etched lines. He was very old, but he would never give his age. His shoulders were hunched and his posture stooped. His large hands were gnarled, and the staff he carried was split by time and weather. Long gray hair bristled in a crown about his bald head, as if desperate to escape the fate of its fellows, and the mustache above his downturned mouth drooped well below his prominent chin. Everything about him whispered of time's passage.

"A bad habit, Druid. One day, it will be your undoing. You will address the air in a rash and reckless manner and something hiding in it will appear to put you six feet under."

"I think you might get there first, old dog. Tea?"

"Tea? For the love of *haist,* would you poison me? Has it come to that? Naught but ale shall pass these lips! Have you none?"

He slouched forward and mounted the porch, choosing a seat on a bench to one side. Drisker swiveled his rocker around to face him, then rose and went into his home to fetch the imp his ale. When he returned, he found the imp had moved over to sit in his rocker.

"I do not mean to impose. But I assumed you would want to provide me with seating offering the greatest amount of comfort since I am such an *old dog.*" He reached for the ale.

Drisker handed it to him and sat on the bench, smiling in spite of himself. "What, then, brings Flinc the Wise to my humble abode? And don't tell me it's to drink my ale or enjoy my company. There might be more to this visit, I think."

"Could be, could be," the other replied. He drank deeply of the ale before setting it down beside him. This was something of a chore since his arms were not very long and the floor of the porch was rather far down from where he sat. Drisker rose and brought a small table to set beside him. "My thanks," the other said quickly. "Although I could have managed."

"Indeed," the Druid agreed. "So?"

"So what?"

"So what brings you here?"

"A change in the winds, *russ'hai*. A shift in the autumn breezes. Something's coming for you, and it isn't something good."

Drisker nodded slowly. The forest imp was prescient, able to sense things that would happen, capable of discerning if they were good or bad. It wasn't an exact skill and was susceptible to misinterpretation. But not often when it came to Flinc. Flinc had much better control over it than most forest imps, and his foresight and willingness to share it had saved Drisker on more than one occasion since the Druid had made Emberen his home.

For there were those who would never be satisfied until Drisker Arc was dead and buried. It was the sort of hatred that transcended reason or the passage of time. His enemies had been justly earned, but never with malice and never with any intent other than to stop them from hurting others and damaging relationships among the Races. Still, they had not forgotten him just because he was no longer High Druid and gone from Paranor. Now and then they sought him out, each time for the same reason and each time with the same result. Now their bones moldered deep in the woods and their voices were quieted.

"Perhaps I should send the girl away," he mused. "She's awfully young to stand against anything like that."

"Which might help her but not you. Besides, she is stubborn, that one. I've seen it as clearly as you. She will not understand unless you tell her of your fears. And then she will wish to stand and fight beside you."

Drisker nodded. Flinc was right. Tarsha Kaynin was not the type to walk away. Another choice was needed.

"I will leave instead, then," he said.

"Only a few days should be required."

"But they will still come."

"Perhaps. But they are not interested in her. She will be safe enough. There are others who will be here to greet them. Others perhaps better suited to deal with such visitors. You have powerful friends, *russ'hai*, though sometimes it mystifies me why. You've certainly done nothing to please them in a way that would make them friends."

Drisker smiled. He did have friends, and they were better friends than those at Paranor had ever been. Those who had been all too willing to consign him to oblivion, to take advantage of his decision to step down as High Druid and make sure he was cast out for good. Even worse, to make sure it was known far and wide that he was no longer one of them, and no longer welcome to return. It emboldened his enemies and left him vulnerable.

The forest imp looked off into the trees. "She waits now," he said quietly.

Drisker nodded. "I expect so. But let her wait awhile longer. It is a part of her training, learning to wait, learning of patience."

The imp pursed his lips. "I know something of waiting."

Indeed. Forest imps had endless patience. For days, weeks, even months on occasion, they could disappear inside themselves and not move a hair. It was in their nature. Much of their time in the Faerie World had been spent in endless waiting. In the war between creatures of darkness and light, they had stepped aside from both. They had not thought of themselves as part of either faction and did not see the point in allying with either. So they kept to themselves while the war raged.

And after? When the dark were consigned to the Forbidding and the light held sway? For a time, they flourished. But then humans came into the world, and the Faerie kind dwindled in numbers until only a handful remained hidden in the deep woods and high mountains and impassable hollows, waiting for the cycle to reach its end and begin anew. They could live a long time, these forest imps. Centuries, in some cases. It was in their nature to survive, to endure when other, more aggressive species burned out and vanished. Instead of refusing to change, the imps evolved and found ways to fit into a world that never remained the same for long.

Flinc was quite old. Older than dirt, he liked to say without a hint of irony or braggadocio. He was proud that he had lived so long and seen so much, and he liked holding that over Drisker with his inferior Druid Sleep that allowed only years and not centuries of longer life. But they were friends, the imp and he, bonded by a shared worldview and involvement in the possession and usage of magic. Friendships were odd constructs, after all, formed in strange ways and maintained for strange reasons. However you saw them, it was hard to dispute that not all of them made sense or offered insights into the lives of the people involved.

Drisker glanced back to where Flinc had been sitting in his rocker, but the chair was empty. The imp had gone back into the trees, his message delivered and his piece said. He was not one to linger. He was not one for casual conversation. Not a bad trait, to Drisker's way of thinking.

The Druid stood and stretched. Time to get under way. He had sent Tarsha out into the forest, instructing her to hide her trail and then wait for him to find her. When he did—not if, but when—she was to circle him once in an open space without allowing him to discover she was there. She could use the wishsong to achieve this and to offer proof she had done as tasked. She could call up whatever other magic she possessed to aid her. She could employ what subterfuges she chose.

A seemingly impossible task in his mind, but then he thought her capable enough of achieving the impossible, even at this point in her training.

He straightened himself and, picking up traces of her body heat still lingering against the air currents, he began tracking her.

• • •

Less than a quarter mile away, Tarsha was resting in a shady glen dappled with ferns and wildflowers and surrounded by giant spruce. She had gone as far as she thought necessary before stopping and no farther. It was pointless to wear herself down by attempting to outdistance or outsmart Drisker Arc. He was more than capable of finding her no matter what she did to try to lose him. Druids were trained to track using heat images, and on a windless day like this one there was little hope that whatever impressions she had left in her wake would dissipate before he caught up to her. She could try to disguise her passage with magic, but he would likely be able to read that, too. Druids, after all, were the prime wielders of magic in all the Four Lands, and you never wanted to underestimate what they could do. Especially someone like Drisker Arc.

So let him come. Let him track her, and when he found her he would discover she had become more talented than he thought. Not that he would underestimate her. But he still thought of her as a novice, even though she had gone beyond that point in their first five days together.

As a tutor, he was formidable. He trained her from dawn to dusk and sometimes beyond. He worked her steadily and methodically, always with a goal in mind, always with a lesson at the heart of every exercise. His method was to challenge her at every turn, and she thought some of this was due to his understanding of her urgency about helping her brother, but most of it was a reflection of his desire to discover if she could fill his need for an assistant. He was not one to drag things out, not one to hold back on the theory that caution was always best. Either you could do this or you couldn't. Either she could measure up and begin the process of learning from him or she couldn't and should be sent home. He wanted a quick answer to that question, and she was prepared to give it to him.

If it was the answer she hoped for, perhaps she would one day be a member of the Druid order. Even if, as he had told her, he was no more than an outcast himself.

In the trees off to her left, something moved. For a moment she froze, gone cold to the bone. Was it him? Had he somehow managed to creep up on her without her knowing? She waited for more, for his appearance, for a word, for an indication she had failed. But there was nothing there.

Or apparently nothing. She had her doubts. This wasn't the first time she had sensed she might have a shadow. She had blamed it on an overactive imagination. But she wasn't entirely sure. Not then and not now.

"If someone is there, show yourself," she called out, standing to face toward the movement she had sensed.

Nothing happened.

Nerves, she thought. *Shades! Am I such a child?*

She sat back again, looking up at the sky, clearing her thoughts and calming herself. Another few minutes and it would be time to prepare. He had said he would give her thirty minutes. But she knew better. He would give her more. He would give her at least an hour because he would want her to wait on him, wondering what he was planning. For he was always planning, always seeking to stay a step ahead. Frequently, he was—although less so as the days passed.

His complexities troubled her.

Sometimes she wondered if his almost alien intuition and pre-science were a direct by-product of his peculiar nature. Living out here alone for more than two years seemed to have given him a strong connection with his surroundings and whatever creatures inhabited them. At times, he talked to things she couldn't see. Or perhaps he was talking to the air or the trees or the sky; she could never be sure. He never offered to explain, and she didn't think it her place to ask. But he clearly believed his behavior was normal, and this was more than a little disturbing. If he was seeing things that weren't actually there, then how reliable was he? If he talked to himself, what did that say about his mental state? And the way he was constantly touching things for no apparent reason. And how he sniffed the air like an animal. However you looked at it, he was exhibiting behavior that suggested his sanity was not altogether sound.

Yet whom else could she turn to if she walked away now?

Better to chance the stability of the known than to risk the unknown. How could she be worse off by doing so?

It was a question she was not prepared to face.

Drisker Arc moved steadily into the forest, tracking the heat images Tarsha had left in her wake, keeping his senses attuned to his surroundings, searching for any sign of the girl. But he did not detect her anywhere close and so did not slow in his efforts to catch up to her. She would have stopped by now and be planning a way to complete her task. She would have found a suitable spot and set herself in place. Because he would be searching for her, she would want to move quickly, knowing she could not expect to fool him for long. Keeping these factors in mind, he was already developing a strategy—refining the details of a plan for tricking her into thinking she had gotten the better of him. He was confident he could do this, his experience and skill giving him the edge over her raw talent. But he knew he must be careful; she was no fool.

He hated to admit it, but he loved matching wits with this girl. The excitement of having to test his skills against those of someone he was teaching was something he had missed since leaving the order. He realized how stagnant his life had grown, and he regretted that he had been so reluctant to do anything to change that until now. It was so easy to let go of everything when you lived alone. He had let it happen almost without realizing it, thinking it was better this way, believing this was how things were meant to be.

After all, hadn't he been the one to abdicate his position as High Druid? Hadn't he been the one to walk away from Paranor? Hadn't he decided that it was all too frustrating and pointless?

Wasn't he the one who had given up?

He banished these thoughts swiftly and returned to the matter at hand. The heat images were fragmenting now, stirred and broken by a sudden breeze. Drisker quickened his pace, surprised that the images were continuing to appear in a mostly straight line. Why wasn't the girl doing more to try to throw him off, to switch directions or offer multiple images? She seemed so confident.

He pressed on, and soon the images grew stronger again, an indication that he was getting close to her. She had not gone as far as he had imagined she would, choosing instead to let him come upon her more quickly than he would have expected. She had a definite plan in mind, certain she had a way she could get the better of him, seeing no point in drawing things out. It was the sort of risk he admired.

On the other hand, she was making this awfully easy on him.

He slowed his pace, sniffing the air, reaching out with his other senses, trying to find what might be hidden from him. But he found nothing unfamiliar or troubling. Everything seemed to be just as it should with no encroachment by scents or appearances or movements that felt out of place. He extended his search to what he could see in his mind, a reaching-out beyond his sight and hearing. Again, he felt soft breezes brush his face. Just a whisper, nothing more. Tiny seeds and bits of lichen blown loose from the trees tumbled about him.

He walked on, slower now, following the traces of herself she had left behind but allowing caution to govern his progress. Fresh breezes brushed his face and the back of his neck. But when he glanced up into the trees he saw no movement in the branches.

And with a reluctant smile, he stopped where he was. "You can come out now," he called to her.

She emerged from the shadows of the woods to his right, her smile firmly in place. "You didn't see me, did you? Or hear me? How did you know I was there?"

He walked up to her and put his hands on her slender shoulders. She was just a girl, but a girl with such promise. "I didn't sense a thing until the breezes. They touched my face but the treetops remained motionless. You were moving without my seeing you, but I felt you. I'm sorry, Tarsha. You've lost."

She shook her head slowly. "I've won."

He frowned, looking into her eyes and finding an undeniable certainty in their steady gaze. "Did you now?"

"You told me I was to circle you once without you detecting my presence. I did that."

"But I called you out before you finished." the Druid pressed her. Then he hesitated, realizing what he had missed. "But I didn't, did I?

You circled me earlier, when I allowed myself to become distracted by my thoughts. I remember the breezes against my face and the seeds and bits of lichen. You circled me then. But how did you manage it? How did I not sense you?"

"I didn't let you," she declared proudly. "That was the point of the exercise. To stay hidden."

He shook his head. "But I should have been able to detect you in some way. I wasn't that distracted."

"You did detect me. You just didn't realize it was me you were sensing. You thought it was just you. I used the wishsong to make myself *be* you for the few moments I required. I disguised myself as you—invisible so you couldn't see me, blending my smell and movements so closely to your own I was just another part of you and you couldn't tell the difference!"

"You have evidence of this? You're not just telling tales, are you?"

She looked offended. "I wouldn't do that."

She stepped back, gestured with a circular motion, and hummed a little of the wishsong. Instantly Drisker Arc found himself wrapped in a garland of silvery seedlings and lichen that clung to his dark robes like tiny stars. He looked down at himself in disbelief, and then laughed heartily.

"Shades, Tarsha Kaynin. My apologies. You have indeed won the contest!"

She rushed in to hug him, then backed away almost hurriedly, afraid she had overstepped her bounds. "Sorry," she said.

He shrugged, his smile broadening. "Oh, please don't be. After what you've managed to accomplish this day, I think you're entitled to a little celebration."

He turned her about, and they began the walk back to his cottage, the Druid asking her to explain her process in disguising herself using the wishsong while he added bits and pieces of advice that might serve her better in the future. Although it was hard to think that she needed much advice now. She had proved herself in dramatic fashion, demonstrably the best young magic wielder he had ever encountered. He was so pleased with her performance—and with her overall progress—that he was prepared to consider her end of the bargain fulfilled. But he didn't want to lose her, didn't want to give her up just yet. It was more than a bargain by now. It was the clear realization that she had helped bring him back to himself when he had given up. Instructing Tarsha had given him a purpose in life that for a long time had been absent.

When they arrived home, an arrow shrike was waiting. It sat in the open-fronted wire cage allotted for its use, a message tied to one leg.

Drisker walked over to the bird, stroked it reassuringly, and removed the message. Tarsha crowded close to try to read the contents over his shoulder, but he shifted his body slightly to block her from doing so.

In ragged Troll dialect, the message read:

> Corrax Trolls destroyed two days past.
> Enemy unknown.
> Come now.
> M.

Drisker studied the message a moment longer and then crumpled it up and stuffed it in his pocket. He needed to know more about this. He needed to find out who these enemies were and what they wanted. He knew the messenger and how to find him. He wouldn't have been summoned if it wasn't urgent. He had the excuse he needed to leave for a while, as Flinc had suggested. Tarsha would be fine without him. She would be well-enough protected in his absence.

He turned to her. "I'm sorry, but I have to go away for a few days. Maybe longer. You'll be here alone. Can you manage?"

She nodded at once. "Of course. What is it? What's happened?"

Drisker hesitated. He didn't want to alarm her until he understood more of what this meant. "Let's just say that a friend has summoned me with news I can't ignore. I promise to explain when I return, but in the meantime . . . You must excuse me." And he turned and vanished into his cottage.

TEN

As Drisker Arc moved through his cottage, gathering supplies for his sudden journey, Tarsha was left alone on the porch to puzzle things through. She had only a short time to do so before he reappeared, a pack slung over one shoulder and a polished black staff in one hand. The staff caught her attention immediately, a gnarled piece of wood intricately carved with runes and seemingly unmarked by usage or age.

He caught her staring and handed it to her. "Take it. Feel its strength, its warmth. Wood like this is rare and precious, Tarsha. This staff is very old, and it has been passed down through the years. The one who carried it first was a Druid like myself, centuries ago."

"It is a beautiful thing," she agreed, handing it back.

He gripped it tightly, studied it himself for a moment, and nodded. "I'll be gone for more than a week. Stay close to the cottage. The fewer who know of your presence here, the better."

"Am I to worry, then? Should I hide?"

He smiled. "Hiding might be taking it a bit far. But caution would be advised. I do have enemies, and sometimes they come calling. Just use your good sense—and your magic if it is needed. But better to hide than fight. Better to keep hidden than to force a confrontation."

She wondered where he was going but knew that wherever he

went it would be in response to the arrow shrike's message. Even so, he still did not offer an explanation but simply turned from her and walked away. She watched him until he was out of sight, gone down a pathway toward the village of Emberen, and then she sat down on the porch to think.

Her thoughts that morning were dark and conflicted. On the one hand, she was pleased with her progress as the Druid's student, particularly after her achievement in this morning's exercise. She had caught him completely by surprise, disguising herself in a way he had not guessed she might try and then draping him in silver stars in dramatic fashion. She had reason to feel proud of how far she had come with her studies of magic in such a short time.

On the other hand, she could not help thinking about the family she had left behind so abruptly, especially her brother. Even the short time she had been gone seemed entirely too long, and she was uneasy with what might have happened in the interim. Four years with her uncle . . . She felt an urgent need to return to her brother and make certain he was well. She wanted Drisker to understand this and to respond to her need, and she thought that at some point soon now he would.

Perhaps on his return from this meeting . . .

She stayed where she was for perhaps an hour, drinking tea and listening to the birds, trying to identify them from their songs, occasionally calling them to her with the wishsong's magic. She could do that almost effortlessly, a skill she had mastered even before coming to Emberen. She had moved beyond that endeavor to find ways to imitate the wind and the sound of a stream's rippling passage and the whisper of leaves in the branches of trees. How to imitate nature. The more she could assimilate with other things, the more accomplished her abilities to hide and blend in would grow.

Of late, she had begun to find ways to make others see her as someone or something other than what she was. A sort of cloaking of herself in a disguise that could not be revealed while her magic was working on keeping it in place. There were endless possibilities where the wishsong was involved. Some were frightening. She knew from studying with Drisker that at various times in the history of the Ohmsford family certain members had mastered the power of life and death over living things, of employing the wishsong to save lives by healing or to take them by force. It was a terrible responsibility to have such power, and she was not at all sure she wanted it. The Druid, however, had insisted skill at her level required she master every aspect of it. You could not back away from what it could do once it was given to you. Management and understanding were the only reasonable options for maintaining control.

But she had not yet been tested in this or thought to test herself. It rankled her even to think about it. Better to let it be until Drisker felt she had learned whatever else he had to teach. So far, he had not asked instances of using magic to manipulate life, and she thought he felt as she did. It would come to her soon enough in any event, and rushing into it before she was prepared physically and emotionally was unwise.

When the tea was gone and the morning with it, she began training once more. Every day she was required to complete certain exercises involving the use of magic. Some of them required that she leave the cottage and go into the forest, but on this day she chose to stay close. Drisker didn't seem to think she was at risk, but she didn't like it that he had felt it necessary to warn her in the first place. So she took his advice to heart and exercised caution, being careful not to do anything that would attract attention.

Her efforts took her mind off her brother and her parents sufficiently that after a time she stopped thinking about them at all and disappeared into her lessons. She spent considerable time persuading a crow that she was her fledgling. In the end the crow hopped right up to her before realizing something wasn't quite right and flying off. She assumed the guise of a tree, disappearing into a skin of bark and a covering of leafy branches, becoming a part of the woods surrounding her. It was hard to tell how successful she was since she couldn't judge her own appearance from inside her covering. But squirrels and birds seemed convinced enough to try to either climb or land on her, and she took that as a good sign.

By nightfall she was exhausted enough that it took what little en-
ergy remained to prepare a meal, eat it, pull off her clothes, and wash
her face before falling into bed and going off to sleep. She slept undisturbed through the night and woke rested and cheerful on finding
the new day sunny and warm.

For the better part of the next week she worked on her magic and
stayed close to home. She kept an eye out for Drisker, but he did not
return. By the seventh day, she began to worry. How far had he traveled? Had he walked the whole way? She found herself wishing she
had asked him for a few details about his plans.

She also wished she had asked him about the eyes.

Ever since she had arrived, she had felt them watching. She accepted that there were creatures living in the woods about them that
she couldn't see and that preferred to remain hidden. She could even
accept some of them were enchanted, drawn to this place by Drisker's
use of magic and now, perhaps, her own. But she was troubled by the
constant surveillance, knowing it was there yet not being able to confirm it. She was troubled, too, by her disappointment that the Druid
had not thought it necessary to tell her.

But there was nothing she could do about any of it, so she resigned herself to biding her time, deciding that when Drisker returned she would confront him and demand that he tell her the truth.

But that night, she found out the truth for herself.

Drisker Arc walked into Emberen to the storage service that kept
watch over his two-man flit. It was a modified model, not new but in
excellent condition. It had space for two where most flits had space
for only one. He used it mostly to haul supplies and equipment because he almost never had reason to carry a passenger. Until now, of
course. Now, it appeared the flit would prove useful while Tarsha
worked with him as his assistant. They would need to travel, and
these days most travel was done using airships rather than horses.

After hauling out the flit with the help of the storage manager and
stowing his pack, he boarded the little craft and flew northeast. He
traveled for the rest of that day and then three more, crossing the

Streleheim before swinging farther north to pass below the upper reaches of the Skull Kingdom, then continuing on past the Razors. On the fourth afternoon, he flew over the city of Anatcherae and by nightfall reached the eastern shore of the Lazareen. At daybreak on the fifth day, he resumed flying, making his way toward Taupo Rough.

Brutal country, he thought as he disembarked and looked around. *Hard on man and beast. Unfit for anyone civilized.*

What he sensed in the cries of birds, in the scents of the morning air, and in the shifting of light and shadows that morning told him something was amiss. It was akin to the premonitions he had been having over and over again of late. But this one was so strong there was no questioning it. Somewhere, death had found an unexpected release.

At midday he reached his destination, a barren patch of ground uninhabited by much of anything beyond insects. There he waited through the rest of the day, unable to go farther than the place where he and the Morsk always met. For now, he must wait on his informant and trust that he would show. It wasn't a given; sometimes he didn't. But he would be patient, in large part because he was greatly troubled by the destruction of the Corrax Trolls. It was odd that it should happen to a Race of people trained to fight almost from birth. Troll tribes engaged in territorial battles regularly, but such skirmishes did not involve the annihilation of one by another. There wasn't a military force in all the Four Lands that should have been able to manage such a feat.

And if such a thing had happened, where were the Elves and their magic and the Federation forces and their war machines? Where were the Druids? Did they not know what had happened? Given the extent of their resources and widespread network of spies and scouts, it seemed unlikely they hadn't heard anything.

Sooner or later, no matter the odds or the challenge presented, someone was going to have to act. That no one had done so thus far suggested that everyone was waiting for someone else to solve the problem. It would be typical of the Southlanders, but not the Elves and certainly not Druids. Paranor, at least, should already be responding in some significant way. That they weren't doing anything suggested their leadership was proving to be as mercurial now as it was at the time of his departure. This was just one more consequence of his decision to shed his responsibility for the Druid order that he had to live with.

It was nearing dark when the Morsk finally arrived. It appeared out of the darkness like the wraith it was, black as night and twice as ghostly, its robes drifting behind it in a shift of wind like the tattered remnants of its unfortunate life. It wore a vaguely human shape, but its features were hidden and its movements so liquid it seemed to lack substance. It drifted toward the Druid silently and settled down across from him, another of night's endless shadows.

Drisker Arc.

Its voice was a hiss in the near silence of their private space, soft and menacing.

"Well met."

You would be the only one to say so. Not many think meeting me a fortunate moment.

"Then it is good I am not of their ilk. What have you learned?"

That winds of death and destruction blow through the Northland and are coming south. That the Races face a danger the like of which they have not faced before. That you should never have ceased to be Ard Rhys. That your counsel and leadership are badly needed.

Drisker closed his eyes and then opened them again. "Could you be more specific about who or what this danger is?"

They are wraiths that appear and vanish at will. They may have magic. These are the rumors of the living—the wives and children of the dead. The Trolls were overwhelmed and destroyed in spite of superior numbers. But I did not see this for myself.

"But someone must have seen them. Are they from another region of the Four Lands? From another country we know nothing about? Someone must know."

The Morsk studied him. *If you are so interested in knowing more, why don't you track them down and see for yourself? But perhaps you should be wary of coming too close to them, considering.*

Drisker Arc sat back. It was not up to him to do this, of course. This wasn't his business. It was up to the Druids.

You are thinking all this should be done by the Druid order. And so it should. But you know they will do nothing.

"You seem certain of this."

They have done nothing so far, have they? Why would that change?

Why, indeed. "How many of these invaders are there?"

I cannot tell. The ground hides their footprints.

This was impossible. "No tracks? No sign of their passing?"

Perhaps they are dead men. Perhaps they are ghosts. Perhaps the rumors are true.

Drisker shook his head. What was going on?

There was a second attack this morning. The Vacchs tribe. They were strong and seasoned warriors. They resisted the invaders, as did the Corrax. Like the Corrax, they are no more.

Drisker remembered his premonition. This confirmed its source. Grim news. Worse than grim. "The Vacchs could not decipher what was happening to them? They could not save themselves? None of them?"

The Morsk shrugged. *Are we finished?*

The Morsk's impatience was obvious. It had come only because it owed Drisker, who had once saved its life when it had been imprisoned and threated with death by superstitious Southlanders in a small village above Varfleet. How they had caught it or managed to contain it, he had never found out. Certainly the Morsk was not eager to tell him, ashamed and furious at its circumstances. But Drisker had discovered it was being held and came out of Paranor to set it free and explain its unfortunate condition to the villagers who saw it as a demon and a dark thing in need of killing.

Afterward, the Morsk had told him something.

I was born into a mixed-Race family, it had said. *My ancestors were both shape-shifters and humans with an Elf or two thrown in for good measure. They were feared and hunted, all of them. They were seen as creatures of the dark. As am I. There is no acceptance or understanding of us, Druid. There never will be.*

Well, perhaps. But for those few moments after freeing it, Drisker tried to persuade it otherwise. And the Morsk had not forgotten his kindness or his respect.

"Where does this enemy travel now?" he said.

A rippling of dark robes and a shifting of its body filled a momentary pause. *Where they will, Druid. The Northland will do nothing more to stop them.*

Drisker imagined not. Not after two Troll armies had been annihilated. But what would they do next? He would have to find out. He would have to do more than that, in point of fact. The Druids would have to be braced. Ober Balronen would have to be confronted. It would not be a pleasant moment, no matter its compelling nature.

My debt to you is paid, the Morsk whispered, its voice sand roughblown against wooden walls. *I am leaving now.*

"My thanks," Drisker replied, bowing in deference, head lowering.

By the time he looked up again, the Morsk had disappeared.

A week after Balronen's last, decidedly unproductive Council meeting, he summoned Darcon Leah to his private study. It was early morning, and the Blade was barely up and dressed when the summons arrived. Dar yawned and stretched and considered taking time to eat something before deciding any delay was a bad idea. Better to arrive promptly and hope to get free quickly. The Keep's inhabitants were awake and moving down the hallways, and the day was bright with sunshine and birdsong. It almost made him think things would go well for a change.

Almost.

But his instincts told him this was going to be another wide detour around the issue of what to do about the enemy marching steadily south toward the more civilized and densely populated sections of the Four Lands. He girded himself for the necessary unpleasantness of having to remind the Ard Rhys of the urgency of acting while not insinuating himself too far into areas over which he had no personal jurisdiction.

Still pondering the possible ways this meeting might go as he approached the chambers of the Ard Rhys, he was surprised to encounter Ruis Quince and Zia coming out. Looks were exchanged but no words. The expression on Zia's face was unreadable, although Quince seemed immensely pleased. They went by him quickly, and he continued on through the open door to find Balronen waiting.

"Close the door." The High Druid gestured impatiently. He stood in the center of the room, facing Dar. He did not offer a seat, did not offer a libation. He did not look happy. "Something's happened that requires our attention."

Balronen turned away momentarily as if looking to see if that something might be present. "There was another reveal of magic early this morning in the scrye waters. A rather demonstrable reveal, much on the order of the one that signaled the demise of the Corrax Trolls. I think we can safely assume there has been another attack. So I have decided to dispatch Ruis and Zia immediately to find out what is happening. I want you to go with them. Can you be ready by midday?"

Dar nodded. "Of course."

Balronen looked back at him in time to catch the nod, but there was something oddly distracted about the look. "That's good. Good." He cleared his throat. "There's something else. I want you to keep an eye on those two; I want you to watch them closely. They have been . . . furtive. There have been suggestions of bad intentions in their meetings with me. Their interactions are . . ." He trailed off.

He was clearly having difficulty expressing himself. After a moment, he continued anyway. "Their eagerness to share this journey troubles me. Ruis was too quick to agree . . . after Zia suggested he lead the delegation. It makes me wonder what else is going on."

Dar stared. "I'm not sure I'm following."

"Come now," the other man said softly. "Surely you know by now that they are lovers. They share a bed; they share secrets."

As a matter of fact, he did know all this. But he couldn't see how it mattered where the mission was concerned.

Balronen seemed to sense his hesitation. "I want to know what's going on between them!" he snapped irritably. "Is that so hard to understand? I would think you would want to know, too. She was your lover before she was his, I seem to recall."

Dar couldn't speak. What was this really about? Was Balronen worried there was some sort of intrigue brewing between the two? He didn't seem interested at all in the delay in finding out why these Troll massacres had happened or who had perpetrated them. His concern was with what he appeared to view as a personal offense against him.

"You saw it, too, didn't you?" the High Druid pressed. "You must have. In that last meeting? The way Ruis maneuvered things so it didn't look like it was his idea? The way Zia accepted his company right away?"

There was a dark look in his gaze that told Dar immediately this was a full-blown obsession the other man had latched on to, brought about by suspicions that had their origins in things the highlander knew nothing about.

"I'm not sure what I saw," he answered carefully. "You recognize such things better than I do."

"Then you must take my word. Yours is a less complicated mind than my own, I suppose. I wouldn't expect you to see the nuances of these types of things. But it was there in the looks they exchanged, in the words they spoke—all slyness, clever avoidance. I must always be on my guard against things unseen. You are my Blade, and I want you to protect me by finding out what they are planning. Can you do that?"

Ober Balronen was talking as if he was deranged. Dar Leah knew he should resign his position on the spot and get out of Paranor. But he hesitated, and Balronen took his silence as an affirmative answer.

"Do so, and I will make you a Druid. You command magic, after all, and there's no reason you should not be one of us. But do not fail me in this. Find out the truth. Any way you have to."

He gripped Darcon's shoulder tightly and squeezed it. "You depart at dawn tomorrow."

Then he released his grip and walked past the highlander and out the door, exiting with long, swift strides. Dar stood rooted in place, trying to make sense of what had just happened and failing.

"Shades!" he whispered to himself.

He waited until Balronen was five minutes gone before leaving the room. Even then, he paused at the doorway and peered out to make sure the other was out of sight. He felt more than a little foolish, but he didn't want to have to face the High Druid again right away. That much suspicion felt like a disease, and he didn't want any part of it.

He was moving down the hall, intent on reaching his quarters, when a voice said, "You look a little worried."

Zia stepped out of the alcove shadows to one side, confronting him. Almost as tall as he was, she wore an intense, determined expression. "Surprised to find me waiting?"

"A little."

"I've made it a habit, I guess. Waiting for you. Now and before. Same reason each time. I keep hoping you won't end up forgetting me entirely."

He smiled and shook his head. "No one could ever forget you, Zia."

She gave him a noncommittal look with those huge blue eyes and brushed back a lock of his reddish hair from his face. "You managed it not too long ago." She held his gaze. "Old news, though. Did Balronen tell you he's finally decided to send Ruis and me north?" Her mouth twisted with disgust. "It took him long enough to act."

"When hasn't it? He makes no decisions until he can see his way clear to whatever benefits he might derive from doing so. Why do you have anything to do with these people, Zia? You don't have to be part of this inner circle nonsense."

She shrugged. "Maybe I like being part of it."

"Oh, of course. No wonder you always look so intensely interested in the meetings."

"Like you, I get bored. But I promised Ober I would stick."

He gave her a look. "You don't have to keep that promise. You can walk away."

Her smile was rueful. "You seem better at walking away than I am."

She was so smart, so quick to see the truth of matters. Sometimes he felt like a child in comparison. It was a bitter reminder of why he had been drawn to her. Her intellect and her deep understanding of others were as compelling as any other aspect of her. For him, perhaps, even more so.

She moved next to him, took his arm in hers, and started walking him down the hall. "I want you to do something for me. I want you to come with me on this mission. Come as leader of the Druid Guard. You can do that. Ask Ober. Tell him you want to be there to make certain things go the way they should. Something of that sort. But come."

"Why do you want me to do that?"

"A sense of things not being right. A suspicion that this expedition won't turn out to be what we expect. I don't know. I think I'm missing something. I can't put my finger on it. I just have a feeling that something bigger is wrong, that this meeting won't be what we expect. There have been two attacks, Dar. I don't like it. But if you were there, I would worry a lot less."

He took a deep breath and exhaled sharply. "I never saw that in you before. You were always so confident."

"Maybe not so much anymore." She kept her head lowered and his arm tightly clutched in hers.

He stopped her, turned her toward him. "Zia, I don't think . . ."

"Will you come with me or not?" she interrupted quickly. "Just say it."

They stared at each other in silence for a long moment. Dar found her as beautiful now as he had when they'd first met. As beautiful as she was on the day he told her he couldn't give her what she wanted. He didn't think he would ever see her any other way.

"As a matter of fact, I'm already going."

She looked uncertain. "What are you talking about?"

"Balronen ordered me to go with you. He thinks something is wrong, too. But he thinks it has to do with you and Ruis. He wants me to keep an eye on you."

He paused, wondering if he should try to explain, and decided he had already said too much.

Zia confirmed his assumption. She was incensed. "He wants you to keep an *eye* on me? What does that mean?"

Dar, never good at lying, didn't try to do so now. "He doesn't trust you. Or Ruis."

A flash of anger crossed her face. "And you agreed?"

"I wasn't given a choice." He paused. "Is there anything you know about this that I don't?"

She stepped back from him quickly, releasing his arm. "Such as what? What are you talking about?"

"Anything about you and Ruis? About you and Ober?"

She exhaled sharply. She was beyond incensed. "What is it to you, Dar? What do you care about anyone and me? You didn't want me. Is it so hard to believe that someone else does? Spy all you want, but otherwise you stay away from me."

Then she wheeled away and was gone.

ELEVEN

♦

TARSHA KAYNIN WAS ASLEEP when the scratching began. She had spent the day training, following her usual routine of exercises and testing, and she was tired from her efforts. It was impossible for her to know how long she had been sleeping, but she was deep under when the scratching sound brought her awake. She surfaced out of a black well of comfort and darkness, her thoughts gathering slowly, her awareness of where she was and what she was doing recalling itself in fuzzy detail as her eyes blinked open.

Although she continued to hear the scratching, it took her a moment to realize what it was. Even then she questioned it. Who or what would be scratching the side of the cottage? What was the point of making such a sound? Through force of habit, she probed the darkness with her senses, searching for the source.

Out from her small bedroom, through the cottage rooms and past the doors and windows into the night.

Out to where dark-cloaked figures closed on Drisker's little cottage, their blades glinting in the pale starlight. She saw them coming toward her from three directions. Ten or twelve, at least. Common sense told her there would be more at the rear of the cottage, as well.

She was up quickly then, pulling on her clothes and boots and slipping from her bedroom into the front rooms where she could peer through the window. She saw one of them immediately, crouched down and looking over to where others crept from the shadows. She took a moment to wonder who they were before deciding it was a pointless exercise. Their purpose was clear: They were searching for the Druid. Drisker had warned her; sometimes his enemies came looking for him. Even if they didn't find him and only found her, they weren't likely to leave her alive.

She experienced a moment of raw terror. There were too many. If they found her, they were going to kill her.

Fear gave her purpose. She had to stand and fight or run. The choice was made before the thought was complete. Drisker had made it plain enough what she should do if confronted with this sort of situation. She backed away from the window, crouching low so as not to be detected, and moved toward the rear door of the cottage. They might well be there, too—probably were, in fact—but she had to find an escape route somewhere. She wore a long knife belted at her waist, but her only real protection lay in the magic of the wishsong. She hummed it to life as she neared the back door, brought it up to full strength, and cloaked herself in shadows.

At the door, she paused. Was there anything she should take with her? Anything important to the Druid? Anything he treasured and could not afford to lose?

Abandoning the wishsong's cloaking, she went back into the living area and paused when she reached the shelving that held the two heavy volumes of spells and conjuring her mentor was endlessly reading when not engaged in instructing her. His favorite books, the ones he seemed to rely on most. Would these intruders try to steal them? Would they even know what they were?

No point in taking chances. She snatched them up, her resolve to save them strengthened by knowing she was doing something important.

She returned to the back door and paused again. She bent close, her head just touching the wooden barrier, and probed with her senses. She detected it right away. Something was out there, but it did not reflect the sounds or smells or feel of humans. She hesitated.

There were no windows in the back wall through which to peer. Time was running out. She summoned the wishsong once more, cloaked herself anew, took a deep breath, and eased the door open. When she saw nothing, she opened it further, then further still and stepped outside.

She nearly fell over the body that lay directly outside the doorway in a pool of black shadows, its head gone. Stifling the scream that threatened to escape her, she forced herself to look more closely. From the look of the clothing, she could tell it was one of the intruders. But who had killed him? Closing the door behind her, she eased past the huddled form, her eyes searching everywhere at once. As she glanced back momentarily, she caught sight of multiple parallel gouges in the door, crisscrossing its surface in regular sets. There must have been a dozen of them.

The source of the scratching sound, she realized.

But what could have made the marks?

When she turned back again, a moor cat was standing right in front of her, lantern eyes gleaming and dark muzzle inches from her face.

This time she did scream, but no sound came out. Her vocal cords were paralyzed and the wishsong was frozen in her throat. Instantly, she became visible again, unprotected and unarmed. The fear that raced through her was paralyzing. Her skin prickled at the animal's closeness, at the size of its head, at the prospect of teeth that didn't show but which she could easily imagine. She had never seen a moor cat before, but she had no doubt she was seeing one now. It was coal black from nose to tail save for twin silver stripes that ran down the very center of its forehead and an odd blaze on its lean chest. Even for a moor cat, it was huge, its head on a level with her own, its body easily more than eight feet in length.

She stood there with Drisker's books clutched tightly against her chest and waited for the beast to do something. But it just stood quietly, seemingly content to stare at her. Then, apparently tiring of the effort, it leaned into her and sniffed, its hot breath on her face and neck. She closed her eyes and continued to wait, not knowing what else to do. She felt it move behind her and shove against her back with its broad head, pushing her toward the woods. She responded automatically, walking in the direction it was nudging her, hugging the books of magic to her breast. When she opened her eyes a second later the great beast was in front of her, leading the way. Her heart stopped pounding as she realized what it wanted, and she followed, staying close.

She understood by now the cat was in some way connected to Drisker. This was who had been shadowing her ever since her arrival. Its eyes were the ones she had felt watching her. Since moor cats could appear and disappear in the blink of an eye, she had never had any real chance of seeing it. The Druid had said she would be looked after in his absence. Apparently, he had meant that quite literally.

They passed a second body sprawled on the ground. This one was missing its head, too.

Then they were into the trees, and the moor cat stopped to look back at the cottage. In the darkness, the cloaked figures seemed to be everywhere, edging about the walls, picking their way through the shadows. One of them found the body by the rear door, bent to examine it, and backed away quickly. Another approached, and a short conference ensued. Other intruders had entered the cottage and were searching. They would find the Druid missing. But they would also find evidence of her presence. She had done nothing to hide it. There had been no time to do so, even if she had thought to try.

A moment later a flickering light rose from within the cottage. It was small at first, but then it grew quickly in size until it seemed to fill the interior entirely. The intruders had set Drisker's home on fire.

For just a moment Tarsha considered doing something to stop this from happening. She almost set down the books and started back. But then she felt the moor cat nudging her once more and realized she had done as much as she could. At least she had managed to save the most important of his books. So she turned away and followed obediently as the cat led her deeper into the woods. All she could think about was what might be lost in the blaze. Surely there were other possessions of importance, other books and papers, other personal effects. With the exception of the books she carried, all of his possessions would be turned to ash. All of hers, as well—what few she had. She slowed and looked back, anger warring with caution. Some of the intruders were standing in a cluster next to the burning cottage, clearly revealed against the soaring flames, staring toward the trees. It was almost as if they were daring her to show herself, to come out to face them. It felt like a challenge.

She considered accepting it, her magic rising within her, hot and raw and eager. But then the moor cat nudged her anew, and she turned again toward the deeper forest.

Behind her, the cottage was engulfed in flames.

She followed the moor cat until they reached a place so far from any-where she had gone before in her wanderings she did not recognize it. The beast lay down in a patch of grass and waited for her to do the same. Without getting too close, she did so. They watched each other in silence, an uneasy alliance.

"Thank you," she said finally.

She had no way of knowing if it understood her or not, but she felt better for having spoken the words. The cat had saved her life. She would have been trapped and killed in the cottage otherwise. She might have lost her things, but she was alive. The cat must have been keeping watch over her to act so swiftly and decisively. It had killed two men to free her. It had opened a path to safety. This was an intel-ligent creature, a friend to Drisker, perhaps even a familiar.

A good one to have, she thought.

She slept for a time after that, tired in spite of the stress and uncer-tainty she was feeling, still not quite believing what had happened. She was too on edge at first, lying on the ground facing the cat and watching its eyes blink slowly. But then it began to emit a deep, steady purring, and her eyes grew heavy as she was slowly lulled to sleep.

It was sunrise when she woke, the light a bright glimmer east through the trees, long gold shafts spearing the dark to chase back the night once more. She sat up slowly and looked around. The moor cat was gone. She searched for signs of it, still uncertain of last night's events, and found a depression in the grasses where it had rested. She tracked its footprints for a short distance, but then they vanished. Apparently, it had done all for her it could.

There was no point in thinking she had somehow dreamed it, especially after she found Drisker's books still stacked at her feet.

She rose and looked about doubtfully. Which direction would take her back the way she had come, back to the burned-out ruin of the cottage? Which way was Emberen?

"Are you lost, little sister?" a voiced inquired.

She turned to find a strange man of diminished size, bristling hair and whiskers, and a slouched posture staring at her. She believed the grimace on his lined and weathered face was a genuine attempt at a smile, although it didn't quite succeed in accomplishing its intended goal.

"A bit, perhaps," she replied, risking a smile in return. "Who are you?"

A shrug. "A friend of the Druid's, like yourself. What matters more is who *you* are. His protégée, his student, his hope for redemption."

Hope for redemption? "Tarsha Kaynin," she said, extending her hand.

"Pleased to meet you." He accepted her offer of a handshake but did not provide his own name. "Can I help direct you back to the cottage? Or to what remains of it?"

She made a face. "Burned to the ground, I suppose?"

He nodded. "But at least you saved something that matters." He pointed to the books. "The Druid will appreciate having those back."

"I would have saved more, if I could. It all happened rather quickly. Who were those men?"

"Cutthroats and assassins of the garden variety. Such men come calling every so often. Mostly, your mentor is here to greet them, and they are so pleased to be welcomed they never leave."

She did not miss the irony in his voice. "Maybe he should move somewhere safer."

"Well, if such a place existed, I'm quite sure he would. As yet, one hasn't been found. Shall we go?"

She picked up Drisker's books and set off through the forest, the strange little man leading the way. All around them the morning was coming alive with birdsong and small-animal activity. Squirrels and chipmunks raced up and down trunks and across limbs. Mice darted through grasses and weeds. Rabbits sat hunched and frozen in place, noses twitching. Once, a badger lumbered by, looking uninterested. The early-morning breezes died and the day warmed.

Before long, the sun had risen sufficiently that the forest shadows had shortened or disappeared. Tarsha was feeling surprisingly good in spite of last night.

As they walked, she spent much of her time trying to figure out what sort of creature was keeping her company. He was not of any species she had encountered, and there was something decidedly odd about him. As if maybe he was not altogether human and perhaps more a creature of the forest. It was in the way he saw things, commenting on this and that animal or bird in a conversational way when she couldn't see what he was looking at. It was in the way he moved, a kind of sliding that now and then caused him to momentarily disappear. She had a feeling he might have use of magic or might simply be magical himself.

"Can I ask you a rather personal question?" she asked finally.

"Nothing too embarrassing, I hope."

"Well, I don't think so. But you can always refuse to answer if it is."

"That I can. Ask away."

"What, exactly, are you? You seem very different to me. Who are your people? Where do you come from?"

"Oh, I see." He nodded to himself without looking at her. "I didn't give you a name, and that troubles you. A name suggests a species or a place of residence. I was able to name you, but you have no knowledge of me! So now you seek to set things right and put us on an equal footing. Well, that's not asking too much, I guess."

She waited, but he stopped talking. The minutes drifted away.

"So?" she said finally.

He looked at her. "So what?"

"So what is your name?"

"Oh, that. Well, what I *am* matters more, so let's stick with that. I am a forest imp."

She frowned. "I've never heard of a forest imp."

"Well, there aren't many of us, and we don't tend to mix with other creatures. We stay where we belong, mostly—here in the deep woods. There are only six or eight of us in this stretch."

"And where do forest imps come from?"

"Far, far away. From a place called Morrowindl, a volcanic island out in the Blue Divide. We lived there for centuries but then some of us came back with Elves who were rescued from an explosion along with the city of Arborlon."

She stared at him. She had no knowledge of any of this. Did she even want to know? She decided not. "What do forest imps do?" she asked instead.

"Oh, pretty much whatever we want. We have no limits to our capabilities, you know. Even the Druid admires us."

"You've been friends a long time?"

"Long enough to get to know each other pretty well. He's not like other people."

"I don't suppose he is."

"I suspect you are not like the rest of your people, either, little sister. I think your magic makes you very special. I have watched you using it under his guidance. I have seen what you can do. You are very talented."

So. Another pair of eyes has been watching. How many more are there that I don't know about?

"Thank you," she said. "You seem to have a lot of free time."

"Nothing but," he said, and his rumble of laughter filled the forest and sent birds and animals alike scattering in all directions.

When they finally reached the cottage, they found it in ruins, a charred and still-smoking heap of timbers and ashes. Tarsha stood looking, a deep sadness stealing through her as she thought of the Druid's face on seeing what had been done to his home.

"You can't stay here," the little man said, glancing over.

"I have to wait for Drisker," she answered. "I have to tell him what's happened."

"He might not be back for quite a while and possibly not until after that. His journey took him far to the north. Come with me. I have a place. I will leave him a sign so he will know where to look for you. Come."

She hesitated, but then grudgingly followed, the books still in her arms. She didn't trust leaving them out in the open. She wanted to give them to Drisker herself. She wanted to show him she had been able to save something that mattered.

They walked into the trees again, this time in a different direction, one that eventually took them into a part of the forest to which she had never been. Here the trees were giants, their limbs heavy and broad, their trunks soaring hundreds of feet into the air. The sun was visible but only just, and the light that managed to work its way through the canopy was diffuse and pale. The air smelled of damp and rotting things, as if although still living this part of the forest was in the process of dying, too. There were huge nurse logs and splintered remains of fallen trunks clogging the forest floor, and the forest imp and the girl had to pick their way through the debris. It was difficult for Tarsha, but the imp seemed to find it easy and his movements were quick and sure as he led her on.

Something else was odd, she realized after a time. There were no birds here—no singing and no signs of flight. She didn't notice any ground animals, either. It was as if they had entered another world. She felt a slight sense of worry nudging at her, but there was nothing to suggest that the forest imp meant her any harm. Could a friend of Drisker Arc's be a danger to her? She didn't see how. So she continued on, telling herself it was all right, that she just needed to be a little cautious.

A little more than an hour later, they had reached a glade shadowed by giant conifers that ringed the space in perfect symmetry. The light was brighter and the air less fetid, and Tarsha felt a sense of reassurance. Without slowing, the forest imp went to one of the trees, reached down, and opened a trapdoor covered with moss and grasses.

"I live here," he advised.

At his beckoning, she went down a set of wooden stairs into a wide, spacious underground chamber framed by tree roots and wooden beams used for shoring up the earth. There was a table and four chairs, a cooking stove, an unmade bed with colorful quilts and pillows, a dresser with drawers partially opened and stuffed with clothes, a work area with benches and cabinetry, and the most wondrous golden chandelier she had ever seen. It hung from a beam at the center of the room, arms gracefully spreading, curious glass bulbs at their tips giving off just enough light to brighten the room.

"Do you like it?" he asked eagerly.

"Of course. It's beautiful." She could not take her eyes off it. "Where did you find it?"

"I didn't find it. I made it."

Then he snapped his fingers, and the glass bulbs brightened further, illuminating the entire chamber from wall to wall. Tarsha smiled in surprise. "So maybe you do know a little of magic," she said.

"A little. Let's eat something. You must be hungry by now."

He trundled over to the kitchen area, removed some meat and cheese from cold storage along with a pitcher of ale, found some bread and fruit, and brought all of it over to set before her. While she continued to gaze around the room, he laid it all out, pouring the ale into two tankards. They ate and drank and talked until the meal was consumed. By then Tarsha could barely keep her eyes open, holding her head up with one hand and running her fingers through her white-blond hair as she felt a deep weariness overtake her.

"Come with me," said the forest imp.

Taking her hand, he led her to the bed and, in spite of her protestations, insisted she lie down and try to sleep. She was exhausted from her ordeal, he said. Anyone would be. Better she be refreshed and awake when the Druid returned.

She did as he suggested, already feeling it was impossible to do anything else—and the minute she laid her head on the pillow he had provided, sleep claimed her.

TWELVE

---◆---

IT WAS ON THE eighth day after leaving for the north that Drisker Arc returned. He flew the two-man flit into Emberen two hours after midday and stabled her with the storage manager before starting the walk home. His thoughts were of the enemy army on its march south out of Troll country toward the Borderlands and the continuing mystery of its hidden intent. That it was an invader come to claim new territory seemed apparent. But who this invader was and where it was going ultimately remained uncertain.

Which left him wishing he knew a great deal more about what was happening than he did.

These invaders had been fortunate in their successes so far because they had been dealing with Trolls, who saw things mostly in straightforward terms of strength versus strength, and had stood little chance against an enemy that utilized skilled military tactics. And quite possibly used some form of magic, as well. But others they would encounter if they continued south would be less vulnerable. Others would be more experienced and would possess better weapons. Others would confront them with greater numbers. It would take more than clever tactics and basic magic to bring them down.

He wrestled with what he was going to do about what he had learned. He had to do something, but the most obvious choice was the one he wanted least to make. To go to the Druids and share what he had learned. To go to them and warn them and hope they would listen to him. To brace Ober Balronen, now High Druid, at Paranor, where he had once held the same position, and risk the sting and shame of being turned away.

He was not at all sure he could do it.

He was less sure still that he could not.

The walk calmed him, banishing the thoughts that had plagued him all the way home from the shores of the Lazareen, bringing him fully back to himself. The familiar smells of the forest, the flashes of color from swooping birds, the buzzing of insects, and the skittish movement of small animals in the underbrush all served to remind him of what mattered—his home and his privacy, his escape from the stresses of his former life, and a reassurance that he was free of the constant feeling that he was serving no purpose as a Druid leader. The dark memories of those years had not faded, and he did not think they ever would. Here was where he belonged. The good feelings of his retreat engendered in him by his walk home only served as a welcome reminder.

And suddenly he was standing at the edge of the clearing where his cottage home had once been, staring at the still-smoking rubble, and everything was swept away in a moment.

At first, he couldn't believe what he was seeing. Nothing remained of what had been there eight days earlier, the whole of it reduced by fire to ashes and debris. He started forward and then stopped again. He needed to make it feel real, yet at the same time wanted it not to be. Because if it was real, then everything that mattered to him was gone.

He wondered suddenly of the girl. Tarsha Kaynin. Where was she? He looked around the clearing, hoping the answer would reveal itself but knowing it would not. He continued forward, scanning the ground out of habit, searching for signs that would tell him who had done this. He circled the rubble twice, eyes cast downward. He found the tracks soon enough, dozens of them. Whoever they were, they had come in force and attacked from all sides. One or two and maybe even more had died in the attack, their blood still staining the ground. But there were no bodies, discarded weapons, or telltale leavings. The attackers had gone back to wherever they had come from without leaving any clue as to their origins.

Of Tarsha, there was no trace at all.

Flinc appeared out of the trees, shambling toward him in that oddly sliding fashion, grizzled countenance wreathed in lines of sadness. One gnarled hand gripped a heavy canvas sack.

"There were more than a dozen," he advised, shaking his head mournfully. "They came last night—searching for you, I would guess. They found you missing and burned your home in retribution. There was nothing I could do."

Drisker eyed the forest imp coldly. "Apparently not. And the girl?"

The little man shrugged. "Dead. They killed her in the first few minutes. I am not sure she even woke before it was over. I tried to warn her, but I was too slow. I did manage to rescue these."

He passed the sack to Drisker, who opened it and pulled out his two most precious books of magic. A small consolation in a desolate moment, but he should have been grateful. "My thanks."

"It was nothing. A small attempt at redeeming myself when I could do so little else." The imp looked immensely pleased, his attempt at humility pathetic. "I have always done what I could for you. You know that."

Drisker felt a surge of rage. "And frequently done what you shouldn't have, too."

He watched Flinc's expression change, saw his gaze shift and his body recoil. It confirmed the Druid's suspicions. That something was not right with all this. That the imp was playing games.

"Do you want to tell me what really happened?" he asked quietly, his voice chilly with menace.

Flinc quickly tried to recover. "I don't understand—"

"You don't understand many things," Drisker interrupted. "Particularly the fine art of lying and making it seem like truth. Let me ask you. How is it that you managed to retrieve these books and yet not wake Tarsha in time to get her out of the house?"

The forest imp stared at him, wide-eyed, openmouthed.

"How is it that you managed to retrieve my books from a house filled with assassins without them seeing you?" Drisker gave him a dark look. "Have you learned how to make yourself invisible long enough to accomplish such amazing things?"

"You besmirch me when all I did was try to help—"

"Besmirch, is it?" Drisker interrupted none-too-gently. "Such a big word for such a little man. Let us pretend you never told me this wildly improbable story. Let us presume that what you intended to tell me has to do with your fascination with beautiful and precious things. Such as Tarsha Kaynin. What then might you have to say about her supposed death? What might you choose to tell me of her present whereabouts? Or should I simply go find her myself?"

Flinc stared at him a moment longer and then stamped his foot in rage. "You always know! How do you do that?" The forest imp threw up his stubby arms. "How can you manage to see through me so easily? You aren't Faerie! You have no innate skills!"

The Druid's smile was cutting. "There is an old saying, friend Flinc. One that has survived even the destruction of the Old World. 'It takes one to know one.' Sound familiar to you?"

And he gave the forest imp a knowing wink.

He found her shortly afterward in Flinc's underground lair, curled up in the imp's bed, sound asleep. It was the sort of sleep he recognized instantly as one induced by strong drugs. Administered, no doubt, through ingestion of food or drink laced with one thing or another. He glanced back at Flinc who stood silently in a far corner of the chamber, his bright eyes filled with frustration and fear.

Drisker shook his head. "I am disappointed in you. It was bad enough to come home to find my house destroyed and my possessions gone. It was even worse to learn that Tarsha was dead. It would have made some difference in my displeasure if you had told me the truth and let me know she was alive and well. What was your plan? Did you intend to keep her prisoner? Did you think I would not find out?"

The forest imp straightened. "I thought she would be better off with me. I thought the remaining assassins would return for you and sooner or later they would find her and she would be killed. I had no plan other than to save her."

The Druid felt a stab of guilt. It was not an altogether misguided piece of reasoning. It was still wrong, but it did not lack merit. "It was not your place to make such a decision," he said finally. "It was hers."

He reached down, scooped Tarsha Kaynin off the bed, and cradled her in his arms. "I will take her now. I think it best if you remain here."

When he reached the stairs leading up, he paused. "I am going to forget this ever happened. I will not tell her what you did or what you intended. But you would be wise not to try anything like this again, Flinc."

He left the forest imp in his underground lair and went back to the village of Emberen with Tarsha in his arms and took rooms for them at a small inn. Leaving her to sleep, he went down to the carpenter's place of business and asked how long it would take to rebuild his cottage. The answer given back was a bit vague but suggested it would be several months at least. Drisker gave him the job and asked that he get started as soon as possible. Then he returned to the inn to sleep.

When he woke the next morning, the sun had already risen and the girl was sitting at his bedside. He nodded in greeting, rising to a sitting position. "I thought I locked that door."

She looked vaguely chagrined but not enough to suggest any real regret. "I was worried about you. I was sure you had seen your home, and I knew you would be upset. I thought I should make certain you were all right." She paused, brushing back several loose strands of her white-gold hair. "Locks do not mean much to me," she added.

"I can see that. Another hidden talent, I guess. Or did your magic open them?"

She shook her head. "Picks. I sometimes had to let myself into my brother's rooms when he locked himself in and was . . . when he needed me."

The Druid nodded. "Well, as you can see, I'm fine. As are you, it appears. So we can examine the situation with some possibility of clarity. Can you tell me what happened?"

She did so in detail, giving him a clear picture of how she had awakened, how she found the intruders circling the cottage, how she got out and encountered the moor cat.

"Is he yours?" she asked.

"One doesn't keep moor cats as pets. They come and go as they please. Fade prefers my company and sometimes keeps watch over things."

"Things like me, for instance. His name is Fade?"

"*Her* name is Fade. Female moor cats are actually bigger than the males. Fade, in particular, is very large. Did she frighten you?"

"Within an inch of my life." She paused. "How did I get here, anyway? To this inn? The last thing I remember is being in the forest imp's underground home, trying to stay awake."

She was surprisingly calm about it, considering the shock she must have experienced on waking in an entirely different place than the one she had fallen asleep in. But Tarsha Kaynin was not one to panic easily.

"I found you and brought you here," he said. "I'll look for other lodgings later today. I'm told it will be awhile before my cottage is rebuilt."

She nodded, her expression speculative. "Can I ask you something? More?"

He gave her a look. "Can I stop you?"

"This is rather personal."

"I should not be surprised."

"About me, not you."

He hesitated. "All right. Ask anyway."

"That forest imp. Flinc. I've been thinking. Something about that whole business doesn't feel right. Fade led me away from the cottage, but then Flinc found me and took me to his home to wait for your return. He said he wanted to protect me. Was he telling the truth?"

He hesitated and then gave her a small nod. "He probably saw it that way."

"But then I fell asleep and didn't wake up again until you brought me here. I never sleep like that. No dreams, no sense of drifting. I was so sound asleep I could barely make myself move even after I awoke here." She shook her head. "I think maybe he gave me something."

"He might have. He might have thought it would help."

Drisker had promised Flinc he would not tell Tarsha of the forest imp's intentions, and he did not see a reason to break that promise. But if Tarsha guessed the truth, he would not deny it. She was already looking at him doubtfully, as if realizing he was hiding something and trying to see what it was. He kept his expression neutral and waited to see where she was taking this.

"He seemed nice enough, but sort of strange, too," she continued. "I can't explain it, but I think he might have had something else in mind when he took me."

His face tightened. "Are you hurt in some way?" Suddenly he was afraid he had missed the obvious. "Is there anything wrong? Are you having bad memories of something?"

She gave him a long, searching look. "Only of those men and what they tried to do to me. But you mean something else, don't you?"

He shook his head. She was too sharp by half. He would have to watch out for that. "Not really." He didn't want to answer her question until he'd had time to think about it more. A small suspicion had taken root and he shoved it to the back of his mind. "Would you like something to eat?"

They went downstairs to the public rooms and took a table. Breakfast was hearty, and both were full long before the food was gone and the tea Drisker had ordered drunk. Tarsha said little as they ate and Drisker, while observing her closely, let her be.

"It was brave of you, Tarsha," he said finally, as they sat together after the plates had been cleared, "to take the time to save my books. That was quick thinking. Those books are very important to me. We have a history together. I would hate to lose them."

She couldn't quite meet his gaze. "I wish I could have saved more."

"You were smart not to try. Those men would have killed you without a second thought if they found you. You were right to get out quickly."

"Who were they?"

"Enemies of the worst kind. The fact that they burned my home suggests they wanted to be sure I was dead. I imagine they thought I was inside."

She shook her head. "I don't know that they thought that at all. They got into the house and searched it before they set it afire. Unless they thought you were hiding in it somewhere, they knew you were gone."

"And they burned it anyway? That's odd. Now I really do wonder who they were."

"The forest imp didn't seem to know, either." She looked away and then back. "Does he have a name? He kept dodging the question when I asked him. Doesn't he want people to know who he is?"

The Druid thought about his answer, not wanting to say too much. "His name is Flinc. He likes playing games. He likes keeping people off balance. He is an imp, after all. There's a bit of trickery in all of them."

She looked at him. "I've never heard of forest imps."

"Few have. There aren't all that many."

"So he said. But is he right about being a Faerie creature?"

Drisker shrugged. "Maybe. He says that's what he is and there are none to disprove it. I let him have that distinction. If he wants to call himself a forest imp, then I guess there's no harm in it."

"Does he have magic?"

"Of a sort. He isn't a practitioner but he has some natural ability. He can do small tricks and enact subterfuges now and then. His skills are limited, but his knowledge is extensive. He has lived a long time, and he knows a fair amount about the Old World."

"He seems to like you."

Drisker's smile was wan. "I suppose so. In his way."

He left her at the inn and went out into the village. After asking around, he found a cottage that was vacant and rented it from an old man who didn't much like him but was willing to take his money all the same. Their negotiations were swift and chilly, and it was clear to Drisker that the other found the entire transaction distasteful. The cottage was a two-bedroom single-story with less space than his own, but adequate for his needs. He paid the old man and left.

He found Tarsha waiting on his return, and together they walked to their new lodgings and settled in. He took note that while they passed a number of Emberen's residents on their way—all of whom looked them over carefully—none chose to speak. He was certain Tarsha noticed it, too, although she did not comment. She seemed to be inured to this sort of suspicious scrutiny, and he suspected that she had endured much the same where her brother was concerned. You could always tell when people disapproved of you.

Again, Drisker left her and spent the remainder of the day questioning any residents of the village who would talk to him in a civil manner, seeing if he could find out anything more about the men who had burned down his home. He was assiduous in his efforts, but in the end he found out exactly nothing. No one had seen the men. No one had seen whatever aircraft they had arrived in. No one had heard anything the night of the attack.

He returned no wiser than when he had left and found that in his absence Tarsha had purchased food and ale and prepared dinner. They ate together in silence, save for right at the beginning of the meal when Tarsha asked him what he was going to do about the men who had escaped Fade.

His shrug was a brisk dismissal. "I'm working on it."

What he thought about as they ate was that he was going to have to shift his attention from what to do about the invaders coming down from the north to the more personal threat posed by these men hunting him. He did not think he could afford to wait around for them to try to kill him again.

After the girl went to bed, he sat alone in the darkness of the living room and continued to think about it until he dropped off to sleep.

Sometime after midnight, the assassins who had come for him before returned.

It was a possibility he had considered and dismissed. He did not think it likely they would come after him a second time so quickly. Having burned down his home and survived an encounter with Fade, they would lie low for a time. That he had underestimated either their determination or their desperation to be rid of him was abundantly apparent. He was not ready for them, but he was also not where they expected him to be, which was probably what saved him. They smashed his bedroom window and riddled his bed with darts and short spears from less than a dozen feet away, and by the time they realized their mistake he was awake.

Seconds later he went after them.

He burst through the front door with his magic alive and crackling at his fingertips, forming a protective shield of pure blue light. The men at his window—a quick count revealed three in all—wheeled back to face him, and seven others rushed out of the trees. Because he was so close to Emberen, there was no help to be found from Fade, who seldom left the deep woods. Nor was Flinc anywhere in evidence, although this came as no surprise. It was highly improbable he would have chosen to intervene, in any case.

Drisker attempted to defend himself against both assaults, his Druid magic a blaze of blue light that exploded in sharp bursts amid the black-garbed assassins. In the midst of this struggle, Tarsha Kaynin flew through the door, her body wreathed in brilliant white light and shards of silver. Her wishsong was a death wail, unbound and hungry, and it sent Drisker's assailants flying like straw men. They were not expecting her, and it was their undoing. Even though their numbers were superior and they were experienced killers, they were overwhelmed. Of the ten they began with, three were dead in the first thirty seconds.

Faced with such ferocity, the rest broke and ran, too frightened now to continue their attack. Drisker went after them. He did not hold back as he did so, did not think for a moment to spare these cowards who came in the darkness and sought to kill him while he slept. By the time he was done with them, they were all dead, and he was spent to the point of exhaustion.

But he had to know who they were. He strode purposefully down off the porch and bent to examine the dead one by one, and his suspicions as to the nature of the men he was dealing with were confirmed. On the wrist of each was a marking he recognized—a pair of closed eyes, bleeding through the lids. These men were members of an assassins' guild called Orsis, which operated out of the Borderlands city of Varfleet. High priced and highly skilled at their work, they had found themselves a bit overmatched in this instance.

Now that he knew who those seeking to kill him were, he wanted to know who had hired them.

He searched for footprints to see if any had managed to escape him. None had. He took a moment longer to be sure and then turned back. This batch had been dispatched, but others would come.

Tarsha ran up to him. "Do you recognize them?" she asked at once.

He gave her a look. "What made you charge out of the house like that? You didn't stop to think about it, did you?"

She reddened, hearing the reproof in his voice. "I was just trying to help. There wasn't time for thinking."

He put a hand on her shoulder and gave her a none-too-gentle squeeze. "If you find yourself in this situation again, pause before you act. Precipitous action is a two-edged sword. Be wary of it."

He started to move away, but she caught hold of him. "Just wait a minute. I don't feel too good about this, either. I killed three human beings. How do you think that makes me feel? I've never hurt anyone! I've never used my magic that way!"

"I'm sure that's true. I'm sorry you got involved. But you should have stayed inside."

"Are you saying I shouldn't have tried to help you?"

"I'm saying you need to be more careful."

"Oh, I see. Better to be cautious than save your life!"

He shook his head. "It's not that."

"What is it, then"

He paused, sighed. "What it makes you feel after you've killed someone? I wanted to spare you that feeling. Doesn't matter your good intentions or the rightness of it. It feels terrible afterward, nevertheless. It feels as if a part of you has been stolen away. I don't want you hurt. Physically or emotionally."

She released him. Her expression was unreadable. If she was bothered by what he said, she wasn't showing it. "What are you going to do about the ones who got away?" she demanded abruptly. "They've come twice now; they'll come again, won't they?"

His reply was brief. "This is Orsis we are dealing with—an assassins' guild. Their reputation is well known. Once they take a contract, they do not give up until it is fulfilled. However long it takes, however many men they must employ, they will keep coming until I am dispatched."

She stared at him. "How do you put a stop to it?"

His eyes turned to flint. "They've had two chances at me now and botched them both. Instead of waiting around to see if they botch a third, I think I should pay them a visit."

He leaned close. "Do you want to come with me? You seem eager enough for a fight."

She nodded at once.

"Then let's find them, you and I, and put an end to this!"

THIRTEEN

◆

AS TAVO KAYNIN STOOD in the open doorway and looked outside, the day seemed very quiet to him. It was midday at the start of a sleepy, windless afternoon. The sun was a bright orb in a cloudless autumn sky, and all around him the deciduous trees were beginning to turn, their riotous colors a stark contrast to the deep evergreen of the conifers. Far in the distance, hawks flew loops and circles seeking prey on the forest floor, but closer to where he watched there were no birds and no birdsong in evidence.

He liked the quiet. It was so much better than the screaming.

He knew he should probably leave, but something held him fast. Not fear, not shock or rage—all those had dissipated in the wake of the killing. He was calm now and at peace. Perhaps that was what kept him there, rooted in place, looking out over the surrounding forest. It had taken a lot to bring him here, a lot to persuade him that this was the right thing to do. Much of his thinking had been so jumbled, so confused over the past few years. But now he felt clearheaded and oddly lighthearted. Those feelings were the result of his efforts at setting things right. He felt so much better now that he had put an end to the source of his problems.

But had he? He wasn't sure. Not entirely.

She was still free, after all. *She* was still out there, somewhere.

He took a moment to glance over his shoulder, and the shock of what he saw caused him to turn away immediately. The inside of the cottage was covered in blood. It was everywhere—on the floor and walls, on the furniture, in some places even on the ceiling. Who knew there was so much blood in a human being? Well, two human beings actually, but still. Where did it all fit? He grinned at the idea of blood "fitting" into someone. It just did, of course. Obviously.

He looked down at himself. A lot of the blood was on him. A whole lot of the blood. It had dried to crusty brownish stains on some parts of his clothing but was still bright red and slick on others. After all, he had taken his time with it, made the purging ritualistic so as to free himself, because otherwise there would be no release for him. How long had it taken for them to die? He couldn't be sure. It seemed as if it had taken forever, but he knew that wasn't an accurate approximation. It might have taken an hour; he didn't think it could have been much more than that.

It was their fault. They shouldn't have abandoned him. They should have cared enough about him to discover what was happening to him, what was being done to him. Instead, when confronted with the truth, they had insisted they didn't know. Parents, claiming not to know. But they had known where he was, hadn't they? Known from the first day they had taken him there and left him to his fate.

And they thought it was enough simply to believe he was in good hands without making any real effort to find out? Well, they knew the truth now. They had died hearing him scream it in their ears. Had heard him describe what his uncle had done to him, what games they had played and what things he had endured. They had heard how his uncle had tried once too often to force him to comply, once too often to bend Tavo to his will.

It had been simple enough to kill his uncle, once he had made up his mind to do so. But killing his parents had demanded more of him. Much more.

Their struggle had been a hard one. He hadn't expected that. He thought they would let it happen willingly, that they would recognize the need for it just as he did. He thought they would accept their complicity in his terrible emotional distress, in his rampant confusion. But they accepted nothing, right up to the end. They fought him as hard as they could, trying to stop him from what he knew he must do. They hurled themselves at him over and over, flinging their shattered bodies at him as if they had any chance of saving themselves when they must have realized they did not.

They called his name. They wailed it. They screamed it.

He walked back into the cottage and looked at them one more time, needing to make sure they were dead. But there was little doubt. There was hardly anything left of them. They were bloodied lumps on the cottage floor, barely recognizable as human. Although he had stopped thinking of them as human a long time ago, such was his disdain for them.

So much blood.

He had not come home to kill them. He had come home to make them come to terms with what they had done to him. But then he had discovered that *she* had gone (he could no longer stand to speak her name, even in his mind) and had demanded that they tell him where. Foolishly, they had prevaricated and dissembled. They had lied outright. They had told him to go back to where he had come from and to stay there until she returned. As if that would ever happen. He had put an end to the man to whom they had entrusted him. That monster. Why would they have put him with such a creature? That he should have been forced to suffer what he had gone through at the hands of that animal was beyond forgiveness. A member of the family? A trusted uncle? A good place for him to be? So many lies! It had brought about their doom. All of them had paid for what had been done to him.

He studied what remained of his work dispassionately, playing back the details of his homecoming in his mind. Their faces when he had appeared at the door, a mix of surprise and fear. Their efforts to save each other, so pitiful and so hopeless. Their cries as they begged him to stop, pleaded with him to think what he was doing. Their feeble hand motions and twisting bodies when their voices were gone and their lives were leaking away.

Their last, desperate gasps for breath.

The man and the woman who claimed to be his parents but never really were. Not in any way that mattered. Not in a way that might have helped him escape or at least cope with the demons that tormented him every single day of his life.

He relived their struggles to escape him. The man had attacked him. Come at him with a knife right there at the end, fought to reach him when he was so broken he could do no more than lurch like a puppet with its strings severed. Come at him as if he actually thought he could hurt him with his puny blade. It was pathetic and hopeless, and he had decided in that moment to finish things. So he had flayed the man alive, his power so great it would allow even this. And while both the man and the woman screamed at him for mercy, he rendered the man unrecognizable and turned his attention to the woman.

Her death had been worse, but then she was supposed to be the one who would always protect him.

Well, enough was enough. Their lives were over, and that was as it should be. They had their chances to try to help him, to understand what he was going through, to find a way to make it better. But they had been frightened and powerless in the wake of his gift.

Only *she* could have helped. *She* had the gift, too, after all. *She* had the use of it, understood its shape and form and knew how to manage it. *She* had even tried to help him for a time, working with him to master it, to keep it in check when its dark shadow enveloped him and stole away his reason and drove him toward insanity. It was a miracle he had survived its power and kept himself whole. It was a miracle that the insanity that threatened almost daily to claim him had not managed to do so. Such insanity eventually claimed others, yet he had survived it.

He frowned, finding something wrong with his reasoning. But its flaw would not make itself clear. *She* would have known had *she* bothered to stay with him instead of running off. His sister; his lifeline.

For a moment tears of rage consumed him. Her treachery was anathema. Her betrayal unsupportable. Unforgivable. For all she claimed to want to help him, in the end she had abandoned him just as their parents had. Just as everyone had who might have made a difference. Now he was adrift and in the grip of his so-called gift. It was instead a curse, and there was nothing he could do but accept his fate and learn to live with it.

He walked to the cottage door and passed through. His life here was over. All the members of his family were gone now save the one. To wipe the slate clean and settle his mind, to give himself a measure of peace from his torment, and to find the quiet that his world so desperately required, he must end her life, too. He must find her and face her and destroy her.

His little sister.

Tarsha.

Suddenly it was easy to speak her name. It would be easier still when she was dead.

He walked away from the cabin toward the houses of his family's neighbors and down the road leading away from the village of Backing Fell. It had helped him achieve his retribution that his home was set so far distant from others. It was a fact that had worked in his parents' favor after his magic had manifested, when they were still hopeful of finding ways to keep him from shaming them. While neither of them had the gift, and his sister suffered no obvious torment from bearing it, he was the embarrassment they could not afford to reveal. His bouts of sickness were constantly surfacing in unpleasant ways, and they did not like it when that happened. He was never sure exactly why this bothered them, but they were very determined to keep his condition a secret from everyone outside the family—and believed their remote location helped with that.

It didn't, of course. Not for long. Others found out quickly enough that he was not like them. Now and then, some of them would test him in unpleasant and invasive ways. He was forced to do what any boy would do and fight back. But his control over his gift was limited, and frequently his response to his attackers was severe. He left a handful of them permanent victims of night terrors that would never leave them in peace. He even killed one, but he had been smart enough to carry the body deep into the woods and bury it where it would never be found. There were suspicions, of course, but no one could ever prove it was his fault.

Only Tarsha had ever seemed able to quiet his demons, sometimes using her own magic to do so, singing to him in ways that only she could, her clear sweet voice attuned to his suffering, offering him healing. But the healing lasted only for the moment and never for good. She could not do more, as much as she claimed she wanted to. Yet even though she had her limits, when he needed her she was always there. It was a battle she could not win. His magic was harsh and cutting. It was debilitating. It stripped him of all sense of self and bore him into such darkness that each time it felt as if this was the last and he would not find a way out again.

Until even she had run from him. Even she had fled him, abandoned him, betrayed him, and left him to his suffering and his demons.

Tears ran from his eyes. *Tarsha!*

Ahead, on the roadway, a figure appeared. Big and shambling, heavy-headed with his shaggy hair and beard, a giant with his great powerful arms and massive shoulders—there was no mistaking Squit Malk. He slowed involuntarily as the other approached. Malk was another of his childhood tormentors, one of the worst. One who had survived his reprisals by being able to shake off the effects of his magic.

Malk saw him approaching and did not change direction. He kept coming, and in his insistence the boy saw his own demons gathering once more, intent on bearing him away.

"Tavo!" the other boomed. "Tavo Kaynin!"

He stopped where he was, feeling anger and hatred stir.

"Where are you headed, boy?" Squit Malk demanded. "Shouldn't be out alone like this, should you? I thought you were locked away on your uncle's farm. How'd you get out of your cage? Other animals throw you out, maybe?" He glanced around. "Where's that snippy sister of yours, the one who keeps you on a leash? Did the smart thing, I heard. Run off and left her brainless brother behind."

The boy shook his head. He didn't like talking. Especially to people he distrusted and even more to people he despised.

"Is that blood on you? There, on your face and arms? That looks like blood to me."

The boy said nothing.

"Humph, still voiceless, are you? Or pretending at it, at least. I've waited five years for this. I should have squashed you the last time we met up, but you tricked me. I think maybe this time things might be different."

The boy's lips tightened further.

You better not try to find out.

"I think maybe you realize what you're up against. Why not take your beating and get it over with? Wouldn't be so hard for a voiceless freak like you to put up with, would it? Come on; let's get it done. You're all alone out here, sisterless and parentless, and there's no one within shouting distance."

The boy straightened slightly.

Which should concern you, not me.

"Hey, say something! Go on, say something! Use that voice you think's so powerful and see what good it does you. Go on! Don't just stand there like a stump."

But Tavo kept silent. He had done what he had come back to do and was on his way out. He wanted Tarsha, not this creature. Time mattered, although he couldn't have said why. He needed to get things done, and Squit Malk was making it difficult.

"Guess I'll just have to beat it out of you," the other growled. "You really shouldn't have come back. You should have known I'd be waiting."

He started forward, fists bunching, shoulders rolling as if he meant to charge. Tavo waited, resigned to what was going to happen.

But suddenly a cart appeared on the path behind Malk, wheels creaking, pulled by a mule and driven by an old woman. "Hey, now!" she called out sharply. "You there, big timber! You leave that other boy alone!"

Malk turned in shock. He couldn't believe anyone was talking to him like that, least of all an old woman. His first reaction was to take a few steps toward her, thinking certainly that to bash her head in would silence her quick enough. But the old woman brought up a wicked-looking scythe from beneath her seat and stood waiting on him, looking very much as if she was ready to defend herself.

Malk stopped and turned back to Tavo. "This will wait. Another time, another place will do for you."

Still Tavo said nothing. He just stood there in silence as Malk trudged past him, heading toward Backing Fell. He watched the other until he was out of sight and then turned to the old lady.

"What's your name, boy?" she asked at once.

He surprised himself. "Tavo."

"Well, Tavo, you come from Backing Fell?"

He nodded.

"Know some people named Kaynin?"

The boy froze. Some part of him recognized that saying anything at this point was dangerous. "I think they moved," he said finally.

The old lady made a dismissive sound. "Odd, since they just placed an order with me for plants and bulbs for a garden. I hauled them all the way here from Yarrow. You sure about them moving?"

He shuffled his feet. "I've got to go."

He started past her on the path, trying not to look her in the eye. If he did, she would see the truth. They saw the truth when he lied. It was in his eyes or on his face or somewhere, but it was always there. He waited for her to ask him, to call him out, to make it clear she knew. But she only shook her head and gave him a shrug.

He was just past her when he remembered she'd helped him. He turned back. "Thanks for standing up for me," he said, eyes downcast as he spoke, already turning away again.

"You watch your back," the old woman called after him. "He's the type doesn't forget. You be careful."

He waved to her in response and kept walking.

That night he slept out in the open in a hay field with great, circular bales gathered and tied with twine and left to season. The weather this time of the year was warm and dry, and even a light rain would cause no problems for the hay. These bundles looked new. Probably the farmer thought to collect and haul them off to market by week's end, but tonight they gave Tavo something to curl up against.

By now, Fluken had joined him, as he knew he would. Fluken appeared just after he stopped by the hay bale, seemingly coming out of nowhere as he always did, a little late, but welcome nevertheless. Fluken was loyal, where too many others were not. It didn't matter that he seldom talked. Tavo always knew what he was thinking anyway, because the two of them were so much alike. Close friends didn't need to talk. They only needed to be there for each other.

Together they lay down. Tavo was wrapped in his travel cloak, wearing nothing underneath. He had removed his clothes and washed out the blood in a creek he had crossed earlier. He would have been content to leave them soiled, a sort of badge for what he had accomplished, a statement of his independence and his retribution, but he knew they would draw attention. Blood always drew attention. He didn't want that. He wanted to be invisible until the very moment he confronted Tarsha.

While his clothes dried, draped over the hay bale he was lying beside, he looked up at the stars and fought to keep from falling asleep. Sleeping was not a pleasant experience for him. He was haunted by dreams, terrible visions brought to life by the curse he carried within him, black nightmares that would not leave him alone. His dreams were warped and twisted things, stark reimaginings of how he had been forced to give way to his demons and use his magic to save himself. All of the deaths and injuries he had caused were brought back to him in new and terrifying ways. It was like being torn apart from within, and no amount of self-reassurance would free him from their relentless grasp.

But when he fixed his gaze on the stars, he could escape his dreams and his inner demons. He could imagine other worlds and other lives, and he could think himself into those worlds and lives and make them seem real. It never lasted, but even a few brief moments provided some relief. He could never use his magic to aid in this, of course. Not in the way that Tarsha could. Her magic was dependable and safe. It allowed her to create without worrying that whatever she conjured would end up broken and lifeless. She could sing anything to life, could make it be so pleasing that anyone would feel comforted.

He could not do that. He could not conjure anything that would not in the end become terrifying. He had tried. Over and over. But his efforts always seemed to turn back on themselves, violent and frightening parodies of what he intended. So he no longer tried to do what Tarsha did so easily. He no longer attempted things he hoped would please people but only caused them to look at him in disgust and horror. He kept his magic a secret, tucked carefully away. He had not summoned it for almost a year. He had not used it even once.

Until his uncle had come for him one too many times.

Until he had returned home and his sister was gone.

Until he knew there was no hope for him.

He was still thinking of this when his eyes closed and sleep claimed him. It was not a kind and gentle sleep, for sleep of that sort had never been his. Sleep for him was familiar enough, but not in a good way. The nightmares came swiftly, snippets of all the incidents that his magic had generated, all the people who had paid the price. And now, too, images of Tarsha slipping away from Backing Fell, disappearing into the shadows, a sly and cautious figure distancing herself from a brother whose very presence she found impossible to tolerate. He was standing there as she left, close enough that she could see him as clearly as he could see her.

"Goodbye, little brother," she was saying as she turned to him. "Find your own way in this world, and I will find mine. But we cannot go together. You are not like me and never will be. You must go alone."

He grappled for her, but she twisted out of his grip, laughing as she did so. Laughing as if she had never seen anything so funny as her brother trying to hold her back.

He woke an instant later, grappling not with her but with someone else altogether.

"Hold still, little man!" a voice hissed in his ear. "I will only break a few of your worthless bones! A few to make up for your disrespect!"

He was in the grip of Squit Malk, who had somehow tracked him down and was grappling with him, intent on delivering the beating he had promised earlier. He tried to say something, but tape bound his mouth so tightly he could not speak. And if he could not speak, he could not use his magic to defend himself.

Fluken had disappeared. There was no help to be found there.

A ringing blow to the side of his head momentarily stilled his struggling. "Better now, isn't it?" Malk continued, groping for purchase. "Perhaps there is a better use for a pretty boy like you. Your beating could wait an hour or so, don't you think?"

Tavo only struggled harder, fighting to break free, desperate to escape. He felt his fear growing as his efforts grew weaker. He was no match for the other, lacking strength and skill both. His magic would not come, although he grunted and groaned through the tape.

Malk had ripped open his cloak and was bearing him facedown on the grassy earth. He could smell the soil and the greenery; he could feel its roughness against his face. *Roughness. Stones and hardpan dry from lack of rain.* He felt a twinge of hope. He rubbed his mouth hard against it, trying to loosen the tape. He ignored the pain as his skin was scraped and torn. He ignored what was happening on top as Malk bore down.

The taped loosened enough on one side of his mouth to let his voice take shape and form, enough to release a tiny shred of the magic fighting to break free.

The force of its escape ripped the rest of the tape free and threw him backward with such force that he dislodged Malk entirely. Tumbling away in a tangle of arms and legs and clothes, he scrambled to his feet, searching wildly for his attacker.

He found him at once, tossed aside like a sack of feed, cursing and shouting and trying to get to his feet. Tavo let him rise, gave him the space and time to do so, consumed by a red haze of ungovernable rage and bloodlust. He was no longer remotely rational. This could end only one way, and he had the power to make that happen.

"Tavo!" Malk howled as he saw him standing there, waiting.

It was a plea more than a cry. It was rooted in what he saw in the other's eyes. He would have run, but there was no time left. There was only time for one last breath.

Tavo Kaynin's magic burst free in a white-hot explosion of sound that ripped into Squit Malk with the destructive force of a thousand razor-sharp shards. His skin tore away from his body, flesh disintegrating like a sand castle caught in a heavy wind. The bones, ligaments, muscles, and soft organs went last, pulped into a gelatinous mass of tissue. Then that was gone, too, liquid sinking into the parched earth.

Where Squit Malk had stood only seconds earlier, nothing remained but tiny particles floating on the air like ash.

Tavo went silent again, the force of his magic spent, its power dissipated. The red haze faded, and the night turned silent and dark once more. The stars shone brightly overhead in the cloudless sky, and the field in which he stood was dotted with hay bales and grasses and smelled of death.

Fluken reappeared. He was smiling. He stood next to his friend, amazed at what he had done.

Tavo smiled back, satisfied with what he had achieved.

Hungry suddenly to discover if he could do more.

FOURTEEN

◆

THE BLACK MOOD OF the trio that set out for the Northland to
fulfill the charge given them by High Druid Ober Balronen was a
perfect match for the weather that approached from the west.

Darcon Leah stared at the skies and then the horizons and
frowned.

Why should I have expected anything else?

The day was cloudy and threatening. Winds swept across the
country through which they flew, sudden gusts sending unsecured
objects—wagons, furniture, farm implements, and small animals—
scattering in all directions. Heavy clouds surged into view, a fore-
warning of an approaching storm that promised steady rains by
nightfall. Colors were leached from the countryside by the storm's
dark shadow, and even the heavy warship that bore them north
bounced and rocked as the winds caught it broadside and twisted it
about like a toy.

Dar was at the helm, the position ceded him because, like all of
the Leahs in the past several hundred years, he had been raised with
airships. If there was something to know of flying, no matter how
obscure or trivial, the Leahs knew it. Dar had grown up with his family's air transport business, a fully engaged member of a shipping
company that had suffered its ups and downs over more than three

hundred years but had come through largely unscathed. Not until he had answered a summons from Drisker Arc and chosen to accept the position of Blade had he even considered leaving a life of flying.

And in truth, he hadn't left it altogether in any case. On most of his assignments with members of the Druid order he was expected to act as pilot. He had kept his hand in through these experiences, always remembering what his father had taught him about airships. He could still recite the words verbatim.

They'll always do the best they can for you, but they'll do better if you're the one at the helm.

He liked being in control, in any case. It gave him a sense of well-being to know that his life and health did not depend on others. That he protected those who accompanied him was just an extension of that responsibility. He knew he was best equipped to keep them safe, not necessarily the most talented or skilled, but by far the most experienced. He had worked hard to succeed at what he did, and his pride and confidence in himself were important to him.

Which made traveling with Ruis Quince a problem.

Ruis did not much like him anyway. How could you blame him? They were men of decidedly different personalities, the Blade driven to resolve life's challenges by action, the Druid by reasoning. Placed together, they tended to move in different directions. Their present circumstances were equally troubling. Dar had been Zia's lover first, and there were clear indications that Zia still favored him. Ruis was no fool; he would have picked up on this. But it went beyond that. Ruis Quince was mindful of competition, no matter its source. His view of Dar was very much colored by his belief that Balronen favored the highlander over him. This was misdirected, in Dar's estimation, because any favoring of Dar was heavily influenced by his position as Blade and his very real responsibility for the safety of the High Druid. Had he chosen to think this through, Ruis might have realized as much. But Quince had a tendency to see what he wanted to see, and nothing he chose to see in this case favored the Blade.

He had already made it his business to tell Dar—pointedly, confronting him in front of Zia—that he was in charge of this expedition and Dar was not to do anything without permission. The command was delivered in Quince's usual dispassionate, calm manner but with an edge underlying the words. Dar could have pointed out how foolish this proclamation sounded, but he decided Ruis was just marking his territory. So he simply nodded and resolved, as always, to do whatever the situation dictated whether he had permission to act or not.

Zia, unfortunately, wasn't much friendlier toward him than Ruis, which was more troubling. She was still angry after their last conversation; she continued to assume he had been poking around in her private affairs. Already Dar was regretting he had ever agreed to go on this expedition, much less try to find out if either Ruis Quince or Zia was scheming in some way against Balronen or the Druids. He still found the idea nonsensical. What plans could either possibly have that would matter to the High Druid?

So he kept himself to himself, even in the company of his companions, and carried out his responsibilities for flying the airship and commanding its crew. That was all he cared about anyway, so it wasn't difficult. The Troll guards, on the other hand, who sensed things in a much more intuitive way than most would give them credit for, exhibited signs of uneasiness that were unmistakable. Dar guessed that if asked they would have told him they wished they were anywhere else but here.

The day wore on toward evening and the storm closed swiftly on their airship. Dar was forced to give his entire attention over to keeping the airship steady while searching for a place to set down. If they were aloft still when the full force of the weather struck, they would be in serious trouble. By now they were across the backside of the Dragon's Teeth and into the Jannisson Pass, pointing toward the eastern edge of the old Skull Kingdom, following a route that would take them squarely between the craggy mountains of the Skull Kingdom on their left and the towering peaks of the Charnals on their right. The corridor was wide enough to let them pass safely if good weather held, but not if the winds blew hard enough crosswise.

When he found a broad stretch of land that opened below the

southern edge of the Malg Swamp, Dar dropped the airship toward a clearing on the lee side of a high rocky slope where they could anchor for the night without worrying about the winds battering their vessel. Already members of the crew were setting the mooring lines, and by the time the ship was down to within six feet of the ground they were over the railing and anchoring them in place. The wind continued to howl overhead and the skies to darken almost completely, but the ship rocked only slightly as the storm passed east and rolled on toward the Charnals.

When dinner was consumed and the Trolls had set a watch rotation and rolled into their bedding, Dar found a spot near the stern that was sheltered enough to offer a bit of comfort from the weather. By now the rains were easing off, and he did not care to go below with Ruis and Zia. He did not care to be anywhere in the vicinity when they were together. His feelings about Zia might have been tamped down by practical concerns, but they were not in the least diminished.

So instead of going below, he sat wrapped in his great cloak and looked out into the darkness with nothing but his thoughts for company.

Because his mood of earlier had not changed appreciably and his current view of his future as Blade to High Druid Ober Balronen was just as dark as ever, he found himself considering a change in professions. It wasn't as if he had no other skills or life choices. He could always go back to what he had been doing before Drisker had recruited him. His brothers would be willing enough to welcome him back into the airship transport business; his skills were no less than they were before. They might even have real need of him if business was as good as they had led him to believe.

The trouble was, of course, he really didn't want to return to the family business. It was never what he'd wanted to do with his life. He had always been too restless, too anxious for something more challenging. He had a craving for excitement, and his position as Blade had given him that. But his enjoyment was being crushed by his dissatisfaction with Balronen's lack of ability to serve as High Druid.

Compared with Drisker Arc's, Ober Balronen's leadership bordered on incompetency. That Dar felt he knew what needed doing better than his employer was deeply worrying—especially when so much was at stake. If a High Druid guessed wrong or made bad decisions, the consequences could prove fatal.

Dar was increasingly certain this was what he was facing by coming here, deep in the Northland, on this fool's errand.

A cloaked figure appeared out of the darkness and sat down beside him. Zia's rain-streaked face looked over.

"You look less than happy," she observed.

He nodded reluctantly. "Probably because I am."

"This whole business is a mess." She scooted closer, as if to be better heard. "We're on our way to getting ourselves killed."

"That's a bit stark, isn't it?"

"Story of my life."

"I don't like to see you like this."

"Really? Since when? Why would you care?"

"Why wouldn't I? I still think there is something good between us."

"I suppose. I just have trouble thinking of what that something is."

He paused. "What are we talking about here? Is this about you and me? Or is this about something else?"

She held his gaze, her eyes fixed on him. "You and I, we had something special. I don't know where it was going, and I really didn't think it important enough to worry about. I just enjoyed having you as my friend and lover. But it wasn't enough for you. I don't understand it."

He took a deep breath. The ache of her unhappiness was palpable. "We've discussed all this, Zia. I don't know what else to say. I felt I wasn't being fair to you. I felt I was leading you on."

"You don't fix things by shoving them aside." She leaned in. "You decided all on your own that things weren't going to work out; you never discussed it with me. I didn't even know you were troubled! You just walked away. You broke my heart. Do you know how that felt?"

He started to speak and then stopped. "Not good, I guess."

"Try 'terrible.' I was devastated. You treated me as if I was worthless. You didn't make me feel better by trying to spare me. That wasn't what happened! It felt like you were doing it for yourself. I was just something in your way."

"I didn't . . ."

"You didn't what? Think? Agreed; you didn't. Behave like a grown-up? Agreed again. Handle it in a compassionate and reasonable way?" She shook her head. There were tears in her eyes. "I thought you loved me. I thought we meant something to each other, something important. I guess I was wrong."

"You weren't wrong. But I didn't want you tied to someone who was at risk every time he left Paranor on an expedition. It didn't feel fair to ask that of you. I thought it was better to break it off. You would forget me. You would find someone else, someone who led a less dangerous life."

"We don't pick and choose who we love, Dar! Don't you know anything? We love people for all sorts of reasons, some of which we can't even explain. It isn't a shopping trip with a list all written up."

He exhaled in frustration. She would never accept his reasoning. All they were doing was tearing pieces off each other's hearts. He wanted this conversation to be over. "I'm not saying it is. But we have to be reasonable about it as well as emotional."

She stared at him. "You want to know why I went from you to Ruis? He was convenient and willing. I can tell you that now because it doesn't matter anymore. I can even tell you he was a poor substitute. I told him we were done just before we left Paranor."

"You left him?" He felt an unexpected jolt of happiness.

"I did. Just like you left me. And I can tell you this: It doesn't feel all that satisfying."

"Look," he said, resting his hand momentarily on hers. She jerked away as if he had burned her. He shook his head. "Zia, we have to let it go, both of us. We have to bury the past. Going over it every time we meet won't bring it back."

"Not that it matters to you!"

"But it does matter!" His voice rose, edged with a bitterness that surprised him. "I loved you, too! As much as you loved me!"

She drew herself up. "Nice to hear you say so. You forgot that part of it when you told me you were leaving. Well, better late than never, I guess. Maybe one day it will mean something to me again."

There was nothing to be gained by responding or by pursuing the matter further, so he simply looked off into the darkness and waited for her to leave. But she didn't move. She just sat there next to him.

Finally, he said, "I asked about you and Ruis that day not because I was being nosy but because I was worried about you. Ober seems to think the two of you planned this expedition for reasons that might not be in his best interests. He told me to watch you and report back. I didn't say anything, and even if there was something to tell I wouldn't."

She gave him a look of disbelief. "He told you he thought Ruis and I might be doing something behind his back? That's a laugh! Do you know what he's really worried about? He wants me in *his* bed!"

"He thinks you and he . . . ?" He flashed on a picture of it and dismissed it immediately.

She stared at him, realizing what he was thinking. "There wasn't any possibility of that happening before, and there isn't any possibility of it now. So you can tell him whatever you like."

He shook his head. "I guess I understand his feelings. I loved you, too, you know."

She gave him a smirk. "So you say. Just not enough, I guess."

"No, it was enough. More than enough. So much so that I was afraid of it. I didn't know what to do!"

The pain he was experiencing at hearing her tell him how much she had loved him and how much losing him had cost her was reflected in his unguarded response. He didn't stop to think about what he was saying.

She laughed. "Oh, well if you were clueless, then I guess it's okay!" Her expression hardened. "Shouldn't I have had a part in making this decision? Wasn't the choice of separating, of ending everything, as much mine as yours? Didn't you consider it important enough?"

"Yes!" he snapped. "I did consider it important enough. But I didn't want to give you a chance to make me change my mind. Listen to me. My family history is bleak. Leahs have always been at risk as swordsmen. Whole handfuls of them have died because of it. I'm just one more example of a potential repeat of history. I didn't want that for you!"

"I wasn't asking that you make a life for us! I was asking for your companionship and love. Anyway, how is what you do so different from what I do? I risk myself, too, every time I use magic, every time I am sent out to face a new threat. That didn't stop me from wanting to love you! That wasn't enough to force me to tell you we couldn't go on!"

He leaned back against the deck wall. His pain was overwhelming. He felt every argument he had once believed solid, every bit of reasoning he had once relied on, slip through his fingers as he tried futilely to hold on to it. He could no longer make himself justify any of it.

"All right. I understand that now. I handled everything badly. No excuses. I threw away something I should have held on to. I probably gave up the best chance at having someone love me I will ever find. I miss you, too, Zia. I hated it when you were with Ruis. I thought about you all the time after I left you, but I didn't see how I could come back. I still don't. Because now it's too late."

She studied him a moment and then got to her feet. "I'm going below where it's warm. You think some more about all this. When this expedition is over, maybe we can talk again."

She started away, but then she turned back. "The trouble is, Darcon Leah, I don't know if you matter enough to me anymore."

Her smile, as she turned away, was filled with sadness.

They continued flying north at sunrise. The weather improved and the sky offered glimpses of the rising sun, a pale and elusive orb through layers of cloud covering. Dar had slept badly, and he was heavy-eyed and irritable. He wanted to keep to himself, and mostly he was able to. Once or twice, Ruis Quince appeared to give him perfunctory orders; mostly it seemed it was just to reaffirm that he was still in charge. As if something might have changed during the night, Dar thought. As if the order of things might have somehow shifted.

And perhaps for Quince they had. He was no longer Zia's bedmate and partner. He was no longer much of anything to either of them— just another member of the Druid order. Dar had no illusions about what this meant. Quince would blame him for Zia's leaving and would be slow to forgive. Few words were exchanged as the day wore on, and it became clear that this was unlikely to change. Dar began to grow anxious. If there was no communication among them, the chances for mistakes in carrying out their assignment increased. Their plan for finding their quarry was shaky at best. They were flying to where the most recent massacre had taken place. From there they should be able to track whoever was responsible until they caught up to them. Even in rocky, barren country their passage should be visible.

But none of the highlander's concerns proved to be relevant. They traveled on for a second day, and it was just reaching midday on the third when a large body of soldiers appeared directly below them. One minute there was only mist and emptiness and the next the lead- ing edge of this horde hove into view. There was no mistaking what they were. Their banners and insignia were unlike anything the Dru- ids or Dar had ever seen. Some carried eight-foot spears and some swords. All were armored and wore helmets that concealed their faces, disguising their features. There were at least a thousand of them. They traveled in formation, yet there was a loose order to their columns that suggested they felt comfortable in their ability to react swiftly to any perceived threat.

Heads glanced up as their airship passed overhead, but beyond that there was no apparent concern for their presence.

"Bring her around!" Ruis Quince ordered suddenly as they passed over the rear lines of the army and flew out onto the empty plains beyond.

Because the Druid was standing right below the pilot box, Dar had no trouble hearing the order—just trouble believing it. Quince wanted to make another pass when the invaders had no reason to think them anything but another airship? What was he thinking? A second pass would surely betray their interest and expose their intentions to even the most obtuse.

Zia, who was standing a few feet away, was quick to challenge the order.

"What are you doing, Ruis? If we pass over them again, they're bound to notice! Are you trying to draw their attention?"

"What would you have us do, Zia? Sneak up on them? See if we can trick them into talking to us?" Quince made it sound like he was lecturing. "Blade, do what I said. Turn around. Fly back so they can see us clearly. Land the airship a quarter mile in front of them. We'll wait for them there."

Still Dar hesitated. "We know nothing about what these people can do. If they get us on the ground, they will have us at their mercy."

"Shouldn't we take the time and trouble to find out a little more about them?" Zia was standing right in front of him. The Trolls looked around to see what was happening. "A little caution might have value!" she snapped.

Ruis Quince turned away. "You have no right to question me, Zia. You threw that privilege away." He glanced at Dar. "Do what I said, Blade. Or would you rather I had you removed from your command and charged with treason!"

Dar stared at him without flinching. "I won't put my airship and crew in danger."

"*Your* airship and crew?" Quince laughed openly. "You have no airship or crew, highlander. Everything you have belongs to the Druids! Even this infatuated girl who cannot seem to realize the importance of who she beds and who she—"

Zia slapped him so hard that Dar could hear the crack of it over the rushing of the wind. Quince rocked back on his heels, his expression one of shock. Zia shoved him hard, pinning him back against the wall of the pilot box. A long knife appeared in her hand as if by magic and pressed up against his throat. "If you ever say anything like that again, Ruis, I will cut out your tongue and take my time doing it. I will make you sorry you were ever born!"

Her words were a hiss of warning that lingered momentarily in the ensuing stillness. She waited a moment to be sure he had heard, ready to act if he should choose to respond. The knife remained at his throat, and her eyes never left his.

But Quince merely rubbed his cheek. "Turn the ship around, highlander," he said one time more. He spoke the words very deliberately, his voice devoid of passion. "That is an order."

He held Zia's gaze until she released him and backed away.

"This is a mistake, Ruis."

"If so, it's mine to make."

She hesitated. "All right. But if anything goes wrong, you'll have to answer for it."

Dar did not find this very reassuring. If he was wrong, they were likely dead. He thought about refusing, thinking this decision ill made and dangerous, worried about what would happen if he obeyed. But there was a limit to what he could do, even as captain of this airship. He engaged the starboard thrusters and felt the vessel begin to turn.

"Chutin!" he shouted in Troll speak to his Captain of the Guard. "Unhood the flash rips and ready them for firing. If we are attacked, you may respond. Put men at all four."

The big Troll nodded and repeated the orders to his men. The flash rips were readied, and the gunners took their positions.

"An unnecessary precaution," Quince said dismissively. "An overreaction, in point of fact. You're showing your lack of confidence in those you sail with. No one is going to attack an armed Druid warship. Who do you think these people are?"

"I'm not sure," Dar replied as the airship continued its turn, its sleek black hull cleaving clouds and mist. "Are you?"

Quince laughed. "Savages! That's who they are. Look at them! Look at their weapons! Swords and spears. Look at them down there. Marching like it doesn't matter if they do so in formation or not. No order to anything. Not even a visible command presence. Do you see any sign of a central command? You can't even tell who leads this pack of animals."

"I can count, though," Zia pointed out, moving into the pilot box beside Dar. She gave Quince a withering look. "There are at least a thousand of them. Have you forgotten what they did to the Corrax? And to another Troll tribe, as well? What do you think they could do to us?"

Quince started to answer and then seemed to think better of it. Instead, he shook his head and made a sweeping gesture toward the army.

"Numbers aren't everything. Where are their airships? Where are their automatic weapons? Do they even possess magic? Real magic? The kinds of magic we have at our command? We can control the elements—wind, fire, water, and earth. We can simply toss them aside. Either one of us could put a stop to their advance in five minutes. They would turn tail and run the moment they were confronted with magic like ours. If all they've faced are Trolls, they know nothing of real power."

He leaned forward. "This is exactly the right time to make them aware of what they are facing. If they can be brought into line before they get any farther south, we should be able to do what Balronen wants and turn them loose on the Federation. They will probably be cut to pieces, but it will cost the Southlanders, too. And it will give our most dangerous enemy something to occupy his time."

His words were persuasive and his voice reassuring. But there was an element of madness, too. The words were tinged with it, the speaker's tone of voice strident. Dar stared openly. What was going on with Ruis? Why was he acting this way?

"That wasn't the mandate we were given!" Zia snapped. Dar could hear the anger in her voice. "We aren't supposed to start a war! We're supposed to scout them and report back. Nothing more. You take this too far."

The other Druid was seething. "I take it as far as I was given leave to take it, Zia. I have authority you know nothing about. I can scout or engage. I am empowered to use my own judgment. Just because you weren't included in the conversation doesn't mean it didn't take place."

Dar didn't like the sound of it. Ruis Quince was not the sort to assume a mantle of authority that hadn't been bestowed on him. But if

Balronen had given him authority to do all he claimed, there was reason to be concerned. The risk of something going wrong was measurably increased. Drisker Arc would never have given another Druid authority to act unilaterally in a situation like this. It was another mark against Balronen's capability to act as High Druid.

He almost turned the ship around once more. But countermanding a direct order from the expedition leader would get him exiled from Paranor or worse. Zia caught his eye and shook her head. She seemed to have decided the same thing. Why, he wasn't sure. Maybe she knew something he didn't.

It was enough to persuade him. He kept the airship on course.

They sailed over the heads of the marching army. More helmeted heads looked up this time, a sea of matching iron faces. The Druid warship flew past once more, headed back the way it had come as hundreds of eyes watched. Dar continued on a bit, then brought the airship down to where she was hovering above a flat stretch of rocky ground and held her there.

Locking the wheel in place, he climbed out of the pilot box to face Quince.

"You intend to wait here for them?" he asked.

Quince nodded. "Let them come to us."

"You'll talk? Bargain, perhaps?"

"Observe. Assess. Act according to what I determine needs doing. What is your point in asking?"

Dar nodded. "The airship stays where she is. I want her ready to leave in a hurry if the need arises. You and I will take four of the guards and go to this meeting. Everyone else stays on board."

Quince bowed his head as if in thought. But when he raised it again there was a dangerous look in his bright eyes. "What did I tell you, Blade?"

Dar felt a sinking feeling in his stomach. "You are in charge."

"I am in charge. But it doesn't sound that way to me. It sounds as if you think you are in command."

"I was just—"

"You were just overstepping your authority," the other cut in.

"Again. Things will happen when I command it. People will do what I say they should do. You will keep your mouth shut."

Dar stayed silent. There was nothing he could say that wouldn't get him in worse trouble still. He watched Zia walk back from where she had been standing by the railing. Her honey-gold hair whipped about her face in the wind, strands of it blowing over her features like a veil. Her eyes were suspicious. "What are we doing?"

Quince didn't look at her. "Taking a short walk. You and I and six of the Troll guards will go out to meet these invaders to discuss their intentions. If they act in a hostile manner, we will respond accordingly. If they seem amenable to cooperation, we will attempt to push them off onto someone else." He paused. "The Blade stays here, aboard ship."

Zia shook her head. "He is our protector! He is supposed to stay with us in situations like this one. He can't do much if he's left aboard ship!"

Quince made a dismissive gesture. "He can't do much in any case. An ancient sword possessing ancient magic? Of how much use can that be? We are far better able to protect ourselves than he is to protect us. He stays here, out from underfoot."

He was doing this for no better reason than to reassert his command over not only the expedition but also Zia, in particular. He was showing her he could still make her do what he wanted, even if they were no longer a couple. Dar almost hit him. He was close enough that he could have done so. But the way Quince looked at him suggested the Druid would like nothing better. Strike a Druid while serving the order and you were out on your ear.

Zia saw the look that passed between them. "Time to go, isn't it, Ruis? We should get down there and be ready when they come." She took his arm and pulled him away. "I will watch your back. You do the talking when these people reach us. But be careful. Don't assume anything."

She started away, drawing Quince after her. But just as she reached the railing, she turned back to Dar. "You can watch us well enough from on board," she said. "But watch us closely."

The expression on her face was an uneasy one, and Dar read more into it than what the words she spoke indicated. She was already preparing for the possibility of things going wrong. She was doing this because she had to, but she wanted to know that someone would be watching out for her.

And not just someone.

She wanted Dar.

She gave him a knowing look just before she turned away again, and then she began to descend the rope ladder.

FIFTEEN

◆

Darcon Leah waited in the pilot box until he saw the Druids and their Troll guards appear beyond the bow of the airship, and then he hurried forward so he could better see what was going to happen. He could already spy the forefront of the faceless invaders appearing over a rise, spears raised skyward to form a forest of wood and iron. He peered out at them through a screen of mist and rain that had suddenly formed, and he searched for their leader. But no one stepped forward to indicate who was in charge.

Dissatisfied with the airship's positioning, Dar ordered that the anchor be let out further so the airship could rise and his view improve. When the ship was somewhere around fifty feet off the ground, he ordered her secured. Still not the greatest visibility, but any higher and he would be in the mix of clouds and mist that had been steadily lowering.

Ahead, Ruis Quince had called a halt. He and Zia were standing in front of their Troll guards, separated from them by perhaps a dozen yards. Dar was instantly uneasy. The distance was too great should trouble arise. At least two of the guards should be warding them closely. As it was, the Druids were unprotected on three flanks.

He thought at once about disobeying Quince and leaving the airship to go down and join them on the flats. At least then he would be there to aid them should things go wrong. But he knew what Quince's reaction would be, and he held off doing anything. The best he could hope for was that only talk would be involved. If things went wrong, he must trust to the power and mobility of the airship to come to their aid.

His Captain of the Druid Guard, Stow Chutin, was still aboard. Quince did not like him any better than Dar, so Zia had not selected him. He loitered close by, hands gripping the ship's railing as if to hold it in place. His face revealed nothing of how he felt about being left behind, but his restless movements betrayed his dissatisfaction.

Dar called him over. "I want this airship ready to go to their aid the minute we sense anything is wrong. When they start talking, I want men standing by to pull up the anchors and engage the thrusters. Hold us at the ready. Can you do it?"

The big Troll grunted. "You taught me, Blade."

Indeed, Dar thought, he had. So he hardly needed reminding. "Carry on," he said.

Chutin walked away and began positioning the ship's crew, setting the stage for a quick response to trouble. He had the gunners stand away from the flash rips, but he left the weapons uncovered and ready for use. Dar watched for a few moments, long enough to be satisfied that everything that could be done was, and then he turned his attention back to the flats and the invading army.

The front ranks had come to an uneven halt, the helmeted soldiers standing in ragged lines with the butts of their great spears grounded, a sea of indistinguishable bodies gone completely still. They stood so far apart from one another that it almost looked like every other man was missing. Something about their formation felt wrong. Dar immediately began to cast about for anything that looked like movement behind or to either side, but he saw nothing unusual.

He turned his attention back to the confrontation. Quince was already speaking, addressing the ranks of the invader, gesturing expansively, his deep voice loud and insistent. It would have been comical if Dar hadn't been so worried about what might happen. The Druid's effort to attract someone's attention failed, and he went silent.

He stood waiting patiently, and the men of the army facing him did the same.

Zia stepped close to him to say something, but he brushed her away. "Does no one lead you?" he roared finally. "Speak up!"

His tone of voice demanded a response.

He got one.

A slender figure draped in a white cloak, face concealed within a closed helmet like all of the other soldiers, stepped into view, appearing as if by magic out of the center of the army's ranks. Behind strode a company of six armored knights wearing scarlet. The party proceeded to within fifteen feet of the Druids and stopped. For a moment, no one spoke, and then the white-cloaked figure gestured toward Ruis and said something. Ruis was quick to answer back, and the tone of voice he used left no doubt as to the nature of his reply.

A further exchange ensued, but in the rush of wind and rain that was sweeping over their surroundings, the words were impossible to decipher. Whatever the speaker in white was saying, it was clear Ruis was responding with anger and defiance. Dar listened in alarm to his rising shouts and sharp-edged threats. Quince was treading on dangerous ground whether he realized it or not. More than a thousand armed soldiers stood not a hundred yards away. Did he think it wise to display such insolence?

He glanced at Stow Chutin, who was standing next to him again, and grimaced. The big Troll shook his head. "He is handling this poorly," he growled.

On the plains below, Zia was looking around in concern at the proximity of the army they had chosen to confront. There were blank iron faces staring back at her from three sides by now, members of the enemy having somehow shifted position while Dar wasn't watching. It had happened very quickly. He watched Zia straighten and then take a step backward from Quince.

Then suddenly no one was speaking anymore. Something had passed between Quince and his counterpart that Dar had missed while looking at Zia and the soldiers. Ruis glanced over his shoulder at Zia and said something, but she shook her head. The white-cloaked soldier stood waiting on him as he turned back, as if giving him a chance to say something more. But Quince had been rendered momentarily speechless by whatever had passed between them.

As if words were no longer of use.

Instantly Dar ordered Chutin and his crew to pull up the mooring lines and the Troll gunners to man the flash rips. There was no longer any reason to take a chance on what was going to happen next. He rushed from the bow to the pilot box, hands finding the thruster levers. Quince had shown neither caution nor tact in his negotiating attempts. He appeared to have misjudged the situation badly. His blunder, whatever its nature, had very likely convinced the white-cloaked soldier he was a fool. Dar was appalled.

He glanced up, and in that instant saw a strange shimmer run through the ranks of the enemy army. There was a kind of melting-away of bodies amid a rippling shift in their formations.

Men were disappearing.

Zia reacted instantly, perhaps already aware of the danger. Her hands swept up, bringing with them a protective covering of magic. She dropped to one knee to make herself smaller, and her arms closed over her head, drawing her magic tighter. When a barrage of arrows and darts rained down on her she deflected them easily.

The Trolls who were there to protect her were not so fortunate. Although they rushed to the aid of both Druids, they were already dead men. Caught in an iron rain of missiles, most were dropped in their tracks. Within moments a swarm of enemy soldiers had charged in from both sides and driven their great spears through the bodies of those Trolls who remained, leaving them sprawled on the ground, bloodied and dead.

They came for Ruis Quince next. But he was a practiced magic wielder and quick to recover from his initial shock. While his attackers faded and materialized all around him the Druid's magic warded him, and he fought back fiercely. Down went the first of his enemies, unprepared for such fury, surprised by the Druid's ferocity. Quince tried to reach Zia but was quickly besieged on all sides.

"Zia!" he called to her, as the rest closed about.

But Zia Amarodian was too busy defending herself to hear him.

She had risen again, bringing her protective magic with her, trying to unleash a counterattack on the enemy fighters swarming around her. She sent several bolts of brilliant blue fire exploding into their midst, but most of those struck were nothing more than images of men who were no longer there.

Seconds later she cried out in desperation and disappeared under a blanket of attackers.

Dar was coming for her, his airship dipping toward the attacking army, all four flash rips firing steadily into the enemy ranks. But as with the Druid magic, their firepower was largely negated by the fact that the targets were mostly empty air. Attacking the main body of the army might have produced better results, but those soldiers were holding their ranks. It was the ones who were swarming Zia and Ruis Quince with whom they needed to deal, not the others.

Abandoning the pilot box to Chutin, Dar charged forward, threw a mooring rope over the ship's railing, and leapt after it. He slid down so quickly he was momentarily thrown off balance when he struck the ground. But he scrambled up and raced for Zia. She crouched just ahead, locked in her protective covering, fighting to hold it intact.

"Leah! Leah!" He shouted the ancient battle cry of his family, a roar of incendiary rage rising above the tumult of the struggle, an attempt to draw the attention of Zia's attackers.

Farther ahead, Ruis Quince had fallen to his knees. His efforts at defending himself had brought down six of his attackers, but his strength was expended. He was not trained to fight as were warrior Druids, and he was poorly conditioned for prolonged struggles. Dar watched the fire of his magic begin to flicker as more and more attackers cut at him.

Then the speaker for the enemy army, white cloak whipped by the wind, armor shining with raindrops, appeared before him with sword in hand and stood looking down. The Druid looked up, and in his face Dar saw resignation and despair.

"Wait!" Dar cried out.

To his surprise, the white-cloaked figure glanced at him momentarily. Then his sword blade whipped about with frightening power, breaking through the Druid magic and driving into the exposed throat of the Druid. Then he gave the handle of the weapon a vicious twist, and Ruis Quince fell away, his head severed from his body.

The faceless soldier looked at Dar again, measuring him.

But Dar did not see that look. He was already moving, fighting his way to Zia, driving back her attackers so that she had space to rise and stand with him. Together they retreated through the dead and wounded enemy, past the bodies of the slain Trolls, to where the airship had descended far enough to allow them to reach a rope ladder. As they climbed to safety, flash rips kept their attackers at bay and within moments both were back aboard.

Dar glanced downward one last time and saw Quince's executioner staring up at him. He experienced a cold chill. Then the airship was turning sharply southward, thrusters shoved forward and parse tubes opened wide to speed it away into the approaching darkness.

To escape from the enemy army and its mysterious white-cloaked leader, Dar Leah turned their Druid warship not toward Paranor but east toward the towering peaks of the Charnal Mountains. It might be that the enemy did not have the means to pursue them by air, but there was no point in taking chances.

"What are you doing?" Zia demanded immediately, watching the compass needle as it swung from south to east. She had recovered sufficiently to stand next to him in the pilot box, although she was still badly shaken.

"Hopefully, what they don't expect!" He had to shout to be heard above the roar of the wind as they gained speed, the thrusters shoved all the way forward, the ship bucking as it was struck by wicked gusts of wind.

"It's the wrong direction!"

"Not if we want to find cover. If we reach the mountains, we can disappear—lose them in the peaks and valleys, or even hide in the forests. Don't you see, Zia? They might come after us. If they have airships close at hand, they can be airborne pretty quickly, and maybe we won't be fast enough to outrun them. If they have weapons like ours, they can bring us down."

"If, if, if!" she muttered, her bitter words almost lost in the wind. "What a mistake this was."

She went silent then, glancing back over her shoulder, watching the land behind them rapidly disappear into shadows and memory. Was it a mistake? Dar grimaced. Sending Ruis Quince had been unfortunate. He had completely misread the situation and was dead as a result. Balronen had misread it, too. He was the one who had sent them on this fool's errand—he and his sycophantic allies, thinking the enemy could be turned to their own purposes, thinking they would be manipulated.

Everyone had been so wrong. But was it simply a mistake?

He wondered. The intrigues at Paranor were like spiderwebs these days, with everyone scuffling about to avoid being ensnared while trying improve their standing in the order. Cooperation was a thing of the past; all that mattered was getting close to Balronen and his inner circle. Drisker had said as much on leaving all those months ago, almost his final words to Dar.

Do what you must, young man, he had whispered. *But watch your back. In the scramble that lies ahead, I fear there will be few you can trust.*

So nothing had been achieved in this outing. All they had to show for it was the senseless deaths of a Druid and the Trolls who had tried to protect him. The pointlessness of it all was stunning. Dar had not even been allowed to put himself in a place where he could help save them, and if it weren't for his compulsive insistence on taking any risk necessary to fulfill his pledge to protect the Druids placed in his charge they would have lost Zia, too. Now they were in flight, and whatever opportunities there might have been for peaceful negotiation were lost. All that was left for them was to get back to Paranor and warn the Druids what was coming.

"So we tack into the mountains and make our way home from there?" Zia pressed him.

He nodded. "Fly low, stay out of sight, get home as quickly as we can and report what's happened. Then prepare for the worst. That army is coming for us."

"Ruis should have seen it. He should have recognized the danger. He just disregarded it."

"It was strange to see him so strident and aggressive. He isn't usually like that. What happened back there?"

She nodded vaguely, looking away. "Ruis didn't even try to be cautious. He just started threatening. Said the Druids would smash them if threatened. Bragged that no one could stand against the Druids, and that they should beg forgiveness for their intrusion into Druid country. Demanded to know what they intended. Insisted they explain themselves. Half of it didn't even make sense. It was ridiculous. The one in the white cloak mostly just listened. Then White Cloak motioned his soldiers forward to surround us, seemed to be indicating we were all his prisoners. Ruis just stared at him; he didn't seem to know what to do. Then we were attacked."

"What in the name of sanity was Ruis thinking?" Dar muttered.

Zia shook her head, glancing back again. "That wasn't Ruis Quince back there. That was someone else entirely."

They didn't speak for a while after that, although Zia stayed with him in the pilot box. The Trolls who remained aboard had stationed themselves at the rail slings and flash rips in readiness for whatever might come against them. They were Trolls, and so their faces showed nothing of their feelings. But Dar knew them well enough that he could recognize the tension in their posture and movements. They were stunned by what had happened back on the flats, not sure how they could have changed things but wishing they had. They cast their eyes back frequently, waiting for what might be coming, uncertain if they could escape.

"We need to eat," Dar said finally. "Will you take the helm while I get us something?"

She was no skilled flier but perfectly capable of keeping the airship on a straight course toward the mountains. Around them, the world was a gray, forbidding place. Clouds hung low across the sky. Shadows painted the land in broad swaths. A storm chased them in a dark line, running north to south on the horizon. They would be into it within the hour.

Dar disappeared below and searched their stores for food and drink, settling on an aleskin and half a loaf of bread. He was thinking they were ill equipped to withstand a sustained pursuit. Their stores were minimal and their craft, while capable enough, was less than suitable for effecting an escape. He kept seeing the white-cloaked leader of the enemy army. He saw him killing Quince all over again, a nasty piece of work for which he showed no emotion. He kept hearing Zia cry out in dismay. He kept thinking about how he would have felt if it had been her instead of Quince.

He paused at the ladder leading up. Perhaps he had been wrong to doubt their relationship. Perhaps he should have given it another chance, a longer chance, to see if things might work. He had been so cautious; he had miscalculated how strongly she felt about him. Immersed in his job as Blade, given over to fulfilling his pledge to protect the Druids, he had failed to protect what mattered.

How much they meant to each other. How fragile the ties that bound them actually were. It was said love could not live in a vacuum. It might be said it could not live in a whirlwind, either.

He went up with the bread and ale and took back the controls. The mountains were growing closer. He glanced over his shoulder and found the horizons west empty of airships but thick with rain clouds. Yet he judged the approaching storm too far back to catch them. Another thirty minutes and they would be into the Charnals, where pursuit of any kind would become much more difficult.

"Did you love Ruis?" he asked Zia, unable to help himself.

"I loved you."

"I know."

"Then why are you asking about Ruis? Had you been paying better attention earlier in our relationship, you wouldn't have to ask me that question now."

Her long hair flew back in the wind, tendrils of honey-colored softness whipping against his face. She was standing very close now, pressing up against him. "Were you worried I might love him?" she asked.

"I guess I was. He wasn't right for you."

"Maybe not. But then it seemed you weren't right for me, either. Or I for you."

"I misjudged. I missed seeing the truth. I was too wrapped up in other concerns."

She looked at him. "Don't expect that to change, Dar. It might not be possible. It would mean you would have to change, and I don't think you can."

He left it there, thinking instead about how he would convince Balronen to seek the aid of either the Federation or the Elves in the coming battle. It seemed more likely than not that the enemy army had bad intentions toward Paranor, and there were serious questions about whether the Druids could stand against them. Balronen would pull out the same tired argument as always, the same old disclaimer. The Druids needed no one. Their magic was sufficient to protect them, their power greater than any combination of human-made weapons. Asking for help compromised their position as negotiators for all the Races. It diminished their standing with the other governments and lands.

It demeaned them. It revealed them as weak.

Such foolish posturing. Such unnecessary pride. But Ober Balronen never saw it that way.

So now Dar must find a way to persuade him to change his thinking. If he failed, the Ard Rhys by his stubbornness risked the destruction of the entire Druid order.

And then suddenly, from astern, a chilling cry arose. "Airships!"

They had been found.

SIXTEEN

Dar turned at once to look, Zia with him, and together they watched as three dots appeared from out of the mists behind them. Fast cruisers, the highlander realized. Built for speed and maneuverability. Warships much more suited for battle than was his.

So the enemy had the use of airships, too.

He stared back at them for long moments, wanting to be sure. Then he turned away again.

The distance between them was diminishing all too quickly.

They were in for a fight.

Pursuer and pursued closed when they were within five hundred yards of the lower ranges of the Charnals, the cruisers coming on fast, the Druid warship backed against the peaks and searching for a way to slip through. Dar was at the helm, with Zia gone to the stern to employ her magic to protect them. He was angling toward Rausk Break, a deep split in the peaks where a narrowing not far within opened into a wider space beyond. Once through, they could turn the airship sideways and bring the entirety of their starboard or port weapons to bear while they confronted the enemy airships in the narrow opening one by one. It was a faint hope, but at this point faint hope was all they had.

Below them, the forests were a rolling green carpet along the lower slopes of the towering peaks, clusters of boulders and dead trees tumbled and turned silver with weather and time poking out like burrowing creatures come up for air. Darkness was descending quickly as the eastern horizon filled with clouds. They had found a fresh rainstorm into which to fly, little more than a squall.

Ahead, a much worse storm waited, a black maelstrom churning within the peaks of the mountains.

As if to signal its ferocity, lightning flashed and thunder rumbled in a long, steady peal, and the weapons of the approaching cruisers began to fire. Ropes of diapson-crystal-generated fire flashed all about the Druid ship, some of which appeared certain to strike the vessel directly. Zia had used her magic to put up a protective screen, and any potential damage was deflected. Even so, the force of the blows rocked the airship, and Dar had to work hard to hold her steady. Aft weapons fired into the enemy, a steady stream of fiery explosions, but the damage was minimal. Too much shifting about as Zia's shield was raised and lowered to allow for any real retaliation. Dar saw how this would go as Zia tired and knew they had to gain the protection of Rausk Break swiftly.

He took their vessel sharply right and downward, then up again in a stomach-churning heave that threw off the charges being fired by their pursuers. Then another surge as a final blow struck their stern, and they were through the gap and into the peaks, their pursuers now forced to follow in single file.

By the time the first of the three enemy airships hove into view, Dar had swung their own vessel broadside, and all of their flash rips discharged at once. Multiple strikes filled the air with fire and smoke, and the stricken cruiser erupted in flames and began to drop toward the rocks below. But the enemy flagship had come in low and quick behind it and was firing its weapons into the exposed belly of the Druid vessel, which bucked and lurched wildly with each blow it absorbed.

Another few hits and she would go down.

Dar pushed the thruster levers all the way forward and shot deeper into the canyon, fast enough to evade further damage from cannon fire but not smoothly enough to evade the ragged cliff walls, striking rocky outcroppings twice, each time tearing holes in the side of the ship's hull. Then they were away again, through the Rausk and into the interior of the Charnals. Dar wheeled their airship left down a long canyon, not even bothering to look back for the pursuit he knew would be there.

"Dar!" Zia was beside him, her face blackened with ash and her eyes wild. "The last two members of the Druid Guard were lost over the side. We're down to Stow and the crew. We have to get out of range of those flash rips!"

"Try to keep them off us for another few minutes," he shouted back. "I have an idea!"

She stared at him, leaned in suddenly, and kissed him full on the lips. "You and me. When we're safe again."

Hope seared through him, and then she was gone, rushing for the back of the airship, already beginning to spin out her protective magic. Dar glanced upward to the airship rigging. Damage everywhere, light sheaths in tatters, spars turned to kindling. Even the masts were splintered and cracked, the smallest almost sheared through about a third of the way up. The deck was littered with debris, and the hull was holed in a dozen places. That the lines to the parse tubes were still intact was nothing short of a miracle.

He stared ahead at the wall of the approaching storm. *Faster,* he thought, trying to urge the ship to greater speed, feeling the nearness of their pursuers. *Fly, you lumbering sloth!*

Then he sensed Zia's magic filling the air behind them, the heat and light of it, the sound of power rising. A quick glance back to confirm one of the fast cruisers was almost on top of them, and then a final push. Flash rip fire lanced all about, but the blows that would have struck were deflected.

Zia staying strong, keeping them safe.

He found the defile he was looking for, a wicked jagged gap with protrusions like teeth, and began to maneuver their airship into its confines. A few feet away, Stow Chutin stood watching the jaws tighten about their craft.

"Zia!" Dar called to her.

She came at once, speeding across the decking, leaping debris as she hurried to reach him. Behind them, their pursuers were momentarily out of sight as they sought to catch up to their quarry without overexposing themselves.

"Can you conjure up a screen of mist so they can't see us until they're right on top of us?"

He was already turning the ship about, pointing the bow back the way they had come. Zia stared at him. "You're going to ram them?"

"The one advantage we have. We weigh a lot more. If we catch them right, they'll go down and we might live to see another day. Can you do it?"

Lips tight, she nodded, hurrying toward the bow as it swung about. Without slowing, she began weaving her hands to summon the elements, turning them to her use and molding them into a heavy mist that rose in front of them and spread outward into the canyon. Dar found a resting point for the airship and held her steady. No movement, no sounds, a predator waiting for prey.

For long moments, nothing happened. Then a shadow appeared in the mists, so vague it almost wasn't there. Dar jammed the thruster levers forward and the big warship began to move. By the time the enemy cruiser was clearly visible they were right on top of it and moving too fast to be avoided. Shouts and cries of warning rose from the other vessel, and Dar could see figures trying to turn the rail slings and flash rips into position to fire on them. But they barely got off a scattering of shots before the fortified bow of the Druid warship slammed into their midsection.

Straight through the center of the cruiser it lurched, splintering decking and hull, staving in masts, scattering soldiers and crew everywhere. With a terrible rending sound, the ship split in two and fell away, taking everyone on board with her.

Dar kept their own ship flying forward, navigating the spiky entrance in an effort to get free again, ignoring the danger to his own vessel, searching everywhere for the enemy flagship.

He couldn't find it.

"Zia!" he called forward. "Can you see . . . ?"

Wham!

It felt as if the world had collapsed atop them. Dar went to his knees, barely clinging to consciousness. Fire rained down, lines of flames exploding everywhere as the enemy flagship swung down from the rocks where it had been waiting and hammered their helpless vessel with strike after strike from its cannons. Smoke and ash and fire were everywhere, and Dar was at the center of the maelstrom. He fell away from the controls, knowing instinctively they were useless. He stumbled from what remained of the pilot box, trying to keep his feet as the warship tilted and started down. He scanned the decks, searching for the others.

"Zia!" he screamed.

No answer. No sign of Chutin, the big Captain of the Druid Guard. No sign of the crew. No sign of anyone.

Overhead, the cruiser was maneuvering into position to finish what it had started. Flash rips were being swung into position and leveled for firing.

Dar Leah hesitated only a moment. Longer, and he would have been incinerated. Racing to the starboard side of the doomed vessel, the Sword of Leah strapped tightly across his back, he snatched up the loose end of the closest mooring line, locked the brake on the spindle, wrapped the line tightly about his arm, and threw himself over the railing and into the misty gloom.

It was an impulsive, reckless, suicidal act, one born of an instinctive need to try to stay alive. In less desperate moments, he would never have even considered it, let alone done it. But desperate moments were all that were left him, so he did it without thinking.

He fell for a long time as he clung to the mooring line—long enough that he began to wonder if he had been mistaken in believing the other end was secured. He tumbled through endless mist and gloom into a void that seemed to have no bottom. To either side, the jagged cliffs flew by, stark and empty and sharp-edged. Birds circled about him, screaming their shrill, mournful cries, engaged in their own pursuits, unmindful of his frightening descent.

Overhead, the Druid airship was ablaze and breaking up, pieces of it already spinning away like shooting stars, barely missing him as they hurtled past, almost as if deliberately intent on seeing him dead before the rope caught. Tears streamed from his wind-whipped eyes. The cliff face drew steadily closer the farther he fell. Much closer, and he would slam into it, but there was nothing he could do to prevent that from happening. He tightened his grip on the mooring rope and waited for the inevitable.

Then the rope played out all the way, and his fall was arrested with such force that it felt as if his arms had been torn out of their sockets. For a moment, he hung there swinging and spinning, gasping for breath and struggling to keep his hold, fighting off the shock to his body. When finally he could manage it, he steadied himself and began to swing toward the cliff face like a pendulum. After several tries his maneuvering brought him close enough to see the jagged surface clearly, and he realized the place he wanted was twenty feet higher up.

Fighting against fatigue and pain, he hitched his way up the rope to an outcropping surrounded by bushes where he hoped he might find concealment from anyone who came searching for him. And he was pretty sure someone would. Even if they believed he was dead, the enemy would take no chances. Their white-cloaked leader would send searchers. He saw the man again in his mind, a faceless vision, so cold and remote, cutting down Ruis Quince where he knelt helpless and unarmed. Dar didn't expect for one minute that he would be spared if the other man found him.

Larger shards of the broken airship began to fall past him, some coming too close for comfort, and he struggled farther back onto the rock shelf and let go of the rope. Pressing himself hard against the cliff face, he watched as what remained of the airship fell past him, the rope going with it.

For a few moments he wondered if perhaps the invaders had missed seeing him go over the side of his doomed vessel, but it was too risky to make such an assumption. He was alive when he should be dead, and there was no point in advertising his presence when they came looking. He was sitting right out in the open, if you discounted the clumps of brush beneath which he had wriggled. All that kept anyone from seeing him were those and the remnants of the mist Zia had conjured during the battle.

Zia. He felt a catch in his throat and a sinking feeling. Almost certainly dead. Along with Chutin and the crew. All of them lost.

He forced himself to quit thinking about it. He would join them quickly enough if his situation didn't improve. He had to try to get out of there. A quick glance around revealed a number of splits and indentations in the rock, but nothing big enough that he could hide in it. He judged himself to be about two hundred feet up from the canyon floor with no quick or easy way to climb down. He thought there might be a place about fifty feet off to the left where he could make a start, but from his current angle of view it was impossible to tell.

"Shades!" he muttered.

He knew he had to try something. And he had to try it soon.

He was still sitting in his brush shelter, thinking about what he should do, when a flit flew out of the mists and pulled up right in front of him, hovering in midair. He stared at the shark fin shape of the bow and the line of embedded flash rips, their muzzles directed at him.

As if determined to make this personal, the white-cloaked enemy leader stood in the pilot box, looking at him. He was close enough that it was possible to see his fingers hovering over the firing triggers, and Dar felt a momentary sense of inevitability. Pieces of debris were raining down behind the enemy flit, some coming much closer than was safe, but the white-cloaked leader never even glanced at them.

Dar waited, knowing there was no escape. He thought briefly about reaching back for his sword, but discarded the idea. He would be dead before he could bring it to bear. The winds had picked up and were surging through the canyon, whipping at him with such force that he was in danger of being dislodged from his perch. He pressed his back firmly against the cliff face and tried to look at his enemy and not the muzzles of those weapons.

The flit dropped a notch and edged a bit closer. The pilot was a skilled flier. He was almost on top of Dar, all but pressing up against him, yet holding steady with no apparent effort. Dar's adversary was studying him, looking at him from out of his featureless helmet, apparently trying to see something in him that was hidden from view.

Or perhaps to make up his mind if there was something to see.

No words were spoken and no gestures offered, and yet in that instant Dar became certain the white-cloaked enemy leader was making a decision.

Abruptly the nose of the flit dropped just enough that they were suddenly eye to eye. While the expression of astonishment on Dar's face must have been apparent, the enemy pilot's own expression remained hidden. Another long moment, and the pilot took the flash rip muzzles off Dar's chest, tilted the nose of the flit upward, wheeled it about, and flew into the haze without a backward glance.

Dar stared in disbelief as the flit disappeared, trying to understand what had just happened.

SEVENTEEN

THE MORNING WAS A clouded, rainy, gloomy shroud, all darkness and shadows and the hint of an unpleasant chill. It was understandable how such a day could affect your disposition—especially if you were one of those people, like Tavo Kaynin, who were susceptible to mood changes and reacted strongly to light and darkness. One minute you could be perfectly fine, the day bright and cheerful and you bright and cheerful with it. Another, and you could find the weather and yourself as unpleasant as anything you could have imagined.

And then you began to think of all the things that troubled you and all the people who had misled and betrayed you. Then the rage would come, strong and knowable and certain, a kind of stiffening of the body and mind, as if a fire burned through your body and you inhaled its power.

And then, if you were the brother of a wicked, deceitful girl like Tarsha, you thought about how you would punish her once you found her.

Tavo Kaynin had been walking for three days—a slog through dark moods and darker silences in which demons surfaced and screamed at him incessantly, awake and in dreams, their voices shrill and demanding.

Do what you must! Hunt her down! Did she not hurt you? You must now hurt her!

The words, piercing and unrelenting, fueled his rage. He welcomed them as old friends, as reminders of what he was about as he traipsed across the Westland toward the Tirfing. They showed him visions of her, revealing the depth of her deceit, suggesting the things he could do to her once she was in his power.

His sister. His nemesis.

Sometimes, she walked with him. She was there at his side when he allowed her to be—never entirely visible, but more of a phantom that he could only glimpse, drifting and surreal. She was there to remind him how she had betrayed him.

Other times, she hid within the trees of the forest, a presence more than an image. In those moments, she would whisper to him—words of succor and reassurance that he knew to be false but wished so badly were not. She was in the shadows and in the rush of the wind. She was in the movement of the clouds overhead. She was even in the flitting of small birds and the scrambling of tiny mice. But she was there, and he saw her.

And sometimes, every now and then, she reminded him of how much she had comforted him during their early years, when she was the only friend he had. She reminded him of how hard she had tried to protect him, even though she was five years younger and so much smaller. He would remember the closeness they had shared, the love she had engendered in him, the sense of peace she was able to bring to him in times so dark he was certain he must go mad. He would remember how she tried to help him with the magic—to control it, to keep it at bay, to not let it rule his life. In those moments, all the bitterness and anger would fall away, the gloom would dissipate, and he would be left with a deep sense of sadness and regret, wondering if there was perhaps a way to reclaim that closeness they had shared.

Then Fluken would appear, and those feelings would vanish once more. Fluken did not like Tarsha. He hated Tarsha worse than Tavo did.

The rain increased, and even his cloak was not enough to keep him dry. He tightened it about him, but the damp and the chill wormed their way into his body and deep into his bones. He wanted a fire. He wanted a bed. He wanted someone to talk to so he could tell his story.

But there was almost no one on the road. He passed the occasional solitary traveler, but only infrequently—traders and trappers, and men and women on their own pilgrimages—all of whom, in all likelihood, journeyed with their own ghosts. He tried making contact, but most simply ignored him and moved on. He let them go because he knew they were right to do so, that no one would want to be with someone like him, someone with blood on his hands. No one wanted to be with someone who saw the dead and wished to send so many of the living to join them.

Now and then, the man and woman who claimed to be his parents traveled with him, wraiths in the gloom. Now and then his uncle was there as well, although he kept his distance. When they appeared, they walked with their heads bowed, returned somehow to the way they had been before he had ended their lives. They said nothing and paid him no mind but simply kept pace. He shouted out at them now and then, demanding they go away and leave him alone. Once or twice he tamped down his rage long enough to tell them he was sorry for what he had done. But mostly the anger and the frustration ruled him. And his rage over Tarsha's betrayal continued unabated. There burned within him a need for revenge that was always present— sometimes a tiny flame, sometimes a fiery conflagration that threatened to engulf him entirely.

It needed tending to. It needed quenching.

Squit Malk was there sometimes, too—a huge ragged thing almost entirely unrecognizable save for his size and bulk. He lumbered out of the shadows now and then, forlorn and lost, a creature with no purpose other than to wander the world of the living in search of his lost life. Tavo did not regret taking that life. After all, Malk had attempted to take his. If he had left well enough alone when they parted on the road and not attempted to kill Tavo in his sleep, he would be alive right now. In fact, it could be said Tavo had done the world a favor, ridding it of such a vile human being, cleaning up one of nature's discards.

Three days, and he had covered so little ground. It would take him forever to find his sister. It might be more than he could manage. Tarsha was strong and clever and willful, and she would likely do what she could to avoid being found. Thus he was given no choice but to hunt her. No choice at all.

On the night of the third day, he slept in a barn with a farmer's animals and found them good company. The lights of the house showed the shadows of the man and woman as they crossed in front of the curtained windows. He thought about asking to be let inside where it was warm and dry, but he knew they would not allow it. He would be driven off and made to feel even worse about himself than he already did.

So he settled for the barn and used the magic of his voice to soothe the animals—a soft singing of their own voices, a talent for reaching out to creatures that he had never quite managed with people. He sang to them and they became calm and quiet within their pens and stalls. His ghosts did not come into the barn with him; not for them the small comforts he relished so. They remained out in the cold and wet.

Even Fluken stayed away, although Tavo could sense his presence close by.

On the night of the fourth day—a day still dark with clouds and wrapped in a steady drizzle, though one less ferociously determined to unnerve him—he reached a village. It was actually more of a hamlet, he decided, on realizing how few buildings there were. The lights that burned through the growing dark were dim and few, but at least they encouraged him to believe there might be something besides trees and hills and bogs and farmland.

So he approached cautiously, realizing as he did so that he yearned for the voices of the living, that he required company, if only for one night. Fluken had been absent all day, and he was feeling lonely. He was a solitary person for the most part, having always been alone due to his dark nature and darker gift. He had always been marginalized or shunned. But even the most reclusive of humans needed the presence of other humans now and then, a reminder of how others could be if given a chance. Not all were infected with evil. Not all were malicious and deceitful and ready to crush your soul.

He found the largest of the buildings and believed it to be a trappers' outpost for those who hunted this region, and he hoped he might find a room and a bed for the night. Just that much would give him strength to continue his search. Perhaps he would even manage to find a meal and conversation.

So he entered, a frail and damaged creature, come in out of the night and the rain. Heads turned upon his entry and conversations lowered or died out entirely. The room was thick with smoke and the smell of unwashed men. He paused at the door, closing it behind him and taking a moment to survey the room. He made out somewhere around twenty men scattered about the room, either sitting at heavy wooden tables or standing at a short serving bar. They were a hard-looking bunch, all bearded and weathered, their clothes of leather held fast by metal stays, their boots so scuffed they no longer possessed a recognizable color.

He nodded to a few as he made his way to the bar, but the eyes that met his stared back without warmth. By the time he had reached the back of the room, conversations had started up again, albeit lowered and guarded. He caught the glint of weapons, handles protruding from sheaths and beneath cloaks. A handful of blades leaned against tables or rested atop them. He knew at once he had made a mistake. This was no trappers' and traders' haven, no inn for travelers come off the road. This was a den for men who made their home in the darkest corners of the world—men whose occupation was not the hunting of game or goods for trade, but the hunting of men.

But it was too late to turn back. Even in his diminished state, he knew that much. To back away would be seen as a clear demonstration of fear, and showing that to men like these was like offering up his exposed throat.

He stood at the counter and waited for the man standing behind it to acknowledge his presence. When the man wandered over, he skipped any sort of greeting and simply said, "Ale."

It was in front of him swiftly and the man gone. He leaned on the bar's scarred surface, sipped at the heady liquid, and thought about his weariness. When he finished one tankard, he ordered a second and turned to face the room. A few eyes glanced up but none lingered. He saw that the man and woman who had claimed him as their child once were seated near the door with his uncle, and that Squit Malk had joined them. They were leaning close to one another, engaged in conversation, the sound of their voices too soft for him to catch. He thought about joining them, then decided better of it.

Where was Fluken?

A woman who was barely recognizable as such wandered out of a back room with plates of food for the men at a table close to him. The food was steaming, and he felt the emptiness of his own stomach as she set the plates on the table. When she glanced up and saw him, there was a startled look in her eyes. When she came over, her nervousness was apparent.

"Do you have business here?" she asked quietly, the words almost lost her voice was so low.

He shook his head. "Just food and a bed."

Her voiced hardened. "This is no place for you. Get out of here."

"Food and a bed," he repeated.

Her face twisted unpleasantly, her eyes frightened as she studied him. "Your choice. I can bring you the former, but we don't have rooms. Eat your food and drink your ale and leave. Go on to the next town. Five miles farther."

She turned and left, moving away with a stiff determination that left him wondering at her purpose in warning him off. She seemed to sense his situation, even if she knew nothing of his journey. To her, he was just a misguided young man who had wandered into the wrong place. He smiled and nodded at the four who sat at the table by the door, watching him. They were ready to leave, too, he could tell. They were dead, but they were somehow anxious about what they feared would happen. He imagined that Fluken was also waiting for him, just outside the door.

He asked for and received a third tankard. This time he held up his hand to detain the barman. "I'm looking for someone," he said.

The barman nodded. "Aren't we all?"

"A girl. Young, hair so blond it could be white, lavender eyes. Pretty, in a deceitful sort of way. I'm looking for her."

"You're looking in the wrong place," the man repeated.

"She would have come through here a few weeks back, traveling alone."

"Not through here, she wouldn't have. Not a girl alone."

"Wait, now," a voice interrupted.

A burly man with coarse, heavy features and massive arms appeared, leaning into the bar and smiling. "I might have seen this girl. Young, you say? And white-blond hair? I think so."

Tavo allowed himself a twinge of hope. "She was here?"

"No, no, not in this place. On the road, out north. Traveling with a family of Rovers. But she didn't seem to be one of them. Didn't have their looks or their dress. Seemed to have taken up with them to share the journey, that was all."

The serving woman appeared with the plate of food and set it down on the bar in front of him. She turned, gave the man an indecipherable look, and disappeared again.

Tavo began to eat. "Did you speak to her?"

The burly man shrugged. "No. Had no reason to. Didn't speak to any of them. Just passing by. I remember the girl because of that hair. Distinctive. You don't see hair like that too often."

"Or never!" someone behind them shouted, and there was a burst of laughter.

"Shut it!" the burly man shouted angrily, turning as if searching for the faces of those who laughed at him. "You bunch don't know what I've seen or not seen, so stay outta this!"

Tavo held his ground, although he knew now that he was in trouble and the man was lying. Over by the door, Squit Malk, his uncle, and the man and woman who claimed him as their son had risen and were moving toward the exit. He wanted to scream to them to stay or even to take him with them. But they were dead, and the dead can't help the living.

"Now, then." The burly man clapped a hand to his shoulder and brought him back around. "I might have a way to help you with this girl you're seeking. Just might. But it will take some of my time and a few supplies because we'll have to go looking for her, you and I. So do you have the means? Credits, to pay me for my trouble?"

The boy shook his head and put his back to the serving counter. "I've no money."

"Aye? And what will you use to pay Harl back there for your drinks and your meal? Will you wash his dishes and sweep his floor?"

Tavo resisted the urge to look behind him. "I'll do what I must."

"You'll do what you must." The man in front of him shook his head. "I don't know that you will. I don't know that you'll ever do anything again if you don't pay me something for the trouble of talking to you. Just trying to help you out, a poor stranger come from another land, and you treat me as if I were a cutthroat after your purse. Well, now, what if I were? Do you think there is anything you can do about it? Do you think it possible?"

Strong hands seized Tavo from behind, pinning him fast against the countertop. Harl, the barman. Tavo knew without having to try that he would not be strong enough to escape those hands. The burly man was already moving to Tavo's backpack, fumbling with the catches. Others in the bar were getting to their feet, as well, sensing there might be a chance for them to share in whatever was found in the pack.

Sensing blood in the water.

Knives came out. Swords were lifted off tabletops. A general shuffling of bodies filled the sudden silence. Tavo caught a glimpse of the serving woman as she peeked out from the kitchen and quickly shut the door, knowing what would happen next.

He heard the front door to the tavern close. His parents, his uncle, and Squit were gone.

He searched for Fluken. No sign.

"Let me go," he said to the burly man.

He said it so quietly that for a moment the other paused in the midst of his rummaging and stared at him, a sudden uncertainty in his eyes. Then he shook it off. "When I'm done."

"You're done now."

The wishsong exploded from Tavo's throat in a red-hot wave of power that slammed into the big man and threw him backward into his fellows. The magic shifted directions and picked up Harl and slammed him to the floor so hard that his head exploded in a red shower of blood and brains.

Free, he turned to the room. "You don't deserve to live, and I don't think I'll let you."

He went after them systematically, in groups where groups were to be found, and one by one when they tried to flee. The wishsong simply encapsulated them where it found them and broke them apart. Bones, organs, and blood flew everywhere, and the room became a charnel house of the dead and dying. He missed no one. Even those who might have thought they could gain the safety of the front or rear doors died trying. They begged and cried for him to stop, to let them live. But he wasn't the sort to grant mercy. His magic was so powerful that its very use was an addictive drug he could not resist. Once he began to use it, he wanted to continue.

And so he did here. All through the room, in every nook and cranny, under tables and behind the serving counter, anywhere a man might hide, he searched them out and put an end to them.

When it was done and no one breathed or moved, and all but one lay dead, he knelt beside the burly man. There was such fear in the other's eyes, such terror and regret. It gave Tavo a pleasure he could not begin to describe. He smiled at the man in a kindly way, seeing the pain etched on the other's face, recognizing a seeping-away of life, a giving-up of hope.

"You should have left me alone," he whispered.

Then he directed the magic to close the man's windpipe and watched as he slowly choked to death.

Afterward, he stood in the midst of the carnage for a long time, taking in the looks on the faces of the corpses, trying to read in their shocked and terror-stricken expressions what they might have been thinking at the end. He found it odd and somehow appropriate that he could create these pained expressions out of his own pain. He was driven to use his magic for this purpose, to help him cleanse his pain and erase his confusion. Always, he wondered how he had come by such power. There were stories, but none seemed to fit. The man and the woman who had claimed to be his parents had never mentioned it. Or were deliberately hiding what they knew. He had thought to learn the truth from Tarsha, but Tarsha had taken whatever she knew with her, away to where he might never find it.

He walked over to the counter and resumed eating. The food was good enough that he was not about to leave it. He ate hungrily, paying no attention to what lay strewn about him. He paused only when he caught a glimpse of the kitchen door opening and the frightened face of the serving woman staring in horror. She did not look at him but softly closed the door and went back inside, possibly to hide or to run. He shrugged it off. It didn't matter to him what she did. He would not harm her. She had done nothing. He didn't harm people who didn't try to harm him first.

Or, like Tarsha, betray him.

He finished his meal and a final tankard of ale. He stripped a pair of boots and a cloak that was almost new from the dead men, hitched up his backpack, and went out the door into the night. To his astonishment, the storm with its winds and rains had passed, and the sky was clear. Stars shone, and a half-moon could be glimpsed through a thin screen of clouds. The chill of earlier was gone, and the air had warmed to a pleasant softness that gave him a sense of peace. He had thought to sleep but found he was no longer tired. He would walk this night until he reached a better place and sleep then.

Sleep until the madness settled. Sleep until the memories of tonight faded. Sleep until the sun warmed the land and the damp had gone back into the earth to nourish the soil.

And then?

I am coming for you, Tarsha. Watch for me.

He smiled to himself. Better days lay ahead.

EIGHTEEN

It was early morning when Drisker Arc walked back toward the village of Emberen to retrieve his two-man flit, Tarsha Kaynin at his side. He was already working out in his head how he was going to go about tracking down whoever was responsible for sending the men from the assassins' guild to kill him. Having identified the guild as one operating out of Varfleet, it would be easy enough to find its lair and not too much harder to lay hands on the men who had come after him. What might prove much more difficult was identifying who had hired them. The guilds were notorious for their secrecy, especially when it came to giving up the names of clients. Once it was shown that you couldn't be trusted with names, business had a tendency to drop off precipitously.

As they walked, Tarsha questioned him about what he had found in the north. "Do you trust this creature?" she wanted to know. "What was it you called him?"

"The Morsk. He's a species of shape-shifter. And yes, I trust him enough to believe he would not lie about this. He has no reason to lie and every reason to be honest. He owes me a favor, and he knows that the danger posed by the invaders threatens him as well as us. What he told me was clearly the truth."

He had been thinking about the previous night, remembering

how fierce she had been, how wild and uncontrolled. He was thinking he would have to watch her closely.

"So we have men who can appear and disappear like ghosts? But what do they want? To conquer the Four Lands? How do they hope to stand against the armies of the Federation? The power of diapson crystal weapons will be too much for them, won't it? The Southland soldiers will simply set fire to everything in front of them and these invaders will be swept away, no matter how hard they try to hide where they are."

Drisker looked off into the trees a moment. "You would think. But I worry there is more to this than we know. I think it would be a mistake to assume anything. In any case, it would be foolish to hope it will not end up affecting us. So we had better find a way to put up a united front before this army becomes too entrenched. The Druids at Paranor should lead that effort. The Morsk was right: They will be most at risk."

She pursed her lips. "Because they have magic, too?"

"Yes. I don't see how we can think otherwise. This enemy will likely consider them their greatest threat."

She did not question him further on this, but let the matter drop. They found the man who cared for Drisker's small airship, and asked to have it brought out and prepared for travel. The man barely spoke two words in response before hurrying off to retrieve the vessel from storage.

Drisker waited a moment and then suggested he and Tarsha have something to eat while waiting.

"Only if you agree to tell me how you think you will find the men who attacked us," she countered.

He doubted she would refuse to eat if he didn't, but there was no reason not to tell her what he knew. So he nodded and started away, heading down the dusty main road that led through the center of the village.

At one of the two inns that served food and drink, they found a table and seated themselves. It was crowded in the dining room, and a few heads turned to look. Not at him, Drisker thought, but at his striking young companion. They would be wondering what she was to him. Drisker ignored them. Let them think what they wanted. He signaled a server and they placed an order. Ale was brought along with fruit, cheese, bread, and pieces of last night's roast pig, and they settled in to enjoy their meal. Tarsha managed to refrain from asking further questions until they were finished; then she started in again.

"Will you tell me your plan now? Is there a way to find out who attacked us?"

He smiled in spite of himself. "So impatient. But, yes, there is a way. All the men bore a symbol on their wrists, a marking of closed eyes leaking blood. It is the sign of the Orsis, an assassins' guild working out of Varfleet. We'll have to go there and follow the thread to wherever it leads."

She frowned. "These people, this Orsis Guild, they won't want to tell us what they know, will they?"

"Not likely. We must use gentle persuasion to convince them. How are you with gentle persuasion?"

She laughed. "I think it best to leave the gentle persuasion to you." She finished off her ale and leaned back. "I do look forward to observing your technique."

Smiling ruefully, he rose and went over to the bar to pay for their meal. When she joined him, they went out the door of the inn and down the roadway to the storage barn and their craft. The two-man was sitting out in a yard behind the barn, cleaned up and ready. Drisker thanked the manager and paid him extra credits for his trouble, then signaled to Tarsha to climb aboard. She did so without comment. She had said nothing since they left the inn, but she had not stopped watching him.

When they were airborne, she loosened her restraining harness and leaned close. "I am not a child, you know," she said quietly. "I don't need to be protected from hard truths."

"Nor will you be," he replied, his eyes directed straight ahead. "If there were anything to tell you—if there is ever anything to tell you—you will be told, no matter the difficulty I might have in doing so. You must do the same for me. You wish to train in the use of your magic, and that requires a sharing of truths. From me to you, and you to me."

"So I am free to be truthful with you?"

Her hair was whipping about her face. "You are *required* to be so."

She sat back and was quiet again. Drisker flew the ship south past the mouth of the Valley of Rhenn before turning eastward toward the dark line of the Dragon's Teeth. The day was warm and windless, the sky mostly clear of clouds, and the landscape below a tapestry of greens and browns with the Mermidon a crooked blue stitching that would lead them eventually to their destination when it joined with the Runne. Now and then, horsemen would appear, sometimes solitary and sometimes warding mule-drawn wagons laden with goods. There were no sightings of anything out of place or threats from the invaders. The enemy army appeared to be in the Northland still, and the Druid wondered just how long that would last.

He had almost forgotten Tarsha when she suddenly leaned into him once more, her head so close to his they were almost touching. "Tell me why you abandoned the Druids?"

He felt a brief surge of irritation. "I did not abandon them. They exiled me. You do know the difference, don't you?"

"Better than you, perhaps. But you exiled yourself, if I remember correctly. Why did you do that? I know you felt powerless in the face of how you were being ignored as High Druid, but why did you walk away? Why didn't you stay and fight?"

"Why did you walk away from your brother and come looking for me?"

It was an unfair comparison, and he regretted making it almost instantly. He felt the hesitation in her response. "We are speaking of you and not of me. Besides, the situations are not the same. You are an experienced magic user. I am not. I was afraid for my safety. Were you?"

He shook his head. "No." He paused. "I apologize for snapping at you. I said we must speak truths to each other, and that is what I must do now. Leaving the Druid order still stings when I stop to think about it. I was High Druid, and I gave that up. I did so for the sake of my sanity and my personal well-being. I left because I was sick and tired of struggling with fools. I left because if I had stayed, something bad would have happened because of it. To them or to me."

She shrugged. "Sometimes leaving is all that is left to us. For you as for me." She was trying to be helpful. "I regret leaving, too. I want to return. Do you ever think of doing so?"

He turned back to face her. "I do."

"Will you take me with you when you do?"

"*If* I do. We'll see."

"Will you allow me to return to Backing Fell?"

He nodded slowly. "I think I must, if I want to keep you with me over the long run. The problems with your brother won't heal by themselves. They will only heal with actions. Your actions. I've known that from the first."

She sat back again. The air displaced by the airship's progress rushed past his ears in a dull roar, and within its white noise he found a kind of solitude. He let it enfold him as he watched the mountains ahead, their dark wall a barrier to Paranor and the life he had left behind.

A life he now knew that he, like Tarsha, might have to return to.

The airship flew on and the hours drifted away in a measuring of his regrets and hopes.

Their journey lasted three days, and on the evening of the third they spent the night in a village just west of Varfleet, their inn of choice positioned right on the banks of the Mermidon and not far west from where the Runne split off and ran south toward Rainbow Lake. It was late when they arrived, and when they entered the dining room to eat they found themselves alone save for an old man sitting in one corner and a pair of drummers occupying the table closest to the fire. Drisker was worn from the day's travel and the assault on his thinking regarding both the disaster brewing to the north and the problem of what to do with the men of Orsis Guild when he found them.

He was counting heavily on the element of surprise once he determined where the guild made its headquarters. If he were to alert those he hunted too quickly, they would go to ground and stay there until he departed. He must find them before they knew he was hunting, and trap them in a place where they could not escape until he willed it. Only then would they be forced to reveal their employer. About the men themselves he had little interest. They were mercenaries who had accepted a job and failed to do it. They cared nothing for Drisker or Tarsha one way or the other. But the man who had hired them clearly cared, and he was the one Drisker was determined to find.

Druid and apprentice ate a meal of stew, bread, and springwater with a plate of fresh cheeses on the side. They ate in silence, conscious of the silence of the room and the ears of the other three who shared their space. Now and then they would glance at each other and then at the men around them, but otherwise they continued with their meal. An unspoken agreement was reached that they would say nothing to each other until they were safely alone.

Eventually the drummers left and then the old man rose and departed, too. The room grew silent save for the crackling of the logs in the fire and the movements of the innkeeper as he cleaned up behind the bar and waited for his last two customers to retire.

Drisker leaned forward. "Are you ready for this? For what it might take to find these men?"

She nodded at once. "I'm not afraid."

"I didn't think you were. But maybe you should be. At least a little. This is dangerous business, Tarsha. These are men who would kill you without a thought if they saw you as a threat. Too much confidence can be your undoing."

She cocked her head at him. "You don't have to worry about me. I can manage. You have to remember, I lived with my brother for years. I always found ways to handle him. I'll do that here, as well."

He nodded slowly, but his mind was troubled. "Maybe you should wait here for me."

She made a dismissive gesture. "Don't waste your time expecting that to happen. Just tell me what you want me to do. Tell me how I can help."

He smiled in spite of himself. A strong-minded girl, this one. Not even fully grown and already so certain of herself. She was on her way to being so when she first came to him, but it was not so evident then as it was now. Maybe his lessons on the usage of magic had helped that confidence to mature and grow.

"All right, let me tell you what I need from you." He leaned close, wanting to make sure the innkeeper couldn't hear. "I need a couple of things. I need your eyes—a second pair of eyes—to search out what my own might miss. And I need you to watch my back. These assassins are trained killers, and they will try to catch us off guard once they know who we are and why we have come. We have to be very careful. If we make a mistake, it could be fatal. Can you do that?"

"I can do it. I'm assuming you will trust my judgment on this? On what needs doing? So I can just do it if there's no time to talk it over?"

"If I can't trust you, then we are both finished." He leaned back again. "I'll make you a bargain. If we discover who is behind the attempts on my life, we will take time to see what can be done about your brother."

"Those two weeks you promised me earlier?" Her face lit up. "Then you think I am ready?"

He looked sternly at her. "Don't get overconfident. And remember, you are still bound by our agreement to serve me as an apprentice. But I can give you time to return home and find out how things are with your brother nevertheless."

"That is more than fair. Why are you doing this?"

He laughed. "Have you decided I am someone who never does anything fair? Goodness."

"You are smart and manipulative, and you always think several moves ahead of those you deal with. Including me. I have seen you work. I have watched how you handle things. You did not become High Druid of Paranor by simply waiting for someone to decide it was a good idea."

He looked at her. "That was a dark analysis of my character, Tarsha Kaynin. I don't think I like it much. Maybe I should take back my offer."

She said nothing, waiting. He continued staring, and then he shrugged. "Well, you are entitled to your opinion. Giving it doesn't warrant rescinding our agreement. But I might think twice in the future. Come. Let's get some sleep."

And he rose and left the room, leaving her to follow when she decided she was ready. She took her time.

NINETEEN

◆

AT DAWN, DRISKER AND Tarsha flew east out of the riverside village where they had spent the night toward Varfleet, watching as the sunrise brightened the morning skies, the day clear and cloudless. Autumn's snap was in the cool air, and leaves were changing rapidly now from green to red and gold. To the south, the Borderlands were a mass of vibrant colors, their canopies spreading like colorful carpets in the receding shadows. To the north, the walls of the Dragon's Teeth loomed dark and forbidding, as if warding Paranor and the entire Northland against this seasonal change.

Tarsha seemed herself again, eager to talk to him, acting as if nothing had passed between them the night before. She showed no signs of being temperamental or out of sorts, had no interest in asking further about his life or his plans for the Druids and Paranor. Instead, she rambled on about the day and the sweetness of the air and the colors in the distance and her own love of nature and its eccentricities. Drisker found himself smiling, even though he had at first wanted to be cross and abrupt, unable to resist her seemingly boundless enthusiasm. It was so easy to forget that in many ways she was still just a girl. Forgiving her for irritations she probably wasn't even aware of seemed a small concession.

After a while, the conversation tapered off and she returned to a companionable silence. The sun was up by now, the shadows of the receding night mostly dissipated. They tracked along the right bank of the Mermidon, Drisker keeping the two-man low and steady as they flew. It was not a long flight, and there was no reason to speed things up since some of what they needed to do would likely have to wait until nightfall. Concentrating on the countryside ahead, forever watchful for things that didn't belong, Drisker spoke to her.

"When we land, we will be in a public airfield. No one will notice us or bother with us after we pay the attendant for the space to park the vessel. After that, we go into the city and speak to someone who knows where the guilds can be found. Once we know the location of Orsis, we wait until dark to pay a visit. There is no reason to think the guild knows who either of us is by sight. Out of our element, they would have no reason to."

"This sounds risky. You're not exactly the type to blend in."

"Everything about what we are doing is risky. But you have a good point. We must watch their eyes and behavior. If anyone recognizes us, we should be able to tell. We just have to be watching for it."

"So how do we go about finding out what you want to know?"

"What we are looking for is the name of the guild leader. Once we discover his identity, we ask to speak with him."

They went silent then, flying on a bit farther with no exchanges until Tarsha leaned forward once more and touched his arm. He glanced back at her, waiting.

"What if we are caught?" she asked. "What if we have to fight to get clear before we discover what we came for?"

One corner of his mouth quirked slightly. "Sometimes that's what happens. If it does, we simply find another way. We can't predict everything, no matter how hard we try. The trick is in staying safe no matter what happens."

He gave her a smile and turned his attention back to flying. He needed her to accept that things didn't always work out. Knowing when to turn and run and abandon a lost effort was part of being a Druid.

And who knew better than he?

An hour passed, and to the south a rain squall swept across the lower edge of the Runne. As the clouds that fueled it passed on, an unbroken rainbow arced through the sky from horizon to horizon. Drisker and Tarsha watched, awestruck.

"A good omen," the girl offered quietly.

"Hmmm." The Druid looked away.

They reached the juncture of the Mermidon and Runne rivers by midmorning and watched the sprawling tumble of buildings and shipyards that marked the city of Varfleet appear in the distance, their colors and shapes muted and distorted by a screen of shifting mists. The city was not pretty or in any way memorable. It was a working-man's city, a conjoining of public and military commerce with goods carried to and from the city by the rivers and the ships that sailed them. It had been so exclusively in the past, but now freighter airships, newly designed and developed, were beginning to steal away some of the river's business. Airfields sitting at the edges of the city offered quicker transportation south to the Federation cities, where airships controlled the bulk of the transport business because the rivers were too small and too frequently separated from one another. Coming down out of the other lands, river traffic was preferred by Elves, Trolls, and Dwarves, who liked the steady dependability of water channels and found airships highly suspect. It was a clear dichotomy of old and new, a preference based not on reason or proven success but on the familiar versus the unknown.

In many parts of the Four Lands, airships were still an oddity. Small craft were accepted pretty much everywhere, but commercial freighters and military ships-of-the-line remained peculiar to the Southlanders. There was a sense of inevitability in their proliferation, even if the other Races continued to drag their heels for as long as they could manage without losing their commercial edge. To date, they had been successful because the Races largely preferred to remain in their own parts of the world. But as with all things, that was beginning to change, too.

Drisker studied the dockyards and piers carefully as they passed over the city toward the public airfield south. It had been awhile since he'd been back, and he felt the need to reacquaint himself with its geography. As well, it was his habit to always be searching for information that, once spied, might be useful.

On this day, he found much he remembered but nothing that gave him pause.

The docks were in heavy use, the cranes unloading supplies, equipment, and consumer goods onto large flat wagons that would take them to the airfields. Airships were not allowed to land anywhere within the city or on the docks. Varfleet understood well enough what it faced once that happened. Dockworkers swarmed the piers to guide what was being unloaded to the proper storage places or sources of transport. Along the piers, transport ships ground against their heavy bumpers, secured by lines and chains to mooring posts. At the land sides of the huge wooden docks, vendor carts and wagons and storefront businesses served the men who worked there with food and drink, clothing and boots, grappling hooks and mauls, and here and there less respectable but more desirable means for getting through the day.

Tarsha wrinkled her nose. "I could never live here."

Drisker had to agree that the smells were appalling. But he had been born and raised in Varfleet, so they were familiar.

They navigated the air above the city with caution, a small vessel in the midst of ones much larger, a speck against boulders. Staying lower to the roofs of the buildings where the big ships could not safely go, Drisker veered among ponderous towers and decorative spires while maintaining his course. As he did so, he pondered his plan for tracking down Orsis. He knew its reputation well enough and understood it to be something of a chameleon. What he found out in daytime would determine what he needed to be wary of later that night. There must be room left for the unexpected. There must be room for improvisation.

He would start his search at the Starving Fat Man, where he would look for One-Eye Quisk.

When they landed at the airfield, Drisker sought out the manager, found one of his many assistants, logged in a space for the two-man, and paid for a two-day stay. He paid extra, as well, for protection against natural disasters, thievery, and vandalism. It was a clear scam, but in this part of the Borderlands it was always better to be safe than sorry, and the extra credits meant nothing to the Druid compared with the reassurance that they could depend on being able to make a quick escape.

When the transaction was completed and the little craft and its contents secured, Drisker and Tarsha started into the city toward one of its rougher districts. When they reached its perimeter, the changes in the look of the buildings and their occupants were noticeable. The buildings were ramshackle and poorly maintained. The obvious inattention to upkeep indicated a lack of interest in encouraging permanent residence. The people, hanging out the windows and lounging in the doorways and streets, mirrored the buildings.

"Why does anyone live here?" Drisker heard Tarsha mutter.

"Maybe they don't have a choice."

"There is always a choice."

"Maybe they don't have the economic means."

She glanced over. "Don't defend them. They are capable of finding something if they're breathing."

He let the matter drop. She was a small-town girl who found large cities untenable. Fine. Let her say what she felt she needed to. He didn't owe the city a defense anyway.

She went silent then, apparently finished with her assessment of Varfleet's populace. They walked on through milling crowds down narrow streets and alleyways, past increasing numbers of carts and small wagons with vendors wailing their sales pitches as if they believed that somehow their individual voices could be heard above the clamor of so many others. The man and the girl were jostled and shoved, obstacles to be brushed aside. They endured their treatment stoically, one with greater forbearance than the other. Drisker wore his familiar black robes, his dark-bearded visage something of a deterrent to those who threatened to come too close. Tarsha, on the other hand, wearing pants and a short-waisted jacket of heavy leather, was an inviting target with her distinctive white-blond hair and violet eyes.

At one point, the two became separated. When Drisker turned to see where she was, he found her pinned against the wall by two men in similar states of inebriation. One had his hand on her arm, the other in a less acceptable place. She was looking up at them as if petrified.

Uttering a silent oath, the Druid started back immediately. He hadn't taken two steps before Tarsha put her knee into the groin of the man who was groping her, and then seized the wrist of the other man and gave it a vicious twist that left his arm dangling. Both men collapsed into the crowd, their cries loud and painful. Tarsha gave them a quick look and moved away. In seconds, she was back beside Drisker.

"What a cesspool," she offered as they set off again.

Drisker shrugged. "You don't have to tell me. I grew up here."

She looked at him in surprise. "You said nothing about that before."

"I thought this time I should."

She looked back once more at the men curled up on the ground as passersby walked around them without interest. "Are you still worried about me?" she asked.

"I guess I shouldn't be."

"Told you."

"But I am anyway."

No one troubled either of them again as they made their way along the narrow passageways of the district to a street lined with taverns, pleasure houses, and cheap eateries. People here were tightly packed together as they tried to maneuver, and the smells were indescribable.

"You can't possibly feel any connection to this!" the girl snapped at one point, grabbing Drisker by the arm so she wouldn't lose him. "This place is an abomination!"

He glanced at her with interest. "I have survived worse than this," he replied. "Remind me to tell you sometime."

She was jostled so hard she almost went down but somehow managed to keep her feet. "I'm not sure I want to know!"

Ahead, Drisker saw the sign he had been looking for, its bold red letters carved into a board hung from chains above heavy wooden doors set into the wall of a building in which no light could possibly have penetrated due to the fact that all the windows were shuttered.

THE STARVING FAT MAN, it read.

Drisker reached back for Tarsha and pulled her after him as he exited the flow of crowd traffic and stumbled through the doors into darkness.

They stood together for a moment, letting their eyes adjust. Voices reached out to them, disembodied conversations between occupants they could barely see in the gloom. Drisker did not want to stand there too long, feeling exposed, and once he could make out shapes sufficiently to identify them, he pulled Tarsha after him and sat her down at a table. "Wait here."

He left her there in the darkness to give her vision a chance to sharpen, and made his way over to the serving bar. The barkeeper glanced up from the far end and wandered over. "Help you?"

Drisker laid some credits on the counter. "Two ales." He waited until the ale appeared, then pushed all the credits toward the man. "Quisk?" he asked quietly.

The server studied him a moment. "He's not here."

Drisker leaned close. "For me, he will be."

The other man hesitated. "Back room, behind the stairs. Game of Old Bones in progress. Five players. Steady customers, so no trouble, right?"

"Not from me. I'm just here to talk."

He picked up the tankards and returned to Tarsha. He sat down across from her and pushed one in her direction. She picked it up and took a swallow. Her expression said it all, but she apparently felt words were necessary, as well. "Vile," she gasped, choking. She pushed it back at him. "What happens now?"

"We're here to talk to someone. Me, not you. You keep quiet. His name is One-Eye Quisk. You'll understand why when you see him, but try not to stare. He should be able to tell us what we need to know."

He got up from the table and waited for her to follow. When they reached the door the barkeep had indicated earlier, a shadow-draped entry under the stairs, he knocked once and then, without waiting, walked in, Tarsha right behind him.

A round table was set beneath a smokeless lamp that hung from the ceiling on a chain. Five men occupied it; they were playing a game of dice. The men were rough sorts, their faces weathered and scarred. Suspicious looks appeared on their faces as they turned to see who was interrupting. No one spoke.

"Quisk," Drisker said quietly, letting the light reveal his features.

It was the big man on the far side of the table who responded, rising slowly to face him. "Everyone out!" he snapped.

For an instant no one moved. Then one by one the other men rose and filed past the Druid and the girl and left the room. Quisk indicated the open door, and Drisker closed it. The two sat down across from each other, and when Drisker indicated the chair next to him Tarsha joined them.

"This must be important," said Quisk, "to bring you out of your Westland bolt-hole and into the light."

His words were edged with a hint of a challenge. He was tall and rawboned, everything looking a little bigger than it should have, from his head to his hands to his shoulders to his voice. But it was his face that drew your attention. Drisker knew the story well. Many years ago, Quisk had gotten into a knife fight with a man in an alleyway in this very same district of the city. It hadn't gone well. The man had been with friends, and they caught hold of Quisk when his attention was on the knife wielder. While they held him fast, the man with the knife cut out his eye, taking a good portion of the surrounding face with it. The resulting damage left One-Eye with a ragged, dark hollow where his eye had once been and the area surrounding it so badly scarred it could never be repaired.

The shock and the loss of blood had nearly put an end to Quisk, and it was mostly good timing and serendipity that he survived. A patrol of City Watch came by only moments after his maiming and chased off his attackers. They then managed to get Quisk to a healing center and necessary treatment before he bled out. When he was recovered from his injuries, he went looking for the men. They discovered when he did what a mistake it was to have left him alive. In a period of less than two days, he caught up to and killed all of them.

But he was left with his face ruined, and nothing could be done to change that. So he chose not to try to cover the damage with a patch but to wear it openly as if a badge of honor.

Drisker gave him a shrug. "Someone tried to put an end to me a few nights back. Twice, as it happens. I wasn't home the first time so they burned down my house. I was there to welcome them the second."

Quisk studied him dispassionately, his good eye fixing on Tarsha. "Who's this girl? And don't tell me she's your niece."

"She's my student. She's studying weaving under my guidance. Shows promise. Back to why I'm here, if you don't mind? A few of the men who tried to kill me didn't survive the effort. They bore the markings of Orsis Guild."

"Didn't quite kill you, I see. Careless of them. And unusual for Orsis. So now what? You're here looking for them?"

"I thought I should have a talk with them, try to straighten out our differences. But I need some information before that happens."

Quisk made a rude noise. "You might be better off chalking this one up to experience. Forget what I said earlier. Orsis has gotten bigger and meaner with the passing of time. Lots of bad men doing lots of bad things. Maybe you should let sleeping dogs lie."

Drisker smiled bleakly. "Not when the dogs are so determined to take a bite out of me. I need to know where they can be found and who leads them. For purposes of our talk, of course."

"Of course." Quisk leaned back in his chair, his ruined face partially disappearing into shadow. "You want to know where these wharf rats make their lair?"

"And which one is the chief rat. The solution to my problem lies in finding out who hired them."

"Usually, that sort of information is hard to come by. Even for Druids. Bad for business when you reveal that sort of thing. Tends to suggest you can't be trusted to keep your mouth shut. And in the assassin business, if you can't be trusted to do that, you find clients much less eager to hire you. But you already know all this. And I presume it doesn't matter all that much to you, or you wouldn't be here."

Drisker leaned forward. "I intend to ask them to make an exception if they want to square matters."

"For you, I expect they will be more than willing." Quisk rose, retrieved glasses from a shelf, and poured an amber liquid the color of thick caramel from a pitcher. Then he carried two of the three glasses over to Drisker and Tarsha and set them down before going back for the third and taking his seat once more.

"Your good health and success in life," he offered, lifting his glass to each of them. "My sincere wish that you do better at achieving both than I think you will."

They drank, and Tarsha made a sound of approval. "This is good. Much better than the donkey piss they're serving out there."

"True, but don't tell the barkeep. He thinks his product is better, and I find it smarter to let him believe so." Quisk gave her a look and turned to Drisker. "Has she got a dog in this fight?"

Drisker nodded. "Very much so."

Quisk drank deeply of the liquid. "You need to go to a pleasure house called Revelations, down on the lower end of Crean Street on the waterfront. Do you know it? No? Bad place to go, but that's what you have to do. The man you want is called Tigueron. But he's hard to find. Smoke and mirrors, mostly. You want to watch yourself, Drisker Arc."

The Druid nodded. "I make a habit of it."

He finished off the contents of his glass and rose. "We should let you get back to your game. Your help is much appreciated. Not many people I can go to these days that I can trust to keep quiet about my visits. The list of those in the city of Varfleet starts and stops with you. Just so you know."

"I feel the same about you." Quisk finished his glass, as well. "Or I wouldn't have told you what I did. I trust that when you are being tortured and asked who gave up Tigueron's name, you will come up with someone other than myself?"

Drisker smiled. "I am more frightened of what you might do to me should I cross that particular line than I am of any member of an assassins' guild. Come, Tarsha. We have another visit to make."

He watched as Tarsha Kaynin emptied her glass. Together they departed the room and the tavern and went back out into the city.

TWENTY

---◆---

DRISKER FOUND THEM AN upscale inn where they could spend the remainder of the day in relative peace and quiet, an establishment that catered to businessmen and government officials and championed food over drink. It was farther into the city, away from the dockyards and waterfront, and the noise was less noticeable here.

They ate lunch in the dining room, a space separate from the bar. Then Drisker left Tarsha behind to rest while he went out to locate Crean Street and determine the particulars of the look and feel of Revelations. The girl did not like the idea of being excluded, but after giving him a look that clearly expressed her displeasure she surprised him by letting the matter drop. He had expected her to argue, certain she would not stand for it. But perhaps she was learning it was necessary to defer to him every now and then. Tarsha Kaynin, he was discovering, was full of surprises.

The innkeeper was able to help with finding Crean Street, offering directions that Drisker found vague but manageable. It took him the better part of an hour to find the street itself, mostly due to the foot traffic that clogged every street and alleyway within six blocks of the water's edge. Carts and wagons and animals added to the congestion, and by the time he started his walk down to his ultimate destination, he was wishing he had taken a carriage.

But a carriage would have been too obvious for this part of the city, and Drisker wanted to remain anonymous. So he suffered the endless walk, the jostling, and the unpleasant sights and smells of the city, thinking as he did that he liked Varfleet these days no better than Tarsha did, birthplace or no. It was odd how what you didn't mind when you were young and growing up became less palatable as you aged. Perhaps that explained his refusal to accept the foolish recalcitrance and pointless obstreperousness of the Druids in recent years. His once-famous patience was frayed and prickly, and he more frequently found the need to settle matters with magic's sharp-edged blade than with the blunt edges of reason and hope.

His walk along the waterfront was rife with sounds and sights and smells, but the deep misgivings of his thoughts kept him from being distracted. While certain of his own abilities and experience, he was wondering for the first time about the girl's. Perhaps he was putting too much faith in her adaptability and quick mind. She was the ideal student, save for her willingness to risk herself so recklessly. It didn't matter that the worst risk she had taken had been for him. It didn't matter that the most recent risk had been with inebriated, drunken buffoons who were clearly overmatched. Her confidence in herself and her determination to see done what she believed right was a dangerous combination. She was good, but there were those who were better. Worse, there was always the chance that her luck would run out.

But he knew that leaving her behind at this point would be worse than including her. It would undermine everything he had worked so hard to instill in her, reduce her confidence to uncertainty, and leave her worse off than when she had set out to find him. That was both unfair and unacceptable. She was better off taking risks while he was there to watch over her than being made to think herself useless.

But for the moment, as he looked along the length of Crean Street, wondering which way to turn and how to locate the pleasure house, he had more pressing problems to occupy him.

"Spare a coin, old man?" a ragged boy asked, tugging at his elbow.

He was young and dirty, and the Druid stared at him openly. "Why should I give you a coin?" he asked.

The boy shrugged. "Maybe because you look like you've got one to spare? Never hurts to ask."

"Tell you what." Drisker bent close to him, ignoring the smell and the sores on his face. "Are you willing to work a bit for this coin?"

"Might be."

"Are you good at finding your way around this district?"

The boy nodded. "Born here. Lived here all my life. You name it, I can take you there."

"You know a place called Revelations?"

"Sure." The boy's mouth pursed. "Though you don't seem the sort who would go to a place like that. It's not safe. Take my advice and stay away. That alone should be worth a coin."

He held out his hand, his gaze steady. Drisker liked him at once.

"It's worth more than that, and I shall pay you accordingly if you guide me there now, and again tonight. Two times, and then you disappear and do not come near it again. What say you to that?"

He dropped a fifty-credit note into the boy's hand. The boy stared at it suspiciously, letting it sit there undisturbed. "You don't expect anything else of me, do you, grandfather? Nothing but what you asked? You're not one of those sorts, are you?"

"I expect nothing more than what I asked. I have business that requires your guide services. Another fifty if you provide them."

The boy nodded eagerly, his hand closing on the note. "Come along then. Try to keep up. I go fast, and I go smart."

And he was off through the crowds.

It was a chase more than a guiding. The boy slipped through the seething masses like water through sand, quicksilver in his movements and certain in his direction. At times, the Druid lost him completely, slowed by his inability to pass through gaps with the alacrity of the boy and his own considerable bulk as an adult. Now and then, the boy had to come back for him, laughing as he did so—although not in an insolent or critical way but with genuine pleasure at the success with which he was able to demonstrate his skills at dodging around and weaving through seemingly impassable obstacles.

The chase wore on, with Drisker growing steadily more irritated and increasingly questioning his wisdom in thinking a guide might help. He would have been better off, he thought, if he had simply continued on alone and relied on his own instincts. Now and then—accepting reluctantly that on this occasion it was unfortunately the former—he found himself wondering if courageous quests and ultimate reckonings were beyond him, and his days of performing the active tasks that being a Druid frequently demanded were drawing to a close.

All of a sudden, as if conjured from the masses of people and with no warning at all, the boy reappeared right in front of him grinning broadly. "We're here!"

He pointed down the street through the crowds to the dark bulk of a structure consisting of towers and spires and flags that hovered over the surrounding buildings like a huge governess over a passel of cowed children. Its windows were shuttered and barred, and the doors off its balconies tightly closed, and there was about it an air of repression and danger that was unmistakable. Those passing by on the streets did what they refused to do at any other point during their various journeys—they shifted direction and gave the building a wide berth while keeping their gazes directed elsewhere.

Even though he was already certain of the answer, Drisker asked the question anyway. "Are you sure?"

"Am I quicker, slicker, and trickier than you, grandfather?"

"I'll take that as a yes."

The boy grinned. "Where do you want me to be tonight when we meet?"

"Do you know the Three Kings?"

"Know it, and keep my distance. They don't like boys like me hanging about. That where you are?"

"Come by tonight. Ask for me at the door. Show me a shortcut from there to Revelations and I'll double your payment."

"Lucky for me, I know one." The boy was grinning excitedly. But then he went suddenly sober. "You're being awful good to me. Why is that?"

Drisker looked off toward Revelations for a moment and then back again. "I was born here, in this district, like you. It was a long time ago. Call it professional courtesy."

"Call it what you like, grandfather. You got my services long as you need them."

"Then go on. Get yourself to somewhere else. Stay out of trouble."

The boy started off. "And what fun would that be?" he called back. Then he was gone.

When Drisker returned to the inn, he found Tarsha sitting at the window gazing down at the busy street below, a curious look on her face. "Did it go as expected?" she asked.

He nodded wordlessly. Something wasn't right. He couldn't put his finger on it, but something was out of place. Then he noticed her face was flushed and her clothing slightly rumpled. "Are you all right?" he asked finally.

"I just need a nap. I couldn't sleep before and went out to look around. Now I'm tired."

She went over to the bed and without another word stretched out and fell asleep. He remained where he was, propped up in the only chair in the room, pondering his uneasiness. What was it she had done? Because she most certainly had done something.

Eventually, he lost interest and his thoughts drifted back to the events of earlier. He had spent time after the boy's departure studying Revelations from several angles, searching for ways to enter and exit the pleasure house, particularly ways to escape it if things should go wrong. There were three doors available—front, back, and a cellar door that opened through the ground on the south side of the bulky structure. Windows were problematic, since they all appeared to be sealed. There were guards at the front and back, warding both entrances against uninvited guests. There would be more guards inside where business was conducted. But without going in, it was impossible to tell in what part of the building the Orsis Guild headquarters were located.

It was just before the girl woke from her sleep that he found the answer he was looking for. She probably wouldn't like it, but it was their best chance for gaining admittance and finding the man called Tigueron. Once they got that far, they would have to rely on instinct and opportunity.

"Feeling better?" he asked her.

She yawned, stretched, and walked over to the basin to wash her face. "You were gone longer than I expected," she said, toweling her face dry.

"I had a hard time getting through the crowds. It would have helped if I'd had some help getting there."

"Perhaps a guide?" she said.

He started to reply, and then abruptly he realized the truth.

"Yes, a guide," he said. "A guide would have helped. But then you already knew that, didn't you?"

She gave him a look. "I did."

"You followed me."

"I did."

"Right from the hotel to Revelations. You saw the boy. You saw everything."

She faced him, unabashed. "I wanted to test myself. I wanted to see if I could manage it without being caught. You never saw me, did you?"

He walked over and sat on the bed. "Is there some reason you are incapable of doing anything I tell you to do? Do you not realize there are reasons for asking for your cooperation, reasons that have to do with keeping you safe? Why are you so obstinate about everything?"

"I don't want to be kept safe. Don't you understand? I want to be educated. I want to learn what you know and do what you do. I want to be what you are, and I can't do that if you keep me shut up in a room."

"You are my student, not my equal!" he snapped angrily. "You aren't entitled to do everything I do. There are skills that will help you find your way there and keep you alive in the process, but you haven't mastered them yet. If you try to take shortcuts, you will eventually damage yourself—maybe seriously. What is so difficult for you to understand about this?"

She came over and sat down next to him. She looked small and beaten, but there was determination etched in her young features. "What is so difficult for *you* to understand? I have a brother who is half mad and on his way to being completely insane. The magic is doing this to him. I have that same magic. I have to learn to understand it quickly, because I don't want to end up like him!"

She refused to look at him and suddenly there were tears leaking from her eyes. She turned away to hide them, wiping at her face with her hand.

"Now look what you've done," she muttered.

Drisker gave her a moment to collect herself, and then touched her shoulder.

"Tarsha, look at me," he said.

When she failed to respond, he reached over, placed his hands on her shoulders, and gently turned her toward him. "Tarsha, I know you are struggling with your brother and the threat of his magic. I know you are worried that time is slipping away from you. But it isn't wise to try to move too quickly, even when it seems you must. You do not help yourself or others by doing so. Thinking you can skip steps and cut corners and ignore risks is foolish. You think I hold you back by asking you to sit tight, but you are wrong. I am trying to teach you. I recognize the need for haste as clearly as you do, but the possibility of harm to a loved one does not excuse rash behavior or disregard for your own safety. You help no one by hurting yourself. You have to step back from these urges and try to trust me a bit. If it is possible to save your brother, you and I will do so. Together."

He paused, taking a deep breath. "Now about this other thing. This is the first I have heard anything about you fearing your own magic. I have had time to study you, to see how you use the magic, to watch you grow as a magic user. If there were any real danger present, I would have recognized it by now. But I've seen nothing. So why have you waited until now to speak to me of this?"

She was already shaking her head, as if to say she couldn't bring herself to answer. But he squeezed her shoulders reassuringly and whispered her name softly. "Tell me."

"I don't want to talk about it."

Petulant, embarrassed.

"Tarsha?"

"No, I can't."

"Tarsha, please! Tell me."

She closed her eyes. "I was afraid you would send me home if you knew."

It caught him by surprise. "Why would you think that?"

"Why wouldn't I? You were quick enough to abandon the Druids when you found them more trouble than they were worth. If I suddenly announced my fears about using my magic, how long would it take you to decide that I was more trouble than I was worth? You were my last hope for helping my brother. I couldn't afford to risk losing that chance by telling you my personal concerns. So I kept quiet."

Drisker was appalled. "But the situations are entirely different, Tarsha! My decision to leave the Druids was based on the actions of people I disliked and distrusted. I don't feel that way about you—nor would I feel that way if you were struggling with your magic. You're not someone who has failed or disappointed me. You've done everything you've been tasked with doing, and you show great promise. I would never abandon you because of your fears. Never."

She studied him a moment. "I don't know if I can believe that. I haven't had much to believe in for a long time. If I'm wrong about this . . ."

"Think about it. If you were wrong, you would be on your way home this very minute. You've told me of your fears, and I found them groundless. I don't see a weakness in you. I don't see any loss of control over the wishsong. I would take no chances with you if I did. There really isn't anything else I can say."

She was looking away again, her face unreadable. He was losing her. He decided to take a chance. "Listen to me. We have to stop talking about this, at least for now. I need you to help me with Orsis Guild. I need you if I'm to do what I came here for. Can you put this other business aside until that's done? I have a plan for tonight, but it needs you to make it work."

Her eyes found his and he saw her sudden interest. "What sort of plan? Tell me."

So with patience and encouragement, he did.

• • •

It was twilight and rapidly turning full dark when the boy appeared at the front door of the inn. Drisker and Tarsha were in their room when word was brought. The boy was asking for the Druid, waiting downstairs for him.

Drisker was on his feet at once. "Are you ready?" he asked her.

Tarsha wasn't sure. She was still upset over their earlier conversation, still troubled by her concerns over what was going to happen. It was all well and good for the Druid to reassure her she would not be sent home after revealing her fears about controlling her magic. But after she had served her purpose and helped him find the men who had attacked him, what reassurance did she have that he wouldn't change his mind? Warring with that particular problem was her displeasure with the plan he had concocted to get them inside Revelations. The only thing that kept her from refusing to participate was her belief that it would probably work.

She rose with him. "Yes, I'm ready."

The boy was standing just outside the front door, a lean and ragged scrap of humanity, another bit of flotsam and jetsam washed up on the shores of the city. Immediately she disliked him. Maybe it was the way he looked, and maybe it was something she sensed about him, but it was there.

"You didn't say you were bringing your daughter," the boy announced, making a face.

"He didn't say he was bringing his daughter because that's not who I am!" she snapped at once.

The boy backed off a step, holding his hands up defensively. "All right, Miss Sharp Tongue. I didn't mean anything by it. I didn't realize it was like that." He paused, giving her a sly smile. "Kind of young to be his bedmate, though, aren't you?"

She almost flew at him, but Drisker stepped between them quickly. "She is my student. That's all you need to know. Can we get going?"

She was still fuming as the boy led them through the city, choosing a route that had so many twists and turns she was lost almost instantly. If she had to find her way back alone, she was certain she couldn't do it. Not that she wouldn't be willing to try, if only to be rid of this obnoxious boy.

They continued on for what seemed an endless amount of time, following a series of winding streets that ran one into the next and never suggesting at any point what direction they were taking. The fall of darkness did nothing to stem the flow of foot traffic; the city of Varfleet was as vibrant and alive at nighttime as during the day. It had been difficult enough for her to follow them when it was light. It was much worse by lamplight, and she had to work very hard to stay close enough that she would not lose them entirely.

She managed it but barely. She grew steadily more convinced the boy was deliberately trying to lose her.

And then they were there, the bulky silhouette of Revelations looming ahead, cracks of interior light seeping through closed shutters, a pervasive sense of gloom and desolation hanging over everything. The boy took them to within fifty feet, keeping to the shadows, being careful not to do anything to expose them to whoever might be watching.

Beneath the awning of a shop across the way from the entrance, he brought them to a stop. "Close enough?" he asked.

Drisker bent to him, his voice soft. "I want you to stay right here. Keep out of sight. Don't do anything to call attention to yourself. Wait for our return. It might be several hours. Can you do that?"

"I'm yours for the night, grandfather." The boy glanced at Tarsha. "I don't know about taking her in there. It isn't a fit place for a young girl."

"I can take care of myself," she hissed at him, unable to keep the irritation from her voice.

He shrugged. "You probably have experiences I don't know about." His eyes shifted back to Drisker. "But be careful in there, grandfather. Bad things live in the shadows."

Tarsha caught a glimpse of the Druid's smile. "Then I'll stay clear of them."

He walked out from beneath the awning with Tarsha at his heels and started across the street. They wove their way through a steady flow of traffic and were almost run over by a cart that barreled through at a reckless rate before arriving on the far side unharmed, if much subdued.

Drisker turned to her. "Are you clear on what's to happen? Any questions about anything we're going to do?"

She shook her head. "Who *is* that boy? What's his name?"

The Druid shrugged. "I don't know. I didn't ask."

"So if he abandons us, we have no way of ever finding him again?"

"I guess that's so. But he won't abandon us."

"Your faith in street urchins is much greater than mine. I suppose you know them better than a country girl from the Westland, though."

"You don't much like him, do you?"

The question took her aback. "He's all right. He's just kind of cocky for someone who doesn't have much."

Drisker put a hand on her shoulder. "In the world of street urchins, Tarsha, you make use of what you can. Come."

TWENTY-ONE

DRISKER LED HER ALONG the walkway fronting the Orsis building, taking advantage of the open space that everyone else studiously avoided. When they reached the front steps, they climbed to an entry within a sheltering alcove, and the Druid rapped sharply on the heavy wood of the closed doors. Minutes passed. Tarsha glanced back at the people in the streets, many of who were glancing at them with undisguised curiosity. In the pale glow of the streetlamps, she thought she could discern expressions of wariness and fear. She stared back boldly until they looked away, and then looked away herself.

The door opened. An old man with scars crisscrossing his face and eyes the color of mud was standing in front of them. He looked as if a strong wind might blow him away. "State your business."

"We seek a meeting with Orsis Guild," Drisker said quietly, sounding as if he were a man seeking discretion.

"Do you have need of their services?" The old man's eyes were sharp with suspicion. "Or is this regarding favors from the pleasure house ladies?"

"We require the guild's services. My daughter was . . ."

A gnarled hand lifted quickly. "The nature of your business is not my concern. Come in. Follow me. Have you weapons?"

Drisker shook his head. Tarsha indicated her long knife, belted beneath her cloak.

"Put it there," the old man ordered, pointing at a table to one side. Tarsha did so. "If you hide others, it will go badly for you," he added.

When neither responded, he beckoned. "This way."

Hunching in the manner of one who has long been lame and learned to make the best of it, the old man led them down a series of hallways and past intersecting corridors and closed doors until they reached a set of stairs. From there they descended until they had arrived at a faintly lit corridor burrowing into the interior of the building. With a perfunctory gesture, their guide beckoned them forward. Tarsha looked around with a growing apprehension. Here the shadows were much more ominous and pervasive, as if the light from the scattering of lamps that dotted the corridor walls was an intrusion barely tolerated. Perhaps the boy had been right. It did feel as if bad things lived in the shadows—though, if so, they were hiding themselves well. She wondered what their purpose was. And how the boy knew they were there.

Wrapped in oppressive silence, they followed the old man through a warren of dank corridors and extended patches of deep gloom. The air was chilly and smelled of mold. At places, the floor and walls showed damp stains and cracks. Tarsha tried hard to memorize their route, preparing herself for the possibility that they might need to find their way back alone. She was certain their present location was several levels beneath the streets of the city, but she was unsure of how many.

At the corridor's end, a widening of the walls indicated something out of the ordinary waited ahead. Sure enough, huge double metal doors barred further passage, heavy and impenetrable. The old man moved to one side and rapped on a wooden panel set out from the stone of the wall. The sound echoed all around them.

A panel in the wall slid back and eyes appeared. "Clients," the old man said, indicating his companions.

The eyes studied them for a moment, and then heavy locks were released and one of the two great doors swung open. A solitary guard, armed and armored, stood waiting. Heads bent close, voices kept low, the old man and the guard exchanged words Tarsha could not make out. Then the old man beckoned, and the Druid and the girl followed him inside.

It felt to Tarsha as if they had stepped into the jaws of a great metal beast. The walls, ceiling, and floor of the room were sheathed in iron plates. There were no windows or doors save the ones through which they had entered—although it was difficult to be sure, because the only light was from a pair of lamps bracketing the entry through which they had passed. Halfway across the room, a forest of iron bars warded a space so impenetrably dark it was impossible to see what lay beyond it. There appeared to be no one else in the room, yet Tarsha sensed immediately that others were present.

The old man retreated through the door and closed it behind him as he departed. "Stand where you are," the guard ordered.

The pair waited. There was the softest rustle of movement in the gloom behind the bars, a whisper of fabric, a scraping against stone. Tarsha was tempted to summon magic that would ward her against whatever was about to happen, but Drisker had forbidden any conjuring except as a last resort. Using magic would reveal more about them than he wished known.

A bank of smokeless lights abruptly appeared in the gloom behind the bars. Three men sat at a table, cloaked and hooded. They wore masks of molded black leather, and they faced the Druid as if they had been carved from stone.

"Explain why you are here," a voice ordered.

Tarsha took a moment to glance over at the guard next to her. He was a huge forbidding figure, cloaked and hooded like the men behind the bars but infinitely larger, with massive arms and a broad chest. She didn't doubt for one minute that he could snap her neck without much effort. This wasn't someone you wanted to cross when all your weapons had been taken away. Which is exactly what the assassins' guild must have concluded when they hired him as their protector.

"We seek redress for a great wrong perpetrated against my daughter," Drisker announced, indicating Tarsha. "A man—a Federation government official—to whom she was pledged in marriage took advantage of her and then canceled the wedding without cause. He left her with child and refuses to acknowledge his responsibility. He has kept her dowry. He is without honor. I seek to secure a contract on his life."

For a moment, no one said anything. Then, from behind the barrier, the voice spoke again. "The cost will be high."

Drisker made a dismissive motion. "No cost is too high. This man is an abomination and must be made to answer for what he has done. My daughter is defiled! I want him dead!"

He certainly sounded as if he did, Tarsha thought. The outraged father determined to avenge his wronged child. It generated an odd feeling in her. It almost made her wish it were true. That he really was her father and she his child. That he cared about her enough to actually feel as he pretended to these men. It caught her by surprise, unexpected and alarming. It was an eye-opening moment.

Then she shook it off, remembering her part. She tried hard to look pitiful in an effort to help convince the men, but false feeling didn't come easily to her, and after a few moments she gave up trying. Instead, she settled for keeping her head down and her eyes demurely lowered.

"Let's be sure we understand each other," the voice behind the barrier said. He named an outrageous figure for payment, but Drisker only shrugged his indifference.

"Credits must be paid in advance," the voice continued. "All of them."

Drisker shrugged a second time. "That will require some assurances from you. Assurances that you will do what you claim you can do and that proof of your success will be provided. And I want those assurances to come personally from Tigueron."

A long pause. "You will do as we tell you." The voice was hard and uncompromising. "There will be no conditions. You do not require assurances."

"Ah, but I do. I have it on rather good authority that you took a contract recently that you failed to carry out. That would suggest you might not be able to fulfill mine."

The pause that followed was much longer. "We have never failed to carry out a contract! Orsis does not fail."

"No?" the Druid said quietly. "Two words. Drisker Arc."

Tarsha forced herself not to look at him. What was he doing? If he gave them away, they would never leave the room alive. He had explained to her the backstory he intended to use to persuade them of the legitimacy of his business, but he'd said nothing of this.

"Who are you?" the voice asked, and there was a dark, unpleasant undertone to it.

"I am a father who is concerned for his daughter. I am a man who is used to getting his way, and I intend to get it here. I will not allow you to bully me or lie to me. I will not pay you without assurances that you can actually do what you promise. You have a fine reputation, and a great record. You should be willing to stand behind it. Will you do so or not? If not, I can easily go elsewhere, although that would pain me. And do not think to harm me because of what I have said. The Prime Minister of the Federation is a personal friend, and he knows I am here."

The men behind the barrier did not respond. Instead, they leaned close to one another and spoke in whispers. But Tarsha noticed something telling in their body language. The men to either side seemed to defer to the one in the middle. She glanced at Drisker and caught his barely perceptible nod of recognition. He saw it, too.

He bent close to her. "Can you disable the guard?"

She stared at him in disbelief. *Now* what was he planning? She took a moment to look over at the monster standing not six feet away, huge and imposing, his armor gleaming in the dim light and his weapons almost as big as she was. Was there any way of doing what Drisker asked? Could she render him unconscious fast enough to prevent him from getting to her?

"Yes," she whispered in reply.

He nodded. "Do so when I give the word."

Fresh movement from behind the barrier drew their attention.

"Drisker Arc is dead," said the familiar voice. "Who said he wasn't?"

The three men were looking out at them again. It was still impossible to tell who was speaking, but Tarsha had already decided the one in the middle was in charge. It would stand to reason that this was Tigueron.

Drisker, however, did not seem satisfied. "It doesn't matter who told me. It matters that you may have failed to carry out a contract. I think we have played enough games, Tigueron. That is you, is it not? The old man who greeted us at the front door said you were here. Pretense and ceremony are fine for those who don't know the workings of the guilds, but I am not one of those men. Give me the assurance I have asked for, and we can get on with this."

The silence was deafening. Tarsha readied herself for whatever was going to happen next. The tension was so cold she shivered in spite of herself. The look and feel of this claustrophobic, prison-like room were deliberate. The materials from which it had been built suggested as much, whispering of unspeakable uses. It was much more than just a place for an interview with prospective clients. Some who entered never left.

She glanced around carefully and for the first time noticed the drains in the floor. Placed there to make cleaning up easier.

It took everything she had to keep from grabbing Drisker and pulling him away.

"Very well," said the voice, a hint of anger and resignation in its tone. "I give you my word that what you pay for will be carried out."

At once Drisker glanced at Tarsha and whispered, "Now."

Without waiting for her response, he extended his hands, summoned his Druid magic, and blew out the barrier separating them from the three men. The iron bars tore from their brackets and slammed into the table and the men sitting behind it, and everything went flying backward into the wall behind.

Tarsha wheeled on the guard, her wishsong sounding a deep, mournful note. She was almost too slow; the giant was much quicker than she would have expected. His massive hands were inches from her face when the magic lifted him from his feet and hurled him away. He struck the wall to the right with stunning force and slumped down, unconscious.

Drisker was still attacking. A hand gesture sealed the door through which they had entered. Another sealed the door on the back wall that served the three unfortunates of Orsis Guild. He strode swiftly through smoke and debris and was on top of them in seconds. One was trying to rise, but the heavy barrier held him pinned in place. The Druid silenced him with a single blow. Another was not moving at all. Tigueron had worked himself free and was trying to reach the sealed door, his frantic movements betraying the terror his masked face could not.

Drisker reached out and yanked the fleeing man backward, holding him up as if he were a toy.

"Tigueron?" he hissed. "Are you in there?"

He yanked off the assassin leader's mask, and as he did so Tigueron's blades appeared as if by magic in his hands. Tarsha used the wishsong in two quick bursts—pinpoint strikes that sent the weapons flying, the hands that held them numbed. Drisker glanced at her and gave an approving nod. "A little careless of me."

Then he shook Tigueron like a rag doll and threw him down. "Stay there," he warned, pointing threateningly.

Tigueron lay still, glaring at him. He was a big man, but the Druid had manhandled him effortlessly. "You won't get out of here alive, you know."

Drisker bent close. "Nor will you, likely. Not after what you tried to do. Did I fail to mention my name? It's Drisker Arc."

There was a flash of genuine fear in Tigueron's face, and Tarsha, standing where she could watch while still keeping an eye on the room, did not mistake its meaning. Drisker was kneeling now, his face quite close to that of the other man, his dark features gone almost black with rage.

"I should kill you and be done with it," he hissed. "Do to you what you would have done to me. But I need something from you. If you give it to me, I will let you live."

Tigueron sneered. "How can I believe that?"

"I don't know. Find a way. It's the only hope you have. Now listen closely, as I don't intend to say this more than once. I don't care all that much about you. I only care about the man who hired you. When did you make the contract?"

Tigueron hesitated, and then shrugged. "Somewhere around six weeks back. I was to wait until the end of the month to fulfill my end of the bargain."

"He paid you, then?"

"Letter of credit. I cashed it the next day to be sure it was good."

"A letter of credit? No gold or silver or coin? You must have been convinced the letter would be honored."

"Convinced enough. And I was right to be convinced. It was a goodly amount—although it ended up costing me too many members of my guild. And now it will likely cost me something more, won't it?"

Drisker ignored him. "Tell me his name."

The assassin leader's face underwent several rapid changes of expression, but in the end it was one of harsh determination. "Go ahead and kill me! If I start naming names, I am a dead man anyway. Your reputation for Druid wisdom should tell you that much. Except you're not a Druid anymore, are you? You're an outcast, an exile, a man shunned by your own kind. Must hurt quite a bit, I imagine."

"You're wasting your time if you think that you can anger me sufficiently that I will put you out of your misery. You're going to tell me what I want to know. Do you know why? Because, sooner or later, whoever hired you is going to find out you've failed. They're going to discover I'm still alive. And when that happens, your reputation as a reliable hire is finished. Likely, whoever finds out they paid for nothing will come after you. I am the only one who can save you. Reveal the name of whoever hired you and I'll silence him. No one needs to know how I found out. That stays between you and me."

He placed two fingers at the juncture of Tigueron's chin and throat, a soft spot on the neck that lacked adequate protection, and pressed in hard on his windpipe. "You are wasting my time. Decide now."

A look passed between them, followed by a long pause. Then Tigueron leaned forward slightly and whispered something. Drisker Arc backed away again, shaking his head. Tigueron whispered something more, and finally the Druid nodded. Then he took his hands away from the assassin's throat, placed them on either side of the other man's head in a curiously gentle way, and gave a vicious twist. Tarsha, standing twenty feet away, heard the snapping of neck bones.

The Druid rose, wiping his hands on the dead man's robes and then patting him gently on the head. Tarsha watched him carefully as he walked over to her. "I thought he told you what you wanted to know," she said. "It seemed like he did."

"Oh, he told me. I just didn't like the idea of giving him another chance at trying to kill me. I didn't think I could trust his word to let things be. Better to end it here." She caught a glimpse of a sad smile. "I suppose my word's not so good after all."

His face was grim enough that she did not think it wise to pursue the matter further.

Drisker unsealed the door leading out by withdrawing the magic that bound it and led Tarsha back through the underground warren the way they had come, accurately following the escape route she had worked so hard to memorize, tracking it as if she were telling him verbally where to go every step of the way. In no time they were back in the front hall. The old man was waiting. He opened the door for them as they left, avoiding eye contact and saying nothing.

Once out on the street again, they crossed through the crowds to the other side and found the boy waiting. "Take us back to the inn," the Druid ordered and went silent.

The return trip seemed to take forever. Some of it was due to the continued presence of heavy foot traffic in the streets and the raucous intrusion of the city's nightlife surging in and out of pleasure houses, gaming parlors, and taverns, the cacophony of the crowds drowning out the possibility of any meaningful conversation. And some of it was due to the reluctance of anyone to speak.

For Tarsha, she was still coming to terms with what she had just witnessed. She could not stop thinking about how swiftly Drisker Arc had dismantled that carefully secured room and gotten to those three men who believed themselves safe behind a barrier of iron bars. She kept seeing him as he sprang into motion—a black-robed dervish, a dark wraith with even darker intentions. He had been a force of nature, a creature of such resolve that he willed what he wanted to happen into being. He possessed astonishing strength, and he was ruthless. He had given his word to spare Tigueron's life and then gone back on it. He had killed the Orsis assassin without hesitation, without a moment's second thought.

What must it take to be like that? What sorts of personal hardships did you have to endure before you became that cold?

She wasn't sure. She didn't know that much about him. There were stories about her mentor, but she wondered how many more remained secret. She thought again of his admission that he had been born and raised on the streets of Varfleet, like their young guide. How many tales of that period in his life lay buried within him? She could not begin to imagine, and she wasn't sure she wanted to find out.

They had reached the inn when the boy turned to Drisker and held out his hand, waiting to be paid. For just an instant—one terrible instant—she wondered if the Druid would go back on his word. If he might even kill the lad. "Grandfather?" the boy said, sensing what she did. "Our agreement?"

Drisker nodded and put his hand on the boy's slender shoulder. "You did well tonight. You kept your word, and you deserve every credit I promised to pay you. My thanks."

He reached inside his cloak and produced a handful of notes. The boy's eyes widened. "This is too much! We agreed on a smaller amount."

"I am changing the agreement. Consider it a bribe. I may need your services again one day."

Tarsha exhaled in relief. She hadn't realized she had been holding her breath.

She was moving toward the inn door when she heard the boy say to her, "You're very pretty."

She blushed deeply and was immediately irritated with herself. Drisker, watching, shook his head.

"I forgot to ask you earlier," he called after to the boy, who was already moving off into the mix of city lights and crowds. "What is your name?"

The boy turned. "Ohmsford!" he shouted back. "Shea Ohmsford!"

Then he was gone, disappearing into the night, leaving Drisker and Tarsha staring after him in disbelief.

TWENTY-TWO

◆

"HE SHOULDN'T HAVE DONE that. He shouldn't have. He shouldn't have done it."

Over and over, like a litany, Tavo kept repeating the words, all as if to measure the steps he was taking along the roadway he was following, a refrain to accompany his progress. He spoke the words in a low monotone, without thinking about them, without tiring. His mind was spinning as he looked back two days to what he had been forced to do in that inn of cutthroats and monsters.

Forced!

It wasn't his fault he'd killed them. It wasn't his fault they were dead. They had lied to him and then tried to rob him. They would have killed him if he hadn't saved himself. He recalled hands and blades and hard looks in a frightening rush of images. They intended to hurt him and he hurt them, instead.

They brought it on themselves!

They had caused it to happen!

Like his parents. Like his uncle. Like Squit Malk. Like all the others, although he no longer remembered who they were. It really didn't seem to matter much anymore.

His concentration broke. He stopped his mumbling and his voice trailed off. "Why did they do this to me?" he said to Fluken.

Fluken did not reply. He never replied, although that didn't much matter because Tavo always knew what he was thinking anyway. Fluken was his best friend—had been since Tavo discovered his magic. Fluken came to him unbidden, but with clear intent. He was there to be his friend. He was there to help him understand. He was there to listen. Fluken was the best friend Tavo had never had. He was always close by when Tavo used his magic and often encouraged him in his efforts. He never criticized, and he never attempted to pass judgment. He never complained, and he never contradicted.

"We have a long way to go," he told Fluken. "We have to find Tarsha."

Fluken gave him a sly look and a wink.

"She hurt me," Tavo added vaguely. "Hurt me inside."

They were walking along in the late-morning hours, on their way to the next village, and he was already starting to feel more than a little tired. "It will be necessary to show her. It will be necessary to hurt Tarsha, too. Not my fault. You can see that, can't you?"

As usual, Fluken just looked at him. But Tavo knew he agreed, and that his continuing presence was an affirmation of his decided course. It was reassuring. It was good to know Fluken would always be there.

Something he had once believed to be true of Tarsha, as well.

He stopped talking for a while, content to follow the road without paying much attention, his thoughts again drifting back to the tavern and the men he had left there, the life sucked out of them. Such men did not deserve to live. They wanted to hurt him. They wanted to steal his money and his possessions and cast him away like garbage. Like all the others, these men hadn't known what he could do or they might have left him alone. How many had there been? Twenty, perhaps? Not that it mattered to him. Not really.

No more than Tarsha mattered now. But he wondered, suddenly, what would happen after he found her. If he killed her, what would become of him then? His home and the people who had tried to claim him as their child were gone. His old life was finished. He would have to begin life over, and he had no idea where to start. Once it would have involved his sister. But if she were gone, he would be alone. This troubled him more than it should have. Suddenly he was crying, the pain of his loneliness excruciating. His stomach clutched and nausea swept through him. He doubled over and retched until his stomach had emptied.

Off to one side, in the sunshine of a small grove of trees, birds were singing. He hated the sound. He screamed out at them, releasing his magic in a fiery torrent that shattered limbs and incinerated leaves. The birds went silent.

Inexplicably, he felt a terrible urge to curl up and die.

He almost gave in to it, but then he remembered his plan to find Tarsha, and the feeling gradually lessened and then passed altogether.

"I can stop using the magic anytime I want," he declared to Fluken as they neared the next village. Dusk was settling in, and there were lights visible on the porches of houses and businesses; the buildings were set close together surrounding a small village green. He wondered again what the name of the village was, but it didn't matter. All it had to offer was a chance for him to rest before going on.

Fluken, as usual, said nothing.

"I can, you know. I can quit. I know how to do it."

He was speaking now to Squit Malk, his uncle, and the man and woman who had been his parents as they walked beside him. Like Fluken, they said nothing. They were growing bolder, he thought. They had never dared to walk this close before. He shivered momentarily. He had no reason to be afraid, but their nearness was troubling. Maybe they wanted something from him. But it was too late for that. He had nothing to give them.

"Get away from me!" he shouted finally, his hatred for them surfacing.

They didn't even bother to look at him, their dead eyes fixed on the empty space in front of them as they walked.

He tried to remember what they had been like in life, but he had already pretty much forgotten. Most of the particulars of the events that formed the building blocks of his early life were lost to him. His mind was fuzzy these days, and the part of it that still worked was consumed with thoughts of Tarsha's betrayal. Everything else seemed unimportant—even the reasons behind what he had done to his fellow travelers.

He traipsed along in sullen silence through rows of silent buildings, peering into the approaching darkness, searching for a place where he might find shelter for a few hours. It had been raining again, although he hadn't noticed until now, and he was soaked through and chilled to the bone. The unpleasantness and discomfort persisted, but his thoughts were on other things, the burning in his heart all-consuming.

Tarsha.

Why?

Ahead, a man was working in his yard, covering planting beds and their fruit-bearing vines and bushes with netting, his own clothes as wet as Tavo's. The man's house looked warm and inviting, and he was tempted to walk over and ask if he could spend the night. But then the man's wife called to him from within and Tavo heard the voices of children and thought better of it. The man turned and waved to him but Tavo just kept walking.

He didn't think he could trust anyone. Even to be dry and warm and maybe be given something to eat.

It seemed that only moments had passed and suddenly he was through the village and out in the countryside. He looked around in surprise, but he did not turn back. There would be no turning back. He trudged on until he saw a dim light ahead, a spot of brightness in the damp dark. It was a fire, lit beneath the boughs of an ancient chestnut, and a man was sitting there, warming himself.

When he drew even, the man looked up. "Hey there, fellow traveler, you are welcome to come sit with me. You can get dry and have a bite of my food. Come on over; I don't mean no harm."

And he beckoned, pausing in the midst of the meal he was consuming to emphasize his insistence.

Tavo wanted to go. The man had a kind face and a gentle voice. He didn't sound like he wanted anything or would try to hurt Tavo. But Fluken was whispering in his ear. *No, no, no.* He hesitated, but then decided he would take a chance. One man, alone, was no threat. Fluken meant well, but he would simply have to understand. That's what friends did, after all.

He walked over to the fire and sat down across from the man. It was dry beneath the big tree's leafy boughs, and the little gathering of wood scraps and twigs blazed cheerfully. Without a word, the man scooped some meat and potatoes out of a small kettle that was hanging over the flames and handed the bowl to him. Tavo nodded his thanks and began to eat. The stew was hot and tasty, and he consumed it with relish. It had been two days since he had eaten anything.

Back at that tavern, standing alone among all those dead men—that was the last meal he had eaten.

Fluken did not come over to the fire with him. He remained out in the rain, although when he looked Tavo could not see him.

"Traveling far?" the man asked suddenly.

Tavo shrugged. "Not sure."

"Where are you going?"

Another shrug.

"Well, you don't need to tell me if you don't know. Stew good?"

Tavo nodded. "Thanks."

"Oh, no thanks needed. I saw you walking out there, soaked through and looking more than a little sad. I knew you needed someone to lend you a hand. Didn't want to stay back there in the village, I gather?"

Tavo shook his head.

"I'm like that." The man ate the last bite of his food and set the bowl aside. "I prefer the outdoors and my own company. Never know what to expect in the villages. Some aren't such good places." He gestured at Tavo. "Looks like you might have found that out for yourself."

Tavo shook his head again, then glanced down at the blood on his clothing. "I had an accident."

"Well, it seems like it might have been a serious one. Not your blood, is it? I hope not. Someone else's maybe; that would be all right, I guess. If they were troubling you."

Tavo was getting tired of all the talking, especially the questions. He shook his head and turned away, not wanting to listen to any more of it.

The man hesitated and stopped himself from saying more. "You must be tired. Why don't you sleep now? Here's an extra blanket. Wrap yourself up close by the fire and rest. Tomorrow's always a new start for those like ourselves."

He produced a ragged blanket and passed it to Tavo, who took it without comment, rolled into it, and lay down next to the fire. In minutes, he was fast asleep.

It was deep in the night when he woke. He wouldn't have woken at all if not for Fluken. His friend was hissing at him, his voice raw and urgent. Something was wrong. The words weren't clear and Fluken was speaking to him from the darkness, but there was no mistaking his tone of voice. Tavo opened his eyes and peeked out guardedly. The man who had fed him and given him a blanket was searching his pack, rummaging through it furtively, pulling things out, looking them over, and slipping them back inside again.

Tavo sat up quickly, facing him. "What are you doing?"

The man wheeled about, startled and frightened, his kind face twisted into a mask of desperation. "Nothing. Your pack tipped over and some of your things spilled out. I was just trying to put them back. The ground's damp, and I didn't want everything to get all wet. Here it is, all of it, safely back where . . ."

He trailed off. It sounded as if he were telling the truth, but Tavo knew he wasn't. "You were stealing from me," he said.

A knife appeared from nowhere in the man's hand, and he lunged forward, blade flashing in the light of the little fire's dying embers. He was far too slow to do what he intended, and with a small series of sounds Tavo stopped him in mid-leap, knocking him backward into the fire. The man lay there a moment, and then leapt up instantly, clothes burning, screaming in terror as the flames consuming his clothing began to lick at his skin. He threw himself down and rolled on the ground, turning over and over until the flames were extinguished.

Then he sprawled panting and sobbing in the aftermath of his failed attack with Tavo standing over him, staring down. "Why did you do that?" Tavo yelled. "I thought you were my friend!"

"No one has any friends on the road," the man whispered. "No one." The words were spoken in a raw, damaged way, as if the fire had gotten deep into his chest. "I was just looking for a few credits." He paused, gasping for breath. "To help pay for the food. I don't have much, and I shared what I had with you."

"I should kill you!"

The man laughed. "You would be doing me a favor."

Tavo hummed softly. The man's arm lifted involuntarily from the ground, turning the knife toward his body. The man began to sob and beg, fighting to prevent what was happening, but there was nothing he could do. The knife drew closer, the point touching his throat.

"All I wanted to do was find my sister," Tavo said, pausing his deadly humming so that the arm and the knife remained frozen in place. "But everyone wants to attack me or steal from me."

"No, please, don't do this!"

Tavo looked down at the man and saw an animal. He saw a predator, turned into prey. He experienced anger and disappointment in equal measures, and his mind hardened as thoughts of retribution crowded to the forefront. But an instant later everything faded as Tarsha's face appeared, and he was again filled with unexpected sadness at the thought of being without her. A part of him understood that if he let her live he would not be without her, but another part understood that this would never happen.

He reached down and took the knife from the man and threw it into the darkness. Without a word, he used his magic to knock the other backward into the ground so hard he lost consciousness. Giving the man a final look, he repacked his bag, rolled up the tattered blanket, and walked away.

He walked until dawn, when he came upon an ancient farmhouse with a few outbuildings that were crumbling and broken, and without even considering what he was doing he went to the front door of the house and knocked.

After a long wait, an old woman appeared in the doorway, staring at him in shock. Gray hair tied back, nightdress beneath an old robe, tired eyes and lined face that marked her as north of eighty years. "Shades!" she hissed.

He was covered in the blood of his victims, his face and hands bruised and scratched and his clothes torn. He had a lank, sodden appearance, his white skin and dark hair giving him the look of a dead man. He stood there waiting, his eyes fixed on her as he waited to see what she would do.

"Come in right now," she said, stepping aside and beckoning him in. "You need to get out of the weather and get warm. Come now. In you go. I have some soup and bread to give you. Some hot apple cider. Goodness, look at you! What happened? Were you set upon by thieves and beaten? Where's your home?"

She did not invite Fluken inside, but then nobody ever did. Fluken belonged just to him. But to his credit, Fluken did not try to warn him against entering. Tavo gave the old woman a wordless nod. Then, offering no explanation, he entered her home and the door closed behind him.

TWENTY-THREE

<hr>

IT TOOK DAR LEAH the rest of the day to climb to the bottom of the canyon and begin the walk out of the Charnals. He found handholds and footholds wherever he could, and used scrub and vines for additional support, but he was forced to give as much time to maneuvering laterally as vertically, and two hundred feet ended up feeling like two miles. At times, he was forced to turn back and start over in a new direction. Frequently, he despaired of ever getting down safely.

It was slow and tedious work, and it gave him too much time to think. He found himself engulfed by memories of the solid, dependable Stow Chutin, Captain of the Druid Guard, the last of an older order that had departed with the banishment of Drisker Arc. He remembered everything he had shared with Zia, who once upon a time had loved him well and might have found a way to do so again. He fought against tears as he ruminated on her courage and her sacrifice, agonizing over what might have been. Perhaps they could have found a way to be together if she had lived. He liked to think so—and he regretted not giving her more of what she needed while taking too much of what he desired for himself.

He thought, too, about the white-cloaked enemy leader, and there his thoughts were disturbing.

Why, he wondered, was he even still alive? The man had found him trapped on a cliff ledge, hundreds of feet above the valley floor. He could have killed him easily, by either using the flash rips in the flit or knocking him off his perch. He had done neither. He had looked at Dar—studied him, it seemed—then simply backed away and left him.

Why would he *do* something like that?

It might have been that he had left Dar in a precarious position he did not think the highlander could escape. It might have been that he had decided that, even if Dar did escape, he would never get back to Paranor in time to make a difference. He might also have believed that it was too late for Dar to do anything that mattered.

But he didn't think it was any of those.

No, he thought it was something else altogether—but he did not, for the life of him, know what that something was.

In any case, it was troubling not to know, to be left wondering why he had been spared. The uncertainty of it, the mystery, left him consumed by thoughts of what it meant even in the midst of his grief for Zia.

Given a reversal of their roles, would he have done the same thing? What would it have taken to make him do so?

It was nearing sunset by the time he arrived at the bottom of the canyon, and fully dark when he began the journey out. He walked south to not only where sunlight through gaps in the peaks had been the strongest but also where he seemed to remember spying an opening through the mountains while flying in. He had not been looking for this feature in particular, but when you piloted an airship, you learned to pay attention to your surroundings. You never knew when you might discover something you would have need of later on.

By midnight he was dead tired and stopped for the night. Wrapping himself in his tattered cloak and huddling within a rocky shelter where the winds were partially blocked, he lapsed into an uneasy slumber. He rose early on a morning of clear skies and brisk winds and started out again. He had no food, but he found water trickling out of the rocks that was clean and cold from the mountain snows. The autumn air sweeping in from the north was chilly, but it made him feel alive and reminded him repeatedly of what he had almost lost.

Upon emerging from the Charnals and following the line of their foothills back down to the flats that provided a corridor between the Malg Swamp and the mountains, he started contemplating what he should do upon his return to Paranor. First and foremost, he must make certain to warn the Druids of the danger posed by these invaders. He must make them understand that they needed to take action to ensure the safety of Paranor.

Also, he had been thinking hard about the new initiate to the order, Kassen Drue. He was remembering how Kassen had been able to disappear so easily during his examination, leaving only an image behind while he moved undetected to another position.

As if he had been born to it.

As if it was a part of who and what he was.

He claimed to be seeking admission to the order as an initiate, but Dar wondered if he wasn't there for some more sinister purpose. He wouldn't have even considered the possibility if he hadn't seen those invaders disappear in exactly the same way. But what if Kassen Drue was one of them? What if the invaders had plans for Paranor and the Druids that were too deeply entrenched to be dislodged? He pondered the possibility as he trudged toward the approaching dark. A spy in their midst? Why not? Kassen had gained admittance to the initiate program almost effortlessly, by displaying skills unsettlingly similar to those possessed by the enemy Dar had just barely managed to escape. If the two were not connected, it was a coincidence of monumental proportions.

His fears propelled him ahead at a much harder and faster pace than he would have set himself otherwise. A return to the Keep, whatever he might accomplish at this point, could not happen too soon.

He walked all that day, following the line of the cliffs south toward the Jannisson Pass and an entry to the forests surrounding the Keep on the north side of the Dragon's Teeth. Nightfall found him still far short of his goal and exhausted from his efforts. He was damaged in too many places to draw on any reserves of strength he might otherwise have found.

He slept that night in a gathering of conifers at the lower edge of the foothills and rose again with the sun. Two hours into his trek, he caught a break. A freight transport flying south from the city of Anatcherae saw him, a ragged traveler walking alone. Responding to his spontaneous jumps and waves and shouts, they landed and took him aboard. Resuming their flight, they gave him food and drink and two days later dropped him close to the borders of Paranor at sunset.

By midnight, he was back in front of the gates to the Druid fortress, shouting up to the guards to be let inside.

Once back inside the Keep, he was taken to the healing center where his injuries were treated and he was given medicine to help him sleep. No bones were broken or fractured—a miracle, if ever there was one—but they refused to let him wake the Ard Rhys or even to leave his bed without a good night's sleep. He resisted at first, insisting he must speak to Balronen, but the healers advised he wait until he had his wits about him. As it was, they pointed out, he was babbling and less than coherent. Dar realized, after a moment's thought, that it might be so, and by then he was so tired he fell asleep almost immediately.

When he woke the following day, he was alone. He lay where he was in his bed and tried to recall everything that had happened. As soon as he remembered the danger to the Keep and the Druids, he forced himself to sit up and then to stand. He wore a Druid sleeping robe and nothing else. His clothes were gone. His sword, as well. He walked to the door and started out but found armed Trolls blocking his way. He protested, insisting he be allowed to see Balronen. One told him to get dressed and then he could have his audience.

Reluctantly, he stepped back, and the door closed.

He found fresh clothes, a cloak, and boots in the closet, and put them on. There was still no sign of his sword. Something was clearly wrong, but he couldn't understand what it was.

He found out soon enough. He was escorted to chambers where

Balronen and his inner circle were already waiting. The Trolls ushered him inside and left at once, closing the doors behind them. He stood at the foot of the table staring at those seated around it, and it was clear from the expressions on their faces that he was not there to be welcomed home.

Only Clizia Porse wore a neutral expression.

"A report, please," Balronen snapped. "Skip the embellishments."

So Dar gave his report, from the time of their initial encounter with the unknown enemy to the death of Quince, the flight east into the Charnals, the subsequent battle and deaths of all of his companions, and his long trek home.

When he was finished, there was a profound silence.

"How is it, Blade, that you failed to protect the Druids placed in your trust, yet you are still alive?" Chu Frenk snapped, not bothering to pretend he didn't find this despicable. "One might wonder if you did anything at all to prevent what happened."

Dar hesitated. For Frenk to speak to him like this, before Ober Balronen had spoken a word, signaled trouble. He would not have done so without knowing he was treading on safe ground.

"I thought I was pretty clear," Dar responded quickly. "Ruis ordered me to remain on board the ship. When things went wrong, I was too far away to reach him. Zia died fighting while I was at the controls of our ship. She was using her magic to keep the others safe. No one feels worse about this than I do, but you have bigger problems."

"You have problems of your own," Frenk noted, turning his gaze on Balronen. "Doesn't he?"

The High Druid looked irritated. "Don't prod me, Frenk!" he snapped. Then, to Dar, "What did you do to be left on board the ship, Dar? There must have been a reason he chose to keep you there."

"Ruis didn't give a reason. He seemed to think I would be most useful if I remained behind. I argued the point. Zia argued it, too. But he was firm in his decision."

"Again," Balronen said slowly, "why were you at the controls while Zia was battling your attackers? Shouldn't she have been at the controls and you doing the fighting? Shouldn't you have suggested at some point that you change places?"

Dar glanced at the others. Most avoided his gaze. There was no help coming from any of them. "There wasn't time for anything like that. It all happened so quickly. I was the better pilot, so I assume she believed it was best if I stayed where I was, while she used her magic."

"Very fortunate for you," Crace Adris observed, earning a nod from Pescarin.

"A warrior stands in front of his men, not behind them," Prax Tolt declared. "That doesn't appear to have happened here."

"Ruis Quince made the choice to go without me," Dar snapped. "I would have gone with him if he had let me. I should have gone with him, as it turned out. His efforts at any sort of interaction failed completely. As for Zia and the others, everyone aboard ship is vulnerable, no matter where they stand. I was just luckier than the others."

"You certainly took no chances, did you?" Frenk gave him a gratuitous sneer.

"Enough!" Ober Balronen snapped. "You were given explicit instructions by me personally, Blade. You were told what was expected of you over and above attending to this encounter with the enemy. Do you have anything you wish to offer on that? Anything further to add to your report?"

So he was fishing for something he could attach to those who were dead. Dar almost said what he was thinking but stopped himself in time.

"I do need to give you warning. Ruis Quince incensed these invaders with his posturing. By aggravating them so, by threatening the might of the Druids as a deterrent, he may have drawn them to us. He may have made Paranor a target. The ease with which they dispatched Ruis and Zia and the Druid Guards suggest they might well succeed. I believe we need to do something to strengthen our position. We need to call on others to stand with us against—"

"Call on the Elves?" Frenk exclaimed in disbelief.

"On anyone who will agree to come! And there's something else. There is an initiate within the walls of the Keep, one newly arrived, and it is possible he is not what—"

Balronen slammed his fist on the table. "Stop right there! Your efforts at speculation are embarrassing. Our Keep has stood for thousands of years against all sorts of attacks. It will not fall now. These savages who invade us, these practitioners of deception and givers of lies, will fail like all others who have threatened! No help is needed to repel such creatures, should they be foolish enough to attack. We can manage well enough on our own. We certainly do not need the services of either the Federation or the Elves!"

He rose from the table and moved around to stand directly in front of Dar. "You allowed two Druids to die unnecessarily. You failed the order, and you failed me. You were asked to be a shield for those who were in your charge and apparently thought only of yourself. Therefore, you are dismissed from the Druid order, and from Paranor. You will depart from here by morning tomorrow; that will give you enough time to gather your things. You are confined to your room until then. Your sword will remain with us. I would confiscate it immediately, but you seem to have left it in your room. No matter. You may be assured you will not be taking it with you. You are not worthy of it. You are banished and exiled."

He made a dismissive gesture as he moved away.

Dar stood where he was, seething with anger but holding it back. This was all planned. He could feel it. This was a scenario conceived and carried out to achieve something he was not privy to. There was so much more he could say, but he knew that none of it would matter. No one in this room cared to hear any of it. No one would take his side.

Of one thing, he was certain. If he was leaving Paranor, the Sword of Leah was leaving with him.

Without responding either by gesture or words, he turned and walked out of the room.

TWENTY-FOUR

◆

THAT SAME AFTERNOON, SHORTLY after midday, Allis took Kassen outside the walls for a walk in the forest. It was a bright, clear sky that greeted them, the sun sending streamers of light through the thick canopy of the trees, a dappling of shadows adding to the charm. She was carrying a basket, and although he asked her repeatedly what was in it, she refused to give him an answer. She was in her usual cheerful mood and he was smiling along with her, her behavior carefree enough that it seemed to require he be carefree, too.

After all, she was working hard to make him feel that way.

The young Druid student had taken great pains to make certain that she remained his closest friend, always happy to see him, always ready to help in any way she could. She had made him her personal project, guiding him about the grounds of the Keep, investing him with a thorough knowledge of the Druids and their order, teaching him the ways in which the members worked to help the people of the Four Lands, and giving him a broader sense of the history of the Races. Every day, she made sure she had something new to impart, and he always seemed willing enough to listen and learn during the gaps that fell between classes or training.

All of this seemed to be bringing him closer to her, and there was nothing she wanted more.

"Are you sure there is no danger of anyone finding out what we just did?" he asked her at one point. "I wouldn't want you to get in trouble."

She had just finished taking him through an underground passageway that ran from inside the Keep to the woods where they now walked—an ancient escape passage that might not have been used in years and may even have been forgotten by most. She only knew about it because her mentor at Paranor, Clizia Porse, had once shown it to her.

"No, no danger. It's one of those ancient secrets only a few Druids even remember. As long as the door is sealed, no one can enter from outside the walls, and that would be the only risk. So there's no reason we can't use it, as long as we seal it up again when we go back. No one has to know we were out here." She grinned. "We can have an adventure."

"What sort of adventure do you have in mind?"

"I can't tell you that! It would spoil the surprise."

He shrugged. "You do whatever you wish, Allis. I am your willing companion. An adventure with you, whatever it turns out to be, is bound to be enjoyable. Just promise me you'll get us safely back inside before my bedtime."

"Worried about bedtime, are you?"

He smiled and winked. "What's in the basket?"

She gave him a look. "That's part of the surprise. You won't have to wait long to find out. Do you want to hear more about the Druid Allanon? He was the last of a much older order at one point, and when he died the Druids disappeared from the Four Lands for three hundred years."

For days now, she had been fantasizing about what sort of relationship they might have. Sooner or later, their studies would be complete and they would go on to become Druids. Perhaps then she could partner with him—a teacher to help him continue his education in his new homeland and a helpmeet to share his passion for magic. She did not let herself think about how he might receive this idea when it became time to suggest it. For now, it was enough to have a goal to work toward. Time enough later to find a way to make it come true. It would be an adjustment for him at first perhaps, but in the end he would become happy with such a life if he truly cared about her.

They reached a grassy clearing surrounded by huge conifers and Allis set down the basket, pulled out a small blanket, and spread it. Then she knelt on the blanket and began setting out bread, cheese, fruit, and cold cuts of roast pig along with an aleskin, humming cheerfully as she worked.

"So the surprise is lunch?" he asked.

She shook her head. "This is called a picnic." She glanced up and saw the bafflement on his face. "They used to have them in the Old World on nice days like this. Families would go to parks and woods and spend the day. They always took food and drink. Sometimes they played games. Sometimes they napped. It was a way to get outdoors and enjoy the weather."

"I am not sure they would have enjoyed it all that much where I come from. They seldom go outside in my country if it doesn't involve work. The weather doesn't allow for it. I've never even heard of a picnic, let alone been on one. Maybe this is an experience I'll want to have more often. So this is our adventure?"

She leaned close. "Maybe. Part of it anyway."

Then she leaned over and kissed him on the mouth. And Kassen kissed her back. He did not try to pull away; it was clear enough he was enjoying it. When her arms came around him, he reached for her, as well. Still kissing, they fell back onto the blanket.

He felt her move closer. "Don't stop," she whispered.

But he did. Giving her a final peck on the nose, he said, "Why don't we eat something? Give me a chance to get used to how this works? This picnic stuff is more complicated than I thought."

He smiled to reassure her, and she smiled back bravely even though she was confused and embarrassed. "I guess I was sort of rushing things."

"No," he said quickly. "It's something else. I've . . . had some bad experiences. The memories still linger. Just be patient with me."

They didn't speak for a while after that, dividing the food and drink and sitting across from each other as they ate. Allis tried not to look at him. She felt she had overstepped herself; perhaps she had even ruined things. But she didn't understand why he had pulled away from her unless his feelings for her were much different from hers for him.

Then, all of a sudden, she was afraid she understood all too well. There were other women within the order who admired Kassen. On occasion, she had seen him with them, heads bent close in private conference. Even more troubling were his occasional disappearances when he was out walking with her. One minute he would be there and the next he would be gone. He was never gone for long, and he always returned with some explanation for why he had wandered. But even so, she wondered. Could he be meeting someone? Could he already have a lover, another woman to whom he felt a deeper attachment?

That was what it was, wasn't it? Of course it was!

A rush of jealousy and anger flooded through her. When he reached over and wiped a corner of her mouth, it incensed her, even though she believed he intended it to be an expression of endearment. She turned away instantly, looking off into the trees and feeling miserable.

A little later, after they were finished eating and she was packing up the basket, she said, "Maybe we ought to go back now."

He shook his head. "I would like to stay here a little while longer. Can we? I'm enjoying this."

She managed a momentary smile. "If you want."

He moved over to sit next to her and put his arm around her. "You have been such a good friend to me, Allis. You've given me so much since I arrived. I would have been lost without you."

"I just wanted to help . . ."

They sat together companionably for a long time, lost in their separate thoughts. Allis did not try to kiss him again, but watched his fair hair ruffle with the breezes, covertly studying his profile, trying to decide what she should do. To attempt to touch him in any way at this point was out of the question. To allow him to touch her even more so. Yet she felt she had to do something.

But it was Kassen who spoke first.

"What do you make of the Blade's dismissal?" he asked.

For a moment she was silent. Ober Balronen's unexpected exiling of Dar Leah was not yet common knowledge.

"You know about that?" she said, confused.

"Word of something so important has a way of getting around pretty quickly at Paranor. What do you think of it?"

She shook her head. "Apparently he accompanied two Druids to meet an army that had wiped out several Troll armies to the north. The purpose of the meeting was to try to find out what these invaders wanted. Things went wrong, and both Druids were killed along with all their guards. Balronen said the Blade was to blame, said he didn't act quickly enough to save them. So he was dismissed from service. He's to leave tomorrow morning."

Kassen considered. "Do you think it's true? What they say about him failing the Druids who were killed?"

She shook her head. "I don't know. He never seemed the sort to back away from a fight, and his reputation within the order is very good. I think maybe the Ard Rhys overreacted."

"That occurred to me, as well. It would be in keeping with what I've been told about Balronen. He is not well liked by the other Druids, rumored to be short-tempered and a bit irrational at times. His abrupt dismissal of the Blade reinforces that impression."

"You're brave to voice those impressions to someone you barely know. What if I were one of his confidantes? What if I were a spy? I would report such talk if I were."

He smiled. "But you aren't, are you? I would like to think I know you well enough to be sure of that. I do, don't I, Allis?"

She nodded wordlessly,

"Let me say something. I lost my nerve with you a moment ago." He gave her a moment to take that in. "I haven't been attracted to anyone for some time. I'm a little confused that it should happen now—and with you, particularly. I like you very much. I don't want to do anything wrong. I hadn't even allowed myself to think there could be something between us besides friendship until today. I guess you surprised me." He paused. "I just want to say that if you asked me, I would like to go on another picnic with you sometime."

She gave him a long, searching look, measuring his words and the expression on his face. "I would like that, too," she said.

And just like that, everything was better.

Dar Leah spent the day in his quarters, confined by order of Ober Balronen, his imprisonment enforced by a pair of Troll guards who never left their post. Several times he opened the door to see if they were still there, and each time they were. It took him far less than an hour to gather up his meager possessions, and then he had nothing to do but sit and wait. It made him wonder. Why had Balronen let him remain in the Keep until tomorrow? The more he thought about it, the odder it seemed. What was Balronen planning for him that he was keeping to himself? Perhaps he still thought to find a way to take the Sword of Leah from him. But Dar didn't have it, and at this point he didn't know where it was.

Food and water arrived, but other than that no one came to visit. Dar paced and fumed and considered various forms of escape but in vain. He spent considerable time trying to figure out what had become of his sword. He was mystified by its disappearance. He was certain he'd still been carrying it when he pounded on the gates to the Keep and was allowed to enter. He did not remember anyone taking it from him. He had searched his room, but it wasn't there. Someone must have it, but who? And why would they take it in the first place? No one could use it but someone born of Leah blood, someone who was a descendant of Rone Leah, who had first immersed the blade in the waters of the Hadeshorn at the urging of the Druid Allanon, all those years ago.

He was still pondering what to do to find it, the sun sliding west across the sky and dusk beginning to settle in, when the door opened and Clizia Porse entered. She was wrapped in her familiar gray robes, her head bent beneath her thick mane of dusky hair, her arms folded across her body like a supplicant. She did not look up until she was almost on top of him.

"Lady Porse," he said with a bow, a courtesy he felt was due her.

"You would be wise to leave here immediately," she responded, her dark eyes lifting to find his. "Before it is too late."

He gave her a look. "Too late for what?"

Her smile was wicked. "Come, now. What do you think, Dar Leah? Have you not wondered at the circumstances of your dismissal? Why were you not sent on your way immediately? Why are you sitting there, twiddling your thumbs? Use your common sense. When someone falls out of favor with Balronen, they tend to fall a long way. Sometimes they fall right out of sight."

Her voice was rough, clotted by age and a passion he did not begin to understand. She was a poisoner, and she had killed many of her contemporaries along the way. He could not help but be wary. Yet her words buttressed his suspicions.

"I should stay and fight the dismissal. The Druid Council will have to hear me out if I insist."

"You won't live that long."

"Is it that bad? Why is he so angry with me? Why so determined to get me out of the way?"

"Who knows what he is thinking these days? Perhaps he is enraged at losing Zia, a prize he desperately coveted. It was convenient to blame you for that loss—you, who were her former lover. And his failure to accomplish anything with his ill-advised mission to these mysterious invaders required that someone other than himself be blamed. You lived while everyone else died, so you drew the short straw."

"No one is to blame for what happened out there!"

"Of course no one is to blame. But in our current culture within these walls, blame must be assigned. If there is a wrong committed, fault must be found. It is how things are these days. Balronen knows this. He would prefer the blame not fall on him, so he has assigned it to you and administered High Druidic justice by dismissing you."

She gave him a hard look as he continued to stare at her. "You should be moving toward the door just about now, not admiring my beauty. I would hate to think I have wasted my warning."

"I would do as you say, but I doubt the guards would be willing to let me pass."

She made a dismissive gesture. "Which guards are those? You might have missed it, but the last watch left early, and the next has not yet arrived. That should provide you with sufficient time to step outside and disappear into the waiting night."

He nodded. "But my sword is missing, and I cannot leave without it." He hesitated, scarcely daring to hope. "I don't suppose you know where it can be found?"

"As it happens"—she reached beneath her cloak and drew out the Sword of Leah—"I do." She handed it to him, and he took it from her gratefully. "I stumbled over it last night on my way to bed. Odd that you should be so careless with it. But then you've been careless about a lot of things lately."

He started to object but then changed his mind and simply nodded his agreement. "Tell me why you are doing this. You owe me nothing. You have no reason to help me."

She shrugged. "That is a matter of opinion. Why don't we consider it a gift? Later, I may ask you for something in return. It makes it harder for you to refuse me when I have done so much for you. You see? I am investing in you. I think you are a good man, Dar Leah, and those are hard to find."

She smiled, but there was no warmth in the gesture. "Also, I do not care for Ober Balronen. Not as a person and not as Ard Rhys. I think his tenure is about over. He is an incredibly foolish man with no sense of himself. He would kill us all if he were given half a chance. I don't care to wait around for that to happen."

Dar nodded but chose not to ask anything more. Her intentions and schemes were her own, and he thought it better that they remain so. The gift of his freedom would likely cost him something eventually. But was there a price too high to pay to save your life?

"Goodbye, then," he told her, moving past her for the door.

When he reached it, she called to him. "I've changed my mind. I think I will call in that favor you owe me. You and I need allies in this business, young man. We need the help of those who think as we do. I hear there is a Druid living in the village of Emberen in the Westland who believes you have merit. You might consider going to him. You might want to ask him if he would be willing to come here and meet with me. Together, we might be able to achieve a resolution to our problems."

She turned away, looking into space as she faced the wall. "I think you will find the west gates your best choice for an exit from the Keep. I would move swiftly, if I were you."

He stared at her for a moment longer—at her gray form, all robes and hair and shadows. Then he was through the door and moving swiftly down the hallway.

Allis and Kassen were just returning from their picnic. It was late in the day with the sun slinking west and the light beginning to fail. They had passed through the underground tunnel once more, the young woman being careful to seal it anew, and reached the ground floor of the Keep. Allis was leading the way, and as they rounded a corner she literally ran into Dar Leah. The force of their impact sent her reeling backward into Kassen's arms and left the Blade stumbling in surprise.

"Allis?" he stammered. "Are you all right? I'm sorry, I was . . ."

He stopped abruptly as he caught sight of Kassen Drue, and for a moment he was left speechless. Allis was suddenly aware that Kassen was holding her in a more possessive way than breaking her fall required.

She righted herself and stepped away from him. "I'm fine," she said, her eyes flitting from one man to the other, not failing to catch the look that passed between them. "I should have been more—"

"We were just returning from a walk," Kassen interrupted, his voice calm and steady. "We should have been paying better attention to where we were going. Please excuse us."

Dar Leah kept his eyes fixed on Kassen. "Out for a walk? Somewhere beyond the walls of the Keep?"

"Allis has been instructing me on the geography of Paranor and the various Druid rules and regulations. A priceless gift to a new arrival, and I am most grateful to her." Kassen smiled.

Dar studied him carefully. "I think there is much more to you than meets the eye, Kassen Drue. Perhaps we should sit down and discuss it."

The other man made a brief bow. "It would be an honor to have that discussion with you, but we must save it for another time. I see you have your sword and a travel pack. We must not interrupt your plans."

Dar frowned, then nodded slowly. "Well, I would hate to think I was leaving when I really should be staying. Things seem very unsettled here at the moment."

The two men eyed each other silently for a moment. Allis, watching both, realized that something important was not being said and what they were saying had another meaning.

Then Kassen placed an arm around her and steered her ahead, past the Blade. "Fate deals us the hand she chooses," he said to the other man. "We are all subject to her whims. I wish you safe travels and will look forward to our next meeting."

Dar Leah said nothing. Allis glanced back over her shoulder and saw that he was still staring after them. Then they rounded the next corner, and she lost sight of him entirely and was left to ponder the meaning of what had just happened.

TWENTY-FIVE

DRISKER ARC AND TARSHA spent the remainder of the night at their lodgings in Varfleet, so exhausted from the evening's events that they went to bed without stopping to discuss anything of what had happened earlier. This didn't prevent either of them from thinking about all of it, however, lying awake until they finally gave in to sleep's welcome embrace.

The Druid was up early the next morning. Tarsha might have slept longer, but he was shaking her awake while it was still dark and she was deep in her dreams. "No point in lingering in Varfleet," he whispered.

His voice was soft and calm but insistent, so she shook off her lethargy and rose without argument. With the dawn still an hour away, they trudged down to the lobby with their belongings in hand and went out into the mostly deserted city, heading for the airfield and the little two-man. Walking was a drudgery Tarsha could have done without, but there were few public carriages working at this hour.

"Who do you think that boy was?" she asked him after they had gotten barely fifty feet from the inn.

"Shea Ohmsford, apparently," he answered.

"So he says. But not the *real* Shea Ohmsford, who's been dead since the time of Allanon. So how did he get his name? Is he family?"

The Druid stared out into the dark, thinking about it. "He might be. Or he might simply have been given the name at birth. Some people still remember the story and revere the name. Parents like to name children after famous historical figures. Or perhaps he decided to take the name for himself. It could have happened like that."

She didn't say anything for a moment. "Big coincidence that he was the boy you chose to guide us, though."

"Coincidences are not unheard of. What difference does it make? Do you think he has use of the wishsong? Or magic of any sort? It didn't seem so to me. Smart, quick, and eager to work but not gifted with magic. I would have sensed it."

She nodded. "Me, too. But it's still strange."

He didn't argue the point, and she took that to mean that he agreed with her. Of all the names to run across while on this expedition to find the mystery man who had hired the Orsis assassins, nothing could have been more unexpected. At some point, she imagined Drisker would want to return and find out about this boy. He hadn't said anything to suggest it, but by now she knew how his mind worked. More to the point, she knew the ways in which he was like her. If she wanted to find out more about this "Shea Ohmsford," it was a good bet he did, as well.

They walked for a time in silence, Tarsha thinking of how much she enjoyed the silence of the very early morning and how much she missed Emberen. She missed the forest—the smells of new leaves and grasses and fresh-cut wood. She hated the city—the raw and acrid burn of ash smoke from factory furnaces, the stench of the rivers where the inlets and bays gathered refuse and waste, the streets littered with trash and strewn with filth, and the dying embers from wood fires smoldering in a thousand barrels where the poor gathered to stay warm.

"Where do we go from here?" she asked him finally, hoping it wouldn't be another city.

"We fly north," he said quietly.

His dark eyes were intense. "To Emberen, you mean?" she asked hopefully.

"No, not to Emberen. We're flying to Paranor."

She felt a twinge of anger. "Why there? They won't let you in, won't talk to you, won't acknowledge you at all. You said so yourself. What's the point?" She stopped where she was and waited for him to turn back. "Is this about finding the man who hired the Orsis assassins to kill you?"

"Yes, Tarsha. I have good reason to think we might find him there."

She stared at him, a look of confusion on her face. "What do you mean, *we might*? You told me that Tigueron gave you his name. Did he or didn't he?"

"He didn't know the man's name. But he gave me a very good description of him. And something just as important. Our mystery man told Tigueron he could be found at Paranor."

"So we can go after him. We can find him from his description. If he's a Druid, we'll know soon enough. We'll finally have him!"

The Druid walked over and placed both hands on her shoulders. "You are a spitfire, Tarsha Kaynin. I like it that you never see any barriers so thick they can't be breached or walls so high they cannot be climbed. But you are getting ahead of yourself. A description alone is not enough. I need something more."

"What? What else could you possibly need?"

"Well, for one thing, I need you to be able to distance yourself from your fixation on gaining revenge for the attacks and try to look at the larger picture."

"What larger picture is that? Hired assassins tried to kill us! I don't think the picture needs to get all that much larger for us to figure out what is needed!"

"Think about what we know for a moment. Twice, these assassins came after us. They burned my cottage to the ground the first time without hurting either of us, and then they came back almost immediately to try to complete the job. So the question becomes this. Who would want me dead that badly? What enemy is so determined?"

"And you think the answer lies at Paranor?"

"I think it is a good place to start. Someone might know something useful—especially once we provide a description of the man who hired those assassins. But we have to ask in the right way."

"Ask, nothing. We should demand the truth!"

"Realities are sometimes very inconvenient." Drisker turned and started walking again, forcing her to follow. "How nice it would be if we could always do just what we wanted without stopping to worry about how to actually make it happen."

"You're making fun of me."

He shook his head. "I just want you to be realistic about the situation. I don't have the standing in the Druid order that I once did. I have few friends left at Paranor. I have fallen far enough that certain men and women feel they can do me harm with impunity. So they try to discredit me and perhaps even send assassins after me. What friends I have and what relationships remain I cannot afford to lose. I have to use good judgment in deciding what questions to ask and whom to ask them of. No amount of wishing will change this. At some point, Tarsha, you will have to learn the importance of moderation. You will have to learn when to back away or at least to bide your time."

She studied him a moment. "I hope you're wrong. I hope I never have to back away when my instincts tell me not to. I don't want to be like that. But maybe it's the wishsong that makes me think this way. Magic is a powerful weapon, and I don't have to back down from anyone or anything."

"Be that as it may, for now you are my student and I am your teacher," he replied, giving her a look. "So you will do as I tell you. We will go to Paranor and we will ask our questions in a disciplined and cautious manner."

A wagon passed them, but it was laden with goods and not made for transport of people. The city was coming awake. A scattering of men and women on their way to work filtered out of the shadows, ghosts in the near dark wrapped in cloaks and jackets, heads lowered against the weight of the coming day's burdens.

Tarsha glanced at those who passed by closest, trying to read something of their lives in their faces. No one looked back.

When they came in sight of the public airfield, Drisker turned to her again. "I know that the chance of Ober Balronen agreeing to speak with me is virtually nonexistent. But there are others who will. The identity of the man we seek might be revealed in the course of this investigation. My path is clear. I have to go, but I want you to come with me."

She straightened, pushing back her white-blond hair from her face. "Well, I am your student, after all."

He smiled. "It does you credit that you honor your commitments. I will try not to keep you away from your real concerns for much longer."

She knew at once what he was talking about.

Tavo.

Drisker understood that her brother was her most immediate concern. She needed to get to him before much longer. Drisker might have imposed a yearlong apprenticeship on her as a precondition of teaching her to expand and manage the uses of the wishsong initially, but he had promised her, as well, he would give her a chance to find her brother before then and make certain he was safe. He had even said he would come with her.

She strode ahead of him, shoulders drawn back, head lifted. She knew the way to the airfield, which was not that much farther ahead; she remembered it from earlier. No damage to her memory as yet, she thought, but her concern about where her life was going was another matter.

They reached the airfield and boarded their craft just before sunrise. Lifting away, they had the pleasure of greeting the sun's appearance as it crested the Wolfsktaag Mountains far to the east in a brilliant display of pink and red turning slowly to gold. The sky flooded with light that revealed a clear blue, cloudless expanse and no suggestion of anything but good weather in any direction. Drisker was at the controls, steering their two-man away from Varfleet and north toward the Dragon's Teeth. Shadows still draped the jagged peaks of those mountains, giving their towering cliffs a scarred, empty look where they rose above the tree line in ragged clumps.

To the west, the leading edges of the emerging sunlight were beginning to creep across the plains country toward the homeland of the Elves. The Druid took a moment to wonder about a people that had been so closely allied to the Druids in years past. Where were the Elves now? An enemy army was invading, battles had been fought and lost in the Northland Troll country, and the Elves might as well have migrated to another continent for all the involvement they'd had. What had become of them?

He sighed ruefully, thinking about it. He would have to address this mystery, as well. Had word not reached the Elves about what was happening? Surely that couldn't be possible. Yet why hadn't they made some sort of response? Why hadn't they acted on a threat that was directed at them, as well, and come north to see what was happening?

Unable to answer any of these questions at present, he turned his attention to deciding whom he could persuade to meet with him. Even that would be hard, for only a few would be likely to listen to anything he had to say. Members of the Druid Guard would be easy enough; the Trolls had always liked and respected him. But it was the Druids who would be most likely to know anything of value regarding enemies and their identities. And it was the Druids he needed to reach.

Drisker shook his head. It was an impossible situation. Aside from Dar Leah and one or two others, he couldn't think of anyone who would disobey the Ard Rhys and speak freely to him, no matter how persuasive he was. The consequences of doing so would likely be severe if Balronen found out, and there were few within the order who would be willing to risk that under any circumstances.

Beside him, Tarsha Kaynin was considering what she would do if her mentor's efforts failed and he decided to postpone the search for her brother once again. He would want her to stand with him or to accompany him on whatever path he chose to take. She did not think she could do this. Not going in search of Tavo would be more than she could bear. He was too important to her. For her, the magic had never been the source of anguish it was to her brother. She was not haunted by it, as he was. She was not given to fits of rage and despair that threatened to destroy the user. And others. All because he could not control it the way it needed to be controlled.

She pictured his face, sad and frightened of what he was, of what he could do without intending it, of how vulnerable he was in the face of such raw power. He must find ways to control those powers. Perhaps by now, even in this short time period, she had learned enough about her own use of the wishsong from Drisker to help Tavo with his. Not to try would be an unbearable failing, and she did not think she could live with the consequences. Her parents were helpless to do much more than talk with Tavo, not having use of the wishsong and not even really understanding what it meant to be its victim rather than its master. She was the only one who understood. She was the only one who could have a positive effect on his life.

She would go to him, she promised herself. Whatever happened at Paranor, afterward she would go to him.

They flew all day through blue skies and sunshine, and by dusk they were nearing Paranor's black towers, which were visible from where they sat upon a broad open rise within miles and miles of dense forestland. Shadows spreading with the slow slide of the sun west layered the battlements and parapets of the Keep, and from atop the walls torches were lit against the coming night. Tarsha felt a menace exuding from the ancient fortress that was troubling. She could not pinpoint its source, only sense it. It seemed to come from everywhere, as if the entire structure and all those housed within were cursed.

Drisker landed their two-man in front of the south wall, and they climbed out and walked over to the huge ironbound gates. From there, the Druid called up to the Druid Guard on sentry duty and asked to speak with Ober Balronen, saying it was urgent. Discretion would be appreciated, he quickly added. The guard on duty greeted him warmly and asked him to wait while his message was delivered, promising to keep it between them. Drisker smiled. The Trolls, at least, still seemed to think he was worth the risk.

He stood next to Tarsha in the failing light and neither spoke, the darkness deepening all around them, the silence a close and vaguely threatening presence. From within the walls came the comforting sounds of life—voices in conversation, laughter, dishes and pans rattling and clanking, the boots of the Troll watch passing across the walkways on the battlements. But out where the Druid and the girl waited, the world felt dangerous.

When the sentry returned, he did not bring good news. He told Drisker that the Ard Rhys refused to speak with him. All within the Keep were forbidden from speaking to him. These were not words he would have chosen to say, he added, if the choice were his. But the choice was not. It would be better if Drisker left now and did not return. It would be better if he left them all with memories of better times.

The words were spoken in the guttural Troll language, but Tarsha understood the gist of it. The rough edges of the words lent them a poignancy that was unmistakable. The Troll who delivered the message did so reluctantly and with no apparent ill will. He was a messenger who clearly wished things could be different.

"Is there no one who would speak with me?" Drisker called back in disbelief. "No one at all?"

The Troll did not respond; then he nodded once and disappeared. They waited expectantly for a few minutes. Drisker shook his head. "Someone will come. We will wait by our airship."

She did not feel the confidence he did and wondered why anyone would speak to them when Balronen was so set against it. She followed him back to their two-man, which by now was little more than a desultory lump swathed in darkness, and they sat down in the shadow of its hull to wait.

Half an hour passed, and no one came.

Another half hour. Still Drisker remained where he was, and because she understood that he was decided on this, she sat with him in silence.

It was an endless vigil that she became increasingly sure would lead to nothing.

Until, finally, she heard a secondary door opening at the base of the walls and saw a momentary sliver of light escape from inside. A shadowy figure appeared in the doorway, silhouetted by the light. They had only a glimpse, and then the door closed and the darkness returned.

Drisker got to his feet and stood waiting. Tarsha did the same.

The figure coming toward them, revealed by the light of moon and stars, was a gray thing, hunched at the shoulders and cloaked head-to-toe. Its gait was a shuffle more than a walk, and the insubstantiality of its body was recognizable even through heavy outer garments. A woman, tall and slight of build, bent perhaps with age and perhaps with something more, face lifted within the cowl so that she was able to watch them closely. She came at her own slow pace, unwilling or perhaps unable to do otherwise, arms lowered to her sides so that she presented no overt threat.

"Clizia," Drisker greeted as she reached them.

"You are surprised, Drisker Arc, that I would speak with you when no one else would? Haven't I always done those things that no one else would dare to do?" The gaunt woman's gaze shifted to Tarsha. "Who are you, girl? What is your name?"

Drisker immediately stepped in front of her. "She is my charge, responsible for helping me with small tasks that would otherwise prove too time-consuming and distracting. Her name is Tarsha. Tarsha, this is Clizia Porse, one of our oldest and wisest Druids."

He said it quickly, cutting off the introduction that Tarsha was about to make. Tarsha didn't miss the warning behind the gesture. *Be careful of this one,* he was saying.

"A helpmeet, is she?" Clizia Porse snorted openly in disdain. "And I am the Queen of the Silver River. You're teaching her magic, aren't you, Drisker? Still a mentor to magic wielders, even if you don't find them here at Paranor anymore. What are your skills, girl? What sort of magic do you have that would interest a man like Drisker Arc?"

Tarsha stayed silent. Drisker took a step closer to Clizia, almost as if to diminish Tarsha's presence. "Why have you chosen to speak with me? There is no love lost between us, and you were pleased enough to see me gone from Paranor. If you could have managed it, you would have succeeded me as High Druid. Your ambitions for advancement are well known. Where is Dar Leah? Surely, he would have been a better choice."

Clizia Porse gave a small shrug. "Once, perhaps. No more. Zia Amarodian is dead, along with Ruis Quince, and Dar Leah is dismissed from service because of it. The truth is this, Drisker. I thought it rude and shameful that no one would come out to speak with you. I despise cowardice. I have no love for Ober Balronen, even though he seems to find my presence in his inner circle comforting."

"Yet you voted with the majority to exile me."

"An entirely different matter. And it does not speak to how I feel about our new Ard Rhys. As you say, I would have preferred that I succeed you. It would have been better for everyone."

"You find him ill suited for the position, too?"

"A fair assessment."

"His decision to dismiss Dar Leah is certainly evidence of this. He was the best protector Ober could have hoped for. What happened?"

"The Blade accompanied Zia and Ruis on a mission to make contact with an invading army to the north, after it had destroyed several Troll tribes. The mission went badly wrong, and the entire delegation save the Blade was killed. He alone escaped to tell the tale. Ober didn't like it that he had lived when all the others had died. Or perhaps he simply wanted a scapegoat to shift the prospect of any blame attaching to him, once wiser heads began to recall that the mission was his idea. A brave man, Dar Leah, but constrained by the nature of his position. He departed two nights ago, at my suggestion. I told him to seek you out. Perhaps he intends to do so. Perhaps he can be your helpmeet, too?"

"Perhaps. That he is banished reinforces my convictions regarding Balronen's lack of wisdom."

"No real surprise. Leopards don't change their spots." She looked around. "Perhaps we could sit while we finish this conversation? My bones ache when I stand about for too long."

They moved over to the two-man and sat within its shadow facing each other in the near darkness. "What magic does this girl have,

Drisker?" the old woman asked once more. As if Tarsha weren't there. As if she didn't matter. "It must be something special to interest you."

"Tell me the rest of what you know of this invading army," he replied without even a glance at Tarsha.

Clizia Porse smiled crookedly. "As you wish." Then she recounted all that Dar Leah had told Balronen and his inner circle, leaving nothing out. She recounted the specifics of the Blade's warnings and the total failure of his efforts to convince the Ard Rhys and his inner circle of the danger.

"Surviving when everyone else dies is sometimes a mistake." Drisker shook his head in disgust. "You have to find a way to convince Ober that he is making a dangerous error. Can you do it?"

She made a dismissive gesture with one withered hand. "He listens to no one but himself these days. That said, I shall repeat your concerns, conveying them as my own. He will listen to me, even if he finds it distasteful. He will do so because he is afraid of me. I might persuade him to change his mind about allies and the safety of the Keep. Is this what you came here for? Dar Leah would seem a poor choice to act as spokesman for your thoughts about this invasion."

Drisker hesitated, as if uncertain whether or not to say more. "The invasion was not the reason I came to find the Blade. I came for a different reason entirely."

Quickly and succinctly, he recounted the attacks from the Orsis Guild assassins and his search to discover who had hired them to kill him. Then he provided a description of the man who had come to Tigueron to arrange for the assassins.

Tarsha listened without comment, knowing the Druid wanted her to stay silent and not give away anything to Clizia Porse. Why he felt that way toward someone from whom he was asking help and to whom he was telling everything was confusing, but she respected his judgment about how dangerous, yet perhaps helpful, this old woman might be.

The seamed face with the depthless black eyes, cloaked and hooded and ghostly, showed nothing as he finished. The eyes spared Tarsha another glance; then the old woman nodded. "I don't recognize the man you've described. I would remember him if I'd seen him." She shrugged. "I think it best you go now. There is nothing more you can do here. I will speak with Balronen in the morning. I will do so without other members of his inner circle present, so they will not be allowed to influence him. If I am successful, I will get word to you."

She reached into her robes and produced a small globe that gave off a faint blue cast that even the darkness could not diminish. "A scrye orb," she told him. "I found it among the artifacts recovered from the sorcerer Arcannen over two hundred years ago. If you warm it with your hands and ask for me, I will feel it. There are two; I will be carrying the other. We can communicate with each other as if we were sitting together as we are now."

"A good sort of magic to have," Drisker observed. "I am surprised you managed to keep it from Balronen."

A sneer twisted her lips. "It has been in my possession a long time. I took it from the archives early on when I decided some talismans were better off with me. You were not yet Ard Rhys, but the order was already frayed around the edges. I see things, Drisker. And your fall and Ober's rise were among them. Here, take it."

He reached out, and she placed it in his hands, adding, "I will expect it back when this is over."

"You shall have it."

She rose. "I should go back inside. If I am out here too long, Balronen will find out. I would rather he does so at a time and place of my own choosing."

He stood up with her, and Tarsha rose with them. "If you should see this man I described or hear any suggestion of who he might be . . ."

"You will be told." Clizia Porse glanced at Tarsha. "I will see you another time, girl."

Then she shuffled away and disappeared into the darkness.

When she was clearly beyond hearing, Drisker said to Tarsha, "Well done."

"But I didn't do anything."

He looked at her and smiled. "As I said. Well done."

TWENTY-SIX

---◆---

THREE DAYS LATER THEY were back in Emberen. They were walking through the late-afternoon sunlight on their way to the cottage when Tarsha made her decision. She had been debating it with herself ever since they had finished their meeting with Clizia Porse and begun the long flight back to the Westland. It was an agonizing process, and she had changed her mind repeatedly as the hours passed.

"I'm leaving tomorrow to find my brother," she blurted out. She surprised herself with the vehemence of her pronouncement and quickly tried to smooth it over. "I mean, what choice do I have? I have to know what's happened to Tavo."

He looked over, and there was surprise reflected on his face.

"I have to," she insisted. "If I stay longer, I will hate myself if things have gotten worse. Hearing from Clizia Porse could take days, and there is no guarantee she will contact you even then. I can't sit around waiting to find out. Nor should you. You promised to come with me. You should do so. Keep your promise as I kept mine."

"You have to make up your own mind on this," he said quietly. "But it is not your place to decide my priorities. I will give the matter some thought. That's all I can promise."

"You can bring the scrye orb with you, can't you? Then she can reach you from anywhere. She can tell you whatever she's learned, and you can return if it is needed."

He studied her a long time before answering. "We have been away from home for over a week. We are both exhausted. Let's sleep on it before either of us makes a final decision. Will you wait a day or so?"

She thought back to the past few days, to the search for the Orsis Guild and the confrontation with Tigueron and his men, to the terrible battle they had fought and to their discovery of the boy's unexpected name. How long had it been since she had not felt tired? She couldn't remember.

In any case, he was right. Decisions of the sort she was seeking to reach should not be arrived at in haste.

So she said no more about leaving, and when they reached the cottage she went straight to bed and slept through the day and deep into the following night. Sleep was so welcome and so all-enfolding that Tarsha did not dream and did not realize the passing of time. Sleep carried her away to a warm, safe place, and all the dangers and threats and feelings of fear and doubt faded into another time and place.

It was only when she finally woke and saw how dark it was that she realized how long she had been slumbering. She lay where she was for a time, luxuriating in the warmth and comfort of her bedcovers, letting wakefulness surface slowly, letting sleepiness drift away at its own pace. When she felt ready to do so, she rose to leave the cottage and go out into the night. She threw on her cloak over her nightdress and walked in silence through the living area of the cottage and out onto the porch, opening and closing the front door quietly behind her.

Around her, everything was silent.

After a moment, she moved off the porch and down into the yard and stood staring at the stars. It was a clear night, and the absence of any artificial light revealed a vast array of brilliant pinpricks and scatterings of milky swatches decorating the blackness of the great beyond. She smiled in the cool of the autumn air at the majesty of this endless firmament, imagining what it would be like to go there, to visit those worlds, to explore those vast reaches. Once, it was said, men did so in airships they crafted from metals and composites and stood upon worlds where no other humans had ever been.

What must that have been like? How many were there? It was impossible to know. Thousands, millions, more?

She closed her eyes and breathed deeply of the forest—of its green life changing with winter's approach, of the fecund earth that absorbed what could be used to create new life when the old began to pass. She breathed and held the smells in her nose and lungs, trying to bring wisdom and understanding out of what she had captured. She wished she were smarter, more capable, and less uncertain. She wished her brother could be kept safe from harm, even knowing it was a wish that could not be granted and would never come to pass. The recognition and acceptance of it were harsh and bitter, and she almost cast it away.

But it was too real and necessary to be recklessly discarded, and she knew she must carry its weight from this moment forward until she had found her brother and done whatever she could to bring him back to her.

Not only in the physical sense but also emotionally.

Not in the hope of a curative but in search of an accord.

When she opened her eyes again to look back at the stars, she found Fade only a few feet in front of her, her huge, sleek body sitting back on her haunches, her lantern eyes bright with intelligence and curiosity. Oddly, Tarsha was not frightened to find the moor cat had gotten so close without making a sound. Her appearance provoked no sense of panic or fear, no response beyond the pleasure she found in discovering she was there. The girl almost reached out to pet the great beast but stopped herself just in time. There were boundaries to be observed with creatures as massive and feral as a moor cat. Presumptions of friendship had no place in the mix. They were alien and mostly unknowable to each other, the cat and she, and an acceptance of this truth was important.

"Well met, beautiful thing," she whispered to the great beast.

To her surprise, Fade began to purr, a rough throaty growl that rumbled up from somewhere deep inside her chest.

"Look at that sky!" Tarsha said impulsively, pointing. "Is it not beautiful?"

But Fade showed no interest in the sky. The lantern eyes remained fixed on her, and only once did they blink, perhaps in acknowledgment of her comment or perhaps just because.

"I would go there one day," she confessed. "I would go there and see what wonders lie beyond our own world, what creatures I would find that I did not know existed, what it would feel like to experience a meeting. I would give anything for that."

Fade stayed put a few moments longer and then rose to a standing position, her muzzle only inches away from Tarsha's face. She saw the cat's nose twitch and realized it was sniffing her, taking in her smells, reading things about her she could only guess at. The exploration lasted several minutes, a slow and leisurely study of one species by another, a consideration of truths to be learned.

Finally, apparently satisfied, the big cat wheeled away and went back into the trees, disappearing a piece at a time as she did so. Tarsha had long heard that moor cats could do this—come and go right in front of you, simply fading away when it suited them, even in broad daylight—but it was amazing to actually see it.

The elemental magic captivated her. It reminded her again of what Drisker Arc could do, of his ability to disappear and leave only an image behind. A magic that she, too, was just beginning to master. It felt right somehow that it was a skill she and the cat should share.

"I never tire of seeing her do that," Drisker said at her elbow. "Disappearing as if she were nothing more substantial than a vision."

Tarsha managed to keep from jumping out of her skin, but only barely. She turned and found him fully dressed and looking off in the direction Fade had gone. "I didn't know you were awake."

"I've been awake awhile, mostly thinking about what to do. I want you to stay, but I realize you very much need to go. I understand, but I don't like it."

She nodded. "I don't much like it, either. But my brother can't be left alone much longer. Not safely."

"Then you must go to him." The dark features tightened around his smile. "You have a strong sense of responsibility, Tarsha. I can't help but admire this. Will you at least stay through this day to see if we hear something from Clizia? If nothing happens, we will go to your brother together, you and I."

She stared at him. "You would come with me?"

"I think I already said I would. I've done what I can for the Druids. Now I have to do what I can for you. I realize how important your brother is to you. I want you to know he is well."

She felt tears come to her eyes as she took his hand and gripped it tightly. "I cannot tell you how much this means to me."

He reached for her then and hugged her tightly. She curled into the warmth of his embrace, thinking it had been a long time since someone had held her like this, reminded of when she was a little girl and her father had done so.

"Dawn is only an hour away," he said, releasing her. "Perhaps we should have some breakfast?"

Together, they walked into the cottage, Tarsha feeling as happy as she had been in a long time.

They prepared breakfast in the predawn and ate it on the porch while watching the sky slowly lighten with the sunrise. Not much was said, the pair content to look off into the forest and the pale-blue arch of the cloudless sky, reveling in the start of another gorgeous autumn day. Already the season was making its presence known, the leaves of the deciduous trees changing color amid the evergreens, the smells of leaf dust and deadwood filling the air. It was a cause for celebration, a reaffirming of life waiting to quicken with the coming of a new season and the ending of an old. Yet for Tarsha there was regret and worry, and any celebration at the prospect of rebirth had an ephemeral feel to it.

They had finished eating and cleaned their dishes and begun a few housekeeping jobs necessitated by their short absence when a lanky figure walked up from the road leading to the village and stopped at the foot of the porch.

"Well met," he greeted Tarsha, who was sweeping off the wooden decking. "I'm looking for Drisker Arc."

On hearing his name, the Druid walked out of the cottage, a smile brightening his dark features when he saw the other. "Dar Leah!" he exclaimed. "I've been expecting you."

"Have you?"

"I'll explain later. For now, come sit with us. This is my student, Tarsha Kaynin. You may speak freely in front of her."

The highlander extended his hand and the girl took it in her own in a brief exchange. She already knew who he was, remembering his name from Drisker's conversation with Clizia Porse. The Ard Rhys's Blade, released from service for imagined failures connected with events that had involved the invaders and the Druids they had slain. She noticed how blue his eyes were, and how browned and seamed by the sun his face. Striking. His grip was calloused and firm. Here was a man who used his hands for physical work, most likely with weapons given the nature of his former position. She noted the black handle of the sword strapped across his back, and the way his eyes shifted as he took in everything around him.

They sat together on the porch with their chairs drawn close and mugs of cold ale in their hands.

"I understand you are temporarily unemployed," Drisker said. "Perhaps you come here seeking work?"

"I can think of worse employment." The highlander smiled. "But I'm not here for work. I'm here to tell you what's happening at Paranor."

"Clizia Porse may have beaten you to it. I spoke with her several nights ago, and she told me of your release as Blade and the story behind it. I already knew of the invaders and their threat to the Four Lands. I tried to find a way to warn Ober Balronen about the danger, but he refused to see me."

"Did you expect anything different?"

The Druid shrugged dismissively. "What else do you have to tell me?"

The highlander bent close, his brow furrowing. "At his best, Ober Balronen is a strange man, but his strangeness seems to have reached new heights. Something is wrong with him, Drisker. I mean, something besides his usual need to assert his authority and seek reassurance of his status on a daily basis." The highlander paused, considering. "Before I left with Zia Amarodian and Ruis Quince for the meeting with the invaders, he told me I needed to keep an eye on both, because he thought they were plotting against him. He didn't elaborate or offer any evidence of this, but he clearly wanted me to find something. When I got back to report them both dead along with all the Trolls who had gone with us, it seemed to matter more to him that I hadn't found out anything to confirm his suspicions. He didn't even seem to care much about the possibility that the rash behavior and words of Quince might have drawn the invading army to Paranor."

Drisker frowned. "Ober has always been paranoid about who might be plotting against him. But Quince and Amarodian were members of his inner circle and supposedly supporters. What do you think?"

"It was nonsense. Zia and Ruis were barely speaking. Ruis went out of his way to embarrass and demean Zia in my presence. There was no indication of any sort of plot. Ober dismissed me from service on the grounds that I failed to protect his Druids, but the dismissal felt arbitrary." He paused. "He doesn't seem rational these days. He seems quixotic and short-tempered and struggling to see things clearly. Have you seen him exhibit this behavior before?"

Tarsha caught a glimpse of recognition in her mentor's eyes. "No. Not in him. But in someone else." He leaned back in his chair. "Before you left, did Clizia Porse speak with you?"

Dar Leah nodded. "She helped me escape the Keep. She warned me that the Ard Rhys might prevent me from trying to leave even though he ordered me to go. She helped me through the gates and out into the forest. She suggested that perhaps I might want to come to you."

"She wanted you out of the way," Drisker said drily. "Did she mention the strangeness in Ober you've spoken about? Anything to suggest she was concerned, as well?"

Dar Leah stared at him. "She touched on it, nothing more. What do you mean she wanted me out of the way? What's going on?"

"Years ago, before your time with the Druids, while I was still Ard Rhys, a Druid with substantial skills in the use of magic and a hunger for power within the order fell afoul of her. I forget the particulars, but he enraged her in a way that was unmistakable. She was already famed as a poisoner, and there were many who thought she might try to put an end to him in the same way she had disposed of others. But curiously, no attempt at a poisoning was made. Though he invited retribution by continuing to disparage her openly, none was forthcoming.

"But then a curious thing happened. The instigator began to act oddly, as though a change in temperament had overtaken him. He made irrational claims and wild accusations against almost everyone. He began to see other Druids as enemies—men and women who had been his friends or at least his compatriots. All of them were shocked by his behavior. This went on rather a long time, and no one could discover a way to put a stop to it. His temperament did not improve. If anything, he slipped further into a sort of self-induced madness. It was terrible to watch. No one could find a cause or a cure, myself included."

He paused, looking off into the forest. "Until one day, he simply threw himself off the walls of the Keep."

"You believe it was Clizia's work?"

Drisker nodded. "I had no reason to think so at the time. But some weeks later, while speaking with her on another matter, she said something that suggested she had played a part in the man's death. She said people should be careful who they choose to anger, because hate has a way of coming back to infect you with its poison."

"So." The highlander paused. "Instead of killing him quickly with poison, she used something that drove him slowly mad?"

"I think she wanted him to suffer."

"And she's doing the same with Balronen?"

Drisker looked at Tarsha, then at Dar Leah. "She wants to be Ard Rhys of the Druid order. She always has. That can't happen while Balronen holds the position. She may think this is the time for him to be pushed out. One way or the other."

"If so, her timing seems incredibly poor," Tarsha declared, unable to stay silent any longer. "What does she accomplish by killing off or removing an Ard Rhys when there are invaders threatening Paranor? Creating chaos accomplishes nothing!"

Drisker nodded. "I don't pretend to know exactly what Clizia is up to. But the circumstances feel too familiar not to be taken into consideration."

"There's something else you need to know," Dar Leah said suddenly. "Something I meant to bring up earlier. I think the invaders have placed a spy inside Paranor. He calls himself Kassen Drue. He arrived very recently to be examined for admittance as a Druid-in-Training and was accepted. At his examination, he was able to shift his position from one side of the room to the other without being detected—even with three Druids watching."

Like Drisker can disappear and reappear, Tarsha thought at once. *And perhaps those invaders? Wasn't that what the Morsk insinuated? That they became like ghosts?*

Abruptly, a suspicion surfaced, hard and quick—a reach that might not have seemed possible before, but now felt almost inevitable.

"Describe this man," she asked the Blade. "Physical characteristics, the nature of his voice, anything at all."

He did so, and even before he finished Tarsha and Drisker were exchanging a look of recognition.

"He's the one, isn't he?" she hissed. "Clizia lied! She must have known who he was from your description. What sort of game is she playing?"

Drisker shook his head. "Who is this man's mentor at Paranor?" he asked the Blade. When he saw the look on the other's face, he stood up instantly. "We need to go to Paranor at once."

Tarsha felt her heart stop. All her hopes of trying to help her brother, her plans for teaching him to manage the wishsong, and her fears and doubts about what was happening to him in her absence were being cast aside once more. As quickly as that, Drisker had broken his promise to come with her to Backing Fell.

She stood up. "What of my brother? What of Tavo?"

Drisker nodded, reminded of his promise. "We can go to him afterward, Tarsha. But we need to address the situation at Paranor first. The threat of what might be going on within the Keep must take priority."

"For you, perhaps. But not for me." She held his gaze. "I will not go with you. I will be going home to my brother. You promised to let me, and now you must. I would have liked it if you had been able to come with me, but I will not hold you to it. Still, I must go."

There was a long moment of silence as the three stared at one another. Tarsha felt a cold place opening inside her as she felt the possibilities of becoming Drisker's associate and friend dropping away. She was giving up everything for a brother who was increasingly a danger to herself and others, and there was no reason to think she would ever get any part of it back.

"You must do what feels right," Drisker said quietly. "If you need to go to your brother, then go. Not with me, but perhaps Darcon Leah will go with you. Someone must protect you if things are not safe for your return."

He turned to the highlander. "Will you accompany her, Dar? There is nothing further you can do for the Druids and Paranor. Only I can do what needs doing now. But I will rest much easier if I know that, while I cannot keep my promise to Tarsha, I can at least be reassured she will not be harmed in my absence. I know I am asking a lot of you, but it is important to me."

Tarsha waited for the highlander to argue or flatly refuse, but instead he nodded. "I will go with her."

She stared at him, searching for some indication of dismay or irritation at having been tasked with acting as her protector, but she found nothing in his expression to indicate either.

"And when you are finished and you have done what you can for your brother," Drisker added, "you will return to me and complete your apprenticeship. A bargain is a bargain, and you must keep it." He rose. "Now I must pack and leave for Paranor."

"Wait!" Tarsha practically shouted the word. The Druid froze.

"Just don't do . . . just wait! This matter is not settled. You presume to make decisions for me, giving me no chance to tell you how I feel. Whether you believe this is for my own good or not, you have no right. I don't want Dar Leah to go with me. I do not need his services. But you most certainly will. Clizia lied! Deliberately! If she has lied once, she will lie again, and maybe worse! She has something planned, and it does not look to me as if it is intended to help you. But Dar can help protect you! He is the only living member of the Druid order who knows anything useful about these invaders. What if they are coming to Paranor? What if they arrive while you are there? How will you know what to expect or do if Dar Leah isn't there to provide advice?"

There was a long moment of silence; then the Blade nodded. "She is right, Drisker. I know what to expect better than anyone."

The Druid looked from one to the other and then nodded. "I suppose Tarsha is right. Very well. Dar will come with me."

He rose abruptly and went into the cottage, leaving the highlander and the girl staring after him—and then staring at each other. For a moment, neither said anything. It felt to Tarsha as if the other was taking her measure. She glared at him challengingly, intimidated by those startling blue eyes, trying to decide what they were seeing.

"Will it be a problem, going back alone?" he asked finally.

"What difference does it make to you?" she snapped, her irritation with him surfacing. "You didn't want to go with me in the first place! Why didn't you just say so?"

His lips tightened. "You know nothing about me and have no right to presume you do. What I want in this matter doesn't necessarily outweigh what *he* wants. I respect Drisker Arc immensely, and I do not presume to know better than he does. Unlike you, apparently, who seem to think you do."

"You're the High Druid's Blade. You belong with him."

"I *was* the Blade. Now I am an exile."

"So we have an exiled Blade in service to an exiled Druid. A perfect fit. You may think him adequate to the task he sets himself, but do not be so certain. I do not think he is who he was when he was at Paranor. Even in the short time I've been his student, I have seen the signs. He was very nearly killed twice last week. You need to be there for him."

Dar Leah nodded slowly. "Perhaps so. But you should understand why he asked me to go with you. He worries about you and needs to know you will be safe if he is not there to protect you. He is concerned that your magic might not be sufficient. You do possess magic, don't you? Of course, you do; he wouldn't be teaching you otherwise. His feelings for you are great enough that he cares about your safety. You should be grateful, and you should let him know it. Attacking me is pointless."

While she didn't care for the dressing-down, she understood that his assessment was correct. Drisker had done this for her. He might not have stopped to consider her feelings, but there was no denying he was focused on how best to keep her safe. It would be incredibly ungrateful of her not to tell him that she appreciated it.

This did not change her belief that it was unnecessary, but it did temper her anger. "You're right," she said. "I apologize for making assumptions about you, and I will speak with him before he leaves."

"Would you consider telling me where it is you are going and what it is you intend to do?"

She saw no reason not to. She was feeling less resentful of him by now, more ready to accept that he cared for Drisker, too. So she explained the circumstances that had brought her to Emberen, and the struggle she was having with her conscience because she had left her brother behind. She revealed that both siblings possessed the magic of the wishsong and needed help with mastering its power—although her brother's need was by far the greater. She confessed she was concerned for his sanity and safety both.

When she had finished, he just nodded. "You show great love and courage, Tarsha. Drisker must have recognized those qualities in you when he chose to take you on as his student."

She gave him a brief smile. "I think he just got tired of hearing me argue over why he should agree."

"So we must promise, the two of us, to do whatever we can to help Drisker and each other in the days that lie ahead."

She hesitated only a moment before nodding in agreement. "I think we must, Dar Leah. If we are all to make it through this, I think we must."

TWENTY-SEVEN

◆

TARSHA KAYNIN LEFT THE village of Emberen the following morning, after the abrupt departure of Drisker and Dar Leah the day before. She saw no reason to leave in a rush or without planning, but took time to pack traveling clothes and food and drink, and to stow emergency equipment in the small flit the Druid had provided for her use. She hiked into the village and retrieved the little craft from the field manager who stored the airship for Drisker's personal use, flew it back to the cottage, and loaded it for the flight. By midday she was ready and set out for the deep Westland.

Her plan was simple enough—find her brother, although she did not know for certain where he might be. She was hoping he was still where she had left him, at their uncle's farm. She would fly to the village of Backing Fell and decide where to go from there. Hopefully, she would also figure out how to set things right with Tavo.

She flew out on an overcast day in which clouds curtained the sky in jagged strips and the sun appeared and vanished again in the wake of their steady movement. A westerly wind propelled them hither and yon, buffeting Tarsha in her flit as she flew crosswise on her passage over forests east of the Rill Song and Arborlon and then south toward Drey Wood and west again into the Sarandanon.

She journeyed onward through the rest of the day, reaching the southern edge of the Sarandanon by sunset and deciding not to go farther that day. Her sense of urgency suggested she should, but her common sense told her she needed to eat and sleep first. It would require another day and possibly two to reach Backing Fell—much of that time passing over wild country with a sparse populace—and she did not want to arrive exhausted and starving. So she set down near a village resting on the north bank of the Rill Song where it channeled its way west, disabled her flit so it could not fly without her and alarmed it, and then walked into town to find an inn where she could eat her dinner and find a bed to sleep in.

For the rest of the journey, this would not be a luxury she could allow herself, for the towns she would pass through were not ones a single woman wanted to be walking around in alone. Granted she had her magic to protect her, but it was always wisest not to tempt fate by using it. So this was probably her last best chance to eat and sleep indoors until she reached home. This would be the last time she could feel safe in her surroundings and not need to be watchful everywhere she went, and she wanted to make the most of it.

Naturally, things did not work out quite as she expected.

Wending Way was larger than she had expected, a town more than a village with multiple streets and a thriving business district that serviced a population of farmers and shepherds and a steady flow of river traffic from trappers and traders. Not far east, a community of Rovers was engaged in salvage operations and airship repairs and restoration. Taken altogether, the surrounding community was a crossroads of commerce.

Tarsha made her way down the streets that led to the center of the village in search of a suitable inn. Nightfall was fast approaching, and shadows cast by the failing sunlight were rapidly spreading over the streets and alleyways. Lights were coming on at the entrances to taverns, their pale glow fighting for purchase on turf already claimed by insistent shadows, their struggle perhaps a warning for the unwary. Tarsha noted the way as she went, but kept her head down and her business her own.

At the charmingly named Cock & Crow, she slowed for a closer look. The building was reasonably pleasant outside, and through the curtained windows she could see tables set with linen and real dinnerware. The second and third floors appeared to offer sleeping rooms. Fair enough. She walked through the door, abruptly stopped, turned around, and walked out again.

A pleasure house! Shades!

She reached the end of that street and turned up another, heading back the way she had come. Darker here, less heavily trafficked, most retail businesses closed for the day. She kept on, searching. Soon enough she found the Wayfarer, which had a less cheerful exterior but was more clearly a normal inn with a bar and stools, tables and chairs, and signs of housing on the upper floors. She entered with fewer expectations, and they were promptly met. A huge bearded man behind the bar called out to her.

"Well met, young lady!" he bellowed. "Come in, come in, all are welcome here, travelers and locals alike. No one turned away. A table for the lady? Right this way."

He thundered out from behind the bar, bearish and round, and guided her to a place by a window. He held her chair for her and pushed it in as she sat. She almost laughed. Who had done that for her lately? "Thank you. A glass of ale?"

He was off as quickly as he had come, filling her order. She watched him with amusement. He probably did not see many single young women come into his establishment. But this inn still felt safe enough to risk taking a room, unlike everything else that she had passed.

She ordered a meal and found the food decent. The patrons mostly ignored her. She ordered a second glass of ale and inquired about a room for the night. The barkeep, who was also the owner, promised her a good room with a sturdy lock. In case she was concerned about being bothered, he added knowingly.

She assured him she wasn't and accepted the room.

She took her time with the second glass, watching the patrons come and go, looking out the window at the street as the night settled in and the clouds thickened overhead, blocking out moon and stars. As the darkness deepened, the people passing by grew more shadowy and less distinct, as if they were being shrouded against the bright intrusion of the lamplight. Tarsha began thinking of her brother, imagining how he would react on seeing her and what she would say to him. Perhaps it would be enough just to be together. Perhaps the words would come naturally, born of the life experiences they had shared for so long. Maybe she would find a bridge to ways in which she could reach out and help him.

Pipe dreams, but she indulged them anyway.

An old woman hobbled by, supporting herself with a gnarled staff etched with markings. She was dressed in a brightly colored robe with tassels and ribbons trailing from the sleeves and hem. Tarsha looked more closely at the markings on the staff. Were those runes? She couldn't be sure in the poor light.

She thought about Drisker Arc, imagining what might be happening to him. Wondering, too, about Dar Leah. She found him refreshingly direct and unpretentious. She probably wouldn't have minded if he had come with her. But he would have been a distraction, and she would have felt guilty about Drisker. Dar belonged with the man he had sworn to ward, Ard Rhys or no. He was the Blade, and that meant he was charged with the responsibility of providing protection to the Druids, not to her.

She sighed, finished the last of her ale, and was about to rise when she glanced out the window.

The old woman she had noticed earlier was standing right in front of her on the other side of the glass, leaning on her staff and staring. Tarsha would have jumped out of her skin if such a thing had been possible, but instead she held steady and stared back. After a moment, the old woman gestured to her empty glass and then the empty chair on the other side of Tarsha's table. Tarsha hesitated and then nodded, beckoning the other inside.

The old woman nodded, and Tarsha could have sworn she winked.

Whatever the case, she hobbled into the inn and without a word to the proprietor or anyone else came over to the table and sat. She said nothing for a minute, apparently content just to rest, her eyes fixed on Tarsha.

"Do I know you?" the younger woman asked, surprising herself with the directness of her question.

"No. We are meeting for the first time. My name is Parlindru. Just Dru, if you please."

She seemed oddly younger once she was sitting close enough that Tarsha could study her. Her hair was gray and chopped short at the shoulders, her body bent with age, her limbs thin and spindly, her hands gnarled, and her shoulders hunched. But her face was almost entirely free of wrinkles and her eyes were bright and alert.

Tarsha was aware she was waiting for a response. "Tarsha Kaynin," she said and held out her hand.

Parlindru took it and held it a moment, her brow wrinkling. "You carry a heavy burden, Tarsha," she said. "And must do so for a while yet. Can you afford to buy me a glass of ale?"

Tarsha signaled the barkeep for two fresh glasses and then turned back to her companion. "Why do you say that?"

No response at first. Dru simply smiled. Then, inclining her head slightly, she said, "Do you know what brought me inside this place? To sit with you specifically?"

"I thought maybe you knew me from somewhere."

"But now you know I don't."

"A free glass of ale?"

"Is that really what you think?"

Tarsha hesitated. "No. I think it's something else."

"But what specifically? Just say whatever comes to mind. Don't stop to think about it. Don't be afraid."

"I'm not afraid," Tarsha declared. But she went silent again as the barkeep appeared with the ale. After he had placed the glasses on the table, she leaned forward. "My brother?"

Parlindru, who by now Tarsha realized was something more complicated than just an old lady, smiled. "Do you know the rule of three?"

Tarsha shook her head. "No."

"Everything that happens in life can be understood if you parse it into threes. All things have three distinct components, and all lives have three distinct destinies. Has anyone ever told you this? Do you believe it to be true?"

"I'm not sure. I never thought about it. Should I?"

Dru smiled, and the smile was so reassuring Tarsha felt all her doubts and irritations drop away. "Give me your hands. Just hold them out. Don't worry. Nothing will happen. You won't be harmed. Just let me hold your hands for a moment."

"Who are you?" Tarsha asked, determined to keep her hands to herself until she knew.

"What I *am* matters more. That is the question you should be asking."

"All right. What *are* you?"

"A seer. All my life, a seer." She paused. "I am forty-one years old. Do I look it?"

"You don't."

"No, I look much older. The gift of seeing the future has done this to me. An irony. It steals life as a reward for revealing time's secrets. Even then, those secrets are not always made clear. I have the gift, but it exacts its price in the way of all magic. You should know, Tarsha Kaynin. You have use of the wishsong."

Tarsha started to deny it but instead stopped herself, wondering how Dru knew this. "So you can read minds?"

Parlindru laughed. "I don't read minds. I read the future. Please listen, young miss. I came into this fine establishment because while I was passing by, your thoughts called out to me. You couldn't have heard them, but I did. You seek answers and solutions, and perhaps I can give you a little of both. But to do that, I need to be closer to you than standing outside a window. I need to be touching you. If you want what I can give you, let me take your hands in mine."

"Perhaps I don't want that."

Dru smiled. "Oh, but I think you do. I think you want it badly."

And Tarsha knew she did. Anything that might allow her to help her brother. Anything that would give her insight into her own life.

Obediently, she held out her hands and let the other woman take them in her own. The seer held them gently but firmly, her fingers pressing into the palms as if to reassure Tarsha of her intentions. All the while, her eyes looked into the young woman's, fixing on them but not really seeing anything, her stare vacant and detached.

Then abruptly the pale-gray eyes became blue and the blue became violet—a slow changing each time—and the heat emanating from them was palpable. At one point, Tarsha felt a burst of warmth in her chest, a sort of spike that was painful but lasted no more than a moment. It let her know that something had happened and she had been part of it. She wasn't sure how long the intrusion lasted; time had stopped. When it ended she could not tell what had taken place, only that something had.

Parlindru released her hands, and there was a look of wonder reflected on her face. Tarsha knew at once the seer had seen something important.

"Rule of three," Parlindru whispered. "So three things shall I tell you and three things shall you know of your future. Listen, now. Hear me and remember."

She paused to make sure she had Tarsha's full attention as she held up one finger.

"First. Three times shall you love and all three shall be true, but only one will endure."

Another finger.

"Second. Three times shall you die but each death shall see you rise anew."

A final finger.

"Third. Three times shall you have a chance to make a difference in the lives of others and three times shall you do so. But one time you shall change the world."

She stood abruptly, taking her staff and looking down at Tarsha with a sad smile. "Your burden is great and will be greater still. Keep true to yourself and remember my words. One day, perhaps, we will meet again."

The old woman motioned to something off to her right, causing Tarsha to look where she gestured, searching for what had drawn her attention. A quick search revealed nothing. But by the time Tarsha looked back again, Parlindru was passing through the front door in a whisper of colored fabric to disappear into the night.

Tarsha sat where she was and finished her ale, thinking over what the strange woman had told her. Rule of three. She guessed she would find out at some point if it was true. She downed the last of her drink and walked over to the barkeep. The man looked up as she set her glass on the bar. "Another?"

Tarsha shook her head. "Have you seen that old woman before?"

"What old woman?"

"The one I was sitting with. The one I bought the ale for."

The barkeep grinned. "You're having me on, young lady, aren't you? There wasn't no old woman sitting with you. Look for yourself. You still got that extra glass of ale you ordered sitting there full up. No one's touched it. You might want to go back and finish it."

Tarsha stared at the full glass sitting at the table and shook her head. "No, I think I'll just leave it."

She exited the room, went up the stairs to her sleeping chamber, closed and locked the door, and slept soundly through the night.

But there were dreams, and the old woman was in them.

TWENTY-EIGHT

◆

DRISKER ARC AND DAR Leah departed Emberen in a rush, not long after the Blade had arrived. Normally, the trip would have required three days, but by traveling straight through the night the Druid believed they could reach Paranor late the following day. It would be an arduous journey, but Drisker was concerned that things at Paranor were spiraling out of control. Ober Balronen's strange behavior was too similar to what Clizia had induced in that other Druid years earlier to be ignored. If this was the result of Clizia's machinations, Drisker had to know.

Because whatever the truth about her involvement with both Balronen's and Quince's strange behavior, her involvement with Kassen Drue could no longer be disputed. She had deliberately lied to Drisker about knowing who Kassen was, and Dar had revealed that lie. Clizia had led the team examining the newcomer for admission. She had witnessed a clear demonstration of his ability to disappear and then reappear somewhere else. When Dar had returned from the ill-fated encounter with the invaders to give his report to Balronen and his inner circle, she could hardly have missed noting the similarity between Kassen's demonstration and what Dar had described the invaders doing. Yet she had done nothing about this, even after recommending Kassen's admission into the order and becoming his adviser. Instead, she had kept all of it to herself and told Drisker nothing. That this was anything but deliberate was impossible.

Drisker knew Clizia Porse well. She seldom did anything without a purpose, and there was no reason to believe she lacked one now, even if he did not yet understand what it was. What he wondered was how much she had to do with the attempts on his life. Had she known Orsis Guild was coming for him? Was she aware that Kassen had hired these assassins? Had she, herself, been behind the attacks, with her own reasons for wanting him dead? He had to assume the worst at this point, and the urgency he felt as a result persuaded him to leave sooner rather than later, and to travel east as fast as he could.

Drisker and Dar Leah flew through the rest of the day and night, taking turns piloting the little two-man—one manning the controls while the other slept. It was an efficient way to make the journey and still arrive at least somewhat rested. Although Drisker thought more than once, as he tossed and turned in the confines of the passenger's seat, that an airship this small was never intended to provide anything approaching comfortable sleep.

Still, he managed to get some rest, as did the Blade, and by early evening they were nearing the jagged spires of the Dragon's Teeth. The day had been cloudy and gray, the air moist with the prospect of rain, and the winds out of the north were crisp and steady. A storm was coming, and they would likely be outside when it struck. But a storm was the least of their problems. Drisker was already worried that any form of entry into the Keep would prove impossible without the use of force.

They landed in a clearing less than a mile from Paranor, the shadows of massive old trees deepening as what was left of the sun sank away.

"We'll walk from here," Drisker announced. "I don't want anyone to discover we're present before we get inside the Keep. If they do, our chances of finding a way in will be minuscule."

They disembarked and began working their way through the heavy forest. It took them only a little while to complete their journey, and soon they were crouched in the concealment of the trees at the western edge of Paranor, staring up at the top of the Keep's walls where a pair of dark figures patrolled the battlements.

"What now?" Dar said quietly.

Drisker shook his head. "Now we look for a way to get inside and speak with Balronen. And try to avoid ending up locked in the cellars." He studied the walls a moment longer. "At least the Keep doesn't appear to be in any imminent danger."

The Blade was sitting back on his heels, his brow furrowed. "I wouldn't be that certain, Drisker. The Druids might be in more danger than they suspect. There's something I haven't told you. Something that happened to me at the end of the battle with the invaders, when our ships were gone and the others were dead and I was all that was left."

Then he told the Druid the entire story of how he had thrown himself from the wreckage of the burning Druid warship to a perch in the rocks of the cliff face, trying to hide from any pursuit. Yet the leader of the invaders had found him anyway, lowering his flit into position with its weapons trained on him, giving him no real chance to fight back—and then left him unharmed, backing off and flying away.

"I'm still bothered by why he was so ready to spare me when he had me trapped like that. He just hung his flit in midair, studying me as you would a bug, and then dismissing me. He could have killed me on the spot. It just seems, thinking back on it, that he really didn't think it mattered if he left me alive. That I was no threat to him. That whatever I did if I made it back to Paranor wouldn't matter."

The Druid stared at him. "I agree it's odd. Certainly there's more to this than we know. It would have been safer just to kill you and put the matter to rest."

He looked up again at the sentries patrolling the walls, thinking of all the men and women inside, wondering if any of them even suspected the danger they were in. He was inclined to think not. At the very least, he had to warn them of what was coming.

"I'm going to try contacting Clizia," he said at last, turning to face the highlander. "I have a scrye orb to summon her; let's see if she will speak with us. If she does, maybe we can learn something about what's happened. I know the danger she might pose to us; I know we can't trust her. It's clear she's lied about Kassen. But we have to do something, and trying to get inside without being seen and without help is a last resort. Still, we need to be cautious about this. I want you to stay out of view while I use the orb. I don't want her to know you're with me just yet. Sit where she cannot see you while I invoke the magic of the orb, and do nothing to give yourself away."

They moved deeper into the trees, safely out of hearing from the guards patrolling the battlements. Dar took up a position facing the Druid after backing away perhaps fifteen feet from where he sat, placing himself where Clizia would not be looking at him when she spoke to Drisker. The Druid waited until he was settled, then produced the orb—a perfectly round milky stone—and held it up in front of him cupped in his hands, warming it to ready the magic.

"Clizia?" he whispered, when he felt the surface of the orb begin to give off heat.

The stone began to glow, and he took one hand away, holding it so that the open side was facing him.

Her face appeared, gaunt and lined and fierce. "Drisker? What is it? I thought I told you to wait until you heard back from me!"

"There's no time left. Paranor may already be compromised!"

"Compromised? What are you talking about? Where are you?"

"Just outside the walls of the Keep. Have you spoken to Balronen?"

"I spoke to a wall that wears our beloved leader's face," she answered, her voice as tightly drawn as her face. "He does not choose to listen to me. He ignores my reasoning. In his skewed worldview, my concerns lack any real merit. *Your* concerns, really, even if I was the one who voiced them. I did what I could, but he continues to play the fool."

"He is displaying irrational and quixotic behavior, would you say, Clizia?"

The sharp eyes fixed on him, suddenly suspicious. "What is this about Paranor being compromised? What is it you know that I don't?"

Drisker glanced at Dar and back at the orb. "There is a man within the Keep, newly arrived, a Druid-in-Training. His name is Kassen. He has abilities that mirror those of the enemy that we suspect marches against Paranor. But you already know this, don't you? I described him to you when last we met. He was the man who hired Orsis Guild to kill me. Why did you lie to me about knowing him?"

There was an uncomfortable silence. "What are you talking about, Drisker? Yes, I know this Kassen. A new initiate. I was there for his examination and saw what he could do. But your description did not call Kassen to mind. It did not match what I know of him closely enough. Be sensible. Why would I send someone to kill you? Why would I bother? I would come after you myself if I wanted you dead."

"Well, that's comforting to know. So you claim not to have made the connection in any way? Not even after hearing that his ability is so similar to that of the invaders?"

"I considered it, yes. I have taken steps to try to convince Balronen of the danger that Ruis Quince may have put us in, though you've already heard what our beloved leader thinks of my opinions. But the similarity in ability is one thing, and connecting your description of the man who hired Orsis is another. Do not confuse them when casting blame on me!"

She leaned closer to the orb. "I am doing what I can. You have to trust me. You have to be patient, Drisker. I have put a watch on Kassen and alerted some of those within the Keep who can be trusted of the danger we might be facing. There are a few—if only a few—who are not fools." She paused. "Now tell me more about the danger to Paranor. Do you have reason to think these invaders are somewhere close to the Keep?"

Drisker shook his head. "I don't think anyone knows where they are just now. Can you arrange for a scouting party to fly out and search for them, perhaps find out where they are?"

She sighed. "I suppose. Prax Tolt controls the airships and their fliers, and he bears no love for me. But he is more sensible than Balronen. He may be willing to listen."

"One thing more . . ."

Her face darkened and her voice turned shrill. "Not now! I told you, you have to wait! I will make contact with you as soon as I know something more. Meanwhile, stay out of sight. I need time to look into this. Be patient while I do so!"

And the scrye orb went dark.

Drisker stared at the sphere for a moment and then tucked it back into his pocket.

"She's lying," Dar said, coming over again to sit next to him.

"Yes, she is," Drisker agreed. "Now what do we do about it?"

The day passed slowly for Allis, who spent her time anticipating the arrival of nightfall. Unbidden, with no warning whatsoever, Kassen had asked if he might come to her bedchamber after hours to see her. He said nothing more, promised nothing, and offered no explanation for this request. But she knew the truth of it, as every young girl does. He could have only one thing in mind, and it was something she welcomed. She had always known he would be right for her, that they would be lovers and partners in life. She had been waiting for a chance to broach the matter to him, but he had saved her the trouble.

So she completed the routines and obligations of the day barely knowing what she was doing; her attentions were elsewhere. She did not see Kassen all day, not even in the classes they shared, so her anticipation was heightened considerably by nightfall. She ate her dinner with friends, barely saying two words, completed her evening chores and studies, and went off to her room to wait.

That he might not come to her did not cross her mind. That he might change his mind—thinking better of such an assignation or losing heart or giving in to unknown fears—was not a possibility she considered. No, he would come to her, and her life would be forever changed. He loved her as she loved him; she was sure of it. It only required tonight to complete the journey that would take them to their destiny and open up the world they had both been waiting to find.

It was not yet midnight when he arrived, slipping silently from the hallway into her room. She was already in bed, waiting for him. He stood there in the darkness just inside her door, waiting for his eyes to adjust. Then he crossed to her bed and knelt next to her.

Gently, he placed his hand against her cheek and leaned forward to kiss her. "Allis," he whispered.

She breathed out his name in response, barely audible even in the silence of the chamber, speaking it into his mouth as she kissed him back.

He broke the kiss but did not move away. "May I stay with you tonight?"

She stared at him in rapture and excitement. "Why?" she asked. She wanted him to say the words. She wanted him to speak them aloud.

"You know why. Will you let me?"

"Do you love me?"

"Like I do the life within me."

She hesitated only a moment, then sat up quickly and pulled him to her. Their kiss this time was long and deep and searching, their arms tight about each other. In those few moments, she knew she was everything to him and that he cared about her as he had never cared about anyone before.

"I can't wait any longer," he whispered.

"I don't want you to," she whispered back.

He pushed her back onto the bed and climbed in to lie next to her, wrapping her in his arms. They kissed some more as his arms and hands shifted beneath her, one hand pulling away for a moment before returning, formed into a fist and pressed against her spine, rotating gently, searching her body.

"I am sorry for this, Allis," he said softly. "But tonight is the end of all things for the Druids."

A spike of pain ripped through her, burrowing deep inside her body, close to her heart. She stiffened and gasped in dismay, and her breathing became rapid and desperate.

"Do you hear yourself?" she heard him whisper. "That is the sound of your death. These are your final moments, and if you concentrate you can feel the life leaving your body."

Her arms tore away from him and began to beat against his back in response. She heaved up against him and tried to twist away. But he held her pinned to the bed with his body, and he was much stronger. She felt her own strength diminishing, fading away into something lethargic and numbing. Even the pain in her side was lessening.

Her eyes opened, looking into his. "You would not like what would happen to you if I allowed you to live," he whispered. "The knife I have substituted is an act of kindness."

She felt him withdraw it from her body and gently push it back in a little higher up on her rib cage. This time something ruptured deep within her and in a matter of seconds she began to feel everything slip away.

She died without ever knowing why.

It was past midnight, and Drisker Arc and Dar Leah were making their way through the forest. The storm that had threatened earlier had moved north, and no rain had fallen. Darkness flooded the empty-seeming land, the silence replaced with night sounds— birdcalls, insects buzzing, the east wind's rush, the voices of those within the Keep and their own increasingly restless movements.

They had already stayed put for too long, for Drisker had hoped to hear something more from Clizia before entering the Keep. But there had been no word since last they spoke, so he had decided they would act now rather than wait any longer.

They were approaching the entrance to the ancient tunnel that led beneath the walls and into the cellars of the Keep when the chaos within began.

Both knew instantly that something was wrong.

They dropped into a crouch, faces intense and worried. "Something's happened," Drisker hissed.

From the walls of the Keep, figures were rushing back and forth, engaged in combat. Blades flashed in the glow of torchlight and bodies tumbled away. Inside the buildings, down farther in the courtyards and passageways, men and women were crying out. Screams rent the air, in staccato bursts and frenzied wails. A battle was being fought. A battle of life and death, with no quarter given and no escape offered.

The Druid experienced a sinking feeling in the pit of his stomach.

He did not need to think twice about what the battle meant. Everything he had feared was coming to pass. It was a moment of such dark clarity that it left him momentarily paralyzed. He felt severed from his past, set adrift by his banishment, and now cut off from all that had once been. No more Druids. No future for Paranor and its wondrous and sometimes fearful artifacts. Magic relegated to legend, become something archaic where once it was so vital a part of everything he knew, vanished with its users. Westland Elves might still make use of it, but those who had curated and safeguarded its most powerful talismans were dead or dying.

"How did they get inside?" Dar whispered.

Then the scrye orb, resting deep in Drisker's pocket where it was wrapped in a piece of cloth, suddenly grew warm with life.

Clizia.

Drisker hauled the orb from its place of concealment and yanked the cloth away, peering at its glowing surface expectantly. When she appeared, Clizia's face was gaunt and fierce. Anger and disgust were apparent in her strong, lean features.

"Are the walls breached?" he asked at once.

"Are you deaf and blind?" she snapped, her voice as tightly drawn as her face. "They were inside before anyone knew what was happening. They are all through the Keep, everywhere, killing everyone."

"But you've escaped?"

"I am old, Drisker, not stupid. Fighting back is impossible. Even with magic, we are overmatched. These invaders, whoever or whatever they are, move like ghosts! You can't see them to fight them! They spread through the Keep like wild beasts, killing everyone. Most of the Druids were caught off guard, either while they were still sleeping or just waking. Prax Tolt fought back with a handful of his warrior comrades, but they went down like wheat before a scythe. Is that clear enough for you?"

She sounded as if she enjoyed describing it, as if she wanted to cause him pain. "So you just watched it happen?" he said. "Then you fled while the others fought for their lives? You're very good at that, aren't you?"

"Spare me your snide comments. You weren't here to watch it happen. I do not engage in fights I cannot win. So stop wasting your time accusing me and start thinking about what we need to do! This isn't over yet."

Drisker's face was dark with irritation. "You apparently have something in mind?"

"As would you, if you stopped to think about it for a moment. We need to rid the Keep of these ghost people and put an end to their plans for occupying our home and stealing our magic. We need to show them what real power is."

He caught his breath as he realized what she was proposing. "You intend to summon the Guardian of the Keep? That's a dangerous choice, even for you. It will kill everyone it finds once it's set loose."

She sneered openly. "Are they not killing us? Do they not deserve the same? I have waited long enough to be certain that everyone that matters is dead, but I cannot do this without you."

Dar Leah had moved close to hear what she was saying, now only a few feet away from Drisker. The Druid gave him a warning look but kept his concentration on Clizia. The expression in her eyes, reflected even through the smoky interior of the scrye orb, was frightening.

"You don't need me to summon the creature that lives in the pit. You are skilled enough to do that on your own. What is the rest of your plan? There is more, isn't there?"

"Ridding the Keep of its occupiers is only the first step. The Druids are dead and gone, Drisker. It will take time to rebuild the order. Decades, at least. We are the ones who must do this, but we do not by ourselves possess the power to hold Paranor safe in the interim. We must seal it and close it away. It must be made to vanish until we are ready to return it to the Four Lands for renewed occupation."

Now he understood. His breath caught in his throat. "You propose to take the Black Elfstone from the archives, and you need me to unlock the vaults. I might be an Ard Rhys in exile, but I am still invested with the power to invoke the codes."

"I see you understand. Yes, I lack the codes. You will have to enter the Keep to help me with the task. Once we retrieve the Black Elfstone, we can summon the creature in the Well. Already, it stirs uneasily. I have sensed it. It knows what has happened and is waiting for our call."

Drisker hesitated. He had not expected this. He had not anticipated such a drastic solution. What Clizia Porse was advocating was risky and could not be reversed once invoked. Her convictions were not misplaced, and her plan to save the Keep and its artifacts was necessary, yet Drisker still had serious doubts. To summon the creature from the Druid's Well to rid the Keep of its intruders was one thing. To seal Paranor away from the Four Lands was something else entirely.

He exchanged a long look with Dar Leah. The Blade gave a determined shake of his head. *Do not do this,* he was urging.

But Drisker had already decided he would. That he must. Even if the Druids were dead, he must save Paranor and its magic. If it fell into the hands of the invaders and they occupied it, everything would be lost. While he trusted Clizia not a jot, he might still require help once he was inside. He knew he must take a chance with her this one last time, for the good of everyone. He just needed to keep close watch on her and remember how dangerous she was.

"Even if the battle is over and all the others are dead, they will keep searching for survivors. How long before they find you?"

Her look was one of disdain. "I am more than a match for these upstart invaders. They will never find me."

"Then stay where you are. Don't move from wherever you are hiding until you have to. I will use the underground tunnel to reach the cellars. When I am inside, I will summon you."

"I would hurry if I were you," she warned.

Then her face disappeared from the orb, and Drisker was left staring at Dar Leah.

"This is madness!" the highlander snapped at him.

Drisker nodded. "Born of necessity, and all other options seem pointless. Wait here for me."

"I'm going with you," the Blade said at once.

The Druid heard the determination in the other's voice, a mirror of his own, and didn't even bother trying to argue. "Come along, then."

TWENTY-NINE

◆

THEY SET OFF FOR the tunnel entrance at once, slipping through the forest like the shadows that draped it, trying not to listen to the sounds that still emanated from within. Through breaks in the trees they could catch glimpses of the fires that burned in the ancient fortress; the flames were consuming everything that wasn't constructed of stone and mortar and metal. The cries and screams had mostly died away, become faint and intermittent. Mostly there were calls and whistles that seemed to be signals. The stomping of boots on ramparts and battlements, down causeways and in halls, was unmistakable. The smells of smoke and ash and blood drifted on the night breezes.

The underground passage that Drisker took them to was unknown to Dar Leah. It had been there, he was told, for centuries, constructed in the early days of the Keep as a way to enter and leave Paranor without notice. Or, in extreme situations, to provide an escape route for the Druids should their safety be compromised. Only the Druids knew of it; only they were privy to the location of its entrance. To the best of Drisker's knowledge, it had not been used in recent memory.

Yet when they found the exterior entrance—a trapdoor set into the ground and concealed by earth and forest grasses—it was immediately apparent to the Druid that it had been opened recently. The ground was disturbed and he was able to detect footprints. A lot of footprints, which suggested recent and heavy use. It appeared likely that the invaders had gained entrance to the Keep this way.

"Who else would have reason?" he said aloud to Dar, once he confirmed the discovery. "It seems too great a coincidence that it should be opened after all these years, and that opening not be connected to the fall of the Keep."

Dar nodded but said nothing. There was no way to know the answer until they found the culprits. "How far do we travel to reach the Keep?"

Drisker shook his head. "Not far. I hope Clizia's right about how things stand. What she proposes assumes that no one will be placed in danger from the summoning, save the two of us. Stand back."

He invoked a form of magic that unsealed the trapdoor. It swung open of its own accord with the soft pop of a seal being broken, and they were staring down into a dark hole in the ground.

"What is this Guardian you spoke of?" Dar asked him. "Is it something magic?"

"Dangerous magic," the Druid answered, a dark expression crossing his face. "The Guardian is an ancient creature, formed when Paranor was constructed in order to ward against enemy intrusion. It is insubstantial and inhuman, a killing beast formed of dark materials and lacking any purpose but to destroy whomever it finds within the Keep. If summoned, it will rise from the Druid's Well and sweep through the whole of the interior of the Keep. All those it finds—and it will find everyone in the end—will be destroyed. It is not clear if even the Druids would be spared. There is a chance they might, since there is no point in killing the Druids if the Guardian's initial purpose was to protect the Keep from enemies. But that assumes it can make the distinction, which has never been proved. Or at least, never been recorded in the Druid Histories."

"Then this magic has been invoked before?"

"No more than half a dozen times in all the centuries since it was created. The Keep has only been breached a handful of times—during the lives of Bremen and Allanon specifically, but one or two other times, as well. It is a final resort, highlander. It marks the end of days for the Druids and their order when it is used. But if Clizia is correct, she and I are the last of the Fourth Order of Paranor's Druids, and there is reason to believe our days are numbered, too."

"There is no other way? No choice besides this one?"

"Clizia does not think so, but I'm not so sure. Still, the seriousness of the threat cannot be denied. This invader is insidious and thorough. It needs to be expunged before it can cause further harm. If it breaches the vaults where the artifacts and talismans are stored, it can do significant damage to the Four Lands. Damage, perhaps, that is irreparable."

He looked at the Blade. "Are you still with me?"

Dar Leah nodded. "Lead the way."

The Druid stretched out his hand, and the Blade clasped it in his own. They gripped each other's wrists tightly for a moment—a reassurance of their unspoken commitment. Their eyes met in the near darkness, and there was an instant understanding between them. Once this course of action was set in motion, there would be no turning back.

Then Drisker clapped his hands once to bring a soft glow to his fingertips, and flames sprang to life against the encroaching dark to provide light to guide them in. Leading the way, he descended into the tunnel's darkness.

Stairs wound downward—old and worn stones set into an embankment that sloped to the tunnel floor. The passageway smelled of damp and ancient roots, as if rotted from within and in danger of collapse. But there were timbers to shore up the walls and ceiling at regular intervals, and the dirt floor looked solidly packed and sturdy. The air was cool this far beneath the earth, and the silence was deep and pervasive. Dar could hear the sounds of their movements and breathing and nothing more. They did not speak to each other as they progressed, their concentration solely on the darkness ahead and the revealing glow of Drisker's light. The passageway wound a bit, skirting the heavy tangle of roots from the ancient trees and the bulky protrusions of boulders embedded within the earth of the walls and floor. Nothing moved in the darkness about them, and the emptiness of the corridor was unmistakable.

It took them longer than Dar had expected to reach the tunnel's end, and when they arrived at a great iron door set into the interior walls of the tower that housed the Druid's Well—walls that extended twenty feet beneath the ground—it caught Dar by surprise. The door was of average size, but its ironwork was every bit as large as the door itself, providing a massive frame on all sides. While there was nothing to indicate how it might be opened, Drisker Arc did not hesitate to act. Once again, he invoked a form of magic, pressing fingers and palms against the door and framework both while muttering under his breath, until the door slowly gave way.

Dar drew out the Sword of Leah in readiness. Light blazed through cracks where the door had opened, bright and challenging, and the distant rumble and clang of the battle being fought above reached out to them.

When they entered the Keep, there was no one about. They found themselves in one of the cellars that formed much of the fortress complex belowground—a maze of passageways and stairs that extended through the earth so broadly and so deeply that the highlander could not begin to guess at its lowest levels.

He looked about expectantly. Nothing. It was as if everything that was happening above them was no more than a dream, and if they surfaced they would find Paranor just as it had always been.

Dar looked at Drisker Arc. "What now?"

"We summon Clizia. Stand where she cannot see you when I use the orb. Let's not give anything away we don't have to."

His suspicions of the old woman were warranted, and Dar did not question them. He knew there was no way to be sure how far they could trust her, given what she may have done. He was deeply troubled by the fact that she had survived when no one else had. Perhaps she was simply clever or lucky. But if it was something more, if there were still other secrets in play, it might be a good idea if one of them belonged to Drisker and himself.

The Druid had the scrye orb in hand, and Dar watched it brighten before his face. It lasted just long enough for the Druid to frown at it before it went dark again. There had been no words spoken, no communication exchanged.

The Druid tucked the orb into his clothing. "She is not responding."

"Perhaps because she cannot? Could she have been found and killed?"

"It's possible."

"So what do we do?"

Drisker shrugged. "We try to find out. Quickly."

Ober Balronen had barricaded himself in his sleeping chambers with Druid Guards stationed at the doorway, both inside and out. He was not so stupid as to think the Keep's attackers, whoever they were, would not come for him. He was frantically trying to figure out a way to escape when the white-cloaked leader of the invaders dispatched the guards outside his chamber almost before they knew what was happening and was through the door, bloodied sword in hand.

The remaining two guards were quickly brought down, as well, and the Ard Rhys of the Fourth Druid Order was alone.

Tall and stooped in his white nightdress, he stood waiting, his sword held out in challenge. His gaunt features were twisted in a mix of rage and disgust. His black hair hung long and loose about his face. Shifting rapidly from side to side as he continued to seek freedom, his eyes glittered with the fear that was consuming him. Though he could not know it himself, he had the appearance of someone already dead. The white-cloaked leader advanced on him, weapon lifting. Balronen's feeble attempt to defend himself failed, his sword knocked from his hand as if it were a toy. His attacker snatched at the front of his nightdress and hauled him close, then struck him on the side of his head and left him dazed and barely conscious.

As he was hauled from the room by his captor, shouts and cries rose from the hallway beyond where weapons clashed and flashes of light revealed the presence of Druid magic. Balronen peered ahead through eyes fogged by pain and tears. What was revealed was pretty much what he had feared. It was less a battle than an execution. The Druids were woefully unprepared for an attack undertaken in the dead of night inside their fortress. Sleep-drugged and confused, they died within seconds of waking, most never making it out of their bedrooms. Some few struggled to stand against their attackers, making a futile attempt to fight back. Prax Tolt, only partially dressed but well armed with sword and the blue fire of his magic, had rallied a few others to him, all of them possessed of similar magic and considerable fighting skills. They battled to hold the invaders back, but in the end were driven back and cut down.

Those Druids still fighting around them saw it happen and realized their fate. Several dropped to their knees and begged for mercy. Chu Frenk, his substantial girth pierced in a dozen places, was screaming for attention, claiming that he could help the invaders, that his services could be valuable. Ober Balronen felt a wave of disgust and fury as the invasion leader yanked him forward. A gesture and a sharp reply and all of those attempting surrender were killed on the spot—including the Dwarf who pleaded for his life even as it bled out of him.

His white cloak blood-spattered and soiled, the leader turned away, scanning a hallway emptied of everyone but the dead and dying as his soldiers worked their way from room to room, searching out the last survivors. There wouldn't be many left by now. Bodies were sprawled everywhere, most of them Druids. The surprise attack had been a complete success. The Druids were all but annihilated. The invaders could do with Paranor what they pleased. What that might be may not have been decided yet, Balronen thought, as the invasion leader brought him to his feet and held him in place, but it was sufficient for now to know to whom the choice belonged.

Drisker Arc and Dar Leah hurried along the cellar passageways toward the archival vaults, where the Druid was convinced he would find Clizia waiting for them. Her plan to hide and wait for their arrival might easily have gone askew, forcing her to rush to their meeting place earlier than expected. Dar did not expect to find her there, however; if she were already in place, she still would have been able to answer the scrye orb summons. But as Drisker said, there was no way to be certain without having a look, so they would make the time for it.

But when they reached the passageway to the rooms that housed the archives, he found it empty and the vaults undisturbed.

Again, Drisker tried to reach her using the scrye orb. Again, she did not respond.

"I think we need to have a look upstairs for her," Drisker said reluctantly.

Dar Leah shook his head. "Too dangerous. Too many chances of being discovered. Besides, you don't need her, do you? Can't we just retrieve the Black Elfstone, summon the Guardian, and get out of here?"

Drisker smiled. "We could. But that would mean leaving Clizia behind. I don't think I want to do that. I think we need to make certain about her, one way or the other."

"She might be dead already. The invaders may have saved you the trouble."

"I know. But she's a tough old bird. I think we have to be sure. I know a way to search for her that doesn't risk that much. And I think I know where she might be."

Dar was not at all happy, but he agreed to give it a try. He respected Drisker enough not to give up on him, or to engage in an argument he already knew he was not going to win. Drisker might be wrong, but he deserved the chance to find out. Dar was not going to let him do so alone, no matter the risks to which he would expose himself.

It was still quiet and deserted as Drisker took the Blade back along the cellar passageways and then up a rear staircase through a miasma of gloom and smoke that had seeped in from the floors on which the battle had been fought. The sounds of the carnage were winding down, but there was still considerable movement everywhere. They crept up the stairs carefully, passed the ground floor, and then went up two more flights before stopping again to listen. There were no sounds, but Drisker wasn't taking any chances. He took them up still another level before they emerged.

The Druid Histories were housed on this floor, and Drisker believed that maybe Clizia had taken refuge here. It would be a logical choice; the room and its contents were concealed by magic, and it was unlikely the invaders had any means of negating the protective spells.

Drisker paused long enough to check the hall both ways before opening the doors to the room. Invoking his magic, he disabled the locks. But when they stepped through, there was no one inside. They took a moment to search the archival vault and the connected rooms, but the chambers were empty.

"I was sure," Drisker muttered.

And suddenly the scrye orb brightened and warmed inside his cloak. When he pulled it out and peered into its glowing face, Clizia Porse appeared.

"Where are you?" she snapped. "I've been waiting."

Drisker exchanged a quick look with Dar. "I've tried to reach you twice, without success. I've looked for you, too. I should be asking you where *you* are."

Clizia shrugged. "No need for that. I'm on my way to the archives now. Meet me there."

The orb went dark again, leaving Drisker frustrated and angry. "Let's get back into the cellars," he growled.

They went down a different staircase this time—one that twisted and wound through the walls and floors like a snake. This was a passage Dar not only didn't know about but had never even heard mentioned. On the second floor of their descent, Drisker hesitated a moment before he motioned Dar ahead once more. They emerged into a hallway that opened out on one side to provide an overlook of the main entry at ground level. There was no one about, but calls and whistles and voices rose from below, so the pair crept to the edge of the overlook railing and peered down.

Below them, the full extent of the slaughter revealed itself. The entryway floor was littered with bodies, and the walls were painted with blood. Most of the dead were Druids, but a few soldiers of the invading force had died, too. The dead were being stacked in piles, while the wounded were being sought out and dispatched if Druids or carried off to be treated elsewhere for their injuries if they were invaders.

To one side, an eight-foot spear had been wedged between pieces of stone flooring like a flagpole. On the point of the spear, Prax Tolt's burly head had been spiked.

Dar caught sight of Kassen Drue standing to one side, watching as the dead and wounded were collected. He grabbed Drisker's arm and nodded toward Kassen. *There,* he mouthed. *Kassen.* The Druid followed his gaze, studied the one indicated for a moment, then nodded in response. The matter was settled. The man who had hired the Orsis Guild assassins to kill him and the betrayer of the Keep were one and the same.

The volume of voices suddenly quieted, and the white-robed leader of the army marched into the center of the room, dragging Ober Balronen by his hair. Almost as one, all the invading soldiers, Kassen Drue among them, went down on one knee. A trilling sound broke from their throats as heads bowed and the butt ends of spears and the pommel ends of swords hammered into the stone in a cacophony of wild sound.

Ajin, Ajin, Ajin! The cry echoed through the halls of the Keep in adoration.

When the cries had diminished, the white-cloaked leader motioned for his followers to rise. Then throwing Balronen to his hands and knees, he drew forth his sword. He waited for the Ard Rhys to lift his head and look at him, but Balronen kept his head lowered, perhaps sensing what was to come. His captor left him as he was, brought up his sword in a wide arc, and sliced downward in a single powerful motion. Ober Balronen's head fell from his shoulders and rolled across the room, eyes wide open and mouth gaping from the shock of his dying.

Again, the cry went up from the invaders. *Ajin, Ajin, Ajin!*

Their leader acknowledged them by lifting his sword and letting the blood of the slain High Druid drip down its length and fall to the stone floor. Then he sheathed his weapon and beckoned to Kassen. Together they left the room, moving down the hallway so that they passed directly beneath the section of the balcony on which Drisker Arc and Dar Leah were crouched in hiding.

Drisker took Dar by the arm and pulled him away. Together they crept back along the hallway and into the stairwell, closing the door tightly behind them. "We'd better hurry," he whispered.

Dar shook his head. "I'm going after them." He gestured toward the two men below.

Drisker stared at him. "Why not leave that until another time?"

"I don't want them getting away. They have too much to answer for!"

"You can't go by yourself!" the Druid hissed. "You don't have any idea what those two are capable of doing. You can't risk it!"

"I can't *not* risk it," Dar insisted quietly. "It doesn't matter what they are capable of. I'm capable of a whole lot more."

The two stared at each other for long seconds, then Drisker nodded. "But listen to me. If you haven't settled matters by the time you start to see trailers of green mist or hear the first screams it produces from those it touches—clear signals that the Keep's Guardian has been released—drop everything and get clear of the buildings and back into the trees beyond the walls. No matter what, you go."

Dar nodded. "If I can, I will."

Drisker's smile was grim. "Remember. There will always be another chance at those two. Don't be reckless."

Dar smiled back. "Don't worry about me, Drisker. Watch out for yourself. I'll meet you beyond the west gates of the Keep when this is finished. I promise."

The two gripped hands and parted. Dar watched the Druid disappear down the stairs leading to the cellars and then turned the way Kassen and the white-cloaked invasion leader had gone and set off to find them.

THIRTY

◆

DRISKER ARC DESCENDED THE back stairway he had come up earlier with Dar Leah until he again reached the entrance to the cellars and hesitated. Glancing back the way he had come, he experienced an odd feeling of leaving something important behind. The feeling was strong enough that it momentarily distracted him from proceeding, causing him to search for a reason for his reaction.

But there was nothing to be found, so he brushed it aside, opened the cellar door, and stepped through. The cellars were dark, and he again summoned a werelight, balancing the flame on the tips of his fingers, adjusting its brightness so he could tell where he was going as he started down the passageway toward the archival vaults.

It seemed to take much longer to reach them this time, as if they were much farther along than he remembered. But it had been awhile since he had been inside Paranor, and he knew better than to rely on memory where time's passage could erase it so easily. He thought briefly about Dar Leah and wondered if he should have given the Blade further instructions. He had told him once he fled the Keep to find shelter in the forest trees and to stay put no matter what happened. He was not to delay his escape, no matter how matters stood with Kassen Drue or the invasion leader. Then he was to hide until either the Druid reappeared or it became clear that he wasn't coming at all.

In case of the latter, he expected the Blade would know enough to return to Emberen and either wait there for Tarsha or set out to find her. The likelihood of the highlander choosing to wait was slim. It wasn't in his nature to sit around, any more than it was in Drisker's. He would go looking, and the best the Druid could hope for was that he would do so with good judgment. It seemed a safe bet. Dar Leah was the best of a ragged and uncertain Druid order, and if anyone could manage what needed doing in Drisker's absence it was the highlander.

Long minutes later, Drisker was at the door leading into Paranor's cellars, the huge iron portal worn and pitted by age and the elements, a barrier to a world he had been banished from and had not expected to return to. He paused, staring at it, and the past recalled itself in painful memories. Lost to him, all of it. Once, if he were caught inside the walls of the Keep without permission, the punishment would have been severe. Perhaps, it would even have been fatal. No more. Ober Balronen and the other Druids were dead, save Clizia Porse. The entire order was gone, and there was no one to catch him out and no one to administer any form of punishment.

The Druid order was destroyed.

The Druids were history.

All that was left were memories of what had been. It seemed impossible. It made Drisker Arc feel as if his life had no meaning and he had no place in the world. His investment in the Druids and in the furtherance of their lofty goals was like a mirage that had faded with a shifting of the light. Where was he to turn, once this was over, that would offer him a chance to rebuild and restore? He could not accept that this was the end of Paranor forever. Surely there had to be a rebirth of the Druid phoenix out of the ashes of the old, as had happened before. There could be a rebirth again. Another order must be founded, and a new beginning in the long and storied history of the Druids started.

He breathed out slowly, as if it were his last breath. He did not know if he was up to it. He could not imagine reconstructing something it had taken so long to create. He could barely accept the idea that it had all been swept away in the blink of an eye, one night's disastrous undoing of so many thousands of years of progress.

Shades, I am getting old.

He brushed aside his musings and turned to the task at hand, proceeding cautiously along the ancient hallways, studying their maze-like confluence and the pools of overlapping shadows that filled them to be certain he was alone. He worried that some of the invaders might have come down into the cellars for a look around, but there was no sign of anyone. Satisfied, he moved over to a darkened corner of the widest passage and brought out the scrye orb.

In seconds Clizia Porse was looking back at him. "Drisker."

"Are you in place?" He did not try to hide his sense of urgency.

"At the entrance to the vaults."

"I'm coming."

It took him less than fifteen more minutes. He saw her step out of the shadows as he approached, all gray and hunched over. A crooked smile played across her thin lips. Her hands were clutched together, and her eyes glowed green in the darkness of her hood.

For one moment, he considered turning back. He did not like the way she made him feel. He did not trust her.

"Better we act quickly now that you are here," she announced. "The Keep is in the hands of its invaders. None of the Druids, Troll watch, or students appear to have survived. The invaders were very thorough. We are all that remains, Drisker. We are all that is left to carry on."

The Druid nodded. "So you would summon the Guardian and seal the Keep away until we can form a new order? Is that still your plan?"

"You have another?"

"I think we would be better served by summoning the Guardian and biding our time on sealing the Keep. It may be that what happens to those inside the Keep will be enough to discourage those without from attempting further entry. Then the Keep would stay abandoned until we formed a new order. We can always choose to close it later."

"That hardly seems a better plan. Mine ties up all the loose ends and leaves nothing to chance." She gave him a dark look. "Still, while I do not favor your approach, I will agree to it. But we should retrieve the Black Elfstone now and not chance the possibility of not being able to return for it later."

He shook his head wearily. "It took something to convince me that coming here at all was worth it. The Druids have been fools. The Keep has fallen, and the order has been destroyed. I am in exile. I am no longer Ard Rhys. I have no official standing or place with the Druids, dead or living. Why should I care about any of this?"

Her muted laugh was deeply bitter. "Oh, please! You would pretend you do not care for the future of the Druid order? You care for it more than anyone! So here is your chance to show how much. I can do everything but open the archives. The codes defy me. But you know them, so use them!"

"Unless they have been changed."

"By Balronen? He was too lazy to change his boots, let alone the codes to a room he believes his personal fiefdom. The codes will be the same. Go and open the door and take the Black Elfstone. Keep it yourself, if you wish. I have no need of it, so long as I know it is safe with you."

He thought about it for a long moment, considering what she was asking and what the results would be. His guard was up; he had every reason to find Clizia duplicitous and scheming. But he saw the wisdom in her plan, and he could not make himself walk away at this point and leave the Keep and all its wildly unpredictable magic for the invaders. Even if they didn't know how to use it now, what was to say they might not learn? And then what use might they make of it in their plans—whatever their nature—regarding the Four Lands? He did not care to find out.

"We must do what we can for the good of the order," he acknowledged.

She smiled. "Lead the way, Ard-Rhys-that-was. Who knows? Perhaps one day you will be the Ard Rhys again."

Drisker ignored the comment and moved out of the shadows and down the hallway, peering into the dark spaces that fell between those scattered islands lit by smokeless lamps. He was mindful of Clizia's limited ability to move with any quickness or dexterity, and so he kept the pace from becoming too rapid. The Keep was as silent as a tomb and had the same feel. From his perspective, Paranor was now a place fit only for the dead, and the living did not belong. If he followed through with Clizia's plan, the invaders would join the dead soon enough.

They descended into the very deepest regions of the Keep's cellars, using ancient stone stairs laced with cracks and worn from use, passing through doors sealed by magic, steadily making their way toward the archives. The location of these chambers had been changed after the sorcerer Arcannen Rai had tricked his way into the Keep in an attempt to loot their artifacts and talismans more than two hundred years earlier. It was decided after his death that a stronger, safer set of chambers was needed to prevent this from ever happening again.

So the archives had been made much harder to locate and less easily breached. There were numerous doors and twisting halls that needed to be navigated just to reach them. It required employing multiple sets of codes to open a series of formidable doors and complex words of magic to release the seals that bound them. It was a fortress within a fortress, and only an Ard Rhys or someone of equal stature could gain it. Drisker knew how and Clizia Porse seemed content to let him lead the way, following dutifully, head down and voice stilled.

At the final barrier, a great iron door set back into the stone of the walls waited, secured and sealed with dozens of locks. They halted and turned to each other.

"You can open it, can't you?" Clizia inquired. When he nodded, the old woman gestured impatiently. "Then get on with it."

Working his way clockwise from top to bottom downward on the right and back up again on the left, Drisker released the locks and seals one by one. It took time, and Clizia seated herself with her back against the passage wall while she waited. Drisker felt her eyes on him, and the weight of her gaze was so strong it was almost visceral. He remembered again his concerns about her propensity for hidden plans, about her still-questionable reasons for sending Dar to see him, and about her history of using poisons. He remembered how she had lied to him about Kassen. He kept vigilant watch against any sort of treachery, not so foolish as to think he was immune. But what was to be gained from harming him? In truth, he was doing exactly what she thought necessary anyway, so it was hard to see what else she could possibly want.

Which was not to say that he was dismissing the possibility she wanted something. Only that he should not obsess over his safety.

When the last of the locks and seals were undone, the huge door swung open effortlessly, revealing the individual vaults within. Drisker looked back at Clizia, but she only shrugged and gestured for him to go on inside. He did so, moving to where he knew the Black Elfstone was locked away within a space hollowed out of the bedrock that formed the chamber walls. He took a moment to study the protections formed of Druid magic—unseen wards set down from before his time as Ard Rhys and left unchanged by Balronen. After he had figured out the order of the releases required, he went to work.

It took him longer than he had expected. There was no rushing this one. A single slip could cause the entire effort to collapse and the locks to meld together in an impenetrable barrier that would take days if not weeks to undo. So he paused now and then, wanting to be sure that he was doing what he should, careful not to make a mistake.

He summoned an opening of the barrier with words and gestures. The barrier melted like frost in the sun, and in the darkness beyond a small wrapped package revealed itself. Inside would be a pouch that could be dated to the time of Walker Boh, who had retrieved the stolen Elfstone from the far-north fortress of the Stone King and carried it back to Paranor. The pouch leather was old and cracked and discolored, a victim of time and nature.

He hesitated before taking it.

There were grim stories about the Black Elfstone—tales to bring a shiver to the spine and a tightening to the throat. It was said to be dark, yet it was the nature of its magic that gave it that reputation. The Stone possessed the ability to absorb and contain other magic. It was the talisman that could negate, at a later time, what his Druid magic might have to do now to seal Paranor and hide it away. On this night, the Guardian in the black pit of the Druid's Well would be summoned. It would rise from its lair and destroy the Keep's invaders and reclaim Paranor for the Druids. But Clizia wanted to go further. She wanted to use magic to make Paranor vanish until a new Druid order was formed. To bring Paranor back after would require using the Black Elfstone to absorb the magic that had concealed it. It was the pathway that Clizia favored—the founding of a new Druid order. Yet Drisker remained unconvinced of her intentions.

I am still not sure, he thought, confronting in the silence of his mind his uncertainty and foreboding.

Yet he reached inside the opening, took the pouch in his hand, and drew the Elfstone clear.

"Hurry!" Clizia was suddenly right behind him. "We have no time!"

Drisker nodded but did not speak. He closed off the concealment that had protected the Black Elfstone, reset the seals and locks, and backed away as if he had committed a violation. Just for a moment, he experienced the strangest sense of having failed.

Then he turned to Clizia, and they went out the door and moved through the cellar passageways toward the door that opened into the pit where dwelled the spirit creature they called the Guardian of the Keep.

It was a given that the creature would be waiting. It would know what had happened and be aware of what was needed. It would be crouched within the green mists that wrapped it like a shroud, waiting for a summoning. It would not act without being called—not so long as there was a Druid presence within the Keep's walls.

And it would know that summons was drawing near.

Clizia seemed revitalized, moving more quickly and surely than earlier, eager to do what was needed to rid the Keep of its occupants. But Drisker was still cautious. The Keep's protector was a most uncertain magic, and it was known to kill friend as quickly as foe. It did not always distinguish one from the other, once released. It was a wild magic barely contained by power the Druids had set in place hundreds of years ago—an act of good intentions that had not entirely succeeded. There were insufficient checks and balances on the creature, and its release was always one of desperation and despair. If it was summoned, Drisker and Clizia both understood they had better be well clear of the walls of the Keep before it surfaced if they wanted to be sure they would still be alive at the end of the night.

They did not speak as they went, dark figures moving to fulfill a purpose darker still. No one happened upon them; they saw no guards and heard no sounds of life. Yet at one point Drisker thought he heard a low expectant hiss snake through the corridors of the Keep. He listened for it again afterward, unable to help himself. Each time the wait was shorter. The Guardian was growing impatient.

When they arrived at the door to the Druid's Well, Drisker turned to Clizia. "Once we do this, there is no turning back. We cannot stop these events if we set them in motion. The consequences will be ours to bear."

She nodded, a deep frown twisting her ancient features. "Is it your intent to talk me to death? Open the door."

He did so, and they stepped into darkness so complete it was startling. They engaged werelights to fend it off, but the light could penetrate no farther than a dozen paces. A dozen paces that, had they taken them blindly, would have carried them directly over the edge of a platform and into the void of the pit. They held their ground, peering into the gloom. The tower was huge, built with smooth stones, which both rose above and fell below an impenetrable blackness. They stood on a metal platform from which a spiral staircase circled upward and downward into the blackness with no end in sight either way. No windows admitted light from without. No other doors were visible from where they stood. The gloom was complete and unrelenting.

"We must work together," Clizia said. "I will follow your lead, Drisker. Weave the thread. I will fill the gaps."

Giving her a nod of acquiescence, the Druid began to recite the invocation that would draw the Keep's Guardian from the pit. He combined words with other, less intelligible sounds and added gestures of power to strengthen the spell. It was a familiar recitation; learning it had been an Ard Rhys's priority since forever to protect against the unthinkable. It had only been used a handful of times in the entire history of the Druids, and then always in dire situations. He had never thought he would see a time when he would be required to use it, to deliberately summon magic that was so dangerous. But it was the unexpected that so often crept up on you when you weren't looking.

Behind him, he could hear Clizia's rough, insistent voice adding to the spell, strengthening it in her own particular way. But her words were strange to him, and he wondered what it was she was doing that was so unfamiliar. No matter. He could not break his concentration now, because the Keep's Guardian was beginning to stir. Low hissing sounded from the depths of the pit, and the first tendrils of mist began to stretch upward like crooked fingers, emanating a wicked green light. The blackness was filled with it, its sickly illumination infusing the dark to mark the creature's coming. It was far below still, but rising steadily. Drisker bore down, anxious to finish the conjuring and retreat to the safety of the world outside Paranor's walls. A sudden surge lifted the mist with a visible heave, and the hissing turned to a long, slow sigh of satisfaction.

"Drisker! Enough!" Clizia was pulling on his arm.

The creature was awake. It was free to do what it had been given to do whenever Paranor was threatened. And now it would destroy its enemies and cleanse its lair.

Drisker stepped back, but as he turned to leave, he felt a sharp sting on his exposed neck as Clizia's fingers brushed his skin. His knees buckled and a sudden weakness flooded through him. He started to fall, and Clizia caught hold of him and held him up until they had reached the opening leading out of the Druid's Well. She guided him through the door and closed it behind them. Then she let him sink slowly to the floor, where he rested limply, his back against the wall.

He saw it then, reflected in her eyes. Her duplicity. Her treachery. Her well-hidden intent. "What did you do to me?" he asked, his voice slurring.

"I stole your strength, Drisker. I took it from you with a needle's prick." She held up her right hand, the nails purple with a potion's coating, studying him as she might a curious insect. Then she reached into his pocket and pulled out the pouch that contained the Black Elfstone. "Here is where we part ways."

He managed a nod, but it was difficult. "You planned this all along."

She shrugged. "You were in the way. I have bigger plans than you know."

His head was heavy, and his chin sank to his chest so that he was looking at her feet. "This will not end well for you."

"Oh, I think it might. But you won't be around to find out. The mist is rising; the Guardian approaches, and the Keep will be cleansed. You, along with the invaders, will pass from memory soon enough."

He could no longer respond, his voice gone, his strength dissipated entirely.

She knelt then, placed a hand under his chin, and lifted his head. "You won't die from anything I do, Drisker. You will die when the mist reaches you and steals away your breath. You should try to think well of me. It will make your death less unpleasant when it comes for you." She paused. "I am leaving you the scrye orb so you can tell me the details of your dying. I would be interested to hear what it feels like."

Then she lowered his head again, rose quickly, and hurried away.

THIRTY-ONE

◆

A DETERMINED DAR LEAH worked his way along the empty hallway on the second-floor level, shadowing the white-cloaked invasion
leader and Kassen Drue where they walked below. He was able to
track them by listening to their footsteps and now and then catching
a glimpse of their reflections in the heavy glass of the tall windows
that lined the lower wall. Their progress was slow and measured, and
the tone and rhythm of their talk suggested it was one of rumination.
Try as he might, however, the Blade could not make out what they
were saying. But what mattered was that he stayed with them, waiting
to see . . .

To see what? What was he doing anyway? He wondered at his
decision to track them through the Keep—a decision that had been
sudden and unexpected, and in retrospect seemed foolish. What was
the point of this exercise? Would he confront them and demand they
surrender? Would he attack them? Was he trying to find out something important by spying on them?

He didn't know. He only knew that he did not want either of them
to escape the consequences of what they had done by destroying the
Druid order. It was one thing to accept that they had done so, as
Drisker had, and turn your attention to preventing any further damage by sealing away the Keep to protect what it contained. It was an-

other to be seeking a confrontation, an accounting, and a resolution of the sort he craved. The loss of Zia was still fresh in his mind, and the two he followed were arguably the most responsible. All he knew at this point, with Paranor undone and its Druids dead, was that someone should pay.

But maybe it was something more, too. Maybe it had to do with his own sense of failure—at not being quick enough or smart enough to find a way to protect and save either Zia or Paranor. And finally, at the end of the day, it had to do with knowing he had escaped their fates in part, at least, because of his failures.

At the first stairway he encountered, he descended to the ground floor and found himself not twenty feet behind them. Here the passageway was bloodstained and littered with debris, but the bodies of the dead and wounded had been dragged away. No one else was about; the main body of the attack force was still back in the south entry to Paranor's main tower. Smokeless lamps were dimmed, and the air was thick with ash and the stench of death.

Dar waited until his quarry was well down the hallway and nearing the broad staircase that climbed to the higher floors. He found himself wondering if they were looking for something rather than simply wandering. The conversation remained muffled, their words vague and indistinct; it was still impossible to know what they were saying. Because it was neither heated nor urgent, he was guessing the two were talking over what would happen after this night. Clearly Kassen was important to whatever plans they had devised; his role in arranging entry into Paranor was undeniably the key to their success in seizing the Keep—and Dar had the distinct feeling things would not stop there.

He was closing in on the pair when a trio of newcomers suddenly appeared from out of the gloom ahead, hailing them, talking in urgent tones. Instantly Dar shrank back against the wall, deep within the shadow of a stone pillar. Those ahead of him were looking around now, scanning in all directions, searching for something.

Right away he knew it was Drisker.

A chill settled in his heart. They must have discovered the Druid.

Perhaps they only knew he was inside the Keep, but perhaps they already had taken him prisoner and were now wondering if there was anyone else who needed finding.

He kept his head, despite a sudden urge to go in search of Drisker. Knowing that if he moved he would likely be seen, he stayed where he was. His hand strayed to the handle of the Sword of Leah and then lowered again. There were too many of the invaders around; the time was not right for an attack.

After a few minutes of further conversation, the white-cloaked leader made a dismissive gesture and the three soldiers disappeared once more. The leader and Kassen remained where they were, heads bent close. Now that Dar had put himself in this position, getting close enough that he could attack them, he had a choice to make. He couldn't just stay where he was. Sooner or later, Drisker would either release the Guardian of the Keep from its confinement or, if captured, be hauled before the invasion leader and killed. If he wanted to prevent the latter, Dar had to act now.

He took a deep breath and prepared to move. But just before he did, the pair ended their conversation and separated, White Cloak continuing down the hallway to ascend the grand stairway, and Kassen turning toward Dar.

The decision had been made for him. Dar Leah reached back over his shoulder and gripped the handle of his sword. He would rush from hiding and try to take the other man alive, a prisoner to question, a hostage with which to bargain. If he could get himself and Kassen safely out of the Keep, Drisker could join them as planned and an important inroad would have been made in their efforts to blunt this invasion and to learn the reason behind it. And if Drisker was now a prisoner of the invaders, Kassen could be used to bargain for his return.

Either way, Kassen would be made to serve a use.

Dar held himself ready as the other came toward him. He would leap out and overpower Kassen before the other could react. Silencing him quickly would be crucial. If Kassen got off a cry for help, others would hear and come to his aid, and that would likely be the end of Dar Leah.

He held himself ready, poised to attack.

But then everything went wrong at once.

While planning his attack, he had failed to notice that the color of the air had begun to change. As the seconds had passed, it had begun to turn greenish. An ugly mist was filling the hallway, swirling idly as it thickened. If his intense desire to take Kassen prisoner had not distracted him, he would have seen it sooner. But now it was too late.

Screams rose from farther down the hallway, where the bulk of the invaders were gathered in the south entry to the building. High-pitched and terror-filled, they exploded through the near silence of the passageway in which Dar was hiding behind a pillar. Instantly Kassen stopped where he was, his face a mix of confusion, fear, and indecision.

Dar did not give the man the chance to act. He leapt from hiding, sword in hand, and rushed to attack. But Kassen was nothing if not quick, and his experience and survival skills allowed him to block the highlander's initial rush. They came together in a frenzied crush, the impact of their bodies knocking the breath from both of them before they skittered apart. Dar wheeled back, waiting for Kassen to call for help, but the other man simply smiled and went into a defensive crouch. Perhaps he realized that his cries would not be heard in the volume of screams. Perhaps he saw no reason to call for help or break for freedom. There was a calm recognition in his eyes that suggested he had known this moment was coming and he was ready for it.

Dar held back, still looking for a way to end this without bloodshed, circling to his left to block the other's escape route. "How goes your training, Kassen?" he asked softly.

The screams nearly drowned him out. The cacophony of voices was deafening, mingled with the sounds of men fighting and dying in their futile efforts to stop what was happening.

Kassen shrugged calmly. When he spoke, it was in the Southland tongue he had so clearly mastered. "We're about to find out, aren't we?"

"You have a lot to answer for. I might give you a chance to do so if you throw down your sword."

"You're awfully sure of yourself, aren't you?"

"It comes with years of practice. But you should know. So clever in tricking your way into Paranor, so eager to betray it."

He made a rush, a feint with his sword. Kassen barely moved, recognizing it for what it was. "You might be overmatched, Dar Leah. Have you thought of that?"

"Not by you I won't be. Why don't you try your disappearing trick? Let's see if I can find you."

Kassen smiled but did not reply. He knew why Dar was taunting him. The air was filled with ash and tinged green by the mist. Some of it would cling to him, even if he tried to conceal himself. It would outline enough of him that Dar would be able to tell where he was.

"What is it you want?" he asked instead, attempting a quick feint of his own, circling left to try to get past Dar. "You can't undo any of what's happened. Is it just my death you seek, Blade?"

"I would take that." Dar blocked his way again. "But what I really want is to find out what's going on. Why don't you tell me?"

The other man shook his head. In the distance, the screams were growing in volume, the sounds more intense, more frantic. The mist was turning a darker green, and there were other ominous sounds beginning, deep and raw, that signaled the coming of something more substantial.

"I think maybe this is where you belong, here among your dead friends and companions," Kassen hissed at him. "Why don't you join them?"

"Not without you for company."

Dar had no idea what made him say this. Maybe it was an attempt to convince the other he was not afraid to die. Maybe it was his determination not to allow himself to be frightened by this man.

Whatever it was, it had an unexpected effect.

"I think you might just be willing to trade your life for mine, Dar Leah. I worry about such mindless commitment. Hold me here long enough, you might be thinking, and whatever's gotten to my companions will get to us, too."

He straightened and sheathed his sword. "The next time I see you, I will kill you. Remember that."

And he disappeared.

Just like that.

Dar couldn't believe it. He stood rooted in place, searching the haze, but he could not see anything. He shifted swiftly right and then left, blade carving through the mist, seeking a target and finding nothing.

But Kassen Drue was gone.

It took Dar Leah a few more seconds of anxious expectation and quick changes of position to realize he was alone. The other man must have chosen to flee rather than stand and fight. The greenish mist was roiling so wildly by now that the ash floating in its midst that might otherwise have clung to him was tumbling everywhere. If he had fled in the opposite direction, any impression he might have otherwise made would have been swallowed up almost immediately.

Dar took a moment to assess his situation—but only a moment, because that was pretty much all he had. Drisker had released the Guardian from the Druid's Well; the screams and greenish mist confirmed it. So the Druid was still free and likely on his way to somewhere safer. And everyone else inside Paranor—himself included—was in danger of being consumed by what had been set free if they did not flee.

Both Kassen and the invasion leader were now beyond his reach, gone somewhere deeper into the Keep or more likely out of it entirely. He felt a moment of deep regret and surging anger. His efforts had failed. There was no reason to stay longer.

He turned away from the encroaching mist and the sounds of the screams and bolted for the nearest exit.

It seemed to Dar Leah, thinking back on it, that it took him no time at all to get clear of Paranor and out into the comparative safety of the surrounding forest. He escaped through a service door cut into the west wall of the Keep, scrambling down hallways to reach it, refusing to look back, closing his ears to the sounds that tracked after him. Once outside the building and across the central courtyard, he made his way through another service door in the Keep's massive outer wall and into the trees. He saw no one on this journey, and even afterward, when he was crouched in the concealment of a stand of conifers, well back from any light cast by moon and stars, no one appeared. He kept thinking someone would—Drisker Arc, in particular.

But the minutes passed, and he remained alone.

Before him, Paranor rose against the eastern skyline, towers and battlements and wind-blown pennants etched against the sky, a lifeless and solitary tomb. The shouting from earlier, loud and frantic enough to penetrate the Keep's walls and reach his ears even within the trees, was gone. Long minutes passed as the silence deepened, and from behind the thick glass of the tower windows, high enough that the walls did not block his view, the dull roil of the greenish mist persisted, spreading from window to window until the entirety of the Keep reflected its sickly hue.

Where was Drisker? What had become of him?

What do I do now?

Dar hesitated within his concealment, unsure.

Seconds later Clizia Porse climbed through the tunnel exit—visible to him from where he was hiding—surfacing from beneath the earth to stand silently in the gloom. Alone. No Drisker. She hesitated, looked around for a moment, and then closed the trapdoor. With a quick motion of her hands, she sealed it. Her movements were hurried and furtive, her constant glances back at the Keep telling.

Something was very wrong, but even though he wanted badly to confront her and ask what had become of Drisker, Dar hesitated. Everything about what he was seeing suggested caution was advisable. So he waited and watched.

It was fortunate he did.

Clizia had turned back to the walls of the Keep, raised her hands above her bent form. Dark clouds formed about her, swirling clutches of mist that hissed and sang of snake poison. From out of their mist, strange forms appeared. They were winged and tiny, but there was no mistaking the red glint of their eyes or the white of their teeth. They surrounded her protectively—a swarm of darting black forms providing a wall between their creator and everything beyond where she stood. As they did so, Clizia began to chant softly, her fingers weaving runic symbols on the night air. Clizia Porse was working a spell, but the Blade had no idea what it was. The casting appeared to require her complete concentration, and for long minutes she was lost in her efforts, paying no attention to anything around her. The black miasma of mist and winged forms bloomed larger, shrouding her completely. Wrapped tightly within its shifting folds, she disappeared, a necessary consequence perhaps of her need to perform her magic.

Then, her conjuring finished, the blackness fell away and she was gone.

Dar searched the darkness for her and then started for Paranor's walls. If Drisker was still inside, Dar needed to find a way to get him out. The mist was dissipating rapidly, the darkness of the night and something more, as well, seeping over everything. But whatever the danger, he was going back.

Then, abruptly, an odd shimmer enveloped the entirety of Paranor—gates, walls, towers, battlements, buildings, even the pennants that flew from their stanchions at the highest levels in tiny flutters on the night breezes. A blast of cold air blew into the Blade, knocking him backward with such force it caused him to stumble and drop to one knee.

He bent his head before its fury and closed his eyes until he felt it pass. Even then, he was cautious about looking to see what had happened. He had reason to be. What he found was so monstrous, so wildly impossible, it took him long minutes to accept that it was real.

By then, his hands were shaking and there were tears in his eyes.

Paranor had disappeared.

Impossible, he thought. But it wasn't there. Nothing was. Only the rise on which it had stood, only the ground on which it had been constructed all those centuries ago. A huge patch of raw, torn earth revealed the imprint of her foundations, still visible at the edges of the dark emptiness where the cellars had once burrowed deep within the earth.

Everything else had vanished into the ether.

A small movement to his left caught Dar's attention. A solitary figure stood outside the edge of the forest almost at the base of the rise, staring at what a few minutes earlier had been there and now wasn't. Wondering, no doubt as he did, what had become of everything, wondering how it was possible for it all to be gone.

The white-cloaked leader of the invaders.

Dar rose from where he was kneeling and started ahead. No reason not to risk it at this point. No reason even to think of doing anything else. All the Druids were dead. All the invaders were dead. Drisker was likely dead, as well. No one was left but Clizia Porse and himself. So now, perhaps, he would get the answers he had sought earlier from Kassen. Now, perhaps, he would find some closure to this devastating turn of events.

His sword came out of its sheath soundlessly, and he was on top of the invasion leader before the other knew he was there. Helmeted and cloaked as before, the leader faced him, Dar's sword pointed at his throat. He made no move to fight or run. He stayed where he was, waiting on Dar.

"We meet again," Dar said, taking the other's measure.

The other man said nothing. He was as tall as Dar, slender overall, not as imposing as the Blade had believed him.

"Who are you?" Dar demanded.

Still no reply.

The highlander was angry now, the adrenaline pumping through him with such force he believed it would take very little for him to do something violent to his passive prisoner.

"Take off your helmet!" he snapped, his voice little more than a rough hiss. "Show me your face."

The other did as he ordered, hands moving to loosen restraining straps in order to lift the helmet away. A splash of moonlight revealed his captive's face with unmistakable clarity.

Dar exhaled sharply.

The leader of the invaders was a young woman.

THIRTY-TWO

INSIDE PARANOR, ALL WAS still. The shouts and screams and cries had been silenced, and the halls no longer echoed with the voices of dying men and women. Nothing moved. The dead sprawled here and there, but none of the living remained. The Keep's Guardian had done its work and gone back into the pit, where it would wait for the Druids to return. Gone as well was the greenish mist that had accompanied its passing, leaving the air clear and free of its presence once more. Beyond the walls of the fortress, the new day was breaking. Darkness was giving way to the coming sunrise, and the sky was brightening. If you looked through the glass of the tall hallway windows, you could see it.

Drisker Arc lay slumped against the wall in the corridor where Clizia Porse had left him and wondered why he was still alive. After all, he should be dead. The Keep's Guardian had killed the invaders and should have killed him, as well. Wasn't that how it was supposed to happen? Wasn't everyone found within the Keep supposed to be eradicated when it emerged from its lair? Hadn't he summoned it himself with that intent, and hadn't he been there when it rose and filled the hall with its greenish presence? Hadn't he been lying there helpless before it, tricked by Clizia into thinking she was his ally instead of his betrayer?

Yet the dark magic had passed him by, the greenish mist rolling over him with no effect and that black thing within it taking no notice. It was impossible to imagine, but it had happened.

He was aware of the rumors of the Guardian's inconsistency and unpredictability, how it didn't always know friend from foe and everyone was at risk. So if everyone might be at risk, the corollary was that maybe everyone might not be.

Druids, for instance, whom the magic was there to ward, might be immune.

He couldn't know for sure. He might never know. What he could be sure of was that its sweep through Paranor's halls was at an end, and he was still alive and beginning to feel the strength return to his body. His bitterness toward Clizia Porse was intense. He should have been more careful and less confident he could protect himself from her. But he had let himself be distracted while summoning the Keep's Guardian from the tower depths. He had left himself vulnerable. And now he was paying the price. He had survived, but she had escaped.

And she had taken from him the Black Elfstone.

He had checked his clothing soon after finding he was not destined to die this day after all. It had been tucked inside his cloak, and now it was gone. But he would catch up to her and take it back. And he would administer a deep measure of revenge . . .

The scope of her treachery was mind-boggling. It had taken him only seconds after she betrayed him to recognize how far it stretched and how deep it burrowed. The signs of its presence were always there. Clizia had been chief examiner on the panel when Kassen Drue was admitted. She had probably arranged to have him admitted swiftly, skirting any of the usual precautions. She would have known all the ways in and out of the Keep, including the tunnel. She would have advised Kassen of this and he in turn would have informed the invader. Once that was done, the Keep and the Druids were doomed.

But there was more. Much more.

She used her potions to alter Balronen's behavior in order to keep him dangerously off balance and unable to function. She would have used them again on Ruis Quince. The reason she was still alive when everyone else in the Keep was dead was because she was directly responsible for everything that had happened.

What had she been trying to achieve? Destruction of the current Druid order so she could rebuild it to her own specifications? An alliance with invaders she believed so powerful it was worth sacrificing Paranor in order to become one of them? Hard to know at this point, but whatever she was seeking was now within her grasp.

Which made him wonder if she had anything to do with Orsis Guild and its efforts to assassinate him. It would make sense, if she had. He was the only one likely to try to stop what she was planning, maybe the only one who might recognize what was intended with the Keep and its Druids before it happened. So she would have let Kassen know where he could be found, and then Kassen sent Tigueron and his cutthroats off to finish him.

Most galling of all was how she had used him to help her achieve her goals. Probably she had always planned to steal the Black Elfstone from him and seal him in the Keep. She had never intended that they should work together to stop the invaders. He was the one who needed stopping.

What a fool he had been. How blind. How gullible.

She must have been planning this for a long time. How long, he wondered, since she had first made contact with the invaders and agreed to betray the Keep? There was no way of knowing without asking her, and he had serious doubts about that happening anytime soon. If ever.

He stopped thinking about it and with great effort forced himself to his feet, standing with his back pressed against the wall for support. A terrible thought occurred to him—one so terrifying that any consideration of it was almost impossible. But the taking of the Black Elfstone, coupled with the continued presence of the curious haze that infused the whole of the Keep, suggested he must.

He looked down at himself, trying to see his arms and legs and body clearly. He could not do so. His vision seemed blurry, as if what she had done to him had affected his eyesight. He looked around. Everything within view was blurry and colorless. He had thought it was the predawn light before, but now he could tell the haziness was everywhere, inside and out of the Keep. As if he were in a different world. As if everything was.

His breath caught in his throat and his stomach clenched.

Shades!

She had done what she had wanted to do all along. She had tricked him into thinking she wouldn't, and then she had done it anyway. She had used her magic to disappear Paranor from the Four Lands, to hide it away where it might never be found.

And by leaving him trapped inside, she had done the same to him.

ABOUT THE AUTHOR

TERRY BROOKS is the *New York Times* bestselling author of more than thirty books, including the Dark Legacy of Shannara adventures *Wards of Faerie, Bloodfire Quest,* and *Witch Wraith;* the Legends of Shannara novels *Bearers of the Black Staff* and *The Measure of the Magic;* the Genesis of Shannara trilogy: *Armageddon's Children, The Elves of Cintra,* and *The Gypsy Morph; The Sword of Shannara;* the Voyage of the *Jerle Shannara* trilogy: *Ilse Witch, Antrax,* and *Morgawr;* the High Druid of Shannara trilogy: *Jarka Ruus, Tanequil,* and *Straken;* the nonfiction book *Sometimes the Magic Works: Lessons from a Writing Life;* and the novel based upon the screenplay and story by George Lucas, *Star Wars*®: Episode I *The Phantom Menace.*™ His novels *Running with the Demon* and *A Knight of the Word* were selected by the *Rocky Mountain News* as two of the best science fiction/fantasy novels of the twentieth century. The author was a practicing attorney for many years but now writes full-time. He lives with his wife, Judine, in the Pacific Northwest.

shannara.com
terrybrooks.net
Facebook.com/authorterrybrooks
Twitter: @officialbrooks
Instagram: @officialterrybrooks

ABOUT THE TYPE

This book was set in Minion, a 1990 Adobe Originals typeface by Robert Slimbach (b. 1956). Minion is inspired by classical, old-style typefaces of the late Renaissance, a period of elegant, beautiful, and highly readable type designs. Created primarily for text setting, Minion combines the aesthetic and functional qualities that make text type highly readable with the versatility of digital technology.